Praise for The Bardic Isles Series

"A creatively crafted fantasy in which magic comes from music itself. A brisk, expertly crafted tale." **– Kirkus Reviews**

"Himeda's prose is engrossing and mesmerizing. Readers most in-tune with this stunning work of fantasy will appreciate its figurative elements and grasp what lies at its core: a pure, exultant celebration of the magic of music." **– The BookLife Prize**

"Filled with fantasy, music, wonderful characters, and deep emotions. A completely captivating story that you will not be able to put down until you finish that final page."
– Kathy Stickles for Reader Views

"The authenticity of the characters and the exquisite capture of emotions create a relationship that pulls at our heartstrings. Beautifully depicted and thoroughly engaging. A complete joy to read." **– The B.R.A.G. Medallion**

"A captivating fantasy novel, richly told and highly unpredictable. A Wishing Shelf recommended read." **– The Wishing Shelf**

"Music is magic in this charming, richly written fantasy. Himeda writes lush, engaging scenes of travel and music-making, in exacting and evocative prose." **– BookLife Reviews**

(audiobook) "What started as short flute, harp, and pipe melodies culminated in amazing, fully-fledged songs, all composed by Marla Himeda. It made me feel as if I were watching an exhilarating stage play. This is a brilliant fantasy that offers both children and adults a lot to enjoy." **– Readers' Favorite**

Master of Music

Book One of The Bardic Isles Series

Marla Himeda

Print ISBN: 978-1-959900-00-9
.mobi ISBN: 978-1-959900-01-6
.epub ISBN: 978-1-959900-02-3
audiobook ISBN: 979-8-868647-50-5
Library of Congress Control Number: 2023900003

Published in Kaneohe, HI, USA

*For my husband, Scott,
whose patience with and faith in my writing
never fails to inspire me*

*And for my daughter, Charis,
for insisting that I bring this tale out of digital obscurity
and share my musical fantasy world with you*

Author's Note

The Bardic Isles Series is set in the time when Druids and Bards made Ireland their home. Although it was not called Ireland or Eire at that time, I've chosen to use Eire as the name for clarity and to differentiate it from modern-day Ireland. I have done my utmost to make the details of my series consistent with this time period and location. Musically speaking, however, I have taken the liberty of making my fictitious group of islands, the Bardic Isles, far more advanced than the outside world was at that time in musical theory and composition, ensemble playing, and in the construction of the flute and harp. This can perhaps be justified on the grounds that, at the time this story begins, the Bardic Isles has enjoyed well over two centuries of musical development in a society where music is the dominant theme of their culture, and the sole fantasy element of my tale. The other Bardic instruments have been untampered with, though please note that the Bardic pipes are not bagpipes, but wooden pipes, similar in construction to pan pipes.

Enjoy your trip to the Bardic Isles!

The Bardic Isles Series

Master of Music
Cry of the Kestrel
Rider of the Wind
Harp of Stone (to be released)

Contents

(continued)

The Bardic Isles

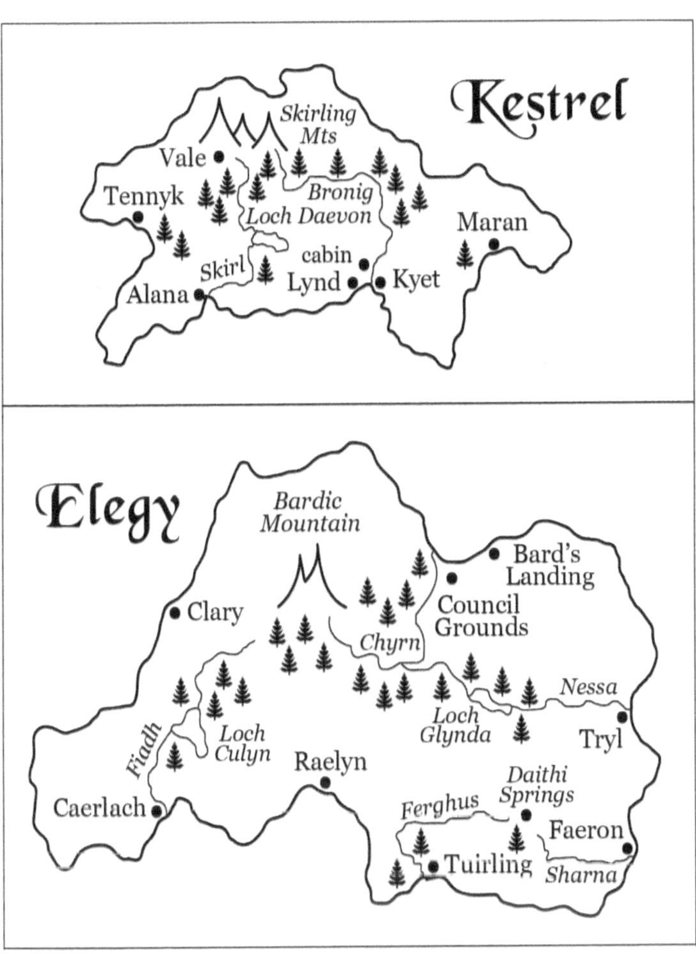
Kestrel
Skirling Mts
Vale
Tennyk
Bronig
Loch Daevon
Maran
Skirl
cabin
Alana
Lynd
Kyet

Elegy
Bardic Mountain
Bard's Landing
Clary
Council Grounds
Chyrn
Nessa
Fiadh
Loch Glynda
Tryl
Loch Culyn
Raelyn
Daithi Springs
Caerlach
Ferghus
Faeron
Tuirling
Sharna

I am leaving here and will not return. The path I walk now is by my own choice and is one that no one can follow. The Gift is dying out in this new land of ours, for reasons none of us understand, though perhaps the horrors that drove us from Eire played a part. Whatever the reason, know that one day, when need calls, it will return. Watch for it and be ready, for the very existence of our new homeland will depend upon it. Watch and listen, for truly, all things are created with music. All things have a song of their own. And one day, one of those songs will be heard, a song that carries the power within it to save us all.

—Master Cyral

Movement One

The Mountains of Kestrel

Chapter 1

High on the cliffs of Bardic Mountain, on the island of Elegy, a kestrel uttered a series of repeated, staccato notes of a single pitch and took flight. He beat his wings into the early summer sky as though pulling himself free of an invisible cord binding him to the lofty peak. His feathers flashed with iridescent splendor in the sun, cornflower blue crowning his head, bronze flowing down his back into the coverts of his wings. As though to emphasize their importance, his primary and secondary feathers were black with white spots, his tailfeathers pale blue with broad black bands accenting their snowy tips.

Catching the wind above, the kestrel soared in glorious freedom, for he was young and strong, the largest of his clutch and ready to fly on his own. He sliced a path through the skies above the woods, streams, and fields of Elegy, the largest of the Bardic Isles, heading north to the coast. Far below him on the remote, rocky beach of Bard's Landing, rock pipits flitted about close to the cliffs and whistling sandpipers pecked their breakfast from amongst the rocks along the shore. To the southeast the kestrel could see the small port of Tryl, shining like a jewel on the eastern coast. The skies were clear in the dawn of this early summer morning, and at this vantage point he could easily make out the island of Eyrie to the west. To the east the island of Lyra raised its own peak into the sky, as did the smallest island of Zephyr just north of it, though neither peak could compare with the supremacy of Bardic Mountain. The kestrel hovered for a moment, critically inspecting the water beneath him. When nothing of interest moved beneath the translucent surface, he continued his journey north, to the second largest island of the five and the chain of mountains that came the closest to matching the grandeur of the mountain he had left behind. To his namesake, though he knew it not ... the island of Kestrel.

Some time later, the adventuring bird flew swiftly west along the southern slopes of the Skirling Mountains, a series of three peaks in the northwestern part of Kestrel. Nestled against the wooded slopes of the westernmost peak lay the village of Vale, known for its excellent wood carvings. Ignoring the villagers bustling about beneath him, the kestrel flew on, gliding smoothly over the northern trees. Movement below caught his eye, and he swooped down to investigate. Perching himself on the branch of a twisted oak tree, he stared down at a young boy crouched at its base. Normally the kestrel would have ignored such a creature, but there was something about this one that captured his attention. The youngster stared intently up at him, and the kestrel felt drawn toward him, pulled by yet another invisible cord as strong as the one that had resisted his flight from Bardic Mountain. The bird cocked his head, listening to the music emanating from the cord. Had the boy held out his arm, the kestrel would have unhesitatingly flown to it. But the youngster abruptly dropped his gaze and returned to his own business, and the kestrel launched himself back into the skies with a piercing spate of staccatos. He would not forget the boy, nor the song that continued to play in his mind. If ever the boy called to him, he would answer.

Far below, the youngster remained crouched among the

twisted roots of the oak. In his hand was a long, narrow bag of sack-cloth. Conflicting emotions darkened the youngster's face as he glanced through the opening at the slender object within. He drew the drawstrings tightly closed, then carefully wrapped the bag in oilcloth. At the place where he knelt, two of the largest roots buck-led upwards, and between them a narrow cavity allowed just enough room for his small parcel. The boy pushed his light brown hair out of his eyes and glanced around to make certain of his soli-tude, then slid the package into its hiding place. He covered it well with leaves, then stood up, brushing dirt from his hands. His amber eyes lingered a moment on the concealing leaves, then he turned resolutely away.

A short time later, he came to a broad dirt road and headed quickly toward Vale. Had anyone glanced through their windows and seen the approaching figure, they might well have wondered, for the day was young and the vendors at the marketplace had just begun to organize their wares. A closer look at the slightly built youngster garbed in faded tunic and worn trousers would have elic-ited wry smiles of recognition. No mysterious visitor, this. It was only, as Holder Gannon often put it, the engaging young scamp whose sole mission in life was to challenge the livelihood of honest Valean vendors. In short, it was only Kaelin.

As the sun rose higher in promise of a fine summer day, the youngster moved among the stalls, deftly complimenting the wares like an expert angler jiggling his line. His observation that the freshness of the rolls in Nyrene's stall would put those of Sharren's, on the other end of the marketplace, to shame, earned him one of Nyrene's warmest smiles and her largest roll besides. The reversed observation, delivered to Sharren, earned the youngster a knowing grin and another roll. A worried comment near the meat stall that one of the rows of spiced meats seemed to have more slices than the others, clearly detracting from the usual artistry of Master Gan-non's platters, made the cobbles ring with Gannon's hearty laughter.

"*Master* Gannon now, is it?" he asked good-naturedly, handing the imp the offending slices. "Be off with you, boy! I'll soon have *paying* customers to see to. And if you return after school to do any bartering of your own, mind your tongue," he added sternly. "I'll be hearing curses aplenty from haggling merchants soon enough, but I'll be hearing none of them from that young mouth of yours, now, will I?"

"No, sir!" The youngster quickly moved on.

Finally, a visit to the fruit stall, followed by a rhapsody of praise in the direction of the ripe melons, added a quarter wedge of fruit to the boy's breakfast. Pleased with his success, Kaelin took his booty and left the village the way he had come, melting unobtrusively into the shadows of the trees. Gannon, catching a glimpse of the youngster as he left, shook his head and sighed. The schoolhouse was in quite the opposite direction.

That afternoon Kaelin made his way to a small, unkempt cottage on the outskirts of the village, pushed open the door, and slipped inside. The small room offered little in the way of furniture. A small, unmade bed stood next to a table bearing the historical evidence of several meals. An old man snored in a chair near the fire, garbed in a faded green robe bound at the waist with a black cord, denoting his rank as a Flutist in the Bardic Order. Kaelin cleared away the dishes, then sat on the floor next to the old man and waited. It wasn't long before the sonorous drone ended in an abrupt cough, and one eye opened. Kaelin grinned.

"Well, youngster, back again, are you?" The old Flutist yawned and scratched his ear absentmindedly. "Can't say I mind. No one but a lad of ten cycles has time to hear the tales I can tell, nor ears to appreciate the music of an old, fumble-fingered Flutist."

"I turned eleven a whole fortnight ago!" Kaelin exclaimed

indignantly.

"Is that so? Small for your age, then, aren't you?" came the tart response. "Well, it's nothing to fret over. I was small for mine as well, but that didn't stop me from becoming one of the best Flutists on Kestrel, you know ... back in my day." He frowned and muttered to himself. Kaelin waited patiently. It was useless to rush the old man, who would get flustered and forget everything, his young guest included. He sighed as the Flutist, in the midst of a confused sentence, abruptly dropped his chin to his chest. His rough breathing settled once more into rhythmic snores.

"Flutist Torin? Sir?" With a sigh, Kaelin moved closer and began to sing of the Bardic exodus so long ago on Eire. It had its usual effect.

The old man's head jerked up and his eyes flashed. "They tried to wipe us out, boy! So they did, but we found a better place, didn't we?"

Kaelin nodded agreeably. Every child in the schoolhouse knew the Bardic Order had come close to annihilation on that day, a story the old Flutist was fond of repeating with the conviction of an eyewitness, though the actual events were over two hundred cycles ago.

"Did I ever tell you why they tried to get rid of us?" Torin demanded.

Kaelin solemnly shook his head. There was always a chance that the Flutist might remember something new.

"It was because of our music!" the old man said, his fist connecting with the arm of the chair so convincingly that it sent him into a fit of coughing. He recovered slowly, then angrily pounded the armrest again for good measure. "The Druids always hated our music, hated the way we helped the people of Eire without asking for payment. The Druids wanted adulation, not to mention coin, for their services. Yet what did they do to earn it? Nothing! They were jealous of the mines our Order found that made us independently wealthy. *That's* what tipped the scale between the two Orders and spelled doom for the Bards."

Kaelin nodded patiently. Every Bardian child was thoroughly schooled in their history.

"And that's not the worst of it, boy," the old man continued. "Why, I've even heard it said that they sacri—" he stopped abruptly, as if recalling the tender age of his audience.

"Oh, please, sir, don't stop now!" Kaelin's eyes shone. *This* had certainly never been discussed by the Schoolmaster of Vale. "Did they really sacrifice people?"

"Well, no," the Flutist admitted reluctantly, "not people, though the Druids of Gaul did. Animals, is what I heard. But they weren't above *murdering* people," he growled with renewed energy. "The Druids snared warriors to their side with promises of coin and a share of the mine's profits, to go up against us. Over a hundred Bards and their wives and families … all of 'em slain by warriors acting under orders from Druid Cathair. No Bards were to be left alive, Bards whose only offense was their music! And such music as contained the legends and history of all Eire. The Druids nearly succeeded, too," he muttered. "Likely not a single Bard left in Eire now, but they couldn't stamp us out completely, thanks to Master Cyral."

"Yes, sir. He saved five ships full of people and supplies, and brought them safely to the Bardic Isles," Kaelin said helpfully, then continued reciting like a model schoolboy. "He established the first Bardic colony on Elegy and brought five more Bardic ships here. He established the five Guilds, for Craftsmen, Tradesmen, Holders, Merchants, and Shipping, governed by their own Guild Law and paying tribute to the Bardic Order."

"And don't forget Caer Wynd, boy."

"Yes, sir," Kaelin said with a sigh, wishing the old man would leave off his history lesson. Everyone knew the prestigious center of learning on the island of Lyra had been established by Master

Cyral for those who wished to study subjects other than music. All Schoolmasters and Schoolmistresses were trained at Caer Wynd and were proficient in all six fields of study: art, writing, healing, history, mathematics, and science. Adepts and Scholars were proficient in all six fields as well, but an Adept was also a Master of at least one of them, a Scholar a Master of at least four. All graduates of Caer Wynd served at least three cycles at Caer Wynd as teachers, to give back to others what Caer Wynd had freely given them. When Kaelin had dutifully recited all this to Flutist Torin, the old man nodded sagely.

"We owe our existence and our way of life to Master Cyral." His eyes probed Kaelin's. "All the Masters of that time were Gifted—couldn't even *be* a Master otherwise—and most of the Bards as well. But Master Cyral was the most Gifted of them all. The power of his music was something to behold, for sure and certain. Why, when Aille-Mara was burning, he brought the rain to put it out! He brought the wind to speed our ships out of the harbor and pushed the warrior ship aground, so he did. Have you ever seen a Master Bard, boy?"

Kaelin, lost in imagining such dramatic events of the past, glanced up, startled. He was silent for a moment, remembering a certain dream. *At least—well, of course it was only a dream!* He shook his head, as much to dispel the memory as to answer the old man's query.

"No, sir. The Master Bard of Kestrel didn't come to Vale two cycles ago, and two cycles before that, I—" Kaelin broke off, feeling his face grow warm. "Couldn't go," he finished lamely.

Not seeming to notice his young guest's discomfiture, the old man landed another thump on the inoffensive arm of his chair. "Well, I've seen *two* of 'em at once!" he stated emphatically. "Went clear to Kyet with my father when I wasn't much older than you, and there they were, playing for all and sundry smack in the middle of the square! Master Bergid was a young Master back then, as was his friend, Master Grened, the Master Bard of Elegy. Flute and harp duets played by Masters ... such music is a thing you don't forget." His rheumy eyes softened with memories, and Kaelin quickly reached over to where the old man's instruments lay: flute, lap harp, and lyre. He picked up the flute and placed it in the Flutist's lap. The aged fingers stroked it lightly.

"This flute." The old man closed his eyes. "I made it myself. I know the feel of it, the details of every key. But in the hands of a Master—" He shook his head thoughtfully. "In the hands of a Master it would come to life. Never would it be the same flute again." His fingers tapped the flute. "There is music trapped in every instrument, boy, music waiting for a Master's hand." He gave his precious flute a final tap and lifted it to his lips.

Kaelin watched intently as the Flutist began to play, clearly at first, then with increasing difficulty. Finally, wheezing in pain, he laid the instrument in his lap. When his breathing grew easier, his jaw dropped open, his eyes closed, and he slept. None of Kaelin's songs could awaken him. With a sigh of resignation, the youngster carefully replaced the flute on the table. He stood looking at it for a while, his face filled with longing. Then, with a last lingering touch, he turned and left.

Brooding deeply, he wandered through the village, thinking of the power Master Cyral's music had possessed to save them all and bring them to this refuge. The Schoolmaster had told them that the Master's Gift had not been seen in the Bardic Isles since, but surely, Kaelin reasoned, that didn't mean the Gift itself was utterly gone. He thought of the flute lying on the old man's table and of what the Flutist had said. *In the hands of a Master it would come to life, lad. Never would it be the same flute again.* The Masters must still be Gifted, then, with something of that power of old. Only fair, he reasoned, for they were responsible for seeing to the welfare of the entire Bardic Isles. What a wondrous thing it must be, he thought enviously, to have such a Gift to use for the good of everyone! Not like him. He grimaced, then stared in dismay at the darkening streets and quickened his pace. There was no sense in giving his sister any more time to worry herself into a temper.

As it turned out, however, it was his own temper that erupted. Kaelin had scarcely sat down at the table when his appetite was destroyed with a single casual comment.

"Craftmaster Arnor stopped by a little while ago." Laena's brown eyes betrayed an excitement not reflected in her voice. She sat back in her chair and twisted a few strands of hair that had come loose from the long, brown braid she kept coiled in a bun on teaching days.

Kaelin almost choked. "What did he want?" He had worked for the Woodcarving Craftmaster for over two cycles, earning an eighth of a copper when the Craftmaster was exceptionally pleased with his work, surplus food from the Craftmaster's garden when Arnor was merely satisfied, and a cuff across the ears when he was not. Since their parents had died four cycles ago, any extra food and coppers were a welcome supplement to the mending Laena took in and the stipend she received as assistant to the Schoolmistress at the girl's school.

Kaelin's older sister took no notice of his discomposure. "He wanted to talk."

"Talk about what?"

"About you, of course."

"Look, Laena, I was only a little bit late yesterday, and I worked hard enough to make up for it, so I don't see what he has to complain—"

"He didn't come here to complain," his sister interrupted. "Although how you could have been late when you left here well before dawn is beyond me." She regarded her brother's innocent expression and sighed. "It's good news, not bad. He came to offer you an early apprenticeship before, as he put it, 'some other fool of a woodcarver takes it into his head to do the same.'" Her eyes danced with merriment. "Of course," she added, "he also made it quite clear that you're an impudent rascal of the first order who scarcely deserves such an honor as being *his* apprentice—" She stopped at the look on her brother's face. "What's wrong?"

He shook his head. "Nothing."

"Kaelin—"

He flushed. "Well, it's just that I ... don't want to apprentice to him."

Laena stared at him. "And just who would you prefer over the Woodcarving Craftmaster of Vale himself?" she demanded.

"You don't understand!"

Laena's brown eyes sparked in exasperation. "No, I certainly don't! Craftmaster Arnor takes only *one* apprentice each cycle, and of all the boys in Vale, he's chosen you, four cycles before you come of age, no less! There's no higher honor you could hope for, Kaelin, and you're going to refuse it? For what?"

"I don't know! But not for being a butcher, or tanner, or apprentice to any other craft in Vale!" He stood so abruptly that his chair fell over backward. He ignored it and pushed past his sister.

"Kaelin, wait!"

He paused, his hand on the door.

"I thought you liked woodworking. You're good at it!"

"What does it matter if I'm good at it, or like it?" Kaelin retorted. "I don't like it enough!"

"Then what *do* you like enough?"

Silence fell like a shroud between them.

"I can't tell you that," Kaelin finally said, his voice rough and laced with pain. "I can't tell anyone."

He left the cottage and wandered aimlessly through the deserted streets, trying to forget the bewildered hurt in Laena's eyes. After a while he left the village and entered the woods. Starlight cast a gentle sheen over the faint path he followed, but the familiar ache deep inside him burned with harsh intensity. He cursed loud and fervently, using every oath he had ever overheard in the village marketplace, but the pain only intensified, as though mocking his blasphemous efforts to bury it in curses. A tear rolled down his cheek and he brushed it angrily away.

Soon Kaelin was kneeling at the base of the oak tree and extracting his hidden parcel. He unwrapped the bag, pulled the drawstrings open, and slid a wooden flute into his hand. It was small and plain, having but seven holes along its length and two beneath, with none of the rods or keys of Old Torin's Bardic flute. Kaelin stared at it for a moment, his other hand clenching into a fist. *Music! What do you want from me? The Bards' and Masters' music does only good, so why can't mine? Why does mine have to do such horrible things?* A spasm of pain shook his slight frame.

The music he would only allow himself to play here in the woods, far enough from his village that no one would overhear him, was both hurtful and healing. If he focused intently on something in the clearing—a rock, leaf, or tree—he could hear its music, wondrous music that seemed to define its very essence. He had never dared to focus on an animal, much less on a person, although he had almost done so with the kestrel he had seen early that morning. Startled by its abrupt arrival, Kaelin had stared at the bird just long enough to begin hearing strains of wild, incredible music, to begin feeling a pull toward the magnificent creature. Then, frightened, he had broken his focus and lowered his eyes, and the bird had flown off.

While Kaelin could safely listen to the music of natural objects, if he attempted to play any of it, pain filled every note and he would break off, gasping. It had been a tremendous relief to discover that he could play variations of such music without pain. He had quickly grown adept at this, listening to the music around him and deftly converting it into one variation after another. These spontaneous variations eased the restless pressure of what resided inside of him, if only for a few moments. For it wasn't only the music of the things surrounding him that he could hear. Kaelin's mind was filled with its own music, as if a composer were trapped inside him, feverishly writing on an intangible manuscript songs that demanded a voice. Yet if he gave in to the pressure to play it, the utterance of every note through his flute was intensely painful, as if each were a sharp knife slicing through the walls of his mind.

Resolutely ignoring the clamor of the music within him, Kaelin thought of the kestrel's music and began to play, weaving the notes into his own variation of what he had heard, music he could play without pain. With the first few notes the cutting edge of his torment subsided, relieving the pressure within him to a bearable degree. He closed his eyes and relaxed, deeply aware, though unable to explain it, that the trees around him listened and tuned their trembling leaves to his music, and the wind swept down to carry the sounds of his inner turmoil away. He played with the movement of the wind for a few moments, scattering notes about the clearing like capricious leaves, then impulsively sent the music soaring upward, far above the trees. He glimpsed the wondrous view the kestrel must surely take for granted, saw the woods and mountains stretch before him across the length of Kestrel. One long, wonderful view of freedom. Then the song modulated under his fingers, the notes weaving wistfully among the trees for a few lonely moments before they died away.

Kaelin lowered his flute and, suddenly aware of the growing shadows of dusk, started to put it away. He paused for a moment, hearing the staccato cry of a kestrel in the distance. The boy smiled, enjoying the fanciful notion that the same bird he had seen this morning was responding to the variation of its own music. "I hope you enjoyed the performance," he murmured, "for you're the only one who will ever hear it."

Since the age of seven, the disturbing music within him had given him no peace, and the only place he found a brief respite was here in the woods, where no one could hear. *Where no one can be hurt.* With a pang of loneliness, Kaelin hid his flute and headed home, wondering, as he so often did, what it would be like to be a member of the Bardic Order, to have the musical training he needed and wanted so badly.

In a remote mountain village like Vale, the chance to apprentice to the Bardic Order was, he thought glumly, nonexistent. It was fortunate for him that the old Flutist had come to spend his last cycles here, but he had stopped taking students long ago. The villages along the coast were inhabited by Harpists, Flutists, and Pipers of the Bardic Order, who gave lessons just as Old Torin had once done. Kaelin sighed as he traveled the path back to his village. There was no point in dreaming about the Bardic Order when he couldn't have paid for lessons from a Flutist even if one were available. And, he thought morosely, why be upset about the impossibility of lessons when he couldn't play for anyone, not even his teacher? Until he solved *that* problem, his only option was to grab his learning in secret wherever he could find it.

And grab it he had, from more than just Old Torin. A few times a month a Bard visited Vale, spending a day or two teaching and repairing any instrument brought to him. Kaelin, though he hovered close and avidly watched every move the Bard made, had never spoken to one. There was, he knew, no point in doing so. Not even a Bard could forbid him to dream, though, and for someone like him, dreaming would have to be enough. And, he told himself, it really *would* be enough if only someone could take away the pain.

In addition to the occasional visits by Bards, the Master Bard of Kestrel visited the mountain villages every other cycle, but he had not done so two cycles ago because of a serious knee injury, and Kaelin had missed the visit previous to that. Hopefully, the Master's knee had healed sufficiently for him to make his scheduled visit this cycle, but there was no telling when that might be.

Halfway home, the boy paused, catching a faint sound carried on the wind behind him. *Flute music?* He listened intently, but only the faint rustling of leaves disturbed the stillness. He stood motion-less, divided between his desire to make it home before dark and a strange compulsion to return to the clearing. Then he shook his head and continued on toward home, a few furlongs west of the village. His sister's patience had limits, and returning home after dark was testing them.

Chapter 2

The dream came to Kaelin yet again that night. As always, it felt more like a vision than a dream, as though he were observing something that had happened in the past or would happen in the future. An old man, dressed in the white robe and gold cord of a Master, trudged wearily up a hill. On his back rested a silken bag, through which the outline of an immense harp could be seen. As so often before, Kaelin found himself fighting the intense longing to see the instrument within, to reach out and touch it ... to play it, though he didn't know how. Feeling like an intruder, he watched as the Master stopped before a vine-covered cliff and turned as though to make certain of his solitude. Always before, the vision had stopped at this point. But tonight, for the first time, the Master looked straight into his eyes.

Kaelin cried out, struggling in panic from his blanket. He sat up, disoriented, his heart pounding, and looked frantically around the small room, as though expecting the Master to appear and demand to know why his journey was being disturbed by some dreaming village boy. *It was just a dream! Just a dream,* he insisted, as much to reassure himself as the unwelcome apparition of the Master. Kaelin lay back down, staring into the darkness, remembering the compelling eyes that had so briefly looked into his. *Amber eyes, just like mine,* he thought wonderingly. No one in

Vale, not even his parents or sister, had amber eyes. He had once fought a boy at school who teased him about having a wolf for a father. Kaelin would have lost that fight if a new student, Erik, hadn't stepped in and thrashed the other boy so thoroughly that no one had ever said such a thing again. All three of them had taken the Schoolmaster's punishment for it, and he and Erik had been firm friends ever since. Kaelin closed his eyes, trying to dispel the unnerving dream, but the image of the Master remained, burning brightly in his mind, forbidding sleep. At last, when his room began to lighten with the approach of dawn, he quietly dressed and left the house.

Kaelin meandered through their small garden, then wandered into the woods, trying to decide what to tell Craftmaster Arnor about his unwelcome offer of apprenticeship. As much as he hated to admit it, Laena was right; it would be madness to let such an opportunity slip through his fingers just because he wanted something he could never have. He and his sister had enough trouble growing food for themselves during the warm seasons. Laena would have no part in accepting charity since their parents died, but packages of food or herbs that mysteriously appeared on their doorstep were not refused, for, as she told Kaelin, how was she to return them? During the winter months Laena increased the mending work she took in, often working late into the night. This, added to her stipend from the girl's school and combined with what Kaelin managed to earn from the Craftmaster and any other villager with a task for him, helped them make it through to spring. As Craftmaster Arnor's apprentice, he would be given room and board and a small but steady wage, not to mention the opportunity to become a wood Craftsman himself someday. He might not want to, but Kaelin knew he had to accept it. He owed that much to his sister, who worked so hard to care for him. After all, it wasn't as though he didn't like the woodworking craft, the smooth feel of wood taking shape under his hands to match the design in his mind. *It's just ... not enough. And it's too soon. I thought I had four more cycles.*

Unaware of his surroundings, Kaelin continued walking, resigned and depressed at the idea of having to accept an apprenticeship anyone else in Vale would have celebrated. When at last he looked up, he was surprised to find that he had climbed a good distance up Skellig Mountain and was not far from the place his parents used to take them on special days. He stopped abruptly. Though Laena had often gone there since their parents had died, Kaelin had refused to go with her. He thought of the clearing where they had picnicked, the willow overhanging a large boulder on the banks of a stream. The names of his family had been chiseled into the flat side of the boulder by his father, Arnor's most talented wood Craftsman. The clear image of the chiseled names shone brightly against the walls of his mind, and Kaelin fought to keep his tears from overflowing. The thought crossed his mind that his father would be pleased to know his son had apprenticed to the Craftmaster. He turned abruptly and headed back.

It was past noon when he arrived back at the road, his stomach rumbling with hunger. For a long moment he stood there, undecided which direction to take. With a sigh, he turned away from home and headed toward the village and Craftmaster Arnor's shop. *Might as well get it over with.*

When he reached the village square, Kaelin glanced around, frowning in perplexity. There was an unusual number of people in the square, all talking excitedly and crowding the cobbled grounds. Kaelin spied his friend Erik among them and pushed his way through, all thoughts of the Craftmaster forgotten. *Perhaps a Flutist or Piper, or maybe even a Bard has come!* It was the only thing he could think of that would cause such a stir. Then he caught a glimpse of white hair, bushy white eyebrows, and a flowing white robe bound with a golden cord. Kaelin caught his breath. In the Bardic Order, apprentices wore grey robes, Pipers cinnamon brown, Flutists emerald green, and Harpists burgundy. Further up the Bardic Order hierarchy, Instrumentalists wore deep sapphire robes, and Bards cerulean blue, known around the Isles as Bardic blue. Only a Master Bard was allowed to wear white.

A Master! Just like the one in my dream. Each of the five Bardic Isles had one Master Bard, and each Master had his own field of expertise. This, then, must be the Master Bard of Kestrel, Master of Composition ... his first visit in four cycles! Little wonder the news had spread like wildfire and the square was full of excited villagers.

Kaelin's eyes were drawn to the intriguing bags lying next to the Master. Bardic blue, with silver tassels adorning their drawstrings. A slender bag certainly held a flute, another looked to be the right size for wooden pipes, and a much larger bag showed the distinct outline of a harp. The boy gazed at the shrouded instrument with awe, knowing that this must be a full-sized Bardic harp, not a lap harp like most Bards traveled with. Even so, this harp was much smaller than the one in his dream. Deep within him, music surged ... begging, demanding, tormenting. Kaelin stared at the Master's instruments and clenched his teeth against his intense desire to touch them, to explore them, to *play* them.

Lost in his fervent desire, he didn't notice that everyone was sitting down until Erik pulled him impatiently to the ground. "Where've you *been?*" Erik whispered fiercely. "Master Bergid has been here since dawn, repairing instruments, talking to everyone, and now he's gonna play!"

Entranced, Kaelin watched as the Master opened the slender bag and withdrew a leather case. Loosening the strap around it, he opened it, withdrew a Bardic flute, and attached its headjoint. The boy stared at the beautifully crafted instrument, wishing he could get a closer look at the intricate keys and rods, which looked even more extensive than the old Flutist's. The Master raised it to his lips, and Kaelin's own mouth dropped open as the sweetest sound he had ever heard floated on the morning air. Old Torin had certainly never produced such a sound as this, nor had any of the Bards Kaelin had ever heard. He caught his breath at the thought that he was hearing the music of someone *Gifted* ... like the Bards and Masters of old, whose music had the power to do untold good. The first notes of the Master moved downward, much lower than Kaelin's small instrument could achieve. Then, with a suddenness that made Kaelin gasp, the music swelled upward, lilting its way to the upper registers like a released bird on the wing. Intricate trills and flawless arpeggios chased each other skyward, unaware that a young boy's spirit eagerly followed them. Then, at its peak, the mood of the music changed, cascading wistfully down minor triads.

Immersed in the music, Kaelin suddenly heard the variation he had played the night before skillfully interwoven in the Master's song. The youngster paled as the music washed over him, music he knew to the last note. *My variation of the kestrel's song! But how?* He shook his head as though to deny what his own ears were hearing. *He must have heard me in the woods last night.* And now the Master was echoing Kaelin's music back to him before the entire village of Vale!

The boy looked about in alarm. *What will happen to them?* But though he searched every face he could see, the expressions were rapt and serene. Craftmasters and apprentices, women and children—all were listening, undisturbed by the conflict raging in Kaelin's mind. *They're hearing my music and nothing awful is happening!* What power this Master had, to turn Kaelin's music into something beautiful and harmless. Music that anyone could listen to. He lowered his gaze in shame.

The music became insistent, lifting Kaelin's theme into the upper register with increased tempo, demanding, compelling his attention. Inexorably, the boy's eyes were drawn upward, and he drew a sharp breath as he met the intense regard of two vividly blue eyes. *Not amber. Not like the Master in my dream.* Kaelin tried to break the contact, both relieved and confused when the melody instantly modulated. It continued for a few moments more, then lingered briefly on the notes of resolution and faded away on the major. Kaelin closed his eyes in pain, feeling as though he had been physically torn from the music and left to bleed. He didn't hear the clapping and shouting around him, didn't notice people getting up and slowly leaving the square, or Erik talking excitedly to two of their schoolmates. Kaelin felt the eyes of the Master Bard resting on him, but did not dare look up to meet them. A moment later, he knew the Master had left.

He glanced up in time to see the white-robed figure leading a well-laden mule in the direction of the woods, his walking staff punctuating the way. Kaelin hurried to follow, paying no attention to Erik's raised voice demanding to know where he was going. Keeping a discreet distance, Kaelin followed the Master as he took the road to Wynd, another small mountain village thirty furlongs east of Vale. The Master followed this road to where a smaller trail branched off north, climbing higher up the slopes of Skellig Mountain. Here the Master paused, then turned and glanced in Kaelin's direction as the youngster hovered uncertainly behind. After adjusting the strap of one of his travel bags, the Master turned his mule onto the narrow trail and was swallowed up by the woods.

Kaelin stood motionless, oblivious to Erik's approach behind him. He had thought the Master would continue his rounds of the mountain villages by going directly to Wynd. *Why would he head north from here? There are no villages further up Skellig. But if he's going to camp up there, maybe I can talk to him in private.* Words of the old Flutist echoed in his mind.

There is music trapped in every instrument, boy, music waiting for a Master's hand.

Kaelin couldn't repress the bitter thoughts that followed. *At least an instrument can't feel the pain of music trapped inside it. I should be so lucky.* He thought of the painful music trapped inside himself and wondered. Dared he even hope that this Gifted Master could free it? *If he can't, I'm no worse off than I am now. But if he can—*Kaelin gasped as someone seized his shoulder.

"What's going on?" Erik demanded. "Are you all right?"

Kaelin turned to meet his friend's bewildered gaze. "No, but maybe ... maybe I could be. If you'll help me."

"Help you do what?" Erik asked.

Kaelin took a deep breath. "I'm going to follow the Master Bard."

"What? Are you crazy? You can't just walk off and follow someone like that, Kaelin! He's a *Master.*"

"That's exactly why I have to! A chance like this—" He forced himself to speak calmly. "I know you don't understand, Erik, and I don't either. But maybe he will. I have to find out."

"So why do you need my help?"

"I want you to tell Laena that I—" He stopped abruptly.

"That you what?" Erik asked impatiently.

Kaelin took a deep breath. "That I followed the Master Bard, and he agreed to take me with him to Kyet to help me find a Bardic apprenticeship."

Erik stared at him. "You can't be serious! Why on earth would the Master do something like that? You don't know the first thing about music!" Kaelin stiffened, but his friend continued, undeterred. "Look, the Master didn't say a word to you. Do you think he'll welcome some scruffy village boy trailing after him?"

Amber eyes flashed. "Does the Master Bard of Kestrel own the woods?"

The defiant question effectively silenced Erik's objections. "All right, then, I'll tell your sister ... not that she'll believe a word of it. I just hope you know what you're doing. *I* sure don't." He turned abruptly away.

"Erik?"

Kaelin's friend paused without turning.

"Thanks," Kaelin managed to say. "For more than just this."

Erik nodded and glanced back. "I hope ... well, I hope you find whatever it is you're looking for," he mumbled. Then he turned and walked quickly away.

As soon as his friend was out of sight, Kaelin hastened into the woods on the other side of the road. It wasn't long before he returned with a narrow bag tied to his belt. He stood motionless for a moment, looking back at the village where he had grown up. He glanced once in the direction of the cottage where Laena would soon learn that he was gone. Then he turned and walked away, following the footsteps of the Master.

When he came to the place where the Master had left the road, he was surprised to find it was little more than a deer path. Did the Master Bard of Kestrel not wish to be seen? Or, Kaelin wondered uncomfortably, not wish to be followed? Moments later, he was relieved to see the light of a small campfire between the trees. As Kaelin cautiously approached, he saw the Master brushing down the mule, whose packs had been removed. The boy quickly hid himself nearby.

As his turbulent feelings calmed, Kaelin began to think. He had been so focused on finding the Master that he hadn't once thought beyond that point. The idea of boldly walking up to that imposing figure and asking for his help was terrifying—preposterous—*impossible*. And yet the hope could not be quenched. Like an invisible tether, it held him in place behind the trees and kept him from bolting home.

Torn between an equal measure of fear and hope, Kaelin surreptitiously watched the Master make a pot of stew, feeling his own stomach rumble with hunger as the savory aroma reached him. Searching his pockets for stray bits of food, he cursed himself for having missed every meal of the day. He watched with envious eyes as the Master finished his meal and sat on his bedroll, silently watching the fire for a long time before banking it and retiring for the night. Kaelin sat motionless in the dark, cursing himself again for his cowardice in not being able to approach the Master he had gone to such trouble to follow. At last, his exhaustion finally overcame his hunger and he fell into a restless sleep, shivering in the night wind blowing through the trees.

The warmth of the sun on his right cheek and the clatter of a pan awakened him early the next morning. Kaelin stretched his stiff limbs and looked cautiously toward the clearing. Master Bergid was readying his pack for travel. Once his preparations were complete, however, he inexplicably reseated himself. Time slowed as Kaelin watched the motionless Master. Dread etched a thin path up the boy's spine, and he withdrew further from sight, trembling with the certainty that the Master knew he was there. Kaelin's memory of his defiant words to Erik mocked him. *Does the Master Bard of Kestrel own the woods?* To remain undetected, he would gladly concede the Master's right to every tree on Kestrel, roots and all.

The color drained from Kaelin's face as the first notes of music drifted toward him. Flute music. *His* music, music that had filled the village square just yesterday. Renewed pressure burned deeply within him. The clear sound of the Bardic flute wrapped around him, the notes pulling him irresistibly, as though trying to reunite with their composer. Then, in the middle of a phrase, the music stopped.

Kaelin lifted his eyes to find himself standing before the Master Bard of Kestrel, though he could not remember having walked there. Alarmed, he stared into vivid blue eyes framed by bushy brows. The eyes were soft with acquired wisdom, but the white brows lifted in his direction were daunting.

"I'm sorry, sir!" Kaelin blurted. "I didn't mean to disturb you."

"Shadows are only disturbing to those who fear them," came the enigmatic reply. "I'm glad to see that this one has substance."

"I—I'll leave if you want me to."

"Certainly not before explaining why you've been following me." The blue eyes held the amber ones firmly. The effect on Kaelin was devastating; this was no Valean vendor he could charm out of his wares with flattery and guile. This was a Master, whose eyes demanded total honesty. Kaelin's mind frantically spouted advice.

Tell him you need to know how he played your music yesterday without anything awful happening!

No, you can't risk him asking questions. Tell him you need help so you can play without pain!

And that's not going to arouse any questions? Tell him—

"I heard you play your flute in the village yesterday," Kaelin said, as much to drown out the escalating conflict in his own mind as to answer the Master. "And I followed you because ... well, because you're a Master, and I was hoping—" Though the words strained to be released, he could not bring himself to free them.

"I played music that was mine ... and music that was not," the Master said, still holding his gaze. "I played the music that was not in order to find its composer. Have I found him?"

The measure of hope fled from the wave of fear that besieged Kaelin. The Master was looking for the composer of dangerous music! *He knows! What will he do to me?*

"I'm sorry, sir!" The apology erupted without warning, earning him a startled look from the Master. "I know I shouldn't have, but I only do it in the woods where no one can hear me! I swear it!"

The Master gave the terrified youngster in front of him an appraising look. "I didn't say you shouldn't have, lad," he said gently.

"It ... wasn't wrong?" Kaelin's expression cleared as hope tentatively crept back. If the Master hadn't sought him out to punish him, maybe he wanted to help him.

"You needn't be a member of the Bardic Order to compose music," the Master assured him, "and you've certainly nothing to be ashamed of in having written such music as that. I am, however, still waiting to hear your reason for following me." The Master smiled whimsically. "Perhaps you intended to take me to task for incorporating your music into my own without authorization."

There was no answering smile on Kaelin's face as he struggled to find his voice. "I followed you to see if, well, maybe—" He floundered to a finish, undecided which truth to tell, shocked when what emerged was the deepest desire of his heart. "I want to become a Bardic apprentice," he whispered.

"Bards and Masters do not take on apprentices, lad. Surely you know that."

"Yes, sir, but I thought you might know someone—a Flutist, perhaps—who does? You must have heard me play, so you know I'm not a beginner. I've learned everything I can in Vale. Becoming an apprentice is the only chance I have to learn more."

"Do your parents know where you are?"

Kaelin hesitated, desperately wanting to answer with a simple yes, but unable to lie to those clear blue eyes. "My parents died when I was seven," he said reluctantly. "I made my friend tell my sister that you agreed to take me with you to Kyet to find me a Bardic apprenticeship. I didn't want her to worry, and all I've ever wanted is music—" His words vanished as quickly as his courage under the Master's bristling brows.

"You began your journey to me with lies?"

Trembling, Kaelin gave a barely discernible nod. His plea for a Bardic apprenticeship was not only going to be refused, he thought despairingly, he was likely going to be sent away with a thrashing as well.

"There is no place in the Bardic Order for someone who lies to get what he wants."

The Master's words stung Kaelin worse than the Schoolmaster's switch ever had. He flushed deeply and tried in vain to look away from those disconcerting eyes. He had the uncomfortable feeling that they were reading him as effortlessly as they would a musical score.

"However," the Master continued, without seeming to notice Kaelin's discomposure, "if you are willing to learn, and accept whatever lessons I see fit to give you, you may stay with me for a trial month as I finish my travels among the mountain villages. *If* those lessons are passed to my satisfaction, I will take you with me to Kyet and arrange a Bardic apprenticeship for you with a Flutist. If they are not, I will take you back to Vale." The Master's brows lifted in challenge. "Are you willing to learn what I choose to teach you?"

"Oh, *yes*, sir!" The Master's eyes released him so suddenly that Kaelin gasped.

"What is your name, lad?"

"Kaelin."

"Well then, Kaelin, your first lesson will be about honesty, however late it may be in coming to you. You will return to Vale, apologize to your friend and sister, and tell them the truth. When you've obtained their forgiveness and your sister's consent, you may come with me."

Kaelin grimaced, knowing that Laena's consent would not be readily given after what he had done. "Will you wait for me here?" he asked hesitantly.

"Yes," the Master replied, "but I have a long way to travel and several more villages to visit, so the sooner you return, the better. I must leave by tomorrow morning at the latest." He continued in a gentler voice. "I think you'll find your return to Vale well worth your trouble, lad. And," he added dryly, "you might consider packing a few other necessities besides your flute."

Kaelin was scarcely aware of his hurried trek back to Vale, his thoughts a confusion of dread at having to face his sister, and hope that she would forgive him and allow him to go with the Master.

Erik's relief at Kaelin's return was quickly replaced with incredulity at the news that the Master Bard of Kestrel had agreed to take an unknown village boy with him for a whole month. When Kaelin asked for his forgiveness, Erik was so flabbergasted that he barely managed to nod. Kaelin left his friend speechless and hurried home, where he found Laena in tears. He stood paralyzed on the threshold; he had not seen his sister cry since the day their parents had died.

"Oh, *Kaelin.*" The relief and joy in his sister's voice struck Kaelin a heavier blow than any the Master's hand could have dealt. In a rare moment of unrestrained feeling, he reached out and hugged her, feeling her arms tighten around him as he stumbled over his apology. Then he began to talk, his words coming with increased strength as he spoke of the Master he wanted so badly to return to.

Laena's eyes widened. Was this her brother, this animated boy with shining eyes and dynamic words? Who was this Master Bard, who could produce a change like this in a single meeting? Clearly, he was a master of more than music alone.

"Music," she said softly. "Is that what you care about more than anything? I never knew music was your dream."

Kaelin frowned and shook his head slightly. "Dreams shouldn't hurt."

"Music hurts you? Why?" When her brother made no reply, she continued. "And why didn't you tell me?"

Kaelin looked up, his eyes filled with such transparent pain that Laena winced. "There was no use in telling anyone," he said hopelessly. "No one could possibly understand or do anything to help me. Master Bergid is the only one who might be able to." He looked at her beseechingly. "But I can't go with him without your forgiveness and permission. Please, Laena! I'm truly sorry." His heart sank when his sister shook her head.

"My forgiveness you have, but I can't give my permission for you to just walk off and leave home, even with Master Bergid, until you're *completely* honest with me."

Kaelin looked at her uneasily. "What do you want to know?"

"Where have you been going before dawn every morning that made you late for school, or not show up there at all? You always gave me excuses that I never really believed. If this Master has taught you honesty, tell me the truth now."

"I went to the woods," Kaelin said reluctantly, "to practice my flute."

Laena frowned. "Flute? What flute?"

"Old Torin gave me a length of wood that I hollowed out and carved into a flute. I've been practicing early every morning, getting breakfast at the marketplace, and then going to school ... most of the time, anyhow."

"And when you didn't go to school?"

"I went to Old Torin's, so I could learn how to play by watching him. It's the only way I could learn, but I can't learn anything more from him."

Laena's eyes traveled to the narrow bag fastened to her brother's belt, and Kaelin stepped back nervously.

"Can I hear—" she began, but Kaelin shook his head before she could finish.

"No! I can't play for you ... it's too dangerous!"

"Dangerous?" Laena echoed blankly. "Why?"

"It just is! I can't explain."

"Why not?"

"Because I can't explain what I don't understand." Kaelin stepped back another pace. It was hardly an answer, but thankfully, his sister didn't persist.

"I won't ask you to play your flute, then," Laena said gently. "But can I at least see it?"

Kaelin nodded in relief, removed his flute, and handed it to her. Laena handled it carefully, then returned it to him.

"You made that?" she exclaimed in astonishment. "Figured out how to play it all by yourself? Practiced in the woods, because for some reason you won't tell anyone, you think it's dangerous for anyone to hear you? And this is why you need the Master's help?"

Kaelin nodded silently.

Laena stood frowning in thought for a long moment. "The brother I knew yesterday," she finally said, "would have lied to the Master and told him he had my permission to follow him. Why didn't you do that? Why come all the way back here to tell me the truth and risk not being able to go with him, when it means so much to you?"

Kaelin flushed. "I would have done that if I could," he admitted, "because I thought it was the only way to get the Master to agree to help me. But I can't lie to him." He frowned, remembering the vivid blue eyes and commanding brows. "His eyes won't accept anything but the truth, and somehow he just pulls it out of you, whether it's what you intended to tell him or not." He dropped his eyes and studied the floor. "If you won't give me your permission, I'll go back and apologize for wasting his time," he said hollowly. "And then I'll go to Craftmaster Arnor and accept his offer." He looked up in surprise when his sister took his hands in both of her own.

"No," Laena said firmly. "Anyone who can do what this Master has done is someone I'll entrust my brother to. Go back and tell him you have my forgiveness and my permission to go with him." As Kaelin stared at her, speechless, she sighed. "How I'm going to miss you, aggravating brother of mine! If you don't pass this trial of his, promise me you'll come home."

The music that suddenly surged inside Kaelin was as clear and sweet as any music a Bardic instrument could produce. "Of course I will!" He gave his sister a knowing grin. "Are you going to join with Donal now?"

His sister's eyes widened. "How did you know Donal and I

were planning to join someday?"

Kaelin's grin deepened with the rare pleasure of seeing his sister blush. "I may be a lot younger than you, but I'm not blind or stupid," he said. "I'd have to be both not to know. Donal's carting business is all the way in Lynd, almost as far away as Kyet, and he used to come through here only twice a cycle. But suddenly, after meeting my *sister* a cycle ago," Kaelin said meaningfully, "he doesn't mind trekking clear across Kestrel to collect wood carvings once a month! And he doesn't exactly hustle his way out of Vale afterwards, either. He hangs around the schoolhouse so he can walk you home after you're done teaching. He brings us twice as much food as he eats when he comes to dinner. And I've seen him drop a copper or two in the coin jar when you're not looking."

"He has?" Laena looked mortified and pleased at the same time.

Kaelin nodded. "I know you love him. And I know you've waited for me to get an apprenticeship before joining with him, so I wouldn't have to move from Vale."

His sister's hand rested suddenly on his. "I never minded the wait," she said softly. "And I would never have made you accept an apprenticeship with Craftmaster Arnor against your will, just so Donal and I could join. Or for any other reason. If you leave the Master later than two months from now, go to Lynd and ask for Donal. I'll be there." She hesitated for a moment. "I won't be able to keep this house when I go. We'll need the coin we can get from it to build a house on the land Donal's leasing for his business. I'm sorry for that, Kaelin."

Kaelin nodded, feeling tears he refused to release. But when his sister reached out for him, he did not pull away.

⌁ ⸙ ⌁

The time it took Kaelin to make his way back to the Master Bard was by no means wasted. Both mind and muscles were exercised to their fullest, and while the latter kept Kaelin's sore legs moving, his thoughts were free for work of another sort. He thought of the village he was leaving. As frustrated as he had been there, it was home, the source of all his memories, good and bad. He wondered if he would ever find another friend like Erik. He thought of the old Flutist, who had helped him so much without ever knowing it, and of his sister. How long would it be before he saw either of them again?

It's strange, he mused as the approaching dusk cast patterns of darkness across his path. He had lied to free himself to leave Vale and follow the Master but had found not even the freedom to look unashamed into the Master's eyes. And that, he knew, was something he badly wanted to be able to do. As he hurried along the darkening trail with the comforting weight of his bedroll and pack on his back, the welcome sound of flute music reached him through the cold mountain air. It seemed to Kaelin, as he moved eagerly toward it, that his life in Vale, both the good and the bad, faded before the brightness of the music that filled his mind from the Master's flute.

A canopy of stars had pricked through the growing darkness above him when he arrived back at the clearing. The Master put aside his flute as the youngster came to stand before him once again.

"I did as you told me, sir, and my sister has given me permission to go with you," Kaelin said. Once again he found himself held by the clear eyes of the Master, but this time felt no desire to pull away.

"And did they both forgive you?" the Master gravely asked.

"They did, sir, but I need to ask for your forgiveness too. I should never have lied to follow you. Please forgive me." Bushy eyebrows no longer bristled at him, and Kaelin looked into blue eyes he knew he could never lie to, nor would he ever want to. Moved by an impulse he did not understand, he knelt on one knee in the

Bardic manner of taking a vow and his faltering voice steadied.

"I will never lie again."

Five words. A promise, given to the Master Bard of Kestrel by a boy who wanted desperately to become a Bardic apprentice. The Master was silent, struck by something in the amber eyes lifted so seriously to him, struck also by the awareness that those five words had somehow changed everything, though he could not have said why or how they had done so. At last, he spoke. "Then you have earned both my forgiveness and my respect."

Kindness shone from the depths of his blue eyes, and Kaelin bowed his weary head over the Master's knee. Hot tears slid across his cheeks and fell onto the white robe beneath him.

Chapter 3

Kaelin awoke the next morning feeling clean and fresh on the inside, stiff and sore on the outside. He opened a drowsy eye, then sat up in panic to find himself alone. Reassured by the presence of the mule and the Master's bags, he stretched and went to build up the fire. A bag of provisions lay next to a cooking pot already filled with water, so he took out his belt knife and busied himself making a stew of carrots, potatoes, and wild onions, seasoned with herbs and chips of dried meat.

"Perhaps you'd like to wash up while I tend to that pot."

Startled, Kaelin turned to see the Master Bard enter the clearing, rubbing his face briskly with a towel. Rainbows danced in the droplets beading his white hair.

The stream was icy cold, but the gushing current refreshed Kaelin and soothed his sore muscles. He returned to camp feeling uncertain and tongue-tied after the events of the previous day, but the Master only seemed interested in breaking his fast and motioned for Kaelin to do likewise.

When they had finished eating, Kaelin took the plates and utensils to the stream to clean them. On his return, they packed up the small camp and carried everything over to the mule. Kaelin hesitantly stroked the light grey animal, and the Master gave the youngster a carrot to introduce himself with.

"Does he have a name, sir?" Kaelin asked.

"Certainly he does. Indeed, I've been remiss in not making proper introductions," the Master said. "Kaelin, this is Poor Oran. Poor Oran, this is Kaelin." The mule turned his head at hearing his name and began nuzzling Kaelin as though expecting to find another carrot hiding in his tunic.

Kaelin tilted his head curiously. "Poor Oran?"

The Master chuckled. "I purchased him on the western coast for this trip. I believe he was named 'Oran' for the unusually light color of his hide, but when the villagers saw how many packs I was loading onto his back, they referred to him as "Poor Oran" so many times that I thought it a rather fitting name."

Kaelin grinned. "Can I take care of him for you?"

"That would be most appreciated, lad. Poor Oran does quite well foraging as we travel, but he enjoys the odd treat now and then, and the daily use of the brush you'll find in that pack. He's a remarkably even-tempered soul, never balks or gives a bit of trouble on the trail. You two should get along fine. Now, then," he said, "before we load him for traveling, I believe you and I need to have a talk."

Kaelin gave Poor Oran a final pat and followed the Master back to their empty campsite.

"Before I decide where to begin your instruction," Master Bergid said, "suppose you tell me about yourself. How old are you?"

"I turned eleven cycles a fortnight ago."

"Eleven? Then you won't be finished with your schooling for another cycle?"

"I finished my schooling a quarter-cycle ago."

The Master's brow lifted. "An excellent student."

Kaelin flushed. "No, sir. Schoolmaster Radnal allowed me to take the test early only because I promised to become a good student if I didn't pass it."

"What were the Schoolmaster's grievances?"

Kaelin's eyes dropped. "Lack of attendance, not paying attention, poor discipline—" His voice trailed off.

"And what were *your* grievances?"

He looked up in surprise. "I needed the time for my flute."

"Wasn't your time at home sufficient to practice?"

"I couldn't—" Kaelin hesitated. "I couldn't play there."

"Perhaps, had you explained the situation to the Schoolmaster—"

"No!" He hung his head, ashamed. "I'm sorry for interrupting you, sir. It's just that no one knows about my flute except you, and now Laena. I told her about it yesterday."

The Master's brow lifted again. "How, then, did you receive any instruction on it?"

"I've never had any. I made it myself when I was seven, and I only play it alone in the woods. An old ... er, Flutist Torin retired to our village, and I skipped school now and then so I could learn by watching him. And whenever a Flutist or Bard came through our village, I studied what they did and then practiced by myself."

"Why didn't you ask any of them for help?"

"I ... couldn't."

For a long moment, the Master regarded him in silence. "Why, then, are you asking me?"

Kaelin swallowed hard. "Because you're a Master. You heard my music and played it and ... nothing happened." He hurried on at the Master's slight frown. "I promise to work hard, sir, and I learn quickly."

The Master nodded thoughtfully. *I played his music ... and nothing happened? What was he expecting might happen, I wonder? The same thing that happened when I heard him play in the woods? But that was hardly an awful thing! This young boy has a Gift the likes of which hasn't been seen in two centuries, and for some reason, he's deeply afraid of it.*

As the anxiety in Kaelin's eyes deepened, the Master decided to leave the matter alone for the time being. "You'll have ample opportunity to prove that during the next month," he said quietly. "Now, I'd like to have a look at your flute. Perhaps you could bring mine back with you as well."

Relieved at the apparent end of the questioning, Kaelin retrieved both flutes. His own was inspected carefully and returned to him with grave respect.

"For a boy of seven cycles with no one's guidance, it's a well-made instrument."

Kaelin's face lit up. "Thank you, sir."

"How did you know where to place the holes?"

"I took the measurements from Old Tor—from Flutist Torin's instrument and adjusted them for the size of this one."

The Master nodded, then reached for his own flute and removed it from its protective case. Kaelin looked longingly at the beautiful Bardic instrument, then emitted a slight gasp when he saw that it was made of rosewood, a rare and expensive imported wood. The one time he had dared to use a small scrap of rosewood in Craftmaster Arnor's shop, he'd been given a sound thrashing for it. Not even the Bards who visited Vale had such a wondrous flute as this one. The magnificent instrument glistened in the firelight, and the boy's mouth fell slightly open in awe of its superb workmanship.

"Your flute," he said in a hushed voice, "must have been made by the finest wood Craftmaster in all the Bardic Isles."

Suppressing a smile, the Master inclined his head. "Such an endorsement from a youngster of Vale, who would of course know good woodworking when he sees it, is quite flattering."

Kaelin's eyes widened. "You made it yourself, sir?"

"All Bards and Masters do, for the bond between a musician and his instrument begins with the making of it." The Master fastened the headjoint securely to the instrument and lifted it. "I'm going to compose a short musical phrase. I want you to duplicate it as accurately as you can."

The Master played a simple phrase of four measures, and Kaelin lifted his own flute and promptly duplicated it. Master Bergid played the same phrase again at twice the tempo, and again Kaelin echoed it back to him with ease. The Master played a complicated rhythm pattern on a single note. Back the lad sent it, fluent and sure. The Master combined the phrase with the rhythm pattern, liberally sprinkling the notes with various articulations. His perfect little echo duplicated each and every one of them.

For the third time that morning, the Master's brow lifted. He played a longer phrase of greater intricacy, choosing notes that the smaller flute was capable of. Once again his music rebounded clearly back to him, the boy grinning up at him afterwards like he was having the time of his life.

Bergid suppressed a chuckle. *Still too easy, is it? Try this!* He quickly composed an advanced piece, keeping it within the parameters of the smaller flute's range, and played it. Then he put his instrument down and looked calmly at Kaelin, whose brows were knit in concentration.

"Could you play it again, sir?" the boy asked anxiously.

The Master complied without decreasing the tempo. Kaelin fingered his flute silently, delight transfiguring his face as he studied the Master's swift movements. Then, taking a deep breath, he lifted his flute to his lips, closed his eyes, and began to play. He played at the Master's tempo; moreover, he missed not a single note, nor the slightest nuance of expressive embellishment the Master himself had used. Even more incredibly, he didn't stop at the end, but continued on, taking the melodic line upward in a swelling crescendo and converting the theme into a variation in the upper register. Deftly inverting both direction and rhythmic pattern, he sent the melody skipping blissfully over dancing staccatos before returning to the opening theme, bringing the piece to an exhilarating close.

The Master was thunderstruck. Not a single Bard could have done what this untrained village boy with the striking amber eyes had just done. *This youngster has flawlessly duplicated a difficult piece he could never have heard before and ended it with a brilliant improvisation! So, not only does he possess an incredible Gift that disappeared two centuries ago, he's also a musical prodigy of the first order.*

His reverie was interrupted by Kaelin's worried voice. "I'm sorry I needed to hear it twice, sir."

"You're sorry ..." The Master's voice failed him.

"And I shouldn't have tampered with it, but I couldn't seem to stop my fingers—" The youngster's head lowered in shame, and the Master laughed.

"*Tampered* with it? I'd say you improved it considerably. When I write this piece down, I'll include that variation of yours and write your name under my own to give you the credit for it you deserve."

Kaelin stared at the Master in surprise. "That was your own music?"

The corners of the Master's mouth twitched. "I was not about to test you on music you might have heard and played before. Surely you know from your schooling that I am not only the Master Bard of Kestrel, but the Composition Master as well."

Kaelin's eyes widened. He had just dared to change the music of the Composition Master of the Bardic Isles? "Yes, sir, I do know," he said in a chastened voice. "I didn't think. I'm sorry for adding my own notes to—"

The Master lifted his hand to cut short a second apology. "Save your remorse for something worthy of it," he advised dryly. "Your variation of my music was excellent and certainly requires no apology."

A thrill of delight ran through Kaelin at the Master's look of approval.

"Now, then," the Master continued, his blue eyes sparkling with humor, "since you've just proven your talent for mimicry and improvisation, perhaps you could demonstrate your ability to compose, as well. I've heard a little of your own music already, but I would like to hear something at closer range. It needn't be long or difficult, just music from within you."

Kaelin's hands tightened around his flute. Had the Master asked him to play the music of anything surrounding them, be it rock, leaf, or tree, he could have easily played him a variation. Instead, he had asked him to play music ... *from within me. He understands, but can I do what he asks? I don't want to hurt him.* The pressure throbbed, its familiar ache intensifying. Kaelin put his flute to his lips, closed his eyes, and sternly lectured himself. *Obey him! He's a Master. He heard you before and nothing happened.*

He rebelled. *That was a variation. He's asking to hear me play my own music!*

If you want his help, you have to be willing to show him your problem. The pain is nothing you haven't felt before, and if he shows any signs of feeling it too, you can stop. So, play!

The single note that filled the clearing trembled, as if resisting being forced through the small instrument. Kaelin gasped, then stopped and chose another, finding it as obstinate to emerge as the first. The note swelled to an incredible length before relaxing into its vibrato. One reluctant note after another was pried free, woven together, bound with rhythm, and brought to life with the essence of the young composer's thoughts. The beginning of an achingly beautiful phrase filled the clearing, then Kaelin began to tremble as he tried desperately to continue. Droplets of sweat stood witness to the pressure within.

The Master watched, fascinated and deeply disturbed by the musical battle enacted before him. This was not the boy who had effortlessly poured his heart out in the woods alone, nor was it the youngster who had so blissfully duplicated and embellished the Master's music. *Something must have happened to this youngster that severely inhibited his Gift, something that caused him to bury it and refuse its expression. Every note is an agony for him! Little wonder he dropped everything but his flute and came to me for help.*

Kaelin broke away from the unfinished phrase with a cry of pain. Silence reclaimed the clearing. A gentle hand touched his shoulder.

"Thank you, Kaelin."

The understanding in the Master's voice brought tears to the youngster's eyes. He fought to keep them from falling. "You *know,* don't you, sir?"

The Master regarded him steadily. "I know," he said at last, "that you are filled with music, that its presence is tormenting you, and that you find its expression painful. I do not know why." The blue eyes looked keenly into his. "Do you?"

The youngster frowned. "I just know it hurts." He looked anxiously at the Master Bard. "My music doesn't hurt you, does it?"

"Certainly not," the Master said in a voice that brooked no contradiction. "Your music may be hurting *you,* lad, but I can assure you it's not painful to listen to. Quite the contrary."

Kaelin drew a breath of relief.

"How is it," the Master asked gently, "that you could play that exquisite song in the woods without experiencing the pain you exhibited just now?"

The boy looked up in surprise. Surely the Master had heard the song of kestrels before and would easily recognize a variation of it. Unless, he thought suddenly, every kestrel had a different song. "That wasn't *my* music," he explained. "That was just my variation of a song."

"You would be hard pressed, lad," the Master said dryly, "to play me a song I've never heard before, variation or no. If you didn't compose the original theme, who did?"

The youngster frowned. "I don't know, it just ... came with him."

"Came with whom?"

"The kestrel," the youngster said matter-of-factly, as though certain he was being asked a question the Master already knew the answer to. "I just did what I did with your music. I made a variation of what I heard."

"From ... a kestrel. A bird whose only cry is a single repeated note?"

Kaelin's anxiety returned. "I just looked at him for a few moments and ... and I heard it. Was it wrong to do that?"

"I didn't say it was wrong, lad." The Master regarded him for a moment. "What else, besides kestrels, can you hear the songs of?"

The youngster looked at him worriedly. "Anything, I guess—rocks, trees, plants—if I focus on them and listen closely. That was the first time I listened to a creature," he assured the Master, "and only because he swooped down to look at me from a branch, so I looked back at him and heard his music for just a moment before I looked away. It was so wild and free," the boy said with a trace of envy, "that later on I used it to make a variation I could play."

"Was the original too complex for you?" the Master gently challenged.

"No, sir," the boy admitted, "though quite a few of the notes were out of range for my flute. I couldn't play it because playing the music I hear from things makes the music inside me hurt, like it wants my instrument for itself. So I compose a variation of the song and play that instead, and it eases the pressure. I can play village songs and make variations of them, too, but for some reason that doesn't help as much."

"What about people?"

"I've never tried listening to a person," Kaelin said, his brow creased doubtfully. "It just seems wrong, somehow … like I'd be invading their privacy. I won't listen to another creature again if you tell me I shouldn't."

"I think it might be best if you don't, lad. At least, for now."

"I promise I won't."

"So then, am I to understand that you can compose and freely play variations of songs that do not originate from you?"

"Yes, sir."

"But the music that originates from you causes you intense pain?"

The youngster silently nodded.

"What about variations of that music?"

Kaelin shook his head. "I can't listen to it long enough to make a variation."

The Master regarded him gravely. "Help in getting a Bardic apprenticeship, then, wasn't the only reason you followed me, was it?"

Kaelin flushed deeply, once again finding himself unable to pull his eyes away from the Master's. "No, sir," he admitted. "I know I can't become an apprentice unless I can play freely. I followed you because I think you're the only one who might be able to fix me so I can." A desperate hope filled the eyes fastened on the Master's. "Can you help me?"

Master Bergid was silent for a long moment. Little was known of the Gift of old, for the Bards of that time had been careful not to allow the Druidic Order to know of its existence. No records were made, no descriptions ever put to scroll. All that was known was what had been written down after the exodus to the Bardic Isles. Few of the Gifted had made it onto the five ships that escaped the destruction of Aille-Mara, for most were helping with the evacuation and were slaughtered by the invading warriors. Ten of the Masters, all of whom were Gifted, made the trip, and probably several Gifted Bards as well. Of the Masters, Cyral's Gift was by far the strongest. After he had used it to bring them to their new homeland, the young Master and his Harp had become a legend of epic proportions. This much was known, but what the Gift actually was, unfortunately, was not.

So, the Master thought, *this Gift we know so little about enables the one who possesses it to hear the songs coming from whatever he listens to? The very music they were created with? Absolutely fascinating! Fully releasing such an inhibited Gift as this, though, must be done with the greatest of care, and only after I get to know this youngster far better. For such a Gift carries more power than this boy could possibly know.*

"I believe I can help you," the Master said at last. He shook his head slightly at the joy that lit the boy's face. "That was not a promise, lad," he gently warned. "Nor will it be easy for you if I decide to do so. Things worth the having seldom are."

"I haven't anything to give you for your time and trouble, sir, but I'll do anything you ask of me."

The Master held Kaelin's eyes a moment longer, knowing he had just won something this boy did not give lightly to anyone. "Trust is a valuable gift. I will not abuse it." He rose abruptly. "Come, we have far to travel."

They made their way through the northern woods all afternoon, following the narrow path that seemed to wind endlessly through the trees, stopping only when the sun began to set. After a dinner of dried fish and vegetables, Kaelin tidied their camp and cared for Poor Oran as the Master settled himself before the fire with his harp. The youngster curled up on his bedroll and listened as the Master sang beautiful songs of the history of the Bardic Isles. Many were gay and carefree, others brought tears to his eyes.

What a wonderful Gift the Master has! Kaelin thought, as music swirled about their campsite like the tendrils of mountain mist through the trees, the fire snapping a rhythmic counterpoint. *I could listen to him forever.* Then the Master began to sing a sad song that Kaelin had never heard before.

If t'were no songs in minor mode,
If sorrow never freely flowed,
If no song spoke of pain, deceit,
Would those in the major sound as sweet?

For into every life, it seems,
Come flowing in these two extremes.
Essential that we taste them both
If we're to come to our full growth.

Enjoy the majors in your life,
The times you're free of pain and strife.
And bless the minor songs you meet,
Or the major ones won't sound as sweet.

The Master stopped singing, and Kaelin, glancing up from his bedroll, caught a look of such transparent pain on the Master's face as he gazed into the flames of the fire, that his own heart twisted. The Master Bard of Kestrel, he saw clearly, was well acquainted with the minor modes. At length, the Master sighed and began playing his harp alone. Listening to the clear sounds of the Bardic instrument, Kaelin fell fast asleep.

During the following two weeks, the two established a pattern that they seldom varied. Afternoons were spent either traveling to or visiting a village, where Kaelin eagerly joined the townsfolk who filled the village square to hear the Master Bard of Kestrel play. His admiration for the Master grew to even greater heights, not just because of his music, but because of the way he talked and laughed with the villagers. He did far more than repair any instrument that came to his hand. He readily gave his aid to anyone who asked for it, and many who were too shy or intimidated to do so. The latter he seemed to have a special affinity for, approaching them himself and talking quietly until, disarmed, they opened up to him. The Master never failed to find a solution for whatever was bothering them, be it a musical trouble or not, and Kaelin was quick to notice that nobody, whether a grown adult or a child of five, ever left without a smile.

Mornings were spent at the campsite, the Master intent on discovering exactly how much Kaelin knew, musically speaking. He did not ask the boy to play his flute again but questioned him thoroughly about theory and composition until he was satisfied that he knew where his instruction should begin. The Master was surprised to discover that Kaelin knew far more than what was usually taught about such subjects in school. He thought of the Flutist Kaelin had spoken of. Torin, he remembered, had long ago refused to take his tests for advancement to an Instrumentalist, saying that he preferred to remain a simple Flutist and teach only that instrument. The Master smiled. Though retired and well on in cycles, the old Flutist had apparently been a rich source of musical information.

One morning, curious about his memory since hearing him duplicate complex musical phrases, the Master handed Kaelin three pages of information on a beginning composition form. Telling the youngster to let him know when he had learned it, the Master returned to his own work. He noticed that Kaelin read through the information twice, once quickly, then again at a slower pace. Then the boy rose and handed the pages back to him.

"I'm finished, sir. Is there anything else you want me to read?"

The Master frowned slightly. "I didn't want you to merely read it, lad. I told you to learn it."

"I—I did," Kaelin stammered in confusion. "Should I learn it again?"

The Master regarded him for a moment. "Tell me what you learned."

With a worried look, Kaelin began to recite. Startled, the Master looked at the sheets in his hand. Kaelin's steady recitation matched them word for word to the end of the last page.

"Have I done something wrong?" The youngster was biting his lip and looking at him anxiously.

The Master shook his head in amusement. "I just realized how you passed the Schoolmaster's tests so early, even with such poor attendance. Have you always been able to memorize so easily?"

"I guess so," the youngster replied, frowning as though thinking back over a lifespan of several decades. "For as long as I can remember, anyhow," he added with a shrug. He wondered why the Master laughed.

"Well, Kaelin, if I apprentice you, it had better be to someone with a mine of information at his fingertips." He paused at the look of distress on the boy's face. "What's wrong, lad?"

"Nothing, sir." A brow lifted in his direction and Kaelin hurriedly continued. "It's just that ... well, I'd rather stay with you."

The Master's brow smoothed. "You would give up the chance to become a Bardic apprentice just to remain with me?"

"Oh, *yes*, sir." His eyes pleaded silently with the Master, who shook his head.

"I think, Kaelin, that you belong *in* the Bardic Order, not out of it." His voice softened a little at the boy's crestfallen look. "But we'll discuss it after your month is over. Now, perhaps you ought to finish up that theory exercise I gave you this morning."

The youngster nodded and went back to resolving dominant seventh chords to their tonics in various inversions, trying to ignore the conflicting emotions that besieged him. Being told by the Master Bard of Kestrel himself that he belonged in the Bardic Order should have sent him wild with delight and *would* have, just two weeks ago. But now ... well, now there was something he wanted more than membership in the Bardic Order. He sternly told himself to stop wishing for the impossible. *Erik was right. The Master Bard has better things to do with his time than taking some scruffy village boy under his wing.* Kaelin forced his thoughts away and concentrated solely on the worksheet in front of him.

The following afternoon the Master and Kaelin continued their travels, heading north to skirt the eastern slopes of Strellig Mountain, the tallest of Kestrel's three peaks. The midsummer day was a fine one, the sun having finally come out after the morning's gentle rain, alpine winds blowing through their hair and making the Master's robe flutter around his legs. After an hour of steady travel, a preoccupied Kaelin missed his footing on the steep slope and fell. To his chagrin, the first word that escaped his mouth was a curse. He climbed back up the narrow path and looked uneasily at the Master.

"Did you injure yourself, lad?"

"No, sir," he replied, his face growing warm.

The Master Bard walked on without further comment. Kaelin followed him, silently castigating himself for having said such a thing in the Master's presence. *It won't happen again.* He was doubly ashamed that evening for breaking his own resolve when a hot pan slipped from his grasp. He sat back, his face burning as hotly as his finger.

"Kaelin."

"Sir?"

"Bring me a switch."

The youngster nodded miserably and rose to obey. At that moment, he would have preferred a beating before the entire village of Vale at anyone else's hand.

The Master silently inspected the switch the boy brought him, then handed it back.

Kaelin glanced at him in confusion. "Aren't you going to

punish me?" he ventured.

"Do you deserve to be?"

Kaelin lowered his head in shame. "Yes, sir."

"And afterwards, would you be better able to keep words like those from entering your mind?"

Kaelin looked up, startled. "I don't know, but … I don't think so," he admitted.

"So, then, you know you deserve punishment, but you also know it will do you no good. Have you been punished for cursing before?"

Kaelin flushed. "Yes, sir, by the Schoolmaster." As the Master's eyes continued to rest on him, he reluctantly continued. "And Holder Gannon caught hold of me once and gave me a thrashing behind his stall. And Craftmaster Arnor punished me for it more than once when my tools slipped … though *he* curses often enough—" He broke off abruptly, as though suddenly realizing to whom he was criticizing the Woodcarving Craftmaster of Vale. "He told me that if I cursed one more time in his presence, he would take me before the village Council to see if that would curb my tongue. I'm sorry I can't seem to learn better," he continued in a chastened tone of voice, "and I know I deserve to be punished."

"Punishment that does not teach is useless, and I am not accustomed to wasting my time. I'm not going to punish you. *You* are going to punish *me*." The color drained from Kaelin's face as the Master held out his left hand, palm up. "Use the switch twice across my palm. If each stroke is not hard enough to leave a mark, you will have to keep doing it until it is."

Appalled, Kaelin took a step back from the Master's open hand and frantically shook his head. "I *can't*. I … I just can't!" He looked imploringly at the Master, whose brows came bristling together.

"Then we shall stand here until your ability to obey me returns to you."

Kaelin stared aghast at the Master's hand. "Please," he begged.

"*Please* don't make me do this! At least let me use it on my own hand. I'm the one who said those words. I'm the one who should hurt for it."

The Master stood as steadfast and silent as the trees around them. Still Kaelin hesitated. His third attempt to avoid using the switch died on his lips with a single raised brow from the Master and a meaningful glance at his open hand. The stricken boy bit his lip and gripped the switch. Then he brought it down across the Master's palm, unable to stop the cry that came from his own throat as he did so.

"That wasn't hard enough to leave a mark. Do it again."

Kaelin clenched his teeth and delivered a harder blow. This time the Master nodded, and Kaelin forced himself to repeat the blow, tears trickling down his cheeks. He closed his eyes and dropped the switch, then clutched his offending hand as though it burned.

The Master closed his own hand and spoke gently. "You found it difficult to inflict pain on someone who had done nothing to deserve it." He lifted Kaelin's chin. "Yet your words hurt me worse than the switch."

Kaelin stared at him through his tears, stunned.

"Sound is a powerful force," the Master told him. "Have you not stood in awe before the sounds of nature? Do you not feel the strength in the music that burns within you? Yet the most powerful sound of all is the human voice. It is the original, primary instrument, the one most capable of pure and nuanced expression because it is a part of us. It should be used with the greatest of care, for it has the power, not only to heal, but to hurt ourselves and others." The Master opened his hand, the welts across it clearly visible.

"The hurt you inflicted with a switch will soon heal. But the hurt you inflicted with your words won't heal so easily, though you cannot see the welts they leave. Such words leave their marks on both mind and spirit, and, as you've already discovered, no one can beat them out of you. The decision never to use your voice in such a harmful way again is not mine or anyone else's to make. It is your own." He released the boy's chin and turned away.

Kaelin cried out and grasped his arm. "Sir, I *have* decided! Please forgive me for hurting you! I won't hurt anyone with such words again."

The Master looked at the remorse on Kaelin's tear-stained face and pulled him close. A silent warning rose within him. *You're getting too fond of this young boy, you old fool. Entirely too fond!*

Chapter 4

Master Bergid and Kaelin spent the next fortnight traveling further east through the Skirling Mountains, stopping at four more villages along the way. The Master often foraged as they went, teaching Kaelin about many of the edible and medicinal plants they came across. Kaelin knew the more common varieties that were readily available around Vale, and which Laena carefully tended in their garden: wild onions, garlic, tubers, parsley, and mint, to name a few. Kaelin kept a sharp eye out for blackberry brambles as he followed the Master with Poor Oran in tow. Though the berries would not ripen for another month, bramble tea, made by steeping the leaves in boiling water, was the Master's favorite morning beverage, and Kaelin took pleasure in making it for him.

One morning, bringing the Master his tea, Kaelin caught sight of his face and frowned. Since leaving Vale, he had become adept at reading his teacher's expressions, and this was one he had not seen before. Kaelin reflected uneasily that, if he himself were the flames the Master was staring at, he would shrink into the ashes under that grim regard. He silently placed the tea next to his Master, then sat down nearby and waited. Whatever was coming, he was sure it wasn't going to be pleasant. He felt himself go cold at the only thing he could think of that would explain the Master's expression. *He's making up his mind to take me back.*

Kaelin closed his eyes against the pain of that thought. He had not played a single note for the Master since his aborted attempt to play his own music for him. He was allowed to play his flute during the hour of free time he had in the afternoons, which helped relieve the pressure of the music trapped inside him. But he'd been given no lessons in his instrument, only an endless string of theory and composition exercises, which he had completed as well and as quickly as he could. And tomorrow his month would be up. He thought of being back in his village again, working as a woodcarving apprentice, if the Craftmaster would still have him, and daring to play variations and village songs only in the solitude of the woods. *He said he could help me, that he would decide before my month was up. Maybe he hasn't given me any flute lessons because he's decided I can't be fixed, even by someone as Gifted as he is. Maybe he's just been waiting for the month he promised me to be over, so he can take me back.* Kaelin's head lowered in despair.

"What's wrong, lad?"

Startled at the Master's voice, Kaelin looked up to find the blue eyes regarding him steadily. "You looked so serious that ... well, I thought—" The boy fell silent and braced himself for the words he dreaded to hear.

"Your month may be up tomorrow, lad," the Master said gently, "but I will not decide what to do with you until I have decided whether or not to help you. It is not something I can do lightly, for it will be very difficult help to receive."

Kaelin bit his lip and silently nodded.

"Are you still willing to accept that help, regardless?"

"Oh, *yes,* sir ... please!"

"Even if it's a longer and far harder lesson than you can imagine?" The Master's brows lifted challengingly.

Kaelin took a deep breath. "The pain has grown worse every

cycle, and now it never stops," he said in a low voice. "I don't know how much longer I can stand it. Whatever you have to do, please do it."

"So be it, lad," the Master said gravely. "If you wish to stop the lesson, you may do so at any time with no fear of reproach."

"How long will it take?" Kaelin asked uneasily.

The Master shook his head thoughtfully. "There is no way of knowing that. All things come in the fullness of their own measure."

Kaelin was silent, realizing for the first time how the Master knew about the music burning inside him. *It's burning in him, too! Only mine is trapped inside of me, and his music is free.*

"Was your music always free, sir, or was it once trapped like mine?" he dared to ask, surprised when the Master readily answered.

"It was partially trapped, but not to the extent that yours is, and it caused me no physical pain."

"And ... did someone give you this same lesson to free it?"

"Yes."

"How long did it take?"

"Three weeks."

Kaelin was silent. If it had taken the one who had become the Master Bard of Kestrel that long to free his music, how long would it take him? *Does it really matter? At least I'll be with him. And if there's a chance, however small, that my music can be set free, I have to take it!* He lifted his head. "I'll accept any lesson you give me."

"You've done so twice against your own wishes," the Master said. "The first lesson taught you honesty, the second the power of words. This lesson will be unlike either of them." The white brows lifted. "You desire knowledge of musical instruments, which is well and good, but never forget one thing. You yourself are the most important instrument you will ever play. A life spent mastering that instrument, whether you ever play a Bardic one or not, is a life well spent."

The Master withdrew his belt knife, picked up a small stick and whittled the end to a sharp point. Then he took a small bag of dark wax from his pack and put a lump of it on the end of the stick. Kaelin watched curiously as the Master held the stick over the fire, turning it slowly until the wax softened. He beckoned Kaelin closer, then pinched off two small pieces of wax and rolled them between his fingers.

"You will soon be unable to hear or see," the Master gravely told him. "From this moment on you are forbidden to speak." He smiled at Kaelin's look of astonishment. "I can't tell you how long the lesson will last," he said gently, "but I promise that I will not leave you." Then he took the softened balls of wax and firmly plugged Kaelin's ears with them.

The sounds of the woods and wind were completely cut off, replaced only by Kaelin's own breathing. He watched in alarm as the Master fashioned small shields with the rest of the wax. These were placed over his eyes and wrapped securely with layers of cloth. No light penetrated the darkness. Kaelin jumped at the touch of the Master's hand on his arm. He felt his pack placed over his shoulder and the end of a rope pressed into his hands. He clutched it tightly as it began to pull him forward. *Feeling is all I have left!*

Even as he thought it, a mighty pressure inside him struggled for recognition. Deep within him, music surged behind the solid walls of a cage he could no longer avoid seeing. Triumphant, turbulent music written by the unseen composer he refused to listen to, the one who incessantly wrote music with notes of pain. *No! I'm deaf! I can't hear anything!* Kaelin concentrated fiercely on the rope that pulled him, denying the music that clamored for his attention until it subsided. He stumbled along in a world of silent darkness, forbidden even the cry of panic that threatened to erupt. His ears strained to hear, his eyes ached to see, and his mind was filled with the irrational fear that his next step might plunge him into a bottomless pit.

Kaelin gradually realized that the Master was taking pains to lead him as gently as possible. No hidden branches slapped his face, no unseen rocks or roots tripped him. One footstep followed another in unbroken monotony until the rope slackened. Kaelin fell to his knees in exhaustion, though he had never found their afternoon treks very tiring before. He found himself turning his head frantically, desperate to know where the Master had gone. *He promised not to leave me!*

To his intense relief, a brush was placed in his hand, and he was led a short distance away, where his other hand was placed against the warm flank of Poor Oran. The youngster laid his face against the mule for a long moment, taking comfort in the stolid animal's proximity, then carefully went over his coat with the brush, feeling calmer as he went about the familiar chore. Afterwards, he was guided to sit by the warmth of a campfire, and a wet cloth was placed in his hands. Kaelin washed his face, hands, and arms with it, wishing he dared reach for the hand that had given it. His thoughts spun in confusion. *How is taking away my sight, hearing, and speech supposed to help me? It only makes everything worse!*

A sudden weight on his lap turned out to be a plate containing bread, a smooth round of cheese, and strips of dried meat. Kaelin ate hungrily and then a firm hand led him to his bedroll. Resisting the impulse to keep hold of the Master's hand, the boy lay down obediently, but his mind, chafing from the increased pressure of the music within him, permitted no sleep. Time became oddly meaningless with nothing but his own breathing to mark its passage. He knew the Master must be somewhere nearby, likely sitting in his accustomed place by the fire where he normally played his instruments in the evenings. But, though Kaelin strained to hear, no music of flute, harp, or pipes broke the unnerving silence.

Unable to hear sounds from without, unwilling to hear sounds from within, he felt utterly alone, as though cutting off his senses had cut him off from every living thing, leaving him adrift in a dark and silent world. When he could take it no longer, the boy crawled off his mat and groped along the ground as quietly as he could, carefully skirting the warmth that marked the location of their campfire. When at last his fingers brushed the Master's bedroll, Kaelin held his breath and curled up as close to it as he dared. This high in the mountains the ground was cold at night even in the summer, but he gave it no heed. He rested one hand against the bedroll's edge. He couldn't be sure the Master was there, but it was comforting to imagine that he was within reach, that he himself was at least touching something the Master was too. He would have been shocked if someone had told him that the eyes of the Master looking down on him at that moment were filled with tears.

A sudden touch on Kaelin's shoulder startled him, then two strong arms pulled him onto the Master's bedroll, a blanket enveloped him in warmth, and a strong hand enclosed one of his own. Kaelin sighed and fell asleep at last, his music pulsing with rhythmic discontent in its prison.

Sometime during the night, he woke up in panic from a nightmare, disoriented and confused at not being able to see or hear, barely remembering in time not to speak. The hand that still enclosed his tightened reassuringly and he lay shaking, unable to prevent his whimpers of fear as the terrifying fragments of the dream slowly dissipated. He was pulled up against the Master, whose arm wrapped around him. Gradually, Kaelin's breathing returned to normal and he fell asleep again.

The Master held the youngster for a few more moments, then released his hold, keeping one of Kaelin's hands covered with his own. His mind alternately accused and defended himself.

What you're doing to him is unspeakably cruel.

Yes, but it's necessary! His Gift must be freed.

If he can bear it.
I'll let him decide for himself what he can bear.
And what about you? Can you bear it?
For this, the Master had no answer.

The next morning, Kaelin did not awaken from the sun's brightness, for he could not see. The scolding jays and clatter of dishes did not awaken him, for he could not hear. But awaken he did, and lay for a moment wondering if he really had. *Please let this be nothing more than another bad dream!* Not knowing if it was morning or night, reality or the continuation of a nightmare, he sat up in the darkness and was given his breakfast, which seemed real enough. He ate slowly, trying to delay the unwelcome feel of the rope in his hands, but to his dismay, it was placed there the moment he finished. He struggled to his feet and was led to a stream, where he washed himself, then used a cloth to dry the breakfast dishes the Master washed. Back at their camp, Kaelin slowly packed their bags, the Master loaded the mule, and they headed out again.

They traveled steadily for several days. Each night, Kaelin's bedroll was placed next to the Master's, and when nightmares woke the youngster, he clung to the strong hand that always lay over his own until his heartbeat slowed and he fell back asleep. His fears when traveling with the rope gradually lessened and he stopped pulling against it, trusting the one who held the other end. In the absence of external distractions, the boy's thoughts turned deeper inward, skirting the fluid boundaries of the music trapped inside him. It surged restlessly behind walls that he had begun to realize were of his own making. *What does it matter who made them?* he thought bitterly. *Behind walls is where it belongs!* Conflicting emotions besieged him; he ached for the music's freedom, yet deeply feared its release. *The Master has trapped me in here with it. I hope he can find me when this horrible lesson is over. I can't even ask him what I'm supposed to be learning.*

Minutes, hours, days – all melted together in Kaelin's mind. Time had been reduced to a mere transporter of moments that all looked and sounded alike. The temptation to end this torment by shouting or ripping off his blindfold plagued him. Only the clear memory of the challenge in the Master's eyes and the awful thought of being taken back to Vale kept him from giving up.

At last, after breakfast one morning, no rope was placed in his hands. Instead, the Master spent the morning building a shelter for them, guiding Kaelin to hold saplings shorn of their branches upright while he lashed them together with wisteria vines. These were set firmly into the ground in a semi-circle, then securely covered with a large tarp. Afterwards, the Master fashioned a makeshift table and two stools from split sections of a log and placed them between the shelter and the firepit.

After dinner, Bergid led Kaelin in a thorough exploration of his surroundings, taking him back and forth between the shelter, table, firepit, and Poor Oran until the boy could navigate around the campsite on his own. It wasn't long before he could take cautious walks along trails the Master helped him become familiar with, until one morning, he took the dishes to the stream to clean them and brought them triumphantly back on his own.

Touch became Kaelin's world, and he concentrated on it in relief. Days were spent sorting a baffling collection of stones by feel. Then he struggled with a mound of feathers and, once that was conquered, a pile of different kinds of tree bark took its place. Everything he touched and focused on brought its song into his mind, which was a welcome discovery, for before this, he had always relied on his sight to do so.

Kaelin had begun to hear the songs of objects he focused intently on when he was five, and it hadn't taken him long to realize that others could not. As he grew older, he thought it was because he'd had the misfortune to be born into a remote woodcarving village that had only one aged member of the Bardic Order living there. Surely, he reasoned, most, if not all, of those who were admitted to that Order must have this ability. Accordingly, he had questioned the old Flutist about the matter and was told that all things were created with music, and whether a person could hear such music or not was clearly their own business, not Kaelin's. The somewhat curt, enigmatic answer had stopped the boy's questioning and led him to believe that this ability did exist in the Bardic Order, but that it was a subject not discussed with those outside the Order.

Since following the Master out of Vale, Kaelin had not dared to question him about it. The sheer beauty of the Master's music, however, and the clear pictures it formed in Kaelin's mind, had further strengthened his belief that those in the Bardic Order had his ability to hear these silent songs. Kaelin had sorely missed them since Master Bergid had blocked his eyesight. To suddenly find that touch could also give him a connection to this music was a welcome discovery, making it far easier to bear the silence imposed on him.

Now, with nothing else to focus on, Kaelin began to pay more attention to the music he heard, and noticed that, although individual specimens of feathers, stones, or tree bark had their own unique song, they were all related to others of their kind, like variations on the same theme. He began to avidly study the many songs his fingers evoked, wondering why he had never heard them this way with his eyes opened. Perhaps, he thought, it was simply because his other senses had been a distraction that was now removed.

One day, after identifying and sorting a collection of leaves by touch, Kaelin felt the Master's hand on his arm. He waited expectantly and a large bag was placed in his hands. Silky tassels brushed his fingers, and he could feel the instrument inside it, which was not in its leather case. Kaelin was startled; surely the Master would not entrust one of his precious Bardic instruments to a boy who couldn't see. He waited a moment, but the Master made no move to take it back. With the utmost care, Kaelin slid the Master's set of pipes onto his lap, awed at being allowed to touch such a marvelous instrument. Without thinking, he focused intently on the smooth, satiny feel of the wood under his fingers, as he had become accustomed to doing over days of sorting objects.

To his surprise, music entered his mind, music that was completely different from the simple melodies that had come from the pieces of wood he had studied and sorted. Those songs, unique to the type of wood he held, were single melodic lines and easily differentiated from each other. Though the Master's pipes were made solely of wood, they emitted a complexity of songs that nearly overwhelmed Kaelin, as though every song ever voiced by these pipes had somehow been ingrained into the wood itself. Deep inside his mind, music instantly responded, battering against the walls of its prison as if trying desperately to release itself through the instrument he held. *No! I'm not going to play you! Even if I were allowed to, I can't. I don't know how to play pipes!*

Shaking with the mental effort of denial, Kaelin gasped and pulled his hands away from the pipes on his lap. The songs flooding his mind from the instrument immediately stopped, and the music behind the walls subsided, as though aware that release was no longer possible. As Kaelin's breathing calmed, he frowned in thought. He had seen and touched his own flute hundreds of times, and never once had his mind been flooded with songs coming from it. Of course, he had never bent his mind to his flute, through either sight or touch, like he had just done with the Master's pipes. Deprived of sight, he had focused intently on the pipes through touch, having no other way to explore them. This focus, it seemed, released the songs the pipes were filled with. Songs that caused an immediate response from the music trapped inside his own mind.

Kaelin swallowed hard. Surely the music trapped within him wasn't sentient, though it certainly seemed so. How could he explore the feel of this instrument without that trapped music surging in response to the songs coming from the pipes? *I have to stop the pipe music from entering my mind.* Kaelin smiled grimly to himself. He was apparently an expert at not allowing music to escape his mind. *Let's see if I can keep it from coming in!*

Cautiously, he placed his fingers on the pipes and focused intently on the wood. Once again, songs seemed to pour from every pipe into his mind. Once again, the music behind the wall surged in response. Kaelin clenched his teeth with the effort to push the songs from his mind. It seemed impossible, like pushing against the current of a river that, no matter what he did, fluidly found a way around his efforts. Angry defiance filled him. *This is my mind, and I decide what's allowed in and what isn't!*

He imagined his will as a block of solid stone between him and the encroaching songs, extending from one end of his mind to the other, then forced the stone of his will outward, pushing the songs out with it. At the same time, the turbulent music within him subsided, as though it had lost its connection to the instrument it was straining to reach.

A backlash of pain filled Kaelin's mind, leaving him dizzy and slightly nauseated. Keeping his hands firmly on the pipes, he waited for the feeling to subside. At last, having regained a measure of peace, Kaelin turned his attention to the instrument's construction. His fingers cautiously explored the wooden pipes, which were lashed together in a curvature toward the player. The Master's pipes were a full set of seventeen, arranged with the largest on the left and graduating to the smallest on the far right. Kaelin thought of the rich, full tones he had so often heard the Master produce from this instrument, and longed to learn how to play it himself. Denied sight for so long, he took pleasure in imagining the sound in colors. The pipes spoke to him in the colors of the earth, dark brown for the largest pipes, melting into orange and ending in upper yellows and amber. Suddenly he saw Laena's warm brown eyes in his mind, looking clearly into his. He bent over the pipes, his sealed eyes hot with unshed tears. After a time, gentle hands took the pipes away.

The next day, another tasseled bag was given to Kaelin, larger than the last. He ran his fingers lightly over the cloth, feeling the outline of the Master's harp. His emotions a blend of awe and fear, he undid the tassels and slid the magnificent Bardic instrument onto his lap. Once again, a wave of music besieged him at its touch, sweet songs from the harp, agitated music from the cage within him, and he gripped the frame of the instrument against the pain of refusing both. *Leave me! I can't play this either!* Again, he erected a wall of sheer willpower to push the songs coming from the instrument out of his mind. He found it harder to do this time, for the harp songs resisted him, as though they recognized how much he wanted to listen to them, how badly he wanted to play them. With a gasp of pain, he finally managed to silence them, and the turbulent inner music subsided. Once again, he had to wait until the resulting dizziness and nausea left him.

Kaelin took a deep breath to calm himself, then concentrated solely on what he held. He explored the harp's frame, tracing the finely etched carvings, opening up clear visions of the designs. His fingers wandered delicately over the strings, automatically sorting them by thickness, length, and tautness. The longest strings were the thickest and vibrated slightly whenever the harp was moved. The strings in the highest register were so tight and thin they left little grooves in his skin. He counted them to keep his mind off the music that moved restlessly in its prison: twenty-nine strings, three groups of seven and one of eight. Kaelin visualized the low harp tones as rich reds and purples, changing to violet in the middle register and a rippling gold in the upper octaves. He had quickly grown to love the sound of this instrument and thought of the many times he had fallen asleep to the strains of the Master's harp, wondrous notes mingling with firelight in his mind. His hands stilled, and the harp was removed from his lap.

The following morning, Kaelin took the slender bag the Master placed in his hands with a confused blend of longing and dread. His desire to open it was intense, but he remained motionless as fear bordering on panic superseded his desire. Anger again came to his aid; his own fear would not keep him from the instrument he most wanted to touch, to explore ... to *play.* He wrestled his fear away, then held his breath as he slid the Master's flute from its travel bag. Kaelin rested the flute on his lap and gently touched the silky rosewood. His hands froze as his mind was besieged with a myriad of songs from the flute, as though all the songs the Master had ever played on it were clamoring for his attention at the same time. He wrestled with the symphonic maelstrom, desperate to silence it. The caged music in his mind surged violently against its walls in a bid to be free, to reach the instrument that could give it voice, as if it knew perfectly well that this was an instrument Kaelin could play.

He came within a few heartbeats of losing the battle. In the end, terror alone provided the strength he needed to push out the many songs coming from the Bardic flute. Kaelin bent over the instrument, shaking with exertion and nausea. Eventually, he calmed himself enough to begin exploring the instrument he loved above all others. And such an instrument it was! He reverently traced every key and rod with sensitive fingers, marveling at its complex construction. He remembered hearing his variation of the kestrel's music come from this flute, expertly played by the Master in the village square, and later to draw him out of hiding in the woods. Kaelin visualized the beautiful tone the Master commanded in shades of blue for the lower notes, rising into shimmering silvers, and he was suffused with the desire to learn, to experience for himself the full mastery of this wondrous instrument.

The Master's flute was gently removed from Kaelin's lap, and he almost cried out to beg for its return. Then his hand was opened and a small, coarse bag was placed against his palm. Kaelin's hands trembled as he opened the bag and removed what lay inside. He couldn't help but notice that the wood was a bit rough under his hands, the holes less than perfectly bored, but none of those imperfections mattered. This was *his* flute, made by his own hands, and that made all the difference. Unlike the Master's instruments, the touch of his own brought no songs into his mind. No music surged, demanding to be released. The sudden, inexplicable silence was unnerving, for the little flute seemed to have fallen silent on purpose, waiting for him to make a decision. One that he knew would change the rest of his life.

The boy sat on the cusp of that decision for a moment that seemed to last forever. Would he deny his own flute the music that was within him, tear off the bandage over his eyes, unplug his ears, and tell the Master that he had given up ... he would return to Vale and never trouble him again?

No! I want to stay with him more than anything.

His mind scoffed. *You can't have it both ways! Which do you want more ... the Master or your fear?*

Startled by his own question, he marveled at the simplicity of the answer. He loved this Master who had taught him so much more than just music, who had freely given him his time, who accepted only the truth, and expected the best he had to give. And if that meant letting go of his fear and facing the music trapped inside him, then that's what he would do. For surely this was why the Master had taken away his sight, hearing, and speech, so that Kaelin would see the cage he had locked his music in, hear the frustrated notes begging him for release, and speak the inner words that would give them their freedom. The panicked thought that this was something he couldn't possibly do was followed by the calm realization that he could. For in that single, suspended moment of time, he understood that what he could not do for himself, he could do for the Master he loved.

Terrified at the thought of what he was about to do, the youngster clung to the thought of his Master, just as he had clung to the hand that helped him recover from his nightmares. Then, for the first time, Kaelin willingly focused on the music inside him, giving in to his desire to see it, to understand it ... to *hear* it. He saw the cage in his mind. The translucent notes within it flowed gently within the constricting walls, for once not surging in protest against them. He listened, and the music that filled his soul was beautiful. He spoke to it silently, giving it permission to simply exist, to be a part of him.

Be free, he told it. To his utter amazement, the walls in his mind shimmered for a moment, then vanished as though they had never existed.

The music within him exploded as his fingers flew of their own accord to the holes of his flute. He froze at the shock of sound that flooded his mind and swept through his fingers, a powerful tidal wave of music he no longer wanted to deny. And in that moment of clarity, he saw that there was no trapped composer in his mind, writing music that must be denied expression. For the trapped composer was none other than himself, a composer who had been constantly writing music in a mind that refused to acknowledge it. His very own, original music, not a variation of something or someone else's. Kaelin's fingers began to move with a life of their own, eagerly playing every note of it. The last traces of resistance were washed away in the wonder of what he heard. For he could hear it, clear and whole, as he had never been able to with his ears.

The Master watched intently as Kaelin fingered his flute in silent ecstasy. *At last, it comes,* he thought in satisfaction. *Denied sight, sound, and articulate expression for so long, he's letting his Gift express itself without inhibition. I wonder what caused him to bury it so deeply in the first place.* He smiled as the boy continued to play in the silent throes of a musical frenzy, his fingers hardly able to keep up with the music sweeping through him. On and on he played, music without sound. Music, every note of which, the Master was certain, was crystal clear to the youngster himself. At long last Kaelin stopped and bent in exhaustion over the flute in his lap. An expression of overwhelming relief transfigured the bandaged face. He slid his flute carefully into its bag and tied the strings securely to his belt. Then he waited, tensely erect, as though bracing himself for having the small instrument taken away.

Bergid reached out and picked up the flute without untying it. He opened Kaelin's hand and placed the small instrument into it, closed the youngster's trembling fingers firmly around it, and pressed it to the young chest. A single, strangled sob came from the boy, tears trickled from the bandaged eyes, and the Master pulled him close, flute and all. Kaelin let the small instrument dangle from his belt and clung to the Master as though he would never let go. Bergid's throat constricted. The day was fast coming, he knew, when he would have to let this boy go, and he was beginning to wonder how he would find the strength to do so.

That afternoon, Kaelin scarcely went an hour without untying the small flute from his belt and fingering it in silent bliss, each time for a shorter period before he relaxed and put it back again. He went nearly the whole evening without fingering it, and did so only once more, just before going to his bedroll. When Bergid banked the fire and went to his own bedroll some time later, he started to reach for the hand he was accustomed to covering, then stopped and chuckled softly to himself. Both of the small hands were clasped around the boy's flute, held possessively against his chest. The Master watched the peaceful face for a few moments, then lay back and relaxed into sleep himself. This night, he knew, there would be no nightmares.

Chapter 5

The next morning, Master Bergid awakened Kaelin just before dawn. He loosened the cloth binding the boy's eyes and removed the wax shields. Quickly, he replaced them with a warm, wet cloth, swabbing gently until the encrusted lids were freed. Then he stood back.

Kaelin opened his eyes and winced against the glaring brightness of a sky that was just beginning to lighten. Blinking, he beheld the most vivid dawn of his life. *Color!* Why, he had obviously never known the meaning of the word. For the earthy colors of the woods were filled with implied pipe music, brilliantly colored flowers sprinkled the forest floor with the strains of a harp, and the cloud-strewn skies above revealed the touch of a Master Flutist. After six long, torturous weeks, an experience rarely achieved in a lifetime of seeing became Kaelin's in a matter of moments.

He turned and impulsively wrapped his arms around the Master's waist, burying his head in the white robe. The silken cord shimmered like liquid gold. The strong hand that had eased his nightmares rested gently on his head. He looked up and touched his lips in mute appeal, but the Master shook his head. The boy nodded in submission and looked around, deeply content. The Master was right. Words would only spoil it.

Kaelin spent the day in the simple joy of using his eyes. He sat at the table and studied the rocks and feathers that had so often frustrated him, aware that he now knew those objects in a way sight alone could never have revealed. He wandered down paths he had learned to navigate easily without sight, gazed at trees and plants he knew so well by touch. He stood surprised by the discovery that what he had thought was a pond was really a large lake, their campsite situated near its eastern shore. The movement of a bird attracted his attention. He couldn't hear the jay's song, but he knew what the bird's feathers felt like from crest to wing. *It's taken touch to open my eyes, silence to free my music.*

The next day, the Master opened a pack Kaelin had never seen before. The youngster had only a moment to wonder where it had come from before the Master removed a set of woodworking tools and watched closely as Kaelin demonstrated his ability to use them. This was an art the village children of Vale learned early and Kaelin had learned far better than most. His talent with wood had given him a position in Craftmaster Arnor's shop as an unpaid learner and, later, the offer of an early apprenticeship. The Master, seeing the boy's proficiency, was soon satisfied. He reached into the pack and withdrew a beautiful, seasoned cylinder of rosewood, of the same diameter and length as his Bardic flute. The Master handed Kaelin the wood and indicated that he was to begin hollowing it, marking its intended thickness.

Kaelin's eyes widened in shock. *He can't mean it!* He sat frozen for a moment, then held the rosewood against his belt, where he kept his small flute tied, and mimicked tying the rosewood to it. He held his breath, hoping the Master understood his unspoken question. Master Bergid smiled, pointed at the rosewood, then at Kaelin, and nodded his head firmly. Had the Master allowed him the use of his voice at that moment, Kaelin would have remained speechless. *A Bardic flute of my own?* He looked up at the Master and willed him to see the gratitude threatening to fill his eyes with tears.

The Master nodded at what Kaelin had not said. Then he laid an encouraging hand on the youngster's shoulder and returned to his own work.

Kaelin selected a tool and eagerly set to work himself, never more grateful in his life for the skills the strict and exacting Craftmaster had given him. Such an instrument would surely take weeks to finish. He wondered if this meant he had passed the Master's trial. Surely he must have, or why would the Master teach him how to make a Bardic flute of his own?

To Kaelin's surprise, they did not resume traveling but remained in their camp. They had left the Skirling Mountains behind them, having apparently traveled some distance south. The Master went alone on his occasional trips to get supplies, making Kaelin wonder for the first time how supplies had been obtained during the many weeks before this. He finally decided someone must have brought them, because he was certain the Master had kept his promise not to leave him, alone and blind. *A Phantom Bard, maybe, doing the Master's bidding,* Kaelin thought with amusement. *If I ever meet him, I'll thank him ... especially for bringing the wood and tools for my Bardic flute!*

Kaelin contentedly worked on his new instrument during the times the Master was gone. He finished hollowing it, smoothed it with a sanding cloth, then applied ten coats of stain, letting each coat dry before sanding it and applying the next. He could hardly wait to begin working on the keyholes. His small flute was his to keep and he often used it, silently fingering the music that flowed freely inside him now. His fear of that inner music was gone, for he had explored it and discovered that it was a central part of him, as crucial as any of his other senses. *It only needs a voice. Someday soon, I'll give it one.*

Two weeks after regaining his sight, Kaelin awoke to find the

Master bending over a kettle of hot towels. The boy spent the better part of an hour holding steaming towels against his ears until he began to sweat from the heat. Loud cracks and grinding noises burst painfully as the wax softened and moved. The Master carefully removed the waxy chunks. Kaelin groaned. After eight weeks of silence, every sound in the woods, every movement of the Master, was magnified to painful proportions. Finally the uproar subsided, leaving the youngster with an aching head.

If his eyes had been filled with a riot of color when they were first opened, his ears were now assaulted with a barrage of sound. He flinched at small noises he would have paid no attention to before. An understanding look told Kaelin that his discomfort had been experienced before by the Master himself. Though Kaelin was free to hear, the Master did not speak or play any instrument. Instead, as his ears adjusted over the following days, Kaelin was struck by the assortment of instruments nature had to offer. Large tree boughs rubbed together in the wind, a groaning bass line for those with ears to hear it. Trilling bird calls, the swirling rush of a stream—how had such a symphony ever passed him by, unnoticed? The music within him yearned for it, blended with it, and became one. Thinking himself alone one morning, Kaelin began to conduct, closing his eyes and beginning with a sweeping downbeat. He was proceeding in grand style until he opened his eyes and met the amused regard of the Master Bard, newly returned from the lake with a string of small trout. Kaelin tried in vain to stop the croaks of laughter that erupted from his dry throat.

Bergid chuckled. "Go ahead and laugh, lad. You've more than earned the use of your voice." He chuckled again at the look of dismay on Kaelin's face when he tried to speak. "Don't worry. Your voice will take a few days to smooth out and sound natural to you again." His eyes shone with approval. "I congratulate you on completing a long and extremely difficult lesson. You've done well, lad. Very well, indeed."

Kaelin responded in a hoarse whisper. "Thank you, sir."

"Let's get back to work on that flute of yours. Your woodworking abilities are impressive for one so young."

Kaelin flushed with pleasure at the unaccustomed praise. His offer of an early apprenticeship notwithstanding, Craftmaster Arnor was not given to compliments.

The Master spent the rest of the day showing Kaelin how to bore holes in his flute without cracking it. Fifteen holes were bored, placed according to the pitch of each tone. Kaelin worked steadily until the Master finally stopped him.

"You did not exaggerate when you told me you learned quickly and could work hard. Such dedication ought to be fed now and then, don't you think? Come, I've prepared a celebratory dinner for you."

Kaelin put the tools and his flute away and hurried to the fire and the waiting meal. "It's not everyone who can say they were served a celebratory meal prepared by the Master Bard of Kestrel himself!" he croaked with a grin. "Not to mention all the times you served me when my eyes were covered. Erik will never believe it."

"Yes, well," the Master said dryly, "perhaps you should keep this unbelievable tale to yourself. The last thing I need is a line of hungry Bards at my door, expecting to be waited on hand and foot."

Kaelin laughed and dug into the fresh trout, roasted tubers, and wild greens sprinkled with pine nuts. The Master had told him they had traveled south along the banks of the Skirl River, partly for the good fishing to be had from it, and were now camped near the eastern shore of Loch Daevon, the largest lake on Kestrel. The Skirl fed into the lake, then continued southwest, to empty itself into the sea near Alana. Loch Daevon had been named after a Gifted Healer, who had come to the Bardic Isles with the refugees from Aille-Mara. Healer Daevon had written several scrolls describing the exodus of the five Bardic ships from the invasion, and their eventual arrival in their new homeland.

After Kaelin had cleaned up the campsite and taken care of Poor Oran, he returned to his flute, then hesitated. He glanced at the Master, who was working on a stack of papers at the table, and went to stand before him, just as he had when he left his village to follow him. The Master looked up in surprise.

"Do you have a question about your flute, lad?"

"No, sir." He bit his lip, searching for words that seemed to be just out of his reach. The Master put down his quill and waited.

"You've done so much for me," Kaelin finally said, "and I haven't even thanked you for it, and I … well, I don't know how I ever can. You've let me stay with you, taught me so much about composition, you're even helping me make a Bardic flute. And you freed my music, sir! I could never have done that on my own."

"I've never enjoyed teaching anyone more," the Master told him, "but I didn't free your music. *You* did that." He smiled at Kaelin's surprised expression. "I provided you the opportunity, yes. I gave you a sense-deprivation test normally given only to Bards, where you had no choice but to confront what was inside you and decide for yourself if you would free it or not. No one but you could have done that."

Kaelin thought about this for a moment. "What if I couldn't have?"

"Then I would have regretfully taken you back home."

Kaelin nodded slowly. "I almost couldn't," he confessed. "Every instrument you gave me to touch made the music surge, trying to get out, and it hurt more than it ever has before." He fell silent, remembering.

The Master nodded but said nothing. He had been aware of the battle Kaelin had fought, a harder one with each instrument he touched.

"Your flute has so much music in it, sir," Kaelin finally continued. "Beautiful music. Touching your flute made me want to play it so badly that, for the first time, I wanted to free my music more than I wanted to keep it safely walled away. When you took your flute back again, I almost gave up and tore the bandage off," he admitted. "But then you handed me my own flute, and everything went quiet in my mind. I realized my music isn't something separate from me that I need to keep behind walls. It *is* me. So, when I tried to cage my music because I couldn't deal with it, I think I just ended up caging myself." He frowned. "Does that make any sense?"

The Master stared at this youngster of eleven cycles who had just stated a truth that the Master himself had not learned until he was thrice that age. "It makes all the sense in the world, lad, and I've never heard it put better."

"I'll do anything you ask of me," Kaelin promised, "for however long you'll let me stay." A shadow seemed to cross his face for a moment, as though he knew how little time that was likely to be. Then he gave the Master a fleeting smile and returned to work on his flute.

The Master sat motionless for a long moment, his brows furrowed in thought, his mind once again divided in opposition.

The time is almost here, and what I'm going to have to do will break his heart. And my own.

Yes, but you can't keep him.

I must keep him! Such a Gift as his cannot be put in the hands of a Flutist or Instrumentalist. They will not understand its importance, will not nurture it like I will.

Nevertheless, you can't keep him.

The force of his own anger surprised him. *Who would dare try to stop me?*

The Council, of course.

It's not against Bardic Law for a Master to take on an apprentice! They cannot forbid me.

You know perfectly well they can forbid whatever they have a majority rule on, and your vote is only one of five! The others will not agree. There is no hope that you can keep him, and the longer you do so, the harder it will be to let him go. You've already kept him far longer than you should have.

Only a Master could have helped free his Gift, and I'm the only one who would have done what was necessary!

And now that his Gift is free, you must let him go.

No. Not yet.

When?

Not until he finishes his flute. I'll allow no one else to help him with that.

For the next several days the sound of his own voice intrigued Kaelin, and he reveled in its use. He talked to the Master, he talked to himself, he even talked to the birds that flew through the clearing. He caught a droll expression on the Master's face and laughed. Except for cajoling the merchants in the marketplace out of their wares, Kaelin had never been much of a talker, accustomed to keeping his feelings as carefully hidden as his flute. This sudden outpouring of speech was exhilarating.

On the flip side of exhilarating was the discouraging realization that he could still not play for anyone but the Master. Kaelin had hoped that fixing one would fix the other; that once his music could be played without pain, he could play for others without fear as well. He knew now, however, that this particular fear had not obligingly gotten up and left when his music was freed. The mere thought of playing for a Flutist in Kyet made his mouth go dry and his hands tremble. His music, he knew, was still dangerous. What it had done before, it could do again.

Since regaining his sight, Kaelin took pleasure in tracking the appearance and disappearance of the pack that had held the tools and wood for his flute, a pack he was certain the Master had not had during the first few weeks of their travels. The apprentice asked no questions about it, preferring to imagine a Phantom Bard trekking back and forth with whatever the Master required. But, though Kaelin kept a sharp lookout, he saw no sign of anyone else near their camp. He chuckled to himself. *Well, and what were you expecting? A Phantom that considerately leaves footprints for you to follow?*

Two more weeks were required to finish his flute. The Master showed him how to fashion a headjoint from a section cut from the original piece. By carving the end of the headjoint narrower at one end, it fit snugly inside the longer section. Moving the headjoint in or out would enable him to control the instrument's pitch. The hole the Master instructed him to bore was not circular, like the one Kaelin had made on his small flute, but slightly oblong to improve the tone.

When the headjoint was finished to the Master's satisfaction, he showed Kaelin how to make rings of wood, some open, others closed. Each had a short handle at one end, bored through the center. Then a long rod with several joints was slipped through them and attached to the flute with tiny pegs. Three such rods were put in place and, with the addition of several levers, enabled the player to control every keyhole. The Master told Kaelin that these were innovations the Instrument Masters of the Bardic Isles had made over the many cycles since leaving Eire, giving the flute a much greater range of notes and earning it a place as one of seven Bardic instruments, a position it had never held in Eire. Finally, the Master showed him how to protect the finished flute by rubbing oil deeply into the wood.

At last, on an afternoon when the wind was capriciously blowing fresh-fallen autumn leaves around their campsite, the Master inspected Kaelin's flute carefully and handed it back with a nod of approval. "A truly beautiful instrument. Perhaps it's time to try it out."

"Oh, *yes*, sir!"

"However, you certainly aren't dressed properly for it." He

shook his head disapprovingly at Kaelin, who looked down at his tunic and trousers in bewilderment. His clothing was clean, if admittedly worn and faded.

"Fortunately," the Master continued, "I have just what you need." He fetched the Phantom's pack and began rummaging through it. "Ah, here it is. To be played properly, a Bardic flute requires a Bardic robe."

Kaelin caught his breath at the sight of the grey robe the Master held out to him, but he did not reach for it.

The Master's brow lifted. "Have I been so hard on you, lad, that you no longer wish to become a Bardic apprentice?"

The youngster looked with longing at the robe. In all the world, there was only one thing he wanted more. "No, sir, I still want to," he began hesitantly, "but I thought you said you would apprentice me to a Flutist."

"I did, indeed," the Master acknowledged.

Kaelin's heart sank. "What if I don't become an apprentice? Would you let me stay with you then?"

"No, I would not," the Master replied gravely, "for that would not be in your best interests. You need the training you can only receive if you join the Bardic Order."

Kaelin dropped his gaze, not wanting the Master to see the tears that suddenly filled his eyes. "Then you'll send me away, whether I accept the robe or not," he said hopelessly. He would have to go to Lynd and find Laena, then, for he knew he couldn't accept an apprenticeship with a Flutist. Master Bergid hadn't been hurt by his music, but surely that was because he was a Master, Gifted with the power to prevent it. Kaelin couldn't take the chance with anyone else. He steeled himself to say the words that would end the best four months of his life.

"I didn't say that, lad." The Master suppressed a smile at the glimmer of hope he saw in the boy's eyes. "I've done quite a bit of thinking in the last few weeks. I considered getting you an apprenticeship with a Flutist, as I told you I would, but if I did that, how would you get the training you need on the other Bardic instruments? An Instrumentalist would be a better choice, being qualified to teach at least three of them, but then how would you continue your training in composition and theory? I've already taught you through the intermediate forms, and there is no Instrumentalist in the Bardic Isles who can teach you the advanced forms." He frowned. "It does not sit well with me to begin something that can't be completed for cycles, until you come back to me as a Bard."

Kaelin stared at the Master. *He thinks I can become a Bard?*

The Master shook his head and sighed. "Quite a problem, lad. I came to the conclusion that the only solution was to defy tradition and place you in the Master of Composition's hands, who can see to the completion of your training in composition and theory and is also eminently qualified to teach all seven Bardic instruments. And, since you're already in those hands, I've no intention of sending you elsewhere." He cocked a brow. "If, that is, you'll accept this robe and put it on."

"You'll keep me?" Kaelin asked incredulously. "You'll ... you'll really keep me?"

The Master looked pointedly at the grey robe in his hand, and Kaelin's face lit with pure joy as he reached for the coveted robe, surprised at how soft and thick the fabric was. This must be a winter robe, designed for warmth against the encroaching cold weather. His mind rose in protest the moment he touched it.

You'll accept an apprentice robe you know you can't keep?

Yes! If that's the only way to stay with him.

You'll lose them both!

But I'll have them now. And any time I can get with him is better than no time at all.

Kaelin quickly pulled the apprentice robe over his clothes. Drawing the black cord tightly around his waist, he looked up with shining eyes and found the Master looking at him as if struck by something he had not thought of until that moment.

"Rassek is going to be downright insufferable," Bergid muttered darkly.

"Rassek?"

The Master sighed. "Holder Rassek, to give him his due title. He farms a Holding near Kyet. He's also a friend of mine who believes I used my 'sorcerous music,' as he likes to call it, to wish up a boy for him as an unsolicited gift last cycle. He retaliated afterwards by wishing a boy upon me, 'a special boy, musically inclined, packed with talent, and cut to a precise Bardic measurement,' as I recall." The Master's eyes smiled into his. "I believe I'm looking at the measure of his retaliation right now."

Kaelin grinned. "I'll be sure to thank Holder Rassek when I meet him." He glanced quickly down at his new robe as if he were afraid it might have disappeared. "Am I really a Bardic apprentice now, sir?" he said wonderingly. "*Your* apprentice?"

"Almost," the Master replied. "You've a Bardic robe and cord now, to go with your Bardic flute, but there seems to be one more thing you're lacking." He reached again into the pack and withdrew a narrow leather case and a grey bag with black tasseled drawstrings and a long strap. "A Bardic instrument also requires a protective case and a Bardic travel bag to match your robe."

Kaelin's eyes widened. *The Phantom Bard has been busy!* He carefully placed his flute inside the case, then slipped it into the bag and cinched it shut, hardly daring to look up at the Master who had given him more than he had ever dreamed of having. He pulled the strap over his shoulder and touched the cord around his waist, unable to speak.

"Now that you're properly clothed, we must formalize our new relationship," the Master said. To Kaelin's surprise, the Master took the end of the apprentice's black cord and the end of his own gold one and entwined them.

"When a student is ready to become a Bardic apprentice," the Master told him, "his teacher takes him to audition before a Bard. If he passes this audition, the Bard gives him an apprentice robe and cord, then formalizes their new relationship by twining the apprentice's cord with his teacher's, just as they did so many cycles ago in Eire and I have done just now. Then the two make the traditional vows. The teacher promises to teach his apprentice to the best of his ability and to always act in his apprentice's best interests. The apprentice promises obedience to his teacher and vows to never use his music, or his position in the Bardic Order, to harm another. Do you have any questions or reservations about these vows?"

Kaelin hesitated for a moment, a bit stricken by the vow to do no harm with his music. "What if harm is caused unintentionally?" he asked.

"That would depend on the circumstances and would be a matter for the Council to decide," the Master said gravely. "In Eire, this vow was taken because those who were Gifted among them wielded power with their music, power that could indeed do harm. Master Cyral, for instance, though he did great good with his music—finding this refuge for his people and bringing them safely here—also drove the warrior ship aground behind them and sank the longboats trying to intercept their path. We can only imagine the horrible choice he faced in doing so, knowing the only way he could save lives was to cause death."

Kaelin's eyes widened. This was something the old Flutist had never pointed out.

"Through all the cycles since," the Master told him, "we've continued to make this vow. For, since music is a form of speech, anything words can do, music can do as well. Indeed, the very fact that it has no words makes it more powerful. When you've been hurt or helped by someone's words, you know and understand it immediately. Music is more subtle, able to affect others without their awareness. Both can be used to stir the soul, to arouse fervor and passion, to bring comfort and healing. They can also be used to stir unrest, to arouse envy and hatred, to cause pain and suffering. Vowing never to harm another with your music is a promise to use it to bring only good to those we serve, to bring balance and harmony to our land."

Kaelin stood silent, more devastated by this answer than the Master could have known. Something was terribly wrong with him, then, that his music caused harm even when he had no intention of causing it. Only the Master, he thought, was strong enough to withstand it and play it safely for others. The boy quailed at the thought of inadvertently causing harm to someone and having to answer to the Council for it. *I'm vowing never to play for anyone but him. He must never know what my music can do, or what it's already done.* He pushed away the guilt that came with that thought. *I'm vowing for the future, not for the past I can't change.*

"Have you any other questions?"

"No, sir."

"Very well." A glint of amusement lit the Master's eyes. "Normally, such an audition takes an hour or two. You, however, have already auditioned before a Master Bard for the unprecedented length of four months and have more than satisfied every requirement to become a Bardic apprentice. You've received your robe and cord. Now you and your Master must speak their vows, your Master first."

My Master! Kaelin had never heard two more wonderful words. He put aside his misgivings. *I'll vow anything to stay with him.*

Master Bergid looked for a moment into the eyes fastened so steadily on his. "I formally take you, Kaelin, as my apprentice. I promise to teach you to the best of my ability. You are not yet of age, so I also take full responsibility for your upbringing. I will treat you fairly, listen to you, and discipline you should you need it. I will always act in your best interests."

It was several moments before the new apprentice could speak. "I gladly agree to become your apprentice, sir. I will obey you as my teacher and Master. I'll work hard and learn as much as I can from you." He paused for a brief moment, then solemnly continued. "I promise never to use my music, or my position in the Bardic Order, to cause anyone harm."

The Master smiled. "All that remains now is for a Bard to confirm our new relationship and, in this case, it will be a Master Bard who does so." He placed his right hand over their twined cords. "I hereby pronounce myself your Master and you my apprentice." He removed his hand.

For a moment they looked at the twined cords, gold and black interwoven like a glistening path the two of them would henceforth travel together. Over and under, around and through, there was no telling where such a path would take them. Music gently filled Kaelin's mind, the notes seeming to come from the Master's golden cord. Then the Master freed the cords, and the music faded.

"You have a rare Gift of music within you," the Master said. "Now that you are free to express it, I will do whatever is necessary to develop your ability. It is fortunate that you have landed in the hands of the Master of Composition, for your music must be written down, and not just left to rattle around in that head of yours." He eyed his new apprentice sternly. "There are many advanced forms of composition and theory, and I intend to drill you in every last one of them until you beg for mercy. We will begin tomorrow, with composition, theory, pipes, and harp lessons. Enjoy the rest of the afternoon, lad," he warned, "for it's the last one you will have entirely free for some time."

Kaelin's face lit up even more. He would cheerfully forfeit all the free time in the world for such wonderful lessons with the Master. Still, he couldn't resist asking about the one instrument the Master hadn't mentioned. "And ... my flute?" he asked hopefully.

His face fell when the Master regretfully shook his head.

"You're free to play your flute during your free time, and I'll answer your questions concerning it, but lessons on it will have to wait."

Kaelin perked up. "Then, eventually ..."

Bergid smiled. "In time, lad. In time. All things come—"

"—in the fullness of their own measure?" Kaelin finished with a grin.

"Precisely." The Master seated himself and gestured toward the woods. "The remainder of the afternoon is yours. Go let all the music bubbling up inside you out through that new flute of yours. The two of you need some time alone to become acquainted. Then come back to me with all the many questions you'll surely have afterwards. An old man like me needs his afternoon rest to withstand such an onslaught." He cocked a bristling brow at Kaelin, who stood motionless.

"Evidently the vow of obedience you just made is slow to take effect," the Master said dryly, then gave an exaggerated sigh when his apprentice still made no move to leave. "I suppose," he grumbled, "despite all the bags Poor Oran is already burdened with, I shall have to add yet another one, filled with switches for use on disobedient apprentices."

The Master Bard of Kestrel was astonished to find himself almost knocked over by Kaelin's impetuous hug. Was it his imagination, or were the words, "I love you," whispered against his chest? Bergid's throat constricted painfully.

The apprentice stood back suddenly and swept his Master a bow. "Poor Oran needn't be inconvenienced, sir. I shall be honored to carry those switches for you myself!"

Amber eyes shone into the Master's for a moment, and then the youngest apprentice in the history of the Bardic Isles was gone, disappearing through the trees, the satisfying weight of his Bardic flute against his back.

Behind him, the first Master in the history of the Bardic Isles to take on an apprentice sat completely still, half of his mind pleased by his break with tradition, the other half shocked speechless by it. Then the latter half rallied and went on the attack.

What insanity have you just committed?

I did what I had to do.

You had to do no such thing! Once the Council hears—

Oh, be quiet! I'll deal with the Council when I have to and not a moment before. No one is taking Kaelin from me.

The faint, clear sound of a Bardic flute wound through the trees, pulling at the Master irresistibly, just as a small flute played by a musically inhibited youngster had done once before in the woods of Vale.

No one.

Chapter 6

Kaelin would remember the following month as a whirlwind of activity. Every moment of the day was filled with learning, and when he finally lay down on his bedroll at night to drowsily listen to the Master play, he was certain that he had never been happier in his life. After breakfast, the mornings began with lessons on the advanced forms of composition and theory. The apprentice quickly absorbed everything his Master taught him, then took down his instructions on the assignments that must be completed by evening, when the Master would review his work and they would discuss it. He rarely had to repeat an assignment.

Lessons on harp and pipes took up the rest of his mornings, and both instruments proved to be more complicated than Kaelin had thought. His fingers, unaccustomed to harp strings, were soon sore from his efforts, and the Master cautioned him to break up his afternoon practice sessions into several short ones.

"Your fingers will toughen up before long," Bergid told his apprentice, "but not if you keep blistering them like that." He withdrew a small tin from his pack and handed it to Kaelin. "Rub a small amount of this salve into your fingertips. It will ease the sting and help them heal."

The Master's full set of pipes were quite a handful for a

youngster of eleven, and Kaelin had soon discovered that blowing into them was nothing like blowing into a flute. He doggedly persisted, determined to please his Master each morning with his progress. Seeing the surprised lift of the Master's brows, and the smile and nod that followed, was all Kaelin needed to spur him on to even greater efforts.

After lunch, he spent the afternoon completing his assignments and practicing harp and pipes. He had one hour of free time, which he devoted to his flute, taking it into the woods and playing the music that sang freely inside him now. He wrote these new flute compositions down whenever he could snatch enough time to do so. He was somewhat taken aback, however, when his Master declined to review them.

"I'll be more than happy to look at them, or hear you play them," his Master told him, "but not in order to critique them. You need an outlet for your music that is free from anyone's scrutiny, even mine. Let your own music come, Kaelin, unimpeded by any thoughts of what you think I might prefer, and write it down exactly as you hear it, using the compositional skills you've worked so hard to acquire. If you wish to stay up an hour later to scribe your compositions or play them, you may do so, but your audience of one will remain silent."

And so Kaelin had done, gladly spending the extra hour writing what he had composed that afternoon. He played each new piece once to check it for accuracy before putting his instrument and writing materials away. Then, giving his Master a hug, he headed for his bedroll, exhausted and thoroughly happy, to fall asleep to his Master's playing.

One evening, Bergid glanced up when Kaelin approached, then set aside his papers and quill at the serious expression on his apprentice's face.

"What's on your mind?" the Master asked.

"I'm just wondering about my Gift." Kaelin replied. "I saw the kestrel during my free time today. I think it was the same one I saw before, the one whose music I played a variation of later."

"There's no shortage of kestrels on this island," the Master said dryly. "What makes you think it was the same bird? Did you listen to its song?"

"Oh, no, sir," Kaelin assured him. "I can't be sure it's the same one, but he's the biggest kestrel I've ever seen, and he has the same markings. Anyway, it got me thinking … now that I can play my own music without pain, I wonder if I could play the music of other things, too, without making a variation first. Nothing living, of course," he hastily added, "just something like a rock or fallen leaf, maybe. Do you think I could?"

The Master was silent for a long moment. This was a conversation he had expected to have eventually, but he'd hoped it would be a cycle or two before Kaelin expressed a desire to further explore his Gift. Bergid suppressed a sigh. His eager apprentice, it seemed, did not wish to wait. "I see no reason why you wouldn't be able to play the music you hear from other things, without pain," he allowed.

The youngster's face lit with excitement. "Would you let me try?"

The Master frowned. He had deep reservations about letting Kaelin explore a Gift that no one in the Bardic Isles, himself included, knew anything about. A Gift that Bardic history proved was inherently dangerous. He opened his mouth, intending to say no, but his apprentice continued enthusiastically.

"I can only imagine what it might be like, but if simple variations are so wonderful to experience, the main themes must be amazing!"

Instead of saying no, the Master said what he knew he would castigate himself for afterwards. "You are young for such an experience, but I think I can allow you to try … under my supervision."

The apprentice's face radiated joy, and the castigation of the

Master commenced.

Did you actually promise him something that could potentially harm him, just to see that look on his face?

I'll be keeping an eye on him.

Of course, you will ... the expert eye of a Master who knows no more about this Gift than anyone else in the Bardic Isles. Which is absolutely nothing!

"Let's have our session tomorrow after your free time, then," Bergid said. "Perhaps you can select an object yourself."

Yes, like that nice, friendly hatchet over there. Perhaps his Gift could levitate it and make it fly about the clearing. What could possibly go wrong?

Kaelin was already heading toward his bedroll.

"Haven't you forgotten something?"

The apprentice turned in surprise.

"How do you expect me to get any sleep tonight," the Master complained, "without a hug from my apprentice?"

Kaelin flushed slightly. "I suppose most apprentices don't give their Masters hugs, do they?"

"Well, since most apprentices aren't you, and most Masters aren't me, I think we can safely ignore what they do or don't do."

Like use their common sense?

"You don't think I'm too old for hugs?" the boy asked hesitantly.

"On the contrary, I shall be devastated the day you stop delivering them."

Kaelin smiled and gave his Master a hug. "Then I'll never stop," he murmured.

The next afternoon Kaelin returned from his free time holding a large feather. The base of the feather was pale blue, lightening to snowy white at the tip, which was accented by a broad black band.

He handed it to the Master. "I think it's from the same kestrel whose music I heard the day before you came to Vale."

"Well, it certainly comes from a large one." Bergid placed the feather on their makeshift table, indicating that Kaelin should take the seat across from him.

Feeling a bit nervous, the youngster sat down and took out his flute. "What do you want me to do?"

"For now, just study the feather and listen to the music you hear coming from it," the Master instructed.

Kaelin laid his flute across his lap and admired the glossy sheen of the feather, wondering what it would be like to soar over the islands with the freedom of a wild kestrel.

The music slipped into his mind as though on wings of its own, and Kaelin stared at the feather in wonder. He had heard this music before, kneeling at the base of a twisted oak in the woods of Vale. His concentration broken by the thought, the music faded. He glanced up at the Master, who was gazing at him with a bemused expression.

"Are all kestrels created with the same song?"

The Master was silent for a few moments. "I think it's safe to say that all kestrels are created with variations of the same song," he finally said. "Their songs are related, but not identical, just as our own songs are." *And may the Maker forgive me if I'm wrong.*

"Then this feather *is* from the same kestrel!" Kaelin exclaimed. "The music is exactly the same." He looked wonderingly at the feather. "What will happen if I play it?"

"That is something best discovered on your own. Listen to the music of the feather again, then duplicate it on your flute, exactly as you hear it."

"Just like I've been doing with the music inside me," Kaelin murmured. His hesitancy gone, he studied the feather again, the beautiful music once again filling his mind. He lifted his flute, closed his eyes, and began to play the music he heard. He duplicated it exactly as he heard it, without variation, confident that if anything went wrong, his Master was there to make it right.

The next moment, Kaelin gasped in surprise as his senses were abruptly taken into what appeared to be an iridescent tunnel. He stared around him, incredulous, barely able to continue playing. The tunnel appeared to be smooth and rounded, light gleaming through its translucent walls. Fractured fragments of rainbows chased each other along its sides. The brief thought that he had somehow entered a passageway to the faery world of Eire gave him a thrill of delight. Further down, he could see other avenues of the main tunnel branching off on either side. Though he knew he was sitting right next to the feather, the music he continued to play on his flute sounded faint, as though it came from a distance. For some time, he stared around him, lost in the scintillating world he had somehow entered. Then he cautiously willed himself forward, surprised when he began moving slowly along the length of the tunnel. He peered into the first branch he came to, finding it similar to the tunnel he was in, only much smaller. When the next few branches were the same, he relaxed and began to breathe more easily. He had just decided to explore one of the branches when the tunnel inexplicably darkened. He looked up to see an encroaching shadow pass over the walls. Startled and frightened, Kaelin stopped playing.

Without warning, the tunnel vanished and Kaelin found himself sitting at the table with his flute on his lap. He was breathing rapidly, as if he'd been running at top speed through the woods. Dizziness and nausea swept through him, and he clutched his stomach as he turned and spewed its contents on the ground. When at last the nausea passed, he looked up at his Master, whose face seemed to have paled a bit as he sat staring at the feather.

"What ... was that, sir?" Kaelin asked unsteadily. "What just happened?"

The Master looked up as though startled by his presence. He

cleared his throat. "Describe to me what you saw."

Kaelin gave him a worried look. "Did I do it wrong and go somewhere I shouldn't have? Has that ever happened to you, sir?"

To hide his utter ignorance, the Master gave his apprentice the sternest look in his repertoire. "My own experiences are irrelevant. Clarity of thought is vital when working with your Gift, and giving me clear, concise descriptions of what you see will aid you in that. Now, I expect you to give me one, as I told you to do."

"Yes, sir." Abashed at this unexpected chiding from his Master, Kaelin described the strange and lovely place he'd seen. "I have no idea where it was. Or *what* it was."

"It was the inside of the feather," the Master told him.

Kaelin gave him a startled look.

"You played the song of the feather exactly as you heard it, did you not?"

"Yes, sir." That much Kaelin was sure of.

"And the song took your senses into it."

"But that's never happened before," Kaelin said doubtfully. "When I played the kestrel's song in the woods, I didn't suddenly find myself *inside* of him."

"That's because you were playing your own variation of his song, not the song itself," the Master explained, sending a brief, petitioning glance toward the heavens. "Thus, your experience of the music only took your senses into what you were remembering or thinking of when you played it. You imagined the freedom the kestrel enjoys in the skies."

"Yes," Kaelin eagerly replied. "I felt myself taken up above the trees for a few moments and could see everything around me, like I was a bird myself! It was wonderful," he ended wistfully.

"I'm sure it was," the Master said. "Taking your senses *inside* the kestrel, however, is something a variation of his song couldn't do, for the original notes have to be precisely duplicated. Thanks to your excellent ability to mimic exactly what you hear, you were able to do that with the feather." The Master indicated the feather's base. "The tunnel you entered was the quill, and the smaller tunnels on either side were the barbs."

Kaelin's eyes widened as he stared at the feather, imagining himself as a tiny person inside the quill. "That fits what I saw," he said at last, "but I'd hate to think of what would happen if I got stuck in there and couldn't come back out. Could that happen?" he asked nervously.

Bergid inwardly winced at hearing verbalized the question he himself was wrestling with. "No," he said firmly, once again petitioning the Maker for forgiveness if he was wrong. "For did you not come back out the moment you stopped playing? Now," he said firmly, "that's enough for one day. It's nearly time for dinner."

Kaelin nodded and put away his flute. He got to his feet and swayed, the earth suddenly seeming a very unstable place. His Master reached him just as he started to fall, and firmly guided him to his bedroll in the shelter, ignoring Kaelin's tired protests that he had a composition to complete.

"The only thing you need to complete right now is several hours of sleep," the Master said sternly.

"But shouldn't I at least clean—"

"I'll clean it up."

"But what about your din—" Kaelin yawned.

"I'm perfectly capable of making dinner," the Master said dryly.

"Shouldn't I at least give you my assign—" The boy's eyes closed, he emitted a soft sigh, and fell sound asleep. He did not emerge from the shelter until late that night, coming to stand sheepishly before his Master, who put aside his harp and smiled at him.

"Good to see you looking more yourself," Bergid said. He reached out and took a well-filled plate from the edge of the fire. "Finishing this off should help as well."

"Thank you, sir." Kaelin gratefully took the meal and sat down. "I must have slept for hours." He took a large bite of fish and chewed contentedly. "Should I bring you my assignment?"

The Master shook his head. "It will keep until tomorrow, and so will that unfinished composition of yours. After you're done eating, you're to go straight back to your bedroll."

Kaelin's fork stopped traversing a path from plate to mouth. "But I'm not—"

"—going to make the mistake of disobeying your Master," Bergid finished, his brow lifting slightly.

"No, sir, I'm certainly not," the apprentice quickly verified. He finished his meal and yawned again as he put down the empty plate. "I don't understand why I'm this exhausted after just a few minutes," he complained. "I can hike or practice for far longer and not get nearly this tired."

"Not inside a feather, you can't," Bergid said wryly. "Nor were you inside it for just a few minutes. It was half an hour."

Kaelin was too stunned to speak. The thought crossed his mind that the faery world of Eire was said to be a timeless place. Indeed, those who foolishly strayed into it and were lucky enough to return could find that the few days spent there had cost them cycles of their own time. He shook his head to dispel the disquieting notion, then rose, gave his Master a hug, and headed for the shelter.

Bergid watched him go, then turned toward the fire.

For the first time in my life, I've taught something under false pretenses!

Perhaps that would matter if someone else could teach him better. But there is no one who understands this Gift at all.

I should at least have admitted to him that I'm wandering as blind as he is.

And give him reason to fear his Gift again, when it has finally been freed?

Do I not demand total honesty from him?

You also made a vow to always act in his best interests. Wasn't it far better for him, in exploring this Gift for the first time, to feel safe while he did so?

And what if he had felt so safe that he had done something foolish, secure in the belief that his Master could keep him from harm? What happened tonight was no small matter! He was utterly exhausted after a half hour inside that feather. What if he had stayed there for an hour or two, apparently having no idea of the passage of time? And who knows what could happen to his awareness inside an object? If something should go wrong, I would be powerless to help him.

Bergid felt himself go cold at the thought of Kaelin's awareness trapped inside something, without the strength to return. It had seemed that simply ceasing to play had brought him out of the feather, but what if that wasn't the case? What if, next time, he continued playing until the flute fell from his hands, and he did not return to himself at all?

He's a young boy who's been through some trauma he's too afraid to tell anyone about. The last thing he should be doing is using a Gift that holds the potential power of Master Cyral's. This is not something I can teach him about, and I'd be a fool to let him continue exploring it on his own. Far better for him if we focus on completing his training. His Gift, whatever it truly is, will have to wait.

Relieved at coming to a decision, the Master banked the fire and went to get some sleep of his own.

⁓ ⸮ ⁓

The following morning, Bergid awoke to find his apprentice already awake and brooding before the fire.

Bergid sat down next to him. "Is something troubling you?"

"Good morning, Master." The youngster gave him a smile.

"Should I make breakfast first?"

"Breakfast can wait, lad. You and I need to talk … but first, tell me what's bothering you."

"I've been thinking about what happened yesterday," the apprentice said. "I was so excited to explore my Gift, and being inside the feather was amazing, even if I didn't know what it was, but then I panicked over a shadow!"

The Master frowned. "What shadow?"

"There was a shadow that darkened the walls of the quill, and it scared me. The next thing I knew, I was back. I don't know if it was my fear that sent me back, or if I stopped playing, and that sent me back." He looked up hopefully, as though expecting to have this explained, then shrugged when the Master said nothing. "It was just a shadow. Now that I know I was inside the feather, I suppose it was nothing more than a bird passing over us, or a leaf blown across the clearing. But it made me start thinking about this Gift, and I realized that, as much as I'd like to explore it, I'm afraid of it, too. Afraid of what it might do … or might have done." He dropped his eyes and hurried on before his Master could question him about the past. "I'm sorry to be such a coward, and I know your own Gift is a wondrous thing, but sometimes," he confessed to the ground, "I wonder if mine isn't more of a curse than a Gift."

Bergid was silent for a long moment, then he abruptly removed his belt knife from its sheath. He held it up before his apprentice, firelight dancing across its smooth surface. "This knife is a very useful tool, is it not? It has a blade strong enough to cut wood and sharp enough to shave the hair from a man's face. Yet this same knife," the Master continued grimly, "can also be used to hurt or kill." He paused for a moment, turning the blade in his hand.

"The knife is but a tool," Bergid said as he slipped it back into its sheath. "It is, of itself, neither good nor evil. If used for good, we do not give it credit. If used for harm, we assign it no blame. Whoever wields such a tool is responsible for how it is used. Your Gift is not a curse, lad. It is merely another tool." He lifted a brow. "If I did not have complete confidence in your intention to use it wisely," he said, "I would never have taken you as my apprentice."

The apprentice stared at his Master. "So that's why you waited so long before deciding whether or not to help me."

Bergid nodded. "Your Gift will not leap up and wreak havoc on its own, any more than your belt knife will suddenly jump from its sheath and stab someone. Your Gift is great, for both good and evil, but how it is used will always be yours to determine. Don't ever forget that."

"I won't, sir," Kaelin assured him, but the Master was not finished.

"That does not, however, mean that you're ready to race off on your own, exploring your Gift in whatever way takes your fancy. You are young and inexperienced in many things besides your Gift, and must gain that experience slowly and carefully, just as you did with an actual knife when you were younger. In the hands of an inexperienced child, the knife might well cause harm. That's why your parents did not allow you to use one until you were old enough to learn to use it safely."

The Master quirked a brow at his apprentice. "Nor will I allow you to use your Gift until you turn of age and have gained the necessary knowledge to use it well and safely. You have much yet to learn, not only with regard to your education in music, but also to gain an understanding of our history, our way of life, of Bardic Law and the laws that govern each of the Guilds. It takes a Bard cycles to gain that knowledge and understanding. You must be given time to gain it as well before learning to implement your Gift in ways that might have unintended consequences more grave than mere exhaustion. And," he continued gravely, "after last night, I also feel it would be best to explore your Gift with a harp, rather than with your flute, so that your own gasps of surprise or amazement don't disturb your playing. It will take cycles to attain full mastery of your harp, which you will need to gain before playing songs that require the utmost precision, not to mention a great deal of stamina." He held his apprentice's gaze as firmly as he had when they first met.

"Therefore, I have decided to forbid you from any further exploration of your Gift at this time. You are not to listen to the music of any living thing. You may listen to the songs of objects and compose variations of them, as you've always done, but you are not to play the unvaried song of anything."

Kaelin sat still for a moment, disappointment warring with relief. The feather had been wondrous, but the shadow still filled him with a nameless dread. He looked at the Master he had so quickly learned to love, the one who completely understood the music that filled his soul, and solemnly nodded. "I promise not to listen to the music of any living thing or play the unvaried music of anything. I will not explore my Gift any further until you decide I'm ready to do so and give me your permission."

The Master nodded, well satisfied with the boy's response. "It is not cowardice," he said, "to question the inherent danger of this Gift, and you show good sense beyond your cycles to be wary of it. I'm sorry to so restrict you," he added gently. "I know how excited you are to discover all you can about it."

Kaelin shook his head. "It will still be there when I'm ready." He smiled at his Master and went to make their breakfast.

The Master fetched his towel for his morning trip to the lake, sending the Maker a stern message as he went. *If I'm wrong ... if the Gift you've bestowed on him leaps up and causes him any harm whatsoever, you will have me to deal with!*

Chapter 7

A month later, Kaelin crunched through drifts of brilliantly colored autumn leaves, following his Master. The surrounding hills were thick with birch, hawthorn, and wych elm, while here and there the russet red of an oak stood out against the shades of yellow. The apprentice, too distracted to notice the stunning scenery, was trying valiantly to stifle the eager questions clamoring for release. In spite of his efforts, another one escaped. "Are we going to travel far, Master?"

"What is far for one is but a step for another."

Kaelin sighed and his Master's eyes twinkled. "Patience, lad. All things come—"

"—in the fullness of their own measure," Kaelin finished with a sigh.

The Master chuckled. "I suppose I've said that a time or two before, haven't I?"

Kaelin shrugged ruefully and took advantage of his Master's attention to allow another question to escape. "Can you at least tell me how many beats are in this measure we're in?"

"As many beats as it takes to get us where we're going," the

Master said unhelpfully as he continued on his way.

Kaelin sighed again and turned his attention to the scenery as he walked, surprised by how much it had changed as they made their descent from the mountains. They had spent the last week moving through the wooded hills east of Loch Daevon, stopping only for the occasional rainfall blown their way from the mountains. Kaelin was still uncertain as to their exact location, though he knew they were far southeast of Vale. Soon they left the woods behind and entered a valley, sunk between gently sloping hills. Several Holdings, their fields already harvested, dotted the landscape. Kaelin breathed deeply of the chilly, fragrant air. Winter was on its way, and it didn't seem possible that it had been nearly a half-cycle since the Master Bard had come to Vale.

They had spent the first half of autumn at their camp, the Master making good on his promise to drill his apprentice unmercifully in composition and theory forms. The apprentice, far from being dismayed, had gladly soaked up every assignment. Just like the woodworking tools that Craftmaster Arnor had insisted he become proficient with before creating works of wood, the assignments of the Master were the tools Kaelin would need to commit the music he was constantly composing in his mind to manuscript.

They made their way through the valley, and at the top of the next rise Kaelin stopped and caught his breath. A large river divided the land from north to south before him. "Is that the Bronig?"

The Master smiled. "Indeed, it is. Which should tell you where we're headed if you paid any attention during your geography lessons." He turned south along the riverbank and Kaelin hurried after him, slightly abashed as he rifled vainly through his memories. He remembered only that the Bronig was the largest river on Kestrel and emptied into the sea on the southern coast. Letting the river's music fill his mind, he effortlessly translated its voice into a flute composition. *Perhaps the harp would be better.* Though his Master still gave him no flute instruction, Kaelin had made good progress on the Master's harp and pipes in the last two months and been promoted to form three on both instruments. His increasing affinity for the harp made him feel disloyal to his flute, though Kaelin told himself that was ridiculous. As much as he had grown to love the first of all Bardic instruments, no harp could ever replace his flute.

As they traveled farther south, a distant, rhythmic sound filled the air, and the tangy smell of salt filled his nostrils. Soon they climbed a grassy bluff and stood at the top, their robes billowing in the sudden breeze.

The ocean! Kaelin stared at it, not quite able to believe there could be so much water all in one place, or that the sky could stretch so far that it became one with it. His eyes became slightly unfocused, and the Master laughed.

"Come, Kaelin. Stop composing oceanic symphonies for a moment. Look there." Lifting his staff, he gestured to the east across the mouth of the Bronig. "Kyet."

To the eyes of a village boy, the town of Kyet seemed enormous, an endless array of rooftops spread along the eastern edge of the bay. A half-dozen docks jutted into the water, three of them with a ship moored alongside. Men busily worked on the docks, loading the cargo of one ship, unloading another. A fourth ship, in full sail, sliced a path toward the open sea. Kaelin stood captivated by its graceful lines and snowy white sails. *Bardic ships!* He turned to find that his Master had tethered Poor Oran and was removing his packs. The apprentice hurried to help.

"Are we staying here?" Kaelin asked in surprise.

The Master smiled. *"I am,"* he said equably. "You, however, will remove your robe, take the ferry you'll find a few leagues downriver, and wait for me at dusk on the other side."

Kaelin's eyes widened. "But sir—" The Master's brow raised a fraction, and the boy instantly subsided.

"Yes, Master." He removed his robe and stowed it in his pack.

The Master handed him a two-copper coin, the largest Kaelin had ever held.

"You'll need part of that for the ferryman," his Master told him. "And if you wish to use the rest in the marketplace, you may. Just keep in mind that whatever you purchase with it must be carried on your own back, not Poor Oran's. And do not forget to meet me at the ferry landing at dusk."

"Thank you, Master! I won't be late." Carefully stowing the coin, Kaelin slung his pack over his shoulder and made his way down the hill.

When he reached the ferry landing, the boy handed over his coin and received a number of smaller coppers in exchange. Heart beating with excitement, he stepped onto the stern of the small ferry as it rose and fell alongside the dock. Before he could reach the railing, however, he lost his balance and fell on his backside, causing a ripple of laughter. Face burning, Kaelin managed to take his place among the other passengers, who seemed to have no trouble staying on their feet. Then he forgot his embarrassment as the ropes were untied and the ferry lurched forward under the combined efforts of the oarsmen. With a firm grip on the railing, Kaelin watched the water divide smoothly before them, leaving a frothing path in its wake. The music of it bubbled up inside him and he stored it away to write down later.

He was soon thankfully on solid ground again and making his way toward the marketplace of Kyet, along with most of his fellow passengers. Kaelin stood staring at the immense square, at least three times the size of Vale's and cobbled with smooth stones. No hastily constructed stalls here; the shops facing the square were well-built structures of wood and stone, spacious and meticulously clean. Many sported glass windows in front, showing a tempting array of the shopkeeper's wares. In the center of the square stood rows of wooden platforms, heaped high with produce. There were customers aplenty, jostling each other and carrying on spirited arguments as they bargained for goods.

The newest arrival from Vale wandered slowly along the shop fronts, staring at everything: candles, soaps, leatherwork, tin ware, and, most of all, woodcarvings. He remembered the Schoolmaster telling his students they should be proud to live in Vale, for it was the chief woodcarving village in Kestrel. Kaelin felt foolish for not realizing that so many of Vale's carvings would find their way to the huge marketplace of Kyet. He watched as merchants busily carted boxes between the docks and the square, feeling a surge of pride in his small village. There was no telling where the fine woodcarvings of Vale would travel ... maybe all the way to the southernmost tip of Elegy or Lyra. Or perhaps, he thought with a thrill, all the way to the northern coast of Gaul, where he knew Bardic ships, altered in construction to mimic the ships of that country, sometimes traded for supplies not readily available in the Isles.

The moment he caught a delicious aroma coming from a shop ahead of him, the youngster promptly forgot everything else. The mountain villages, Vale included, usually had a small bakery, but they hadn't visited a village since Kaelin's sense-deprivation test three months ago. Nor were those bakeries anything like the one he entered now. It was crowded inside, but he didn't mind the wait, looking with mouth-watering appreciation at the array of fresh-baked breads, filled rolls, tarts, and confections he had never seen before. By the time the shopkeeper turned a harried glance in his direction, Kaelin had made his choices and hoped he had enough copper pieces to pay for them. The shopkeeper deftly packaged his order, slipped a spiced meat roll into it with a conspiratorial wink, and handed it to him. Kaelin was pleased to leave with most of his coppers as well; his Master had been more than generous.

He ate the spiced meat roll as he perused a few more shops. When the sun began dipping toward the western side of the bay, the apprentice made his way back to the ferry and sat against a tree to enjoy the rest of his purchases, saving the two best tarts for his

Master. As it grew darker, he became drowsy and had almost drifted off to sleep when a voice startled him.

"I see you enjoyed your trip to the marketplace."

Kaelin looked up into his Master's amused expression and hastily brushed the crumbs from his face. "It's so *big,*" he said as he got to his feet. "There were so many shops that I hardly knew where to go first, but the bakery's where I ended up." He fished out the remaining coppers from his pack and handed them to his Master with the extra tarts.

Master Bergid thanked him for the tarts but refused the coppers. "Keep them, lad. You may have need of them now and then."

Kaelin's eyes shone as he stowed them away. "Thank you, sir!"

"Did anything else besides food command your attention?"

Kaelin grinned and removed a small object from his bag.

"A wood carving? I should think you would have seen plenty of those in Vale."

"This one is special." He handed it over and watched as the Master gazed at the intricate carving of the village square of Vale.

"Do you miss your village?" the Master asked quietly, his eyes still resting on the carving.

"No, sir, though I miss my sister sometimes. And there's a picture of inlaid wood my father made and hung in my bedroom that I wish I'd thought to bring with me when I left. It was a picture of a place ... a special place we used to go as a family." He bit his lip, remembering, then nodded toward the carving in the Master's hands. "I bought that because it's where I first saw *you.* I wouldn't trade that moment for a hundred Vales." Blue eyes shone into his, then he suddenly realized his Master had only his instruments and a single pack with him. "Where's Poor Oran?" he asked.

"The Ferrymaster has a boarding stable on the other side of the Bronig, where Poor Oran will be quite comfortable until our return," his Master told him as he handed the carving back. "Come along, now. We've still a short way to travel."

As Kaelin took up his pack and followed his Master through the dark and deserted streets of Kyet, he wondered. Did the Master Bard of Kestrel not wish to be seen? *Maybe it's his apprentice he doesn't want seen, and that's why he made me remove my robe.* He frowned and slowed his steps at the thought. His existence couldn't be kept secret forever, so why bother trying to hide it? He pushed aside his wondering and hurried to catch up to his Master. To the north of Kyet they followed a well-cleared path up a hill overlooking the seaport. The largest house Kaelin had ever seen stood prominently at the top, and he briefly wondered who they were going to visit at such a late hour and why there were no lights coming from the many windows. To his surprise, his Master unlocked the door and lit a lamp.

Kaelin stood still, struck with wonder. He had never seen such a beautiful, spacious living room, two open archways to his left promising further rooms beyond. Between the archways was a massive fireplace, with several chairs arranged invitingly before it. On the opposite wall another archway revealed a kitchen at least half the size of the cottage Kaelin had grown up in, complete with oak cabinets, a large oak dining table, and eight matched chairs. He pulled his eyes back to the main living room, admiring the gleaming walls of split pine and the thick rugs adorning the floor. To his left, an immense table that could seat a dozen people stood in front of tall windows looking out over Kyet and the bay beyond.

Kaelin turned his gaze to the opposite side of the room, where a large desk stood, framed by a window that revealed the woods behind the Master's home. Near this stood a smaller desk, possessed of many interesting drawers and cubbyholes. To the left of the comfortable chair standing in front of it, four instruments hung in their travel bags from a beautiful oak pedestal. A matching pedestal stood to the right of the desk, empty and presumably ready to receive the harp, flute, and pipes the Master had traveled with. Several manuscripts, most of them filled with music, lay on the desk's gleaming surface. An inkwell stood next to a wooden holder filled with an assortment of quills, ready for use. The apprentice caught his breath. *A composition desk!* His eyes traveled upward, to the manuscripts that filled the myriad cubicles affixed to the wall above the desk. Kaelin hadn't thought there was so much music in all the world. He stood staring until a low chuckle made him turn, to find the room brightening with the soft glow of firelight. His Master stood next to the fire, regarding him with a smile.

"Welcome to my home, Kaelin. As my apprentice, it is now your home as well."

The apprentice gave him a startled look. "Truly, sir?"

"Most truly."

Kaelin gave his Master a smile, then he glanced at the instruments hanging by the Master's composition desk. "Are those your other Bardic instruments?" he asked curiously.

"Yes, my lap harp, lute, lyre, and kithara, the Master replied. "Two or three instruments are generally enough of a load to travel with. When we go to Elegy for Council sessions, we keep spares of the other instruments in our cabins there."

Kaelin's eyes wandered back to the music shelves. "I've never even imagined a home as wonderful as this one," he said in a hushed voice. "I'm surprised you could bring yourself to leave it at all."

"Well, I must admit that this past cycle has been spent more in the woods than out of it, but I normally spend most of my time here. After all, the Bards of Kestrel can't be searching the mountains every time they need to talk to me." The Master settled himself at his desk. "I have a great deal of work to do and messages to leave. We'll stay here a day or two, but no longer." He picked up a quill. "There are pegs over there for your cloak and instruments, unless you prefer to keep them in your room. If you go through the archway to the left of the fireplace you'll find two guest rooms on the left side of the hall. The sliding doors on the right are storage rooms, and the door at the end of the hall leads to my own quarters. You can choose whichever guest room you like for your own."

Kaelin tore his gaze away from the composition desk. "Where does the other archway lead?"

"A similar hallway, with more storage rooms on the left, two practice rooms on the right, and a large ensemble room at the end of the hall." Bergid smiled as his apprentice's gaze gravitated back to the shelves of music above his composition desk. "If you would like to look through any of that music, you may," the Master told him. "The cubicles on the right contain forms, or levels, of instrumental music. First forms on the bottom shelves, moving up to the higher forms, one column for each Bardic instrument. The column in the center contains solo works from various composers. The cubicles on the left contain my own compositions. Just keep in mind that whatever you take out must be put back precisely where you found it." He opened one of the scrolls on his desk and began to read.

Kaelin stared incredulously at the dozens of cubicles on the left. All that music, his Master's own? He hung his instruments up and walked eagerly toward the beckoning manuscripts.

Some time later the Master looked over to find his apprentice surrounded by several piles of music. "You seem to be enjoying my compositions, Kaelin. I trust you remember where they all belong."

The apprentice looked up, startled. "Oh, yes, sir! They're wonderful." He picked up one of the manuscripts and handed it to the Master. "Especially this one. It's not difficult, but ... there's just something special about it."

Curious, the Master opened it, unsurprised to find that it was a flute piece. He scanned the music, remembering the writing of it, then abruptly handed it back.

"May I play it?" Kaelin asked eagerly. "I know it's late ... but just once?"

The Master hesitated, then nodded permission. He watched

as Kaelin took out his flute. After looking the music over, the apprentice closed his eyes and began to play.

Kaelin was well accustomed to using his own feelings to fashion a mental picture of whatever the music suggested to him. This time, however, a picture came to his mind completely unbidden. He saw a man sitting alone in the woods. At first he thought it was his Master, but the man was much younger, with blond hair. He was dressed in a Bard's robe of light blue, bound at the waist with a silver cord. And tears ... tears shone against his cheeks.

The music died softly away. Kaelin turned to see the grief he had just witnessed reflected on his Master's face. Rivulets of moisture on the Master's cheeks glistened in the light of the fire. Stunned, the boy quietly put away his flute, then carefully replaced all the music he had looked through. Leaving the Master to his silence, he fetched his pack and went to look at the two guest rooms. Both were spacious, with windows looking out over the lights of Kyet and the bay beyond. Choosing the room closest to his Master's room, he placed his pack on the desk by the window and fell asleep in what he was certain was the softest bed an apprentice had ever had the luxury of sleeping in.

That night Kaelin dreamed of a tall, strikingly beautiful mountain. Its two peaks were sharply defined, the right higher than the left. A river shone in the sunlight, winding its way south from where Kaelin watched, then curving northwards back toward the mountain.

The vision faded and Kaelin found himself in his Master's living room, his Master asleep at his desk. There seemed no reason for the dread that crept over Kaelin as he watched the still room. Faint strains of music reached him over his Master's soft snoring. *Harp music.* His eyes fastened on the desk. Though it seemed scarcely possible, the music came from one of its drawers. The lyric melody swelled in a compelling crescendo, pulling him unwillingly forward. The music modulated, sending waves of alternating arpeggios across the room, bringing him ever closer to the desk. The drawer glowed, pulsing in rhythm to the music. Helpless to stop himself, the apprentice reached out and opened the drawer.

Kaelin cried out, lunging halfway out of his bed. Before he could get his bearings, his Master was beside him. "It's all right, lad, it's only a dream. It's over now."

Kaelin shuddered and shook his head. "No! It's just beginning!"

The Master frowned but said nothing. He waited until Kaelin was calm, then listened as the boy told him his dream. "Which drawer did you open?"

"The second drawer on the right."

"Did you see what was in the drawer?"

"I caught a glimpse of a book," the boy replied, a troubled look passing over his face. "A golden book. I don't know if it was truly gold or if the firelight made it seem so. The music came from the book. It scared me and then I woke up."

The Master said no more and sat beside him until the boy fell back to sleep. Then he rose and returned to his desk. He opened the drawer Kaelin had dreamt of and removed the slender volume that lay inside. He sat for a moment, watching the golden cover shine in the firelight. Then he replaced what he held and closed the drawer. He didn't need to open the tome, having long since memorized every piece of music it contained. It was an old and valuable collection of harp music, penned by none other than Master Cyral himself. Master Bergid frowned thoughtfully. *He dreams of Bardic Mountain, having no idea of its identity, then is drawn unerringly to the one drawer that has a book of music from the greatest Harpist in Bardic history? Hardly coincidental. Moreover, his dream was quite right about me being asleep at my desk. What, I wonder, have I found in the mountains of Kestrel? Is prescience an offshoot of the Gift as well?*

In the morning, no mention was made of Kaelin's dream.

Master Bergid's decision to spend the day indoors, allowing no instrumental playing, elicited no protest from his apprentice, who happily immersed himself again in his Master's music. That night no dream disturbed their slumber. Well before dawn, the Master roused his apprentice and they left Kyet as unobtrusively as they had arrived, crossing the Bronig on the ferry in separate trips and heading back upriver with Poor Oran.

An hour of steady travel brought them to a small, wooded hillside. The Master led the way up a narrow side path that twisted between the trees to where a small cabin lay nestled out of sight of the main path below. The Master opened the door and motioned his apprentice inside. "My Bards always keep this cabin clean and ready for my use," he said. "I'll make us some tea while you settle Poor Oran in the shed out back, then we'll get settled. This is where we'll spend the winter months. And perhaps a bit longer."

Kaelin nodded and set his packs in the corner, glancing around curiously as he did so. Not that there was much to see, for the single room held a bare minimum of furniture. At least, he thought, there was an extra bed and desk for him to use, though it left little in the way of floor space. Why his Master preferred spending the winter months here, rather than in his large, comfortable home in Kyet was a mystery to the apprentice, but he merely shrugged and went to take care of Poor Oran. He would happily take up residence in a frigid cave all winter, if that's where his Master planned to spend it.

The weather continued to be unusually mild, with only a few flurries of snow to softly carpet the ground. Kaelin, used to the far more severe winter conditions in Vale, was delighted with their new residence and enjoyed being outside as much as possible. Mornings were spent in the cabin, the Master instructing Kaelin through the advanced composition forms, then leaving him to work on his assignments while he tended to his never-ending stack of paper-work. This, the apprentice noticed, was apparently replenished from the Phantom Bard's pack that continued to mysteriously appear and disappear on a regular basis. After lunch, Kaelin spent his hour of free time in the woods with his flute, not only to give his music an outlet, but to give his Master time and space to himself. When he returned, his Master continued his instruction on pipes and harp. After dinner, they built a bonfire in the clearing outside the cabin nearly every clear evening, the Master wrapped firmly in his winter cloak and sitting close to the fire. Kaelin spent most of the evening practicing the Master's pipes and harp. When he grew too tired to continue, he sat with his head resting against his Master's knee while the Master played one song after the next. Sometimes they toasted honeyed slices of jerky over the flames and enjoyed the crispy snack before retiring for the night. Kaelin had never been happier in his life and fervently wished that they could stay at the cabin forever.

Not that everything went smoothly, for the apprentice had discovered over the last few months that learning two new instruments was not nearly as easy for him as memorizing the rules of composition and theory. Kaelin had made steady progress on the Master's pipes over the last three months and had mastered the first two harp forms with only a little difficulty, but he was struggling with form three. His Master, observing his increasing frustration one evening, put aside his own work and beckoned to him.

"Come, lad, bring my harp and your music over here for a moment."

The apprentice flushed, ashamed of his impatience, and did as the Master said. "I'm sorry, sir," he apologized. "I just can't seem to get my fingers to do what I want them to."

"Perhaps that's because you're trying to play something you haven't learned yet."

Kaelin frowned. "Don't I need to play it, in order to learn it?"

"Playing is what you do *after* you learn a piece, not before." The Master looked at him keenly. "Learning a new piece on a new instrument is a matter of training your hands and arms. From the moment you were born, you began training them to respond to mental commands ... to pick up that rock over there, for instance. If you tensed all your muscles before doing so, though, would you be able to pick it up?"

"No, sir. Not easily, anyhow."

"Would it make sense to get upset with your muscles for this failure?"

Kaelin grinned ruefully. "It would make more sense to relax them."

"Just so. Now, then, once you've given the message to your relaxed arm and hand to pick up the rock, your mind will be free to send another message, like bringing your arm back as far as you can reach, then another one to throw your arm forward, yet another to release the rock, and then a final one to walk over to me for a stern lecture on throwing rocks this close to the cabin window, not to mention your Master's unprotected head."

Kaelin chuckled. "Yes, sir."

"You are not yet experienced enough in sight reading to look very far ahead in the score, so when you attempt to learn something by *playing* it, you don't know what's coming next, which causes tension, the very thing you can't afford." The Master motioned toward the music. "Let's reduce the complexity by looking at only the first phrase. Check the rhythm first, then play the notes of each hand separately in the air, without the harp, to that rhythm."

Kaelin looked at him in surprise, then did as he was told.

"Now play it with the articulation, holding an imaginary harp in your hands. Recognize the notes and corresponding strings, see how the right hand plucks the first four notes, then transfers the next four to the left hand. Allow no tension in your hands, for after all," he shrugged, "you're only playing the air."

Kaelin did so, imagining the strings in front of him, his relaxed weight able to draw them firmly and evenly toward him. He grinned at the Master. "I believe I just played that phrase flawlessly!"

"Let's find out. Take up my harp now and feel the strings you'll need to play that phrase, feel the two changes in hand position it will require, and when you feel comfortable with those movements, play the phrase the way you did in the air."

A few moments later, a perfectly played phrase from harp form three filled the air of the clearing. The Master cocked a brow. "Do you see now how much better it is to learn something *before* trying to play it?"

"Yes, sir, I do."

"Continue learning the rest of the piece in the same way. If you get frustrated again, stop and do something else. Come back to it when you're calm and relaxed, or you will simply be reinforcing bad habits."

Kaelin nodded ruefully, and the Master smiled. "And don't be so hard on yourself, lad. The elementary forms are the hardest to learn on any instrument, for you need to learn the fingering and technique, something a more advanced player has already mastered. Keep at it, and you'll soon be enjoying the pieces that are frustrating you now."

Kaelin picked up the music with fresh determination. "Are there other ways to learn new material as well?" he asked.

"There are as many ways as the imagination can invent. As you advance through the levels, your knowledge of them will increase. Remember, as the music becomes more complex, that nothing is so difficult that it can't be broken down into smaller, simple pieces. When you look over a new piece, the first thing to do is break it down into those far simpler pieces and master them. Reassembling them is what enables a musician to play music that is, at first glance, overwhelmingly complex."

Kaelin nodded, thinking this over and seeing the wisdom in his Master's words.

"And," his Master added, "knowing different ways to learn the same thing is essential to becoming a good teacher, so it pays to have a lot of tools in your arsenal."

The apprentice gave his Master a startled look. *"My* arsenal?"

The Master cocked a brow in his direction. "You don't plan on being an apprentice forever, do you, lad? Eventually you'll need to choose between becoming a Harpist, Flutist, or Piper, taking students who pay for their lessons. The better a teacher you become, the better the students you will attract. And a talented student can audition for admittance to the Bardic Order as your apprentice, which is decided upon by a Bard." Amusement lit the Master's eyes. "Or, in your particular case, a renegade Master."

Kaelin grinned, and the Master continued. "Assuming some of these students are approved, you will then have several paying students and a few non-paying apprentices who earn you a stipend from the Order. When you attain proficiency of at least three Bardic instruments, you can test with a Bard to become an Instrumentalist. Passing this will command a higher teaching fee and stipend."

"What comes after that?"

"Eventually an Instrumentalist can apply to one of the Masters for taking the tests to become a Bard, the next step up in the Bardic Order hierarchy. Doing so takes several cycles of study and an advanced level of playing, which is form seven or higher, on at least five Bardic instruments."

Kaelin considered this. "How does a Bard become a Master?" he asked curiously.

"Masters are chosen from Bards who have satisfied the requirements of all five Masters they've served rotations under, and who have achieved an advanced level of playing on all seven Bardic instruments." The Master chuckled at his apprentice's expression. "You look as proud as if you'd just accomplished the feat yourself."

Kaelin shook his head. "I'm proud to have a Master for my master. No other apprentice in all the Bardic Isles is as lucky as I am."

The Master looked meaningfully at his harp. "Well, then, perhaps my lucky apprentice ought to get back to his practicing before his luck starts running out."

"Can I ask one more question?"

"Just one."

"How much of a stipend are you paying the renegade Master who dared to take on an apprentice in your jurisdiction?"

The Master looked into the amber eyes laughing into his and did his best to assemble a frown. "Not nearly enough," he growled.

Chapter 8

The winter days passed by swiftly for the two inhabitants of the hidden cabin on the Bronig. In the evenings, the Master often sang by the fire, either inside or outdoors, depending on the weather. Kaelin never tired of listening to the Master's songs and tales of Bardic lore. When the youngster made a disparaging remark about the Druids one evening, however, his Master shook his head.

"If your Schoolmaster or Flutist Torin gave you the idea that all the Bards of Eire were good, and all the Druids evil, lad, I can assure you that such was not the case. Most Druids wanted what was best for Eire, just as most Bards did. And historically, the two Orders are variations on the same theme, after all."

"The Bards and the Druids, sir?" Kaelin exclaimed.

The Master chuckled. "We might not wish to acknowledge the relationship any more than they do, but it's true, nevertheless. Many centuries ago, three branches of the same Celtic tree came to Eire: Druids, Bards, and Ovates. The Druids were judges and teachers, the Bards were keepers of songs and stories of lore, and the Ovates were healers and seers. They worked together as one and got along just fine."

"I've never heard of Ovates," the apprentice said with interest. "What happened to them?"

"They were eventually assimilated, the seers into the Druidic

Order, the healers into the Bardic Order. Either Schoolmaster Radnal was remiss in covering this," the Master added dryly, "or you were in the woods with your flute that day."

Kaelin flushed. "I suppose I might have missed that lesson," he mumbled.

The Master chuckled. "Were you in attendance the day he described the massacre of Aille-Mara and the exodus from Eire?"

Kaelin brightened. "Yes, sir, and Flutist Torin described it for me a hundred times like he saw it himself!"

The Master's mouth quirked. "Did he? And what, exactly, did Flutist Torin tell you?"

"Oh, everything, sir! Except he didn't explain *how* Master Cyral used his Gift to do all those things."

"That's because no one knows," the Master told him. "All we know is that he used his Gift to accomplish those feats, amplified by the use of his Harp. Many of our records tell of the great Harp the Master brought with him from across the sea. It was powerful and could be handled only by the Master—"

"You mean he was the only one who could play it?" Kaelin interjected.

"Yes," the Master replied, "although no one knows why. Master and Harp were both lost to us forty cycles after he arrived with it on Elegy."

"Flutist Torin told me that, but he never explained what happened to them."

"No one knows that either. The Master left home with his Harp one day and never returned. He left dozens of verses and songs behind that have become part of our lore, many of which are considered prophetic. Those, however, are not fully understood, and we suspect that some pages were lost over time. The entire island—*every* island—was searched for over a cycle, but Master Cyral and his Harp were never found." The Master looked pointedly at his pipes, lying unused across Kaelin's lap. "Now that the more serious gaps in your knowledge of Bardic history have been filled in," he said dryly, "perhaps you should fill in the gaps in your knowledge of form four's exercises for pipes."

Kaelin grinned and picked up the pipes, but his Master was not quite finished.

"And the next time you find yourself condemning an entire Order for the actions of a few, stop and think. Our own Order wasn't perfect then, either, and had its own share of members who did not act in the best interests of anyone but themselves. If such individuals did not exist, Bardic Law would not be needed, then or now. Human nature is not defined by the color of a person's robe, or their membership in a guild, trade, craft, or Order. It is the same across all professions and across all times, now as it was then. No one is exempt from it."

The apprentice frowned. His Master, he was certain, was exempt from all but the best that human nature had to offer.

A smile flitted across the Master's face. "None of us is perfect, lad, even those we revere. Master Cyral was a legend in his own time, but were he living among us in some anonymous guise, we would find him to be a person like any other. He would prove to have good traits and bad, endearing qualities and quirky habits, and the ability to make mistakes now and then, just like we all do. We might even be surprised to find that he did not enjoy his status as a living legend. Indeed, for all we know," the Master added whimsically, "that's the very reason he disappeared."

Several weeks later, the Master Bard of Kestrel stood frowning southward along the cold, foggy banks of the Bronig. He was expecting Flynn to bring him the latest stack of reports from his Bards and update him on the last Council meeting. The Bard that was making his way toward him, however, was certainly not Flynn, for a slightly shrill, off-pitch whistling accompanied his progress, and an extra thump against the ground accented his gait. He was too far away for his features to be clearly seen through the fog, but the Master had little doubt of his identity. Styrian, messenger of the Master Bard of Elegy, was the only Bard he knew who used a walking stick he had absolutely no need of and whistled incessantly. The Master winced. *One would think a full-fledged Bard could keep his own whistling in better tune. No wonder Grened chose him as a messenger.* He could well imagine the crusty Master's desire to keep Styrian's presence on Elegy to a bare minimum.

The Master frowned, wondering how Grened had discovered his whereabouts. Flynn would not have told him, and Bergid was certain that none of his other Bards had any idea where their Master was staying, much less that he had taken on an apprentice. None of them had any reason to investigate the Master's cabin on the Bronig. However, the Bards assigned to the Northwest Territory might well have gotten wind of the fact that the Master Bard of Kestrel had been visiting the mountain villages in company with a young boy. Kaelin's sister, too, might have let it be known that her brother had gone off with the Master Bard. Bergid grimaced. He'd had no reason to keep Kaelin's existence a secret then, having had every intention of apprenticing him to an Instrumentalist in Kyet. And if there was one thing the Master Bard of Kestrel knew, it was that rumors had wings. And one of them had apparently flown to Grened.

Bergid sighed. At least his efforts to stay out of sight had not been completely in vain. He had managed to keep Kaelin's existence a secret from the Council for over half a cycle, though he had hoped for even more time. The Master snorted in amusement as he headed off to meet the messenger, knowing full well the contents of the missive he carried. Grened must have been upset indeed not to wait until warmer weather before demanding a special Council session, which all five Masters would be required to attend. The eastern foothills of Bardic Mountain, where the Council Grounds were located, would certainly not be comfortable in mid-winter, even one as mild as this. Wincing, Bergid quickened his pace. The sooner he met the whistling messenger, the fewer sour notes he would have to endure.

Unaware of the meeting taking place, Kaelin looked over his manuscript in satisfaction. *That ought to please him.* He ran a practiced hand across the harp strings in a triumphant arpeggio. He hadn't thought that he could enjoy any instrument as much as his flute, but his Master's harp was becoming a close rival now that his fingers had accustomed themselves to strings instead of keys. The Master's unfailing patience had kept him from discouragement; his smiles of approval led Kaelin to practice harder and longer. Recently advanced to form four, he was beginning to love the instrument for its own sake and dream of someday making a Bardic harp of his own.

The apprentice carefully put his Master's instrument away and went to build up the fire. He would welcome the arrival of spring. Once every week the Master left for a day or two, tending to whatever affairs Masters concerned themselves with, leaving his apprentice alone in the cabin. Kaelin was content in his occasional solitude, although he was still receiving no instruction on his flute and was forbidden to write down his own music for pipes or harp. He was free to play his flute on his own time and was allowed to compose his own music for it, but he longed for the day his formal instruction on it could begin.

Kaelin sat immersed in his own thoughts, returning to the present only when the Master returned, a blast of cold air in his wake. The apprentice stood to greet him and take his cloak. The Master thanked him and went to the fire to warm himself before settling into his chair. "Well, lad," he said with a smile, "let's see what you've managed to make of your composition exercise this time."

Kaelin watched nervously as Master Bergid read his manuscript, hearing it in his mind without need of an instrument. Then the Master handed it back and closed his eyes.

"Is there something wrong with it, sir? I thought, well—" Kaelin's voice trailed off.

"I believe I would like you to play this exercise of yours for me, please."

"Yes, sir." He fetched the Master's harp with a worried frown and began to play. As music filled the room, Kaelin relaxed, his thoughts drawn back to Vale, to the day he and Erik had skipped school and been caught in a summer storm high in the mountains. He smiled wryly, remembering the difficult trip back, their relief at meeting the men of the village who had been scouring the woods for them. He remembered his sister's own relief at his return, relief which had quickly turned to an anger more formidable than the storm. He finished the piece, and still his Master sat with his eyes shut, saying nothing.

"I'm sorry," Kaelin ventured, "if it wasn't exactly—"

"An exercise?"

Kaelin flushed, though the Master's words were not spoken in rebuke. "I followed the chord progression you gave me," he said in a small voice.

"You did, indeed, and more besides." Still the Master's eyes remained closed. "Kaelin, when a musical composition, even when disguised as an 'exercise,' takes the listener to a place he has never been before and describes the scenery so clearly that he can see the leaves on the trees, hear the raindrops falling off the branches, feel the vibration of a clap of thunder—" The Master Bard took a deep breath and directed a keen look at his listening apprentice. "When a composition does *that*, the response will not be instant applause or a gush of adjectives. If it is, the listener was never there, never saw, heard, or felt it." He tapped the sheets Kaelin held tightly in his hands. "My silence after experiencing this was a compliment of the highest order."

The music within Kaelin surged. He opened the Master's hand and placed his manuscript in it.

The blue eyes smiled at him. "I should not like to take your only copy."

"I have another in my mind that can't be torn or erased."

"Then I gladly accept your gift. Further, I release you from the restriction against writing your own compositions for harp and pipes." He lifted a hand at Kaelin's look of delight. "You are, however, now forbidden to compose for flute. Up until now, I've left that instrument alone because I knew the music inside you needed an outlet. You've worked hard and have attained enough proficiency on harp and pipes for them to be a sufficient channel of expression, as the composition you've just given me conclusively proves. That will leave me free to begin instructing you on your flute." He shook his head slightly at his apprentice's cry of joy.

"Let me warn you that these lessons will not be as wonderful as your imagination is painting them. On harp and pipes, I had a fresh student to work with. You had never handled them before, so I could instruct you properly from the beginning. But you have played your flute for cycles and, though I will not deny that you have become an accomplished player in many ways, you have never had any formal instruction. Because of this, you have unknowingly developed several habits that are obstructing your further progress." The Master's brows lifted. "I can remove those obstacles, Kaelin, but I must have your full cooperation. There is little sense in teaching you new techniques if you're busily reinforcing old ones during your free time. Which is why I require your promise not to play anything on your flute except what I give you, no matter how elementary it may seem to you. Sometimes, in order to move forward one must take a few steps back."

"You have my word, sir," Kaelin said, willing to promise anything for the lessons on his flute he had coveted since following the

Master out of Vale.

Bergid nodded. "I promise you the reward for doing so will be great." He held up the manuscript Kaelin had given him. "You'll be pleased to learn that this is your last composition exercise. You've mastered every form I've given you and passed every test with excellent scores. Now the most important thing to do is to forget them all." He chuckled at the flabbergasted look on his apprentice's face.

"Not *completely* forget them, mind you, but keep them only as a background of knowledge against which you will develop your own distinct style." The Master gestured toward his apprentice's flute. "The compositions I've heard you play on that instrument of yours are excellent, Kaelin. Better, perhaps, than you can know, like hearing a wild kestrel singing its heart out. Now it's time to tame those compositions with the discipline and knowledge you've gained. Tame and capture them on manuscript, and from there they will one day reach the hearts and minds of people all over the Bardic Isles."

Kaelin was silent. It would take time to absorb his Master's words, but he knew now that his life was bound to music as a bird was bound to its feathers. He had spent months in a nest of learning, and it was time now to stand up and flex his wings. With his music he would one day rise up and fly, as free as a kestrel, yet tamed by the hand of one who had been far more than a teacher to him.

Two hours later Kaelin put his flute away, wondering why he had ever taken it out. He was exhausted and he hadn't played a single note. All he had done throughout the lesson was breathe, or try to breathe, correctly. His Master insisted that a good tone came only from a diaphragm of cast iron.

"No foundation? No stable building! No deep well? No lasting water!" he said emphatically. "You will never produce the tone and musical expression your compositions demand until you learn to produce a properly compressed air stream to support them. Now, let's begin again."

And on Kaelin went, faint with dizziness, expanding his lungs and dropping his diaphragm again and again, sometimes lying flat on his back with a sack of rocks balanced on his chest. How could the simple act of breathing be so tiring? Feeling like he'd walked the length of Kestrel in a single afternoon, the apprentice threw himself on his bed with a sigh and closed his eyes.

"Kaelin."

He opened his eyes wearily. "Yes, Master?" Perhaps he'd sighed incorrectly.

"I met a messenger from Master Grened today on my walk."

Kaelin sat up at once, all weariness forgotten. Master Grened, he knew, was the Master Bard of Elegy and Master Harpist of the Bardic Isles.

"I've received a summons to attend a special Council session on Elegy," Master Bergid continued. "It seems that word of my unusual activities this cycle has finally reached them." He chuckled at the look of alarm on Kaelin's face. "Don't worry, I'm guilty of nothing worse than treading on tradition's toes." His blue eyes sparkled with humor. "I've quit my usual domicile, was last seen visiting the mountain villages with a youngster in tow, and then mysteriously disappeared from public view with not even the Bards of Kestrel knowing my exact whereabouts." He smiled wryly. "I imagine some of my more conservative colleagues are wondering if I've quite lost my mind and wish to inspect it for themselves. I've been expecting a summons, but it's come sooner than I'd hoped for. So, I've sent word back that, due to my advanced age and the bitterness of the season, I'll be happy to answer their questions at our usual Spring Council at the end of spring. That will fool no one, but it will give me time to prepare."

"Prepare what, Master?"

"Prepare you, Kaelin."

The Master turned toward the fire, and Kaelin lay back down, wondering. *Prepare me? Prepare me for what?* He knew his apprenticeship was an unusual one, but weren't Masters free to do as they liked? He resolved to work even harder at his lessons.

"Master?"

"What is it, lad?"

"Can they make you send me away?" Kaelin held his breath as he waited for the answer.

The Master turned to him, blue eyes glinting. "Nothing could ever make that happen."

Reassured, Kaelin closed his eyes and soon fell asleep. He woke up once during the night to the sight of snowflakes falling outside the window, illuminated by the firelight within and the sound of his Master's voice singing softly to the sweet strains of his harp.

Over sea and over stone,
Over cycles yet to be,
Lies a Bardic treasure caught
In time, for need alone to free.

Come, you Pipers, blow with might!
Come, you Harpists, play!
Masters, keep the land of song
From silence in that day.

Where, oh where, the young sprig growing
On an old tree, so alone?
Awake the Harp, the Master's Harp,
That lies forsaken, trapped in stone!

Spring came early that cycle, an occurrence that seemed to amuse the Master Bard of Kestrel. He would often stand at the door of the cabin in the early morning, gazing out at the dappled sunlight filtering through the trees and chuckling to himself. One morning, Kaelin rushed to his aid solicitously, opening the door for him and taking his arm as though to help him walk through it.

"Careful, Master!" he exclaimed. "That's a pretty steep step, and considering the 'bitterness of the season' and your 'advanced age' and all—"

"Impudent scamp!" the Master growled, to his apprentice's delight.

Kaelin missed playing his flute the way he used to, but he did not break the promise he had made. After several days of arduous breathing exercises, he graduated to playing single notes, carefully controlling their pitch, volume, and vibrato, excited with the improvement he was hearing in his tone. He progressed rapidly through the flute forms, and by the end of winter had begun absorbing the advanced ones, where he found it difficult to match the rapid, complex fingering to the constantly changing articulation. His Master, observing his frustration one afternoon, put aside his work and asked him what he was having difficulty with.

"I'm trying to match my fingering with the articulation," Kaelin said ruefully, "and I'm not having much success. In fact, I think it's getting worse."

"Then stop trying to match them," the Master unexpectedly advised.

The apprentice blinked. "But they need to match each other, don't they?"

"Yes, but as you're discovering, the more you try to focus on them matching, the less matched they will be. That's because you're trying to focus on two things simultaneously. Instead, focus on the one thing both have in common." His brow lifted inquiringly. "Which is?"

Kaelin frowned, thinking. "I don't know. They're both different and change constantly."

"Finger the notes of the phrase you're having trouble with, without blowing."

The apprentice lifted his flute and did so.

"What are you focused on matching it to?"

"Well, the pulsation ... the beat."

"And you found the fingering easy to match to it. Now articulate the phrase without touching the mouthpiece."

Again, the apprentice complied.

"And the articulation was also easy to match to the beat, wasn't it?"

"Yes, sir."

"Well, then, if the fingering matches the beat, and the articulation matches the beat, does it not stand to reason that the fingering and articulation will effortlessly match each other?"

"So, I should focus only on the beat?"

The Master nodded and returned to his work. Kaelin lifted his flute and relaxed, thinking only of the pulsation of the phrase, and began to play. A beautiful, complex phrase, fingering and articulation perfectly matched, filled the cabin. He stood for a moment, looking at his Master reproachfully, and Bergid looked up inquiringly.

"Is there another problem?"

"I'm just wondering why you didn't tell me this an hour ago," Kaelin said in an aggrieved tone.

"Because an hour ago, you would only have been doing it to obey me. Now you'll be doing it from conviction and will apply the technique to all future pieces without me having to remind you."

The apprentice chuckled. "So, you put up with an hour of my frustration just to better teach me a skill I wouldn't forget?"

The Master smiled. "Thus saving a great deal of time."

And so the days went, filled with teaching and learning. Time, having once dripped at a leisurely pace, began to flow with the strength of the Bronig. Kaelin found himself wishing he could slow it down, could somehow delay ... *delay what?* He shook his head, confused by the sensation that time was sweeping him toward something he did not wish to meet. More often than not, he spent his free time practicing his flute, rather than roaming the banks of the river or exploring the woods. Of this sudden change the Master made no comment, but Kaelin thought he detected a glint of approval in the blue eyes.

A week before the official arrival of spring, Kaelin awoke to find his Master packing his belongings by lantern light. He glanced out the window; not even the birds were up yet. He hurriedly rose to help, but the Master shook his head.

"You'd best start packing your own things, lad, and what's left of our supplies. We'll be leaving the cabin exactly as we found it."

"We're traveling again?"

"Only as far as Kyet. This is the cycle and season Bard tests are given, and this cabin is too small to accommodate them. The tests take a full week, and I have twenty-four Bards to test, so they come in four rotations of six Bards, one from each of the six territories of Kestrel." He glanced around the tiny cabin with amusement, as though imagining six Bards with packs and instruments crammed into it. "In Kyet I reserve three rooms at Gannet's Inn for their use during the testing."

Kaelin thought of Kyet and swallowed nervously. Since leaving Vale, the Master had been his sole companion. The thought of sharing his Master's home with six different Bards every week for a month was intimidating. *What will they think,* he wondered, *of finding an apprentice in their Master's home? And what if one of them hears me play? If only we could just stay in this cabin forever!* He put aside his uneasiness and concentrated on clearing the cabin, making their breakfast, and loading Poor Oran for the short journey.

When they were ready to leave, his Master closed the cabin door and turned to find his apprentice looking at it wistfully. He chuckled. "I thought you'd be happy to leave here and return to 'the most wonderful home you've ever seen,' as I believe you described it."

"I am. But I'll miss being here, too, with just you."

The Master nodded. "So will I, lad." He slung his pack over his shoulder and began walking down the path leading to the banks of the Bronig.

Kaelin took hold of Poor Oran's lead and followed, close to tears. He couldn't shake the strong feeling that they would not return to this place, and that even if they did, it wouldn't be the same. *Why must things always change? Life flows from one key signature to the next with so little warning.* He sighed and followed the Master, lost in his own thoughts until they reached the ferry. His Master instructed him to lead the mule into the nearby stable and return with only his own pack and his Master's instruments. He did as he was told and emerged to find his Master making arrangements for the rest of their baggage to be delivered to his home. Then the Master unexpectedly turned and led the way down a broad road heading west, away from the ferry. Kaelin hurried to follow him.

"Aren't we going home, Master?"

"As a matter of fact," Bergid replied, without slackening his pace, "I had a sudden urge to visit Lynd for an hour or two first. It's a small village a bit northwest of here and won't take us too far out of our way. We'll be back to take the ferry late this afternoon."

"Lynd?" Kaelin said in excitement. "I think my sister is living there now! Do you think we could find out where she is? Maybe even stop there for a few minutes? If there's time, sir?"

The Master halted and turned to his hopeful apprentice.

"I know where Laena is, lad. I've had one of my Bards keep an eye on your sister since you left, and also let her know you were fine, so she wouldn't worry about you." He smiled as Kaelin's hopeful expression gave way to surprise. "She and a young man named

Donal joined together a few months ago, and they moved to Lynd, where Donal's carting business is located. I thought you might like to see her before we go home." The Master strode on. A small hand inserted itself into his. The Master gave no sign that he noticed, but he did not let go.

Kaelin never forgot the look on his sister's face when she glanced up from the peas she was shelling and saw him standing in the open doorway. Her joyous eyes widened at the sight of the Bardic apprentice robe he wore, and the flute bag slung over his shoulder. Before she had time to recover, the imposing figure of the Master Bard filled the doorway, and her mouth dropped open in shock.

Kaelin laughed and ran to hug her. Then, remembering his manners, he introduced his Master. The love and pride shining in his eyes did not escape his sister's notice.

She looked at Master Bergid. "Thank you, sir," she said simply, "for all you've done for my brother."

"Kaelin's Gift of music has been a privilege to develop," the Master told her.

Laena smiled. "I didn't mean only regarding music, Master Bergid," she said. "And Donal would also thank you if he were here. His business has been unexpectedly good this cycle."

"I'm sure he has only his own hard work to thank for that."

"Not to hear Donal tell it."

Master Bergid frowned slightly. "Tell it to whom?"

"Oh, only to me, sir," Laena assured him. "Surely it's better for him to be known for his hard work, than for any ... fortuitous references he might be receiving."

The Master's blue eyes lit with humor. "I can see that Kaelin's quick intuitiveness runs in the family," he said. "Have you an undiscovered Gift for music as well?"

Laena laughed. "I only sing."

"Very well, too, Master," Kaelin put in proudly. "My sister has the best voice in all of Vale, and I'm sure no one in Lynd or Kyet could outdo her, either!"

The Master looked at Laena approvingly. "The voice is as much an instrument as any other," he said. He glanced at the throng gathering outside and cleared his throat. "My services seem to be desired, so I'll leave the two of you alone for a while." He smiled and took his leave, removing his pipes from their tasseled bag as he went.

Kaelin turned to see his sister watching him. "You love him," she said gently.

He nodded, unable to speak.

"And has he fixed whatever it was that needed fixing?"

Kaelin nodded and recovered his voice. "He helped me free my music so it doesn't hurt anymore, and I can play it for myself now, and for him."

Laena looked at him shrewdly. "But not for me?"

Kaelin looked at her uneasily. "I can't play for anyone else," he finally said.

"How do you know? Have you tried?"

"I don't dare."

"Then you're not really fixed yet, are you?"

A spasm of pain crossed his face. "Some things can't be fixed," he said hollowly.

"Why not?" his sister asked gently. "What happened that was so terrible it ... broke you?"

The apprentice dropped his gaze. "I can't tell you that. I can't tell anyone."

"Not even Master Bergid?"

"Especially Master Bergid."

"Why not? Maybe he can fix it."

"He can't." Kaelin said flatly. "There's no fixing this, and if he knew, he'd send me away, even if he didn't want to. And that—" He broke off, unable to say it.

"—would break your heart."

Kaelin turned away and didn't answer. Laena reached out and touched his arm. "I think you may be underestimating your Master."

Kaelin frowned and shook his head, and Laena continued. "I hope what you fear never happens, then. But if it does, you know you can always come home."

It was a moment before Kaelin spoke. "I don't think I could live so close to Kyet and know I can't see him," he said in a low voice. "Or, even worse, happen to cross his path in the marketplace and—" Kaelin's eyes clouded with pain. "Please don't tell Master Bergid what I've told you. If you do, he'll ask me about it, and I'll have to tell him, and then—" He broke off at the thought of seeing those blue eyes look into his with shock, then fill with sorrow. Of hearing the voice he had grown to love above all others take his robe from him and tell him he must leave the Bardic Order—and his Master—and not return.

"I never imagined this would happen when I followed him," Kaelin continued softly, as though to himself. "I just wanted him to fix me. But then he started giving me lessons, in more than just music, and I didn't want him to just fix me anymore. I wanted him to keep me." He bit his lip hard. "Then he offered me the robe and wouldn't let me stay with him unless I accepted it. So, I did. I shouldn't have, but I did."

"Why shouldn't you have?" Laena asked.

"Because there's no place in the Bardic Order for someone like me," Kaelin barely managed to say. "It was so much easier in the mountains and in the cabin, with only the two of us. Now that we're going to be staying at his home, with groups of Bards coming and going, eventually he's going to want me to play for someone. When I refuse, he'll want to know why ... and I'll have to tell him, and then it'll be over. I just want as much time with him as I can get before that happens. And after that, I don't know where I'll go or what I'll do when I get there. But if I lose my Master," he said hollowly, "it won't matter."

"I'll not say anything to anyone, Kaelin. Not even Donal." She squeezed his arm gently. "It's okay if you can't tell me what happened, but I hope that someday you're able to tell someone. Whatever this burden is, it's too heavy for you to carry alone."

Kaelin nodded, and his sister turned the conversation to lighter matters, telling him about Donal's business, then relating amusing bits of gossip from Vale. Kaelin listened and laughed in all the right places, but part of his mind remained fixated on the horrible prospect of losing his Master.

When Master Bergid returned for him and they set out for Kyet, the Master glanced at him curiously. "Did you enjoy playing for your sister?"

Kaelin looked at him uneasily. "I . . didn't play for her, sir. I wasn't sure if it was allowed."

"Certainly, it is. I'm sure she would greatly enjoy hearing you play."

Silence.

"Perhaps next time," Bergid said quietly.

Still Kaelin said nothing, and they continued walking, each of them immersed in their own thoughts. The Master's were disturbed. Although the sense-deprivation test had freed Kaelin's Gift, the boy was apparently still unwilling to play for others, not even for his own sister. *This is more than mere nervousness could account for. His deep-rooted fear is still there. Freeing his Gift did not remove it, and he won't confide in me.* The Master frowned. The Spring Council was less than three months away. Kaelin would need to overcome his fear before then. Bergid came to a halt and his apprentice glanced at him in surprise.

"You know that you've played your own music for me countless times since you became my apprentice, and not once has it caused me the slightest harm," the Master said quietly.

Kaelin nodded slowly.

"It will not harm your sister, either."

Conflicting emotions crossed Kaelin's face. "But you're a Master, sir," he said at last, his voice barely more than a whisper.

"Do you really think that makes a difference?"

Silence.

The Master held the boy's eyes for a long moment, seeing the deep fear and unspoken pleading in their amber depths. He sighed.

"Whatever the problem is," the Master continued, "this is something you must eventually face, lad, like you did the cage inside you. Until you do, it won't matter that your Gift is free, because *you* are not." He released the youngster's eyes, and Kaelin dropped his gaze. "When you're ready to tell me what happened," the Master said gently, "I'll be ready to listen." He walked on, and after a moment, Kaelin silently followed.

Before long they were standing on a hill overlooking the ocean and the seaport of Kyet. The apprentice looked up inquiringly, then gave a knowing look as his Master headed purposefully toward the Bronig. There would be no waiting for dusk this time, no need for the apprentice to remove his robe, no taking the ferry in separate trips. His existence as apprentice to the Master Bard of Kestrel no longer needed to be hidden now that the Masters had learned of it. Kaelin grimaced at the thought of the Masters he had never met and mentally addressed the Council.

You needn't worry. I doubt my Master will have an apprentice for you to object to for very much longer. He knows now that I won't play for anyone but him, and he won't accept silence as an answer for long.

Kaelin shifted the packs on his shoulder and hurried after his Master, his depressing thoughts clinging to him like the burweed growing along the sides of the path. He pushed his thoughts away, choosing instead to remember the words his Master had spoken

when his apprentice first entered his home.
As my apprentice, it is now your home as well.
His spirits lifted.

Movement Two

The Seaport of Kyet

Chapter 9

A few days after the Master and Kaelin arrived back at the Master's home in Kyet, the first day of Bard Testing began. Kaelin knew the testing given on each island was the same on each day, except for the first and fifth days. Today, his Master had told him, voice would be tested by Master Rial on Lyra, Harp by Master Grened on Elegy, and flute by Master Marek on Zephyr. Master Talan would be testing the making of instruments on Eyrie, and here on Kestrel, Master Bergid would be testing composition and theory.

Barely a moment after breakfast was over, a firm knock resounded through the living room. Kaelin, obeying a nod from his Master, took a deep breath and went to answer the door. The six Bards who stood on the Master's porch stared at him as though he had dropped onto the threshold from the clouds above.

Kaelin, not having expected all six Bards to arrive together, recovered his wits enough to give the sea of light blue robes and silver cords a bow. "Welcome, sirs," he said faintly, having no clear idea how to address such a prestigious group.

The oldest looking Bard gave him a nod. "Thank you," he said with a smile. "My name is Flynn."

"My name is Kaelin, sir," the apprentice said, looking anxiously at his Master, who had walked over to stand next to him. All six Bards immediately bowed to the Master and chorused a greeting.

"Good morning, Master Bergid! It's good to see you, sir."

"It's good to see all of you as well," the Master said warmly. "I've been remiss, however, in not instructing my apprentice in the proper etiquette of greeting others in the Bardic Order." Ignoring the shock on the faces of every Bard except Flynn's, he turned to his apprentice. "It is my lapse, Kaelin, not yours. When you greet one of higher rank whose name you don't know, you do so with a bow and a welcome, just as you did, and tell him your name. He will then thank you and tell you his name, as Bard Flynn did. You respond by repeating his name with his title, looking directly into his eyes as you do so, and, in this case, inviting him into our home."

Kaelin immediately turned to Flynn and looked directly into his eyes. "Bard Flynn. Please come in, sir."

With a smile and a nod, Flynn walked into the house, whereupon a tall, sandy-haired Bard nodded to Kaelin. "Thank you for your welcome, Kaelin. My name is Tyrian."

"Bard Tyrian. Please come in, sir."

Four more Bards entered in the same manner, and Kaelin closed the door in relief. His impromptu instruction in Bardic Order etiquette, however, was not quite finished.

"Now that you know everyone's names," the Master told him, "you can speed the process up considerably by giving a single bow, naming each of them with one title if they are all the same, then following that up with whatever is appropriate. They will collectively thank you and enter. If they are not of the same rank, name the higher ranked individuals first. If you know one is older than the others, the elder is named first. Perhaps you could demonstrate that for us now."

"Yes, sir." He bowed to the group of Bards, then looked directly at each of them as he named them. "Bards Flynn, Tyrian, Brent, Gryndl, Niall, and Bran. Welcome, sirs, and please make yourselves comfortable. I would be happy to take your cloaks for you."

The Bards nodded and chorused a thank you.

Flynn looked at him curiously as he handed Kaelin his cloak. "I can understand knowing I'm the eldest, with my thinning patch of hair, but how did you correctly guess the order of everyone else?"

"I thought seniority might have played a part in the order in which you entered."

Bran laughed. "And here I thought it was my youthful good looks that gave me away."

Flynn chuckled as he slid a pack off his back and went to hand it to the Master. "Almost empty at last, sir," he said cheerfully. "Only a page or two inside ... nothing of consequence."

The Master smiled as he removed the papers and handed the pack back to Flynn. "I'm sure you'll be happy not to be carting this all over Kestrel any longer," he said.

Kaelin stared open-mouthed at the familiar pack that had apparently just made its last appearance, then turned a wide-eyed gaze toward Flynn as he went to take his place at the table. *The Phantom Bard!*

Tyrian cleared his throat, and the apprentice hastily turned to take the Bard's proffered cloak. "Well, it might have been a surprise to find an apprentice in Master Bergid's home," Tyrian told him, "but it's no surprise to discover that he's a courteous one. The only reprimand I've ever earned from your Master," he added with wry amusement, "was for discourtesy to a troublesome merchant, whom I thought deserved it. Master Bergid swiftly disabused me of the notion. It was a well-deserved lesson, one which I doubt you will need."

Kaelin hung up another cloak and flashed a rueful grin at Tyrian. "No, sir. I've already received one."

Tyrian laughed, and Flynn looked at Kaelin curiously. "Who could you possibly have been discourteous to?" he wondered. "You haven't been in Kyet long enough to meet anyone but us, surely."

The other Bards looked at Flynn in surprise, as though wondering how he knew anything of the apprentice's existence, much less his whereabouts.

Kaelin glanced at his Master, who had gone to retrieve the test papers from his desk. "On the way here, an elderly woman using a walking stick arrived late to the ferry, and I neglected to give her my place at the rail, as I should have done."

"Ah, I see," Flynn said with a smile. "I would imagine that a single frown from your Master quickly remedied the lapse."

"It would have, but he didn't frown at me," Kaelin replied uncomfortably. "He smiled at her and offered her his own place. When she said it wasn't fitting for her to take the place of a Master, he said that, Master or not, it was very important for a man of his advanced cycles to remain spry and able to keep his balance, and he would consider it a favor if she would give him the opportunity to practice. She laughed and accepted his place."

"That sounds exactly like Master Bergid," Flynn said, chuckling. "What did you do then?"

"I was ashamed," Kaelin admitted, "and immediately offered my place to my Master. He said he couldn't take the place of someone with so little experience of ferries. So, I said that it was important for an inexperienced and discourteous person such as myself to learn to keep his balance and show courtesy to his elders, and I would consider it a great favor if he gave me the chance to practice both. Everyone laughed, and he nodded and took my place."

"And this taught you to practice courtesy?"

"Yes ... but it also taught me that my Master understood the meaning of courtesy and that I didn't."

"What, then, taught you its meaning?" the Bard persisted.

"The lesson I received for it later." Seeing his Master's pointed gesture toward the archway leading to the bedrooms, the apprentice bowed to the Bards with relief. "It was a pleasure to meet you, sirs, and I look forward to seeing you after this morning's testing."

The Bards nodded, watching as Kaelin quickly picked up his work from the table and headed for his room.

"Now, then," Master Bergid said, gesturing to the table. "Let's begin."

The Bards took their seats, bemused expressions on some faces, repressed questions on all. Flynn glanced at the Master, amusement dancing in his brown eyes.

The Master sighed. "You're quite right, Flynn. Best, perhaps, to deal with the issue right away." He glanced around the table. "Before we begin with the testing, then, I shall answer some of the questions I see hovering over your heads. Yes, Kaelin is indeed my apprentice and has been for several months now. Yes, there are reasons why I have apprenticed him to myself and not to an Instrumentalist. No, I will not discuss those reasons with anyone, nor will any of you speculate amongst yourselves, or with anyone else. The subject is strictly off-limits, not only here on Kestrel, but also on Elegy during the Spring Council. Kaelin will be accompanying me there." At the faint sounds of surprise that greeted this, the Master paused for a moment, allowing his Bards time to digest this unexpected news.

"You will all have the opportunity to get to know Kaelin this week and during any future visits to my home. At the Spring Council, you will undoubtedly be hounded by curious Bards from all the other islands for information concerning my apprentice, and you will steadfastly refuse to give it," the Master said firmly, "even if that questioning comes from another Master. The Council will receive their information directly from me at the appropriate time, not by hearing rumors that often grow into falsehoods. This stricture will remain in place until the Bard assignments are posted at the end of the Spring Council, when the need for the stricture will end. Is that clear?" He looked around the table, accepting the hasty nods of assent, then glanced at the oldest of the six Bards.

"Flynn, you have my thanks for keeping your own counsel on this matter, as I asked you to do. You've been a great help to me this cycle and have kept my affairs moving far more smoothly than they otherwise would have. You've been my ears and my eyes, both here and at the Council meetings I could not attend, and I'm aware," he added wryly, "that those meetings could not have been easy for you. Withstanding the pressure of four Masters insisting that you tell them where I was and what I was doing was asking more of you than I had any right to. I appreciate your discretion, and I won't forget it."

"It was my pleasure to assist you, Master Bergid."

"I did not expect to see you today. You are eligible for promotion to a Master, having served all five islands and passed all your tests, including these. Did you come only to meet my apprentice in person?"

"I'll admit I was curious about your apprentice," Flynn replied with a grin, "but I came to take the tests again, if it isn't a bother. I've been working hard on my compositions to see if I can raise my score, and I think I can. Your instruction on that subject—on *all* subjects—is excellent, sir."

"Far from being a bother," the Master replied, "it pleases me that you choose to better your skills. There is no one who is so good at what they do that they can't improve, regardless of rank or test scores." His eyes scanned the group. "I apologize for not being as available to all of you as I normally am. This cycle has been quite unusual, beginning with my tour of the mountain villages and my unexpected acquisition of an apprentice. All of you have stepped up to the challenge and handled many of my affairs extremely well on your own. You have my sincere thanks for that." He picked up a stack of papers and began passing them out.

"We will begin with the composition test this morning, followed by the theory test this afternoon. Niall, Tyrian, Gryndl, and Bran will be taking the test for the intermediate level. Brent and

Flynn, you will be taking the test for the advanced level. Please place the composition test in front of you, face down, and take out your quills." He seated himself at his desk, waited until everyone was ready, then nodded. "You have three hours to complete all three sections of the test. Starting now." The Master reached for the hourglass that sat on his desk and turned it over. The sand from the upper glass globe began to trickle slowly into the lower one.

The Bards flipped their papers and set to work. Their week of testing had officially begun.

Two flips of the hourglass later, the Master collected the test papers. "Bran, would you please ask Kaelin to come help prepare lunch?"

"Certainly, sir." Bran left and soon returned with Kaelin, who went to the kitchen and began preparing the meal. The Bards hurried to help him, and they were soon seated at the table. The Bards ate with good appetite and talked animatedly, telling the Master all about the many events, small and large, that had occurred during his absence. Master Bergid listened intently to each of them, laughing at many of the stories and offering advice when it was asked for.

The apprentice sitting with them said nothing, a bit overwhelmed by the constant stream of rapid talk. He was suddenly reminded of his sense-deprivation test and the confusing cacophony of noises that had filled his ears when they had finally been unstopped. When the meal was over and everything cleared away, the Master brought out the theory tests to distribute, and gave the completed composition tests to Kaelin, who took them in surprise.

"Take these to my composition desk and correct them for me, please," the Master told him. "It will give me time to attend to some paperwork."

"Yes, sir." Kaelin went to do as instructed, pretending not to see the shocked expressions of the Bards. He sighed inwardly, hoping every day of the month to come was not going to be as uncomfortable as this one. If only he and his Master could have stayed in the cabin instead of here, surrounded by Bards who were now eye-ing him with varying degrees of distrust as the Master passed out the theory tests. *I guess it isn't easy for them, either,* he told himself. *After all, their Master has been too busy with an apprentice to give them his full time and attention for three seasons. And now that lowly apprentice is scoring their composition tests! At least in a month all this testing will be over, and then maybe things can go back to normal.* The apprentice suppressed another sigh. If living in the hills with the Master Bard of Kestrel was his definition of normal, nothing was ever likely to be normal again. There was no longer any reason for them to return to the cabin.

Kaelin went carefully through the compositions, correcting them in the same way his Master had always corrected his own work, circling any discrepancies in the cadences and indicating the correct notes in the margins. He was surprised to see that most of them did no more than follow the indicated cadence, adding little embellishment or development of their theme. Kaelin made some carefully-worded suggestions, then scored the tests as well as he could. Then he returned the stack to his Master, who was reading reports at his work desk, while the Bards labored their way through the afternoon theory test.

The Master took the corrected papers from him and told Kaelin he was free to do what he wished for the remainder of the afternoon. Gratefully, the apprentice fetched his flute, pulled on his cloak, and went outside. The weather was cold but fair, and he looked forward to finding a place to practice where no one could hear him.

When Kaelin returned in the late afternoon, he could see the Bards through the window still taking their tests, so he stood outside, unwilling to interrupt. When the Master announced the end of the test, the apprentice quietly opened the door and slipped inside. He moved toward his room, but his Master glanced at him and shook his head. The apprentice stood where he was and watched the Master collect the theory tests and hand out the scored composition tests from the morning. Three of the Bards looked pleased with their scores, especially Flynn, who let out a soft whoop of victory, two of them looked resigned but not unhappy, and one of them frowned deeply.

"Is there something wrong, Niall?" the Master inquired.

"Well ... yes, sir, there is." The disgruntled Bard did not glance at Kaelin. "Surely our tests ought to have been scored by *you,* sir, the Master of Composition, not by an inexperienced apprentice!"

Silence fell as the Master's brows lifted and his eyes held Niall's. "And on what grounds," he said evenly, "do you accuse my apprentice of compositional inexperience?"

Five Bards dropped their eyes and studied their test scores as though the numbers were a mysterious code that required lengthy deciphering. Niall, however, did not back down. "I'm not accusing him ... apprentices are inexperienced by definition! He can hardly be expected to know enough to score Bard tests in *any* subject."

"I see. Well, then, the other five Bards at this table are indeed fortunate that my inexperienced apprentice somehow managed to come up with the exact same score that I did."

Niall blinked. "You scored them too?"

"I reviewed every test Kaelin corrected," the Master replied sternly, "and agreed with his scoring on their tests completely. The only score that I did *not* agree with was your own. Perhaps you are right, and I ought to take my inexperienced apprentice to task for generously overlooking your lack of articulation and merely making a suggestion to include it next time. I would have docked you an additional five points for that." He turned his attention to his apprentice. "Why did you not do so, Kaelin? You know perfectly well that such an omission carries a penalty of five points."

The apprentice shifted uncomfortably. "It was already a failing score, Master, so I felt that a comment regarding it was sufficient."

"I see. Though it was kindly meant," the Master said mildly, "you would do better to give the score that is deserved, lest another Bard comes back with a valid objection over the five points he himself was docked for the same omission."

"Yes, sir. I ... hadn't thought of that."

"And what, exactly, made this test deserving of a failing score?"

Kaelin inwardly groaned; surely this Bard was not going to be pleased to have his mistakes paraded before his colleagues by an apprentice. He took a deep breath. "In the first section, four-part harmony, the first line had three errors in the cadence chords." He hesitated. "Would you like the specifics, sir?"

"By all means. I'm sure Bard Niall will appreciate a thorough demonstration of my apprentice's inexperience."

"Yes, sir." Kaelin kept his eyes on his Master. "The first error was in the fifth of the dominant, which should have been a C sharp, not a C. The second error was in the minor six chord, the third of which should not have been sharped. The third error was in the fifth of the four chord, where the E should have been a D." He paused, then continued when the Master raised an inquiring brow. "There was also a discrepancy in this line in how the dominant seventh resolved to the tonic," he added reluctantly. "Since the dominant seventh was in root position, it should have resolved to the tonic in second inversion, not first inversion."

Niall stared at the first page of his test, his mouth slightly open, his eyes widening as the apprentice's detailed recital of errors continued to the bottom of the page.

"Would you like me to continue to the next page, Master?" Kaelin asked, his eyes begging to be allowed to stop.

"I believe I'll leave that up to Niall," the Master replied, looking inquiringly at the disconcerted Bard, who took a few moments to find his tongue.

"No, Kaelin, that won't be necessary," Niall said at last, then turned to the Master and spoke deferentially. "I've been sufficiently put in my place, and rightfully so, sir."

"As you can see," the Master told him, "there is good reason why my apprentice has my full confidence in his ability to score a composition test. But, if you prefer," he said in a steely voice, "you can pass your test over to me and I will adjust your score to what *I* would have given you."

The Bard lowered his head. "No, sir. Please forgive my objection. I spoke rashly. It was just … embarrassing to be failed by an apprentice."

"Then perhaps you ought to study harder," the Master suggested dryly.

"I have, sir, truly!" Niall protested. "I'm sure I can pass the other tests. I'm just not very good at composition and theory."

"Considering whose island you are currently serving, that is indeed unfortunate. Have you requested help from someone who is? I may not have been fully available this cycle, but there were three Bards in your territory whom you could have asked for help."

The Bard dropped his gaze again. "No, sir. I'm very sorry I did not."

The Master surveyed his chastened Bard for a moment, then rose and went to his composition desk. He withdrew a scroll from one of the many cubbyholes and returned with it and his flute. "I'm going to play a composition that is based on this same cadence. At the end of it, each of you will be expected to score it." He lifted his flute and began to play a lively rondo.

As the rollicking music began to fill the Master's home, smiles lit the faces of every listener save one. Under the table, feet unconsciously began tapping in time, as though wanting to take their owners up and into the dancing music filling the air. At the end, the Bards enthusiastically applauded the composition.

The Master placed his flute on the table and looked at Niall. "What is your opinion of this composition?"

"That was a wonderful piece, sir!" Niall said admiringly. "An excellent theme, fully developed, well articulated, with a superb ending." There was a chorus of agreement around the table.

"And how would you score it?"

"I would give it full marks," the Bard said without hesitation.

Master Bergid looked inquiringly around the table and received the same perfect score from everyone else. He turned his attention back to Niall. "You refused to ask for help from your own colleagues. Would you willingly take lessons from the composer of this piece?"

The Bard's jaw dropped. Lessons from the Master Bard of Kestrel himself? "Of *course*, sir! It would be an honor to learn from someone as gifted in composition as you are."

"Perhaps you should ask him if he is willing to take you as a student, then," the Master said. He motioned toward his apprentice, who flushed deeply, studied the floor, and fervently wished he had stayed in the woods.

All eyes swiveled to Kaelin. Niall's smile vanished. "That was composed by your apprentice?" he asked incredulously.

"That was the composition he wrote on the third section of the test you just failed. I quite agreed with your assessment and gave it full marks."

Niall's was not the only flabbergasted face at the Master's table. "Are you saying, sir," Niall asked, "that your apprentice has taken the intermediate composition test for *Bards?*"

"If that were all he had taken, I would certainly not have asked him to score the advanced level," came the dry rejoinder. "Kaelin has taken all three levels of the composition and theory tests for Bards and passed them all without error." At the stunned silence that fell over the table, the Master's brows lifted. "Perhaps you have a better understanding now why he is not currently apprenticed to an Instrumentalist." Six sets of wide eyes turned again to the apprentice, who chewed on his lip and continued his assiduous study of the floor.

"Kaelin?"

The apprentice looked up, startled at hearing himself addressed by Niall. "Yes, sir?"

"Would you be willing to give a failing Bard lessons in intermediate composition?" the Bard asked humbly. "I would consider it a great favor."

The apprentice's eyes widened. He glanced at his Master, whose gaze remained on the Bard. Clearly, the decision was Kaelin's own to make. "I would not presume to give lessons to a Bard," he replied deferentially, "but it would be an honor to help you in any way I can, and I will gladly do so as my Master permits."

Niall straightened in his seat and nodded. "Thank you, Kaelin, and please forgive my thoughtless words. They were discourteous and quite undeserved. I ought to have been upset with myself, not you, who did nothing more than obey your Master."

"I took no offense, sir."

"You must tell me, then, if there is anything I can do for you in return for your help."

Kaelin's face lit up. "Oh, yes, sir, there is!" The watching Bards couldn't help but smile as the apprentice eagerly continued, suddenly looking every bit a youngster of eleven, unexpectedly presented with his choice of treats at the bakery. "My Master has told me that you're an excellent Piper! Perhaps, at the end of the week, you could play a song for me before you leave? I hope to improve my own playing by hearing yours."

Niall chuckled softly. "I'd be happy to play a song for you, Kaelin." Then the Bard turned to the Master. "I ask for your forgiveness as well, Master Bergid. The difference between what I wrote and what your apprentice wrote is considerable. I deserved a lower score than the one I was given, and I will learn to do better. Nor will I hesitate to ask for help again from those who know more than I, no matter their rank. And your apprentice was far more gracious to me than I was to him. I deeply apologize for my behavior."

"Then you have my forgiveness," Master Bergid said, "and you may work with my apprentice at the end of the day for the remainder of the week."

"Thank you, sir."

"Congratulations to the rest of you for passing your composition tests," the Master said approvingly. "Your testing tomorrow morning will be on the geography, territories, villages, flora, and fauna of Kestrel, followed in the afternoon by testing on Caer Wynd's responsibilities, including their libraries, hierarchy, and the various disciplines taught there. You are dismissed, and except for Niall, may return to Gannet's Inn."

Five of the Bards rose and bowed to the Master, then collected their packs from under their chairs and filed out, placing their instruments near the door and taking their cloaks from Kaelin's hand. The apprentice turned to find Niall still sitting at the table, looking at him expectantly. The apprentice glanced at his Master.

"Our dinner can wait, Kaelin," the Master told him. "I have something to attend to in Kyet first, and will return in an hour or so. You and Niall may work together until then."

"Yes, sir. Would you allow me to review Bard Niall's theory test? It would be helpful in knowing what to focus on first."

The Master nodded permission and left. Kaelin fetched the Bard's theory test and quickly glanced through it. Then he replaced it with the others and took a seat next to the Bard, who stiffened slightly, as though steeling himself for an unpleasant ordeal.

"I suppose I failed that as well," Niall said glumly.

"Yes, sir," Kaelin said regretfully, "but scores don't always tell the whole tale."

The Bard frowned. "A fail is a fail," he said flatly. "What other tale can my score possibly tell?"

"It's more about what tale your score *can't* tell," Kaelin

replied. "If you look only at your score tomorrow, it will tell you that thirty-eight points were docked from it."

The Bard winced.

"However," Kaelin continued, "if you look at your errors, you'll see that there aren't nearly as many."

Niall frowned. "What do you mean?"

"You only made a few errors. Your low score simply reflects making those errors repeatedly in various ways. If we repair your understanding of those few things, you'll pass the test without any problem and have the tools you need to develop your compositions." Kaelin indicated the Bard's composition test. "Your score on that doesn't tell the whole tale, either, for points are only docked for what you did wrong with your tools, not added for what you did well with them. The theme of your composition is excellent, the best one of all those I reviewed. It's deserving of development with the best tools possible." He looked up into the Bard's astounded face. "I meant what I said, sir, when I told you it would be an honor to help you in any way I can."

It was a few moments before Niall was able to speak. "I thought perhaps, with your Master gone—" He shook his head and smiled. "Never mind what I thought. Lead on, Kaelin ... this Bard will gratefully follow."

They worked together for almost two hours until Master Bergid returned, and then the Bard gathered his notes and stowed them in his pack. He stood to bow to the Master, then he turned to the apprentice and bowed with nearly equal depth. Kaelin quickly rose and returned it.

"Thank you for a very instructive lesson," the Bard said sincerely. He turned to the Master. "Your apprentice is an excellent teacher. I'm sure it's because he has one himself. Thank you for the privilege of learning from him."

"I think," the Master observed quietly, "that perhaps you've learned more today than just musical composition and theory."

"Yes, sir, I have, and I thank you for it. I will not forget." Niall took his leave, Kaelin hurrying to give him his cloak and open the door for him. When at last the apprentice closed the door, he turned, leaned wearily against it, and slid to the floor with a deep sigh.

The Master chuckled. "You look as though you had taken those tests yourself today."

"I don't think I'd pass them if I took them right now," Kaelin said ruefully. "I had no idea teaching was so exhausting! I doubt I'd recognize the notes of a diminished seventh chord at the moment."

"Really?" the Master said, his brows lifted challengingly. "So, if I stacked up G, Bb, D, and E on *my* test paper—"

"I'd fail you, sir," Kaelin said promptly, giving his Master a reproachful look, "and not bother looking over the rest of your test. The Composition Master of the Bardic Isles is not allowed to make *any* theory mistakes, and that's a D *flat*."

The Master laughed as he seated himself at his desk. "Things will go more smoothly for you tomorrow, now that you've gained their full respect." He indicated the remaining stack of theory test papers still sitting on his desk. "After dinner, you can spend some time correcting those for me, while I get through the rest of the reports I need to read and respond to. Then I'll look over the trio you were told to finish today. And," he added sternly, "I won't be as forgiving of articulation lapses as *you* apparently are."

Chapter 10

The next morning, during the testing on the history of Eire and the Bardic Isles, Master Bergid was called away to Kyet, leaving Kaelin to finish timing the test and collecting the papers.

"I should be back before the afternoon testing begins," the Master said as he hurried to the door. "If I'm not, the afternoon tests are in the left drawer of my desk. I would appreciate it, Kaelin, if you would distribute them and allow three hours for completion."

"Yes, sir," Kaelin said. Two hours later he called the time and collected the morning tests, then went to help prepare lunch.

Flynn glanced at him as he sliced bread. "I'm curious, Kaelin, about the lesson that taught you courtesy. Whatever it was, I must say you learned it well."

Before the apprentice could answer, Niall frowned at Flynn and intervened with a reckless wave of the ladle he was using to stir a pot of soup. "You don't seriously expect him to give us a detailed description of his own switching, do you?" he demanded.

The others glanced up in surprise at hearing Niall defend the apprentice.

Flynn rolled his eyes. "Of course not, but I don't think he received a switching. Did you, Kaelin?"

"No, sir."

Flynn glanced at Niall. "He didn't say he was punished, he said he was given a lesson. I've known Master Bergid far longer than any of you. He's a believer in lessons that teach, and the ones I know about have been inventive and highly effective. I'll bet the lesson Kaelin received was equally so, and I'd like to hear about it. Not from idle curiosity, or to embarrass him, but because I can think of no one I would like to emulate more than Master Bergid. If you're willing to tell us, of course," he added with an apologetic smile at the apprentice. "Niall is quite right to remind me that this is your own business, not mine."

"I don't mind telling you about it, sir," Kaelin replied. "When we got back here after taking the ferry, the room was filled with all the baggage that had been delivered here before us. I started to unpack, but Master Bergid told me it could wait, there was something more important to tend to first. He sat down in his chair and told me to come stand before him. I thought I was about to be punished, or at least lectured for what happened on the ferry, but all he did was ask me to define 'courtesy' for him. I tried to think of a definition, but it was harder to do than I thought." Kaelin shrugged helplessly. "I finally said it was being polite to people who were older than you, or of higher rank. He asked if he'd ever been discourteous to me, and I told him no, he never had been, not even once. And he asked if I didn't think that was strange, for I was certainly not older nor of higher rank than he was. So, if my definition were correct, I would be required to treat him with the utmost courtesy, but he would be free to treat *me* as badly as he liked. I didn't know what to say to that, so I said nothing."

The Bards chuckled appreciatively. "And then what did he do?" Flynn asked.

"He told me he could hardly expect me to treat others with courtesy when I didn't understand the definition of the word, so he would teach it to me. He told me to remove one of the ropes from the boxes and bring it to him. He tied one end of the rope to his belt and the other end to my own. Then he forbade me to speak but said that otherwise I could do whatever I wished. When I understood the true definition of courtesy, I could tell him what it was, and the lesson would be over."

By now, all the Bards had stopped what they were doing and were avidly listening. "What happened then?" Gryndl asked.

Kaelin shrugged ruefully. "We just stood there. I couldn't talk, and I didn't know what to do, tied to him like that. I had to unpack my things and the supplies we brought back, so I finally moved toward the packs, tugging the rope as I went, and he followed along behind me. I unpacked and started putting things away, and he helped me. I tried to stop him and take the things from his hand, but he shook his head and smiled, like he was perfectly happy helping his apprentice work. No matter where I pulled him, he patiently followed, helping me with everything I needed to do. Pretty soon the bags were all unpacked and put away, except for his own, because I didn't know where his things belonged, and I couldn't ask. So, I left those and pulled him into the kitchen to make our dinner. He helped with that, too, and then we ate." Kaelin grimaced. "Well, at least *he* did. By that time, I was too upset to eat anything." He paused for a moment, remembering. Not a sound disturbed the room.

"I felt terrible," the apprentice continued in a low voice, "pulling my Master around like he was Poor Oran so I could take care of my own work, while he cheerfully helped me do it and wasn't able to do any of the things I knew he wanted to do. And it occurred to me that I'd been pulling him around for a couple of hours, thinking only of myself, and he had never once pulled me anywhere, even though he could have and certainly had the right to. So, after dinner I pointed to his packs, and he smiled at me and nodded. We walked together, neither one of us pulling the other, and I helped him unpack. When he was done, I motioned toward his room, then helped him take his things there and put them away. He likes to compose in the evenings, so I pointed to his composition desk, and he smiled. He sat there and started composing, while I stood next to him and did some thinking."

"Did you come up with a better definition?" Tyrian asked.

"Yes, sir. He finished his composition and pointed to my flute, but I shook my head and stood in front of him. He asked me if I had a definition to give him, and I said that courtesy was more than just acting polite to people. It was paying attention to other's needs and doing what you could to help them, because whatever we do affects all those around us as much as if we were all connected with ropes."

"And what did he say to that?" Flynn asked.

"He said it was the best definition he had ever heard, untied the rope, told me to get myself some dinner and eat it this time, and the lesson was over."

"You're right, Flynn," Tyrian said, impressed. "That's the best lesson in courtesy I've ever heard of. Most apprentices would have just been switched for discourtesy, as most of us assumed Kaelin was, and would have learned nothing from it except a fear of being rude. Kaelin's courtesy, on the other hand, is genuine because he understands what it means and why he should practice it."

"Well, then," Gryndl said pointedly, "perhaps you could all practice a little courtesy and let me eat some lunch before I lose my appetite thinking about the hundreds of responsibilities of the entire Bardic Order hierarchy we're about to be tested on."

A chorus of groans signaled unanimous agreement. The Bards took the food out to the table and began a lively conversation rehashing that morning's history test. Bran, who was sitting next to Kaelin, slathered a slice of bread with butter and turned to the silent apprentice sitting next to him.

"I've noticed that you take your flute with you when you leave in the afternoons," the Bard said conversationally. "Is that your primary instrument?"

Kaelin swallowed the bite of cheese he had just taken and

nodded. "Yes, sir."

"It's mine, as well. Yet we've never heard a single note from yours."

Kaelin glanced at him uneasily. "I wouldn't want to distract anyone during their testing," he said hesitantly.

Bran smiled easily. "I'm sure we all appreciate that, Kaelin." He took a bite of his bread and followed it up with a spoonful of soup. "What flute form are you currently working on?"

"I'm not working on any flute form right now."

The Bard's eyes widened. "No? What form, then, were you working on before you stopped?"

Kaelin glanced around the table, where the other Bards had fallen silent and were waiting for his answer. "Perhaps, sir," he said at last, "you should ask my Master."

"Why can't *you* tell us?" piped up Brent. "Surely it's not a secret. You needn't feel intimidated if that's the problem. After all, you're an apprentice. We're certainly not expecting you to be at a high level of playing."

"Like we didn't expect him to be at a high level of composition or theory?" Niall asked dryly.

Brent chuckled. "Point taken. Nevertheless, most Bardic apprentices are far older than you, Kaelin, and they all begin with form one, just as every one of us did."

"True enough," said Gryndl, "and there are a few Bards who aren't much further along than *that* yet," he said, looking pointedly at Brent, who glared at him.

"I'll have you know," Brent said defensively, "that, with Master Bergid's and Bran's help for two cycles, I've reached the fourth flute form, and I think the next time the Master hears me, he'll pass me to form five."

"Not bad for a level nine harpist," Gryndl allowed. "If you get released for rotation this cycle, you might yet survive your rotation with Master Marek. He doesn't release any Bard from Zephyr until they've reached form seven on flute."

"Then perhaps," Brent said evenly, "you should keep in mind that Master Grened has the same high standards for *my* primary instrument. Which I believe you have yet to—"

"I still want to hear what form *Kaelin* was on before he stopped studying them," Bran interjected, glancing at the disconcerted apprentice. "If you haven't started the flute forms yet," he said in a gentler tone, "there's no shame in that. I'm sure you'll do well once you begin, especially with such a fine teacher as Master Bergid."

Kaelin chewed on his lip, not knowing what to say. The silence became uncomfortable as the waiting Bards stared at him, and then a voice from behind him released the boy from their scrutiny.

"My apprentice stopped studying the flute forms," Master Bergid said quietly from the doorway, "the day he finished mastering them all."

As every head swiveled in his direction, Kaelin quickly rose and bowed to his Master, avoiding six flabbergasted faces. "Welcome home, sir. I'll bring you your lunch," he murmured, and fled to the kitchen. He could clearly hear the voices at the table as the stunned Bards recovered, stood, and belatedly greeted the Master's return.

"Kaelin has mastered *all* the flute forms?" Bran asked incredulously as they reseated themselves. "Even form ten?"

"Is that a problem?"

Bran gave the Master a wry smile. "No, sir. But I imagine it's yet another reason why he isn't studying with an Instrumentalist."

"Just so." The Master surveyed the empty dishes reprovingly. "Now, if you'll clear this all away, we can get started on the afternoon testing."

The Bards quickly rose and cleared the table, then helped Kaelin tidy up while the Master ate his lunch. The kitchen was unusually silent, though the eyes of more than one Bard rested appraisingly on the equally silent apprentice. When they were finished, the Master excused Kaelin, and the apprentice slung his pack and flute over his shoulder and gratefully left the house. He stayed away until he saw the Bards leave, then he reluctantly returned to give Niall his composition lesson. To the apprentice's relief, the Bard made no mention of flute forms, and they enjoyed another productive session together. The moment Niall left, Kaelin went to the kitchen to prepare a dinner of lamb chops, broccoli, and roasted potatoes, which he took to the table.

The Master picked up his fork, then, noticing his apprentice looking gloomily at his own plate, set the utensil back down. "What's bothering you, lad?" he asked gently. "I hope it's nothing worse than my pack of prying Bards."

Kaelin was silent as he tried to sort out his thoughts. "I've never loved anything more than learning from you, sir," he said at last. "The moment I master a new skill, your look of approval makes we want to learn a new one, and another one after that, until I ... guess I passed all the composition and theory tests without even knowing they're for Bards." He sat back in his chair and looked at his Master in confusion. "So why do I feel guilty for those skills now that the Bards have found out about them? Bard Bran told me there was no shame in not having started the flute forms yet. So why do I feel ashamed that I've finished them?"

His Master's hand suddenly covered his own. "Never feel ashamed for what you've accomplished, or the knowledge you've worked so hard to acquire," he said firmly. "Regardless of where you are on the path of learning, lad, there will always be those who know more than you about some things, and those who know less. And there will always be some who feel threatened by someone so young being further along the path than they are." He looked keenly at the youngster, whose eyes were fastened on his. "That's *their* insecurity, Kaelin. Do not make it your own."

The apprentice nodded thoughtfully.

"Some," the Master continued, "will even grumble that it's 'not fair' for the Maker to have given more talent to one person than another, as though a person's own hard work had nothing to do with it. And yet many a hard-working Bard can outplay a lazier one who was born with more natural ability, but less motivation to develop it." He smiled at Kaelin's look of surprise. "Talent is a wonderful thing to possess, but it's certainly not the only factor that determines how well someone will eventually play. Talent that is not accompanied by dedicated hard work is useless, in *any* field."

Once again, the Master picked up his unused fork, then set it back down when his apprentice showed no inclination to pick up his own. "Now, then, what else is worrying you?"

It did not seem at first that the youngest apprentice in the Bardic Order would answer. He sat for a long moment, chewing his bottom lip and thinking. At last, he looked up. "It's just that, now that they know I've finished all the flute forms, I'm afraid they'll ask me to play for them the next time they catch me alone."

The Master frowned and did not reply. His curious Bards, he knew, were likely to do exactly that.

Kaelin's voice rose with anxiety. "I'm just an apprentice, sir, and they're *Bards,* three whole ranks above mine! I'm required to obey them. What will they do to me when I won't?" His shoulders slumped when the Master remained silent. "I hardly went a week in Vale without a switching from someone," he said glumly. "Usually from the Schoolmaster for skipping school, or Craftmaster Arnor if I wasted too many pieces of wood trying something new. Even widow Sorcha gave my hand a switching for talking back to her." He shrugged hopelessly. "I probably got more switchings than anyone else in Vale ever did. It was like the whole village took it on themselves to keep me in line. But not even *I* ever earned six switchings in a row!"

The Master stifled a laugh.

Kaelin was scowling down at his own hands. "If all six of them switch my hands, I won't be able to practice for days, and three more groups of Bards are coming for testing!"

A strangled sound came from the Master, but his apprentice was too distracted to notice.

"Do you think," Kaelin asked hopefully, "they would switch the back of my legs instead, if I asked them? At least then I could still practice." He glanced up, startled at the sound of a sputtered laugh. The apprentice gave his Master a reproachful look. "Fine thing, sir, that my Master finds the thought of his apprentice being switched six times in a row every week for a month amusing."

The Master conceded defeat and laughed outright. Kaelin lapsed into a wounded silence. At last, the Master regained a semblance of gravity. "I don't suppose it's occurred to you to simply do as they ask," he suggested, already knowing the response he would receive.

"I can't," Kaelin said in a low voice.

"Can't?" The Master gave him a keen look. "Or won't?"

Kaelin flinched. "Both, sir." His head drooped when he saw his Master begin to speak. "Please don't," he whispered.

The Master was certain he had never heard a more pitiful, heartfelt request in his life. "Please don't what?" he asked gently.

"Please don't ask me why. You said, when I was ready—" His voice trailed off.

"And you're not yet ready?"

"No, sir, I'd rather be punished for disobeying them." Kaelin stared at his hands unhappily, and the Master laid a reassuring hand on his shoulder.

"Very well, Kaelin, I won't ask you why, nor will I command you to play for them against your will," he said. "When you're ready to explain, I'm still ready to listen. You have nothing to fear from my Bards, though, for they would not punish you, no matter what offense you committed. They would simply take you to your Master, as they would any disobedient apprentice, and leave the burden on him to switch you ... even six times in a row." He suppressed a smile as Kaelin looked up at him hopefully. "And," the Master continued regretfully, "since that's far too much switching for my aged hands to bear, I would do no such thing. So you see, you have nothing to worry about." He smiled as Kaelin left his chair and hugged him, whispering words of thanks against his chest. The relieved apprentice returned to his place, and the Master picked up his pristine fork for the third time.

"However," the Master said, "perhaps I can make things easier for everyone." He shook his shining utensil at his apprentice and spoke sternly. "From now until the end of the month, you are strictly forbidden to play any instrument for anyone other than myself. If anyone should attempt to persuade you otherwise, you are to inform them of the stricture you are under and refer them to me if they have any objections. Is this clearly understood?"

A smile flitted across the youngster's face. "Yes, sir." His eyes returned to his uneaten meal. "Thank you for understanding."

"Perhaps I understand more than you think."

"You do?" Kaelin looked up uneasily.

"If you can't use your hands, I won't have anyone to fetch and carry for me. I won't have anyone to correct composition and theory tests for me, either, and worst of all—" the Master sighed heavily as he speared a piece of cold broccoli, "except for lunch, which my Bards can continue seeing to, I'll have to make all our meals." He gave his apprentice a scandalized expression. "We can't have *that*, of course."

Kaelin grinned. "No, sir. We sure can't." He picked up his own fork and began to eat.

⤚ ⸭ ⤙

Late that night, the Master sat alone before the fire, deep in thought about his young apprentice. Since Kaelin had refused to play for his own sister, Bergid had often wondered what had happened to convince the boy never to play in anyone's presence. He thought of the vows Kaelin had taken. The only vow the youngster had questioned was the one to do no harm with his music. Though nothing was recorded that explained what the Gift of old was, it was a matter of Bardic record that the Gifted of Eire had once commanded great power with their music. Power that could be used for good or for harm, as Cyral's actions at the bay of Aille-Mara decisively proved. And now, after all these cycles, Bergid had found a boy born with the same Gift, a Gift no one understood, not even the boy who possessed it. The power and potential danger inherent in such a Gift had prompted the Master to forbid Kaelin's exploration of it until he came of age.

Bergid tapped the armrest of his chair thoughtfully. Was it caution that stayed his hand, or cowardice? If Kaelin's Gift was ever to be of use, it would need to be developed fully, not held back by his Master's own doubts and fear of a Gift he did not understand. He thought back to the day he had chanced to hear the boy play in the woods of Vale. *What an experience that was! An experience that no one would ever believe.* The Master frowned, struck by a sudden thought. Perhaps he hadn't been the first to hear Kaelin play. Perhaps there had been another listener, someone who happened to be walking near the edge of a cliff, or climbing a tree, or swimming in a river. The Master paled. If someone had been harmed in such a way, it might well have convinced Kaelin that his music was too dangerous to be played in anyone's presence.

Whatever the cause, Bergid knew he must discover the root of the boy's fear soon, before the Spring Council. He knew Kaelin would not refuse him an explanation if asked for one, but Bergid was reluctant to coerce him. With a sigh, the Master rose to bank the fire for the night. There was yet time. He would not force the boy's confidence unless he had no choice. And, he reflected wryly, there was always a choice.

Chapter 11

The following morning was the fourth day of testing, Bardic Law in the morning, followed in the afternoon by the Guild Laws of the Trades, Crafts, Holders, Merchants, and Shipping. As soon as the testing on Bardic Law was finished, the Master left to check on another issue in Kyet. No sooner had the door closed behind him than the madly curious Bards shooed the apprentice out of the kitchen.

"We'll take care of making lunch, Kaelin," Bran said, "if you'll entertain us while we work."

Kaelin nodded agreeably. "How would you like me to entertain you?"

"Hmm, flute music sounds good," Bran said suggestively, while the other Bards chuckled and nodded agreement as they got out the food.

Kaelin's shoulders slumped. "I'm sorry, sir," he said regretfully, "but my Master has strictly forbidden me to play for anyone other than himself right now, on any instrument."

All preparations for lunch suddenly ceased. "Why would he do that?" wondered Tyrian.

The apprentice shrugged. "He didn't give me a reason. He gave me a command, and I don't question my Master's commands. I obey them."

"Well, of course you do," Bran said, as the Bards sighed with disappointment.

"If it's entertainment you want, I can do cartwheels straight through the living room," Kaelin said helpfully.

"And if you end up in the fireplace, which is fortunately not lit yet?" Tyrian asked archly.

The apprentice grinned. "Then I'll end up matching my robe, and you'll be even more entertained!" The Bards laughed and went back to their work. Only Flynn's eyes continued to rest thoughtfully on the apprentice as Kaelin began slicing the last of the winter apples.

Late that afternoon, as the Bards were wearily filing out, Flynn, who had told the others to go on ahead without him, asked Kaelin if he could speak to him outside for a moment. Master Bergid, sitting at his desk reviewing tests, made no sign that he had heard. Niall, who was collecting his theory materials in preparation for Kaelin's tutoring, glanced up in surprise.

"Certainly, sir," Kaelin replied, then turned to Niall. "While I'm gone, could you write a short composition on the same cadence that was in your test, using E major instead? We can use it to discover how far you've progressed."

"Consider it done," Niall said cheerfully, and pulled a fresh sheet of manuscript paper out of his pack. "How long do I have?"

"A theme of sixteen measures, with a variation of equal length, done in the time limit of a half hour, should give us enough material to go over." Kaelin gave the Bard a bow, then turned and followed Flynn out to where the trees shaded the path leading to Kyet.

"You know," Flynn said with a smile, "most apprentices would relish the chance to lord it over a Bard who knows less than they do. I want you to know that the unfailing deference you give to Niall is appreciated, not just by him, but by us all, for he is our colleague and friend."

"He's a Bard, sir," Kaelin said simply. "I owe him deference for the difference in our rank. And," he added wryly, "if I thought otherwise, my Master would swiftly teach me better."

Flynn chuckled. "He would, indeed. But I detect more than due deference. You also treat him with respect ... and respect, regardless of rank, must be earned."

"Bard Niall earned my respect the moment he agreed to be tutored by an apprentice who failed him."

Flynn smiled. "I'm glad to hear that."

"You also have my respect, sir," Kaelin said. "Not just because you've treated me with it from the moment we met, but also because of what you've done for my Master and me for the last half cycle."

The Bard's eyes widened at the apprentice's knowing look. "How could you have known? I never once came to your camp. Master Bergid felt it would be best, in case any rumors of your existence began to circulate, if I could honestly claim to have never seen an apprentice in his company."

"There was a certain pack that kept appearing and disappearing, and my Master kept pulling things out of it that he wouldn't have traveled with. Woodworking tools, a cylinder of rosewood, an apprentice robe and cord, not to mention reams of paperwork ... and I'm pretty sure supplies that kept him from needing to leave me during the weeks I was blind." He shrugged. "I figured a Phantom Bard must be responsible, faithfully trekking back and forth with whatever he required."

Flynn laughed, and Kaelin gave him a grin. "I'm happy to finally meet him and give him my thanks."

"You're more than welcome." The Bard looked at him thoughtfully. "I realize that you barely know me, Kaelin. Though this robe gives me the right to question an apprentice and expect him to answer, I want you to know that you needn't answer me or tell me anything you don't wish to."

Kaelin nodded uneasily and glanced at the house as though wishing he could transport himself back to the safety of his Master.

Flynn, following his gaze, spoke gently. "I've known your Master for many cycles, and this is not my first rotation to Kestrel. This past cycle I've gotten to know him even better, and I'm pretty certain he would not have forbidden you to play your instruments for anyone but him."

Kaelin flushed. "I didn't lie to you, sir. He has forbidden it. Truly ... you can ask him yourself if you like."

"I know you wouldn't have lied to us," the Bard assured him, "which means that he did it because *you* don't want to play for us, and I can't help but wonder why." He surveyed the silent apprentice, who was studying the ground as if it fascinated him. "If it's performance anxiety that's stopping you, perhaps I could help you with that."

Kaelin made no reply.

"My niece, who is five cycles old, lives here in Kyet," Flynn persisted. "She loves listening to music, and I was thinking that if, instead of playing for an intimidating audience of Bards, you played just for her, it might—"

"No!" The refusal burst from Kaelin into the Bard's astonished face, and the apprentice lowered his head and immediately apologized. "I'm sorry, sir. What you're offering to do for me is kindly meant and I appreciate it. But I can't play for her, or for anyone other than my Master."

"Because Master Bergid has forbidden it?" the Bard quietly challenged him.

Kaelin shook his head. "No, sir," he admitted. "He forbade it for my sake, because he knows I won't play for anyone else."

Flynn considered him for a moment. "I see. Does Master Bergid know why you refuse to play?"

"No, sir. He hasn't asked me to tell him."

"And if he does?"

"I will tell him the truth."

"Yet you will not tell a Bard who asks?"

Kaelin shook his head. "No, sir, and I would deeply appreciate it if you didn't force me to disobey you."

Flynn raised a hand. "If Master Bergid is not forcing the issue, rest assured that I certainly won't. Nor will I relate any part of this conversation to anyone. What you've told me is in confidence."

"Thank you, sir," Kaelin said in relief.

"It can't be an easy thing to have no one of your own age to confide in and be surrounded by Bards who have never known what that's like. I'm nowhere close to your age, but I have an excellent pair of highly trained ears. So, if you ever need someone besides your Master to talk to, about this or anything else, I hope you'll feel free to confide in me."

Kaelin, fighting back unexpected tears, barely managed to nod.

"I also hope that whatever the problem with your playing is, you find a good solution for it." Flynn gave the disconcerted apprentice a smile and turned to leave.

"Bard Flynn?"

The Bard stopped and turned toward him.

"When my Master finally asks me why I won't play for anyone else ... the answer will hurt him. I never wanted that."

"What did you want?"

"Just to stay with him." Kaelin swallowed hard. "But that was selfish, because I knew that eventually I'd have to remove this robe and leave him. I used to think that would only hurt me, but it's going to hurt him, too, and I don't know if I can stand to do that." His voice grew rough with emotion. "Sometimes I think it would be better if I just disappeared. If he got up one morning, and I—" he broke off as Flynn pulled him close, and the next moment he was crying harder than he had in cycles. Mortified, he tried to stop, but Flynn just held him closer.

"Let the tears come, Kaelin. Let them come."

And come they did, in a wave of intertwined sorrow and regret that left the youngster trembling when he finally stood back, stumbling over words of apology that the Bard waved away.

"I won't presume to tell you what you should do when I don't know the problem. But before you do something as drastic as disappearing from your Master's life, take some time to think on this. If there's one thing I've learned over the cycles, it's that we can't hurt someone else without hurting ourselves, and we can't hurt ourselves without hurting the ones we love. So, hurting yourself by disappearing, to spare your Master, will only cause him more pain." He looked keenly at the silent apprentice. "I hope, for both your sakes, that you don't have to learn that the hard way, as I once did. And if you decide to do so anyway, don't disappear. Come to me, at least. I'll see that you get to wherever you wish to go, and I'll let Master Bergid know you're safe. That won't prevent him from being hurt, but it will keep him from worrying and upturning every stone on Kestrel to find you. Promise me this, for his sake."

Kaelin nodded agreement. Then, saying no more, Flynn continued down the path to town, leaving the apprentice standing motionless in the shadows of the trees.

⤜ ⸳ ⤛

The fifth day of testing, like the first, was different on each island. Master Rial would be testing ear training on Lyra, Master Talan instrument repair on Eyrie, and Master Grened the lap harp on Elegy. On Zephyr and Kestrel, Masters Marek and Bergid would be testing ensembles. The music would be the same on both islands, and new to all of the performers being tested. Kaelin, whose only experience with ensembles was playing duets with his Master, was looking forward to hearing the performances and asked permission to stay and listen.

"I'll sit in the farthest corner and not make a sound," the apprentice promised hopefully the night before the testing. "And I'll make up my own work after dinner."

187

"You don't mind losing your free time in the afternoon?" the Master asked.

"Not if I can hear the ensembles. And I'm using my free time to practice now, which I can do in the evening instead."

"Actually," the Master said, "I had something more in mind for you tomorrow than being a passive listener." He went to his desk and brought out a thick sheaf of papers. "These are the ensembles that will be played tomorrow, and the adjudication sheets for them. I've made extra copies for you to use. I want you to sit next to me tomorrow and critique the ensembles you will hear."

Kaelin was horrified. "But sir! I've never even *heard—*"

His Master raised a hand. "You won't be scoring them, at least not yet, and only my own adjudications will be given to the Bards. However, there is no better way to train your ear than to listen critically to each part and determine how it contributes to the whole. You'll need to listen for balance, pitch, rhythmic and note accuracy, technique, their cohesion as a group, and musical expression. Even without scoring them, you'll be very busy making comments. You'll do the same in the afternoon, so will have no free time ... but no assignments or lessons, either. Instead, we'll spend the evening comparing and discussing our assessments. If you learn as much as I expect you will, we'll follow the same procedure for the instrumental testing on the following two days, and perhaps you can learn to score them as well."

Kaelin frowned at this, and the Master continued. "I know you haven't yet been instructed on three of the four instruments that will be tested, but that doesn't mean you can't learn a great deal by critiquing what you do know, which is everything except the actual technique of playing them. Rhythmic and note accuracy, phrasing and expression, tone quality, dynamics, and articulation all play a part in solo scoring, and you are well able to critique such things and learn how to score them."

Kaelin's eyes lit in anticipation. "Sounds like fun!"

The Master snorted. "Tell that to your writing hand tomorrow night, lad, and see what *it* thinks about continuing the 'fun' for two more days."

"Is it as bad as being switched six times in a row, sir?" Kaelin asked mischievously.

"I wouldn't know," his Master said dryly, "but if you'd like to find out, I can release you from the stricture you're under and give my Bards permission to handle any insubordination from my apprentice on their own." He chuckled at Kaelin's frantic head shake and handed him one of the papers. "Look over this adjudication sheet and then we'll discuss it. After that, you can read through the scores to familiarize yourself with the music they'll be performing. Listen well tomorrow and do your best to give helpful suggestions in each category. It will be good experience for when you begin playing ensembles yourself."

Kaelin nodded and stared unseeingly at the sheet in his hand. *He expects me to play ensembles?* His mind instantly rose up and began sarcastically lecturing him.

What did you expect, you idiot? That you could just stay at his side forever, refusing to play for anyone else but him?

He refused to answer himself, but the voice would not be silenced.

You're in the Bardic Order now, or haven't you noticed that robe you're wearing ... you know, the one you should never have accepted? He's training you to eventually become a Flutist or Instrumentalist! They take paying students for a living. Just who do you think is going to want lessons from a teacher who won't play for them?

Kaelin stoically maintained his silence.

Wake up and use your head! How long do you suppose he'll accept your refusal to play for anyone else?

This provoked a protest. *He said he won't command me to play against my will!*

That was a promise for the month of testing only, and you know it! Sooner or later, he's going to demand some answers, and you're going to have to give them.

I have at least a month before that happens. I don't have to think about it until then.

For a moment, the idea of simply disappearing at the end of the month held enormous appeal, but the memory of Bard Flynn's words quickly stopped this line of thought. He would not hurt his Master more than he had to, just to avoid having to face him while he did it.

Would he really upturn every stone on Kestrel to find me? As his heart twisted in his chest, Kaelin forced himself to concentrate on the adjudication sheet in front of him.

Chapter 12

The tall archway to the right of the fireplace in the Master's home led to two practice rooms on the right side of the hall and a large ensemble room at the end. Each practice room had a large northern window looking out into the woods behind the Master's home. The ensemble room boasted three such windows with the same view and another six facing west, tall enough for a good view of not only the woods, but the hills beyond the Bronig as well. In the winter, when many of the trees were bereft of their leaves, the glistening river could be seen below, winding its way south toward the bay of Kyet. In front of these windows were three chairs and stands for the performers. Facing this was a large table with two chairs, which would serve as an adjudication table. Along the southern wall were six chairs with plenty of room between them for instruments to be placed. A full pitcher of water and six glasses stood ready on the table. This is where Kaelin led the Bards on the first morning of ensemble testing. They took their places, readied their instruments and music, and waited for the Master to enter and tell them who would be playing the first trio. The room fairly resonated with nervous energy.

The six Bards had come to Kyet one week before their testing so they could study and practice, unhindered by their usual duties. Upon arriving at Gannet's Inn, they had each been given a single part to four numbered trios of various, unknown combinations of instruments. They were free to practice their own part but forbidden to rehearse or discuss them with anyone. Each Bard would also play his primary instrument in a three-movement trio they had been allowed to rehearse. These prepared trios would be performed in the afternoon session.

Master Bergid entered the room, and the Bards rose and greeted him. He returned their greeting and took his seat at the adjudication table. The Bards could not quite disguise their horror when Kaelin was given a stack of adjudication sheets and told to sit next to the Master and critique their ensembles. This prodigy of Master Bergid's might have passed all ten flute forms, but surely he couldn't be an expert in the other six Bardic instruments as well. Moreover, the apprentice was apparently under a stricture not to play for anyone but his Master, so what could he possibly know about ensembles? Certainly not enough to adjudicate them! Visible relief swept the group when Master Bergid told them his apprentice was doing this as an exercise and that only the Master's scores would count.

"Brent, Tyrian, and Niall will be playing the first trio this morning," the Master announced. The three Bards rose and quickly took their places at the front of the room.

Kaelin opened his copy of the score and watched with interest. His Master had told him that each Bard would only be playing an instrument they were proficient on, having reached form seven or higher. Since no one could become a Bard without first attaining proficiency on at least five of the seven Bardic instruments, there were numerous combinations the Master could select for testing. This first ensemble had Brent on pipes, Tyrian on harp, and Niall on flute. The three Bards stood, bowed to the Master, then reseated themselves. Tyrian made eye contact with Brent and began playing. Niall waited, smiling appreciatively at the fluent arpeggios Tyrian sent across his harp, and the woodsy notes of Brent's pipes below them. Then the flutist lifted his instrument and joined in, effortlessly rising above them both.

Before the first phrase was over, the listening apprentice forgot all about critiquing. His quill rolled out of his hand to the table, his mouth fell open and he listened spellbound to his first Bardic ensemble, the likes of which had surely never been heard in the village of Vale. Kaelin was well used to the wonder of listening to his Master and was convinced there was no better soloist in all the Bardic Isles on any instrument. He had also enjoyed playing the duets of each form with his Master. The form duets, however, were fairly one-sided conversations, with one player chattering on and the other barely getting a word in edgewise. The trio he was listening to now was a completely different experience.

At the beginning, the harp and pipes had set the mood for what promised to be a dance. A few measures later the flute obliged, dancing onstage and flitting above them as though daring the others to catch her. The pipes swept up on the crest of the harp's arpeggios and pulled the flute playfully down. The harp took immediate advantage with undulating waves of arpeggios, a beautiful melody plucked with firm clarity above them, intent on proving that it, too, could command the skies with a melodic line. The flute, clearly disgruntled at being deposed, argued dissonantly with the pipes over who was going to put the harp back in its place. At last, abandoning the stoic pipes, she climbed up the undulating arpeggios in a sneak attack, emerging high above the harp's melodic line and triumphantly taking the lead again. Over and under, around and through, the three instruments conversed, creating a story in Kaelin's mind that swept him completely away from the unmarked adjudication sheet before him.

The three Bards finished the trio and bowed to the Master, who nodded with a brief glance and smile from the writing he had been engaged in during their entire performance. Brent glanced at the motionless apprentice and chuckled. "I think our apprentice has fallen in love with ensemble music," he whispered to the other two as they collected their parts, "and can't be bothered with such mundane matters as scoring them."

"Well, of course he has," Niall said with quiet satisfaction. "He's a flutist. Such excellent flute playing would naturally sweep him off his feet."

"I believe it was the mesmerizing *harp* arpeggios that took his wits from him," Tyrian countered. "Perhaps we ought to snap him out of it before his Master upbraids him for not doing as he was told."

"Too late," Brent murmured. The Master was tapping his quill against the desk.

"Kaelin!"

The apprentice came to himself with a gasp. "Master?"

"I believe you were told to compose a commentary. You have five minutes left to do so. And your comments had better be cogent, or you'll lose every minute of your free time for a week."

"Sorry, sir!" Kaelin snatched up his quill and began feverishly writing. The Bards chuckled.

"You called him *our* apprentice," Tyrian murmured to Brent as they set down their instruments and took their seats with the others.

"Did I?" Brent looked mildly surprised. "I suppose that's how I've begun to think of him." He glanced at his colleagues. "What do all of *you* think?"

"He's unfailingly courteous," Bran pointed out.

"He's doing everything he can to help Niall," said Gryndl approvingly.

"Never flaunts his talents," Niall said.

"Worships his Master," put in Flynn.

"And best of all, he has impeccable taste in music," Tyrian said.

Brent nodded thoughtfully. "Well, then, yes, I believe he's *our* apprentice now."

"And the Bards coming after us had better treat him well," Niall said with a scowl, "or they'll answer to us!"

"Remind me," Flynn said wryly, "not to get on the wrong side of someone whose name means 'champion.'"

Gryndl chuckled. "I agree with the champion, though. He's our apprentice," he said firmly, "and nobody messes with him."

An ominous tapping came from the adjudication table. "If you're all done whispering amongst yourselves," the Master said pointedly, "I'm ready to hear the second trio, and my fellow adjudicator," he said with a meaningful glance at Kaelin, who was still frantically writing, "had better be also."

The three Bards who hadn't yet played rose and took their places, but before they could begin, Gryndl suddenly rose. "I'm terribly sorry, Master Bergid," he said apologetically. "I forgot to bring my music." He walked back to fetch it, then reseated himself. The three Bards picked up their instruments.

"One moment," Bran said, putting down his kithara. "I seem to have forgotten my plectrum." He glanced at the Master, who was regarding him impassively. "My apologies, sir." He walked to the table and began searching through his pack for the hard leather pick. "I know I saw it in here just this ... ah, here it is!" He removed it triumphantly and walked back to take his place. The trio once again picked up their instruments.

Flynn lowered his flute, stricken by a sudden coughing fit.

"Perhaps you should go get a drink of water," the Master suggested dryly.

"Yes, sir," Flynn managed to sputter. "I'll just be a moment." He went to the table, poured himself a glass of water, drank a few sips from it, then returned to his seat. "I believe we're all ready now," he said, glancing at his colleagues. "We're very sorry for the delays."

"Oh, I doubt very much that any of you are the least bit sorry," the Master said evenly. "Now, then, if you're quite finished giving my apprentice the time he needed to avoid getting into trouble, let's see if the three of you can play well enough to avoid getting into it yourselves."

Kaelin glanced up in surprise, then gave the trio a grateful look as a murmur of amusement came from the three Bards sitting at the table.

"Yes, sir." Flynn raised his flute and gave the downbeat.

That evening, after his composition session with Niall, Kaelin brought his adjudication sheets to the Master. "I also added some more comments on the first trio during lunch," he said apologetically.

"Let's have a look at them." Bergid took the papers Kaelin handed to him and glanced over his comments on the first trio, then looked up and nodded. "Not bad, especially for a first attempt. You missed a few things, of course, but you listened well, even if it was from somewhere up in the clouds. A good commentary," he said approvingly. "Now, defend it."

"Defend it?" the apprentice echoed in surprise.

"Do you think my Bards will meekly accept whatever score I give them without analyzing every point of it? If my scoring does not match my comments, I'll have a line of Bards at my door pestering me with endless questions." He indicated one of the lines on Kaelin's sheet. "As an example, you wrote that the balance was off in the development section. What was off about it?"

Kaelin scrambled to remember. "Well, the pipes were too loud for the flute's melody to come through as well as it should have."

"And whose fault was this? The piper's or the flutist's?"

The apprentice frowned in thought. "Mostly the piper's."

"A significant lapse in balance, which this was, carries a penalty of five points. How many of them belong to the piper? How many to the flutist? What about the harpist?"

Kaelin's brow furrowed. "Three to the piper, two to the flutist," he decided. "None to the harpist."

"Why?"

"Because, although the piper should have been softer there, the flutist could have projected his tone better as well, since he had the melodic line. The flute fingering there is difficult, which caused the flutist to be too tentative. That's hardly the time for the piper to increase his own volume and nearly drown him out. The harpist did nothing to disturb the balance, so shouldn't be penalized."

The Master nodded in approval. "Then that is exactly what you should have written, and what I, in fact, did. The comment you made was not specific enough for the players to know why, if you were actually scoring this, you docked more points from the piper than you did the flutist, and none from the harpist. Make sure your ensemble comments very clearly explain your scoring by imagining reading them from the point of view of each player."

Kaelin nodded ruefully. "No wonder your hand is hurting, Master." He had noticed his Master rubbing a balm into his hand after dinner.

"And yours doesn't hurt as much as it should," the Master said sternly. "See what you can do to rectify that tomorrow."

"Yes, sir."

"Now, let's go through the rest of your comments, and then I'll explain the scoring system you'll be using for the solo performances."

They worked together until late that night. Finally, the Master's sheets were put safely away, to be distributed to the Bards in the morning, and Kaelin's sheets went to feed the fire. Soon he was leaning against his Master's knee as they looked into the flames together.

"You enjoyed my ensembles," the Master observed.

"Did you write all that music?" Kaelin asked in awe.

"It's the only way to ensure that no Bard taking the test has ever heard the complete ensemble before."

"I've never heard such wonderful music, especially the trios with everyone playing his primary instrument! It was like listening in on a musical conversation." Kaelin sighed, his eyes traveling to his flute, hanging in its travel bag on the wall.

"It won't be long before you can be part of the conversation yourself," the Master told him. He was not surprised when Kaelin made no response but pressed closer against him as though for comfort. Bergid rested his hand on the boy's head and sighed. The Spring Council was only ten weeks away. He thought of the cage Kaelin had created in his mind to keep his music safely walled away. That cage was gone, the music inside it freed. Yet the boy himself remained paralyzed, crippled like a kestrel whose broken wing forbade it the sky that was its birthright.

Solo testing on the remaining Bardic instruments was given on the final two days, with lute and lyre tested on the sixth day, pipes and kithara on the seventh. On the sixth morning, Kaelin sat next to his Master, looking curiously at the lutes that each Bard was tuning in preparation for their adjudicated solos. Each lutist would be expected to perform two solos of different styles from a list of acceptable solos for the level of playing they were attempting to pass. Kaelin knew, from the copies of the solos his Master had given him to study the night before, that four of the Bards were taking the intermediate test, two of them the advanced.

The lutes themselves were fascinating stringed instruments of differing sizes and shapes, made by each Bard to suit his own style of playing. All of them had a long, slender neck and a deep, pear-shaped sound chest with a hole above it that the strings were stretched across. Although his Master had explained that the neck could be either fretted or unfretted, all six of the Bards preferred fretted, as Kaelin thought he would himself for easier finger placement. The strings were attached to pegs at the end of the neck that could be turned to tighten or loosen the tension of the strings, thus changing their pitch. The strings themselves were arranged in groups of two, called "courses." Kaelin could see that the four intermediate lutists had lutes with six courses, a total of eleven strings, since the highest string was not paired. The two advanced lutists had added two more courses to their lutes, giving them fifteen strings that were positioned closer together over the hole. Each course was customarily tuned to the same pitch, but they could also be tuned in octaves.

Kaelin stirred himself from his study of the lutes as Master Bergid asked Niall to play first. The Bard came forward, bowed to the Master, then sat down and began to play without stand or music, for all solos must be memorized. Niall played a lullaby for his first solo, beautifully suited to the soft instrument, then launched into a lively dance, using a plectrum to pluck the strings. Kaelin wrote quickly, mindful of his Master's advice from the night before. According to his scoring, the Bard had easily passed the test for form six. He wondered what score his Master had given and looked forward to an evening spent comparing and discussing his own work as a fledgling adjudicator.

As the Bard stood and bowed to the enthusiastic clapping from his colleagues, the Master looked up. "I asked you to go first, Niall, so you can now go to the practice room and retake your theory test."

The Bard was too stunned to speak.

"You're welcome," the Master said dryly. "I'm giving you this second chance because Kaelin has assured me that you can pass it. I trust you will live up to his assessment."

"I'll do my best ... thank you, Master Bergid!" Niall quickly put his instrument away, then took the theory test from the Master and left. He gave Kaelin a grateful glance as he passed, and the apprentice grinned encouragingly.

The rest of the morning passed quickly, Kaelin too busy writing to notice anything more than the music and his increasingly aching hand. When the performances were finished, he felt that all the Bards had passed their test, Bran by a slim margin, and that the two advanced lutists, Flynn and Gryndl, had done exceptionally well. He was grateful when his Master excused him from helping with lunch and brought him some balm to rub into his hand. When lunch was ready, it was time to get Niall, and the Bard handed over his test with nervous relief.

The Master scored it himself and handed it to the Bard as they sat down to eat. "Quite an improvement," he said with a smile. "You not only passed it, you did so with an excellent score. You have my congratulations ... and my permission to retake the composition test tomorrow during the testing on pipes, which you are not required to take as a level ten piper."

Niall looked at his score with delight as his colleagues on either side of him enthusiastically pounded his back. "Thank you, Master Bergid! I'll gladly retake the composition test, but I think I'll pass your congratulations over to the one who deserves them more than I." He looked at the apprentice. "Thank you, Kaelin," he said with heartfelt sincerity. "I am deeply in your debt."

"Not for long, sir," Kaelin replied with a grin as he dipped a roll in his chowder. "I'm looking forward to collecting on your promise to play me a song after tomorrow's testing is over."

The Bard laughed. "So am I!"

After lunch, testing on the lyre began in the same manner. Kaelin saw that, as with the lutes, each lyre was slightly different. An ancient instrument, the lyre had a hollow sound chest, usually made of tortoise shell, that rested on the lyrist's lap in the same way a lap harp did. A crossbar over the top of the shell made the bridge, which transmitted the vibration of the strings. Extending from the ends of the sound chest were two raised hollow arms that curved both outward and forward. These were connected near the top by a second crossbar. The strings, made of sheep gut, were affixed to both crossbars, and since their lengths did not vary much, different thicknesses produced the different pitches. With no fingerboard, the plectrum came into constant use. It was held in the right hand to pluck the strings, and when not in use, it hung from the lyre by a thin cord. The fingers of the left hand were used primarily to silence the strings. His Master had told Kaelin that in Eire, lyres had but four strings, tuned to create a tetrachord, a series of four tones filling in the interval of a perfect fourth. Those used in the Bardic Isles doubled the tetrachord, giving the lyrist eight strings to use.

This time it was Tyrian who played first, two lilting pieces well suited to the graceful instrument. Kaelin, busily making detailed comments, briefly wondered if the limited range of the lute, lyre, and kithara was the reason all six of these Bards had chosen harp, flute, or pipes as their primary instruments. He filed the question away to ask his Master later and focused on critiquing. Despite its limitations, the lyre music was pleasant, and he enjoyed the rest of the afternoon, though his hand did not. The salve helped ease it, and that evening, after his last composition session with Niall, his Master reviewed Kaelin's adjudication sheets and smiled.

"Much better! Very good comments, and detailed enough to support the scoring you gave. Once you learn to play the lute and lyre yourself, you'll be able to critique the technique as well."

"Is my scoring anywhere close to your own, Master?" the apprentice asked curiously.

"In each category that you scored, you were never more than five points different, a very good beginning."

"And if the other Masters had scored them?"

"We would all have been within a point of each other. We hold joint adjudications once a cycle, with Bards selected by lottery performing in the Council Grounds, a coveted place to play. This gives the Bards an opportunity to earn a critique from all five Masters. It also serves to keep our scoring in line with each other, so a Bard who thinks he's done well under one Master doesn't suddenly find his scoring ten points lower under another."

The apprentice nodded thoughtfully. "I always thought Bards were done with all that."

"Done with all what?"

"With being tested. I figured they were already amazing on their instruments and just went around playing for everyone, like you did when you visited the mountain villages."

"Just went around playing—" Bergid shook his head. "Instrumental excellence is not the only thing Bards need to master, nor is playing for others the only thing they do. They work with all of the councils, lending aid from our Order and collecting tributes when it does not strain the resources of any given area to do so. They see to it that every town and village has at least one Healer in residence, and they must know enough of the healing arts themselves to aid that Healer when needed. They make sure that youngsters with musical promise are given the chance to study under a Bardic teacher. If the family can't afford the lessons, the Master of that island subsidizes them from funds set aside for that purpose." He smiled at the surprised expression on his apprentice's face.

"You would have discovered this for yourself," the Master told him, "had you revealed your ability to a Bard." He continued without waiting for Kaelin to reply. "They must also mediate disputes between all the guilds. If that mediation is not successful, they refer the matter to me for arbitration. So you see, the rigorous testing they're being given in so many diverse subjects is necessary, and all of that knowledge is actively used."

It was a moment before Kaelin found his voice. "I didn't realize how much they have to do. It's a wonder they have any time left to practice. They must have less free time than I do!"

The Master chuckled. "Perhaps that explains why there are many Bards who have not yet reached the level my apprentice has on his flute. But that doesn't mean they should stop progressing, just because they're busy. Becoming a Bard requires a commitment to learning that doesn't end with becoming a Bard or Master."

Kaelin's eyes widened. "Masters take tests?"

The Master smiled. "Not those given to them by anyone else, no. But they constantly test themselves, increase their own level of playing, challenge themselves to become better than they were the day before. You may have graduated from school over a cycle early, but you will never graduate from learning. The day that you do, you will stop becoming all that you can and should be."

Kaelin nodded, and for a few moments the two of them were silent, watching the flames. "So that's why you play every night?" the apprentice asked. "To increase your own skills?"

The Master nodded. "And to instruct you. But more than either of those reasons, I do so for the love of it, for what is the point of learning to play music otherwise?"

"What do you love about it most?" Kaelin ventured to ask.

"Our instruments," the Master said thoughtfully, "are more than their components. We carefully craft them out of wood, strings, pegs, keys, rods ... but when we're done and take them in our hands to play them, they become far more than the sum of all their parts. They become our voice, intimately connected to the essence of who we are. A voice that can translate the truth of our feelings, our innermost emotions. A voice that can say more than we could ever say in words alone. And that," the Master said quietly, "is what I love most about music."

Kaelin was silent, absorbing the truth of what his Master had said.

Bergid chuckled softly. "What are you wondering about now, lad?"

"I was just wondering if you love playing because you became good at it, or if you became good at it because you love it."

"Can't both be true?"

"I guess they can."

The Master gestured toward his instruments hanging on their pedestals around his desk. "Then perhaps you should take whatever love you have for my pipes and go practice, so you can love them all the more!"

Chapter 13

As though in celebration, the last day of Bardic testing on Kestrel dawned clear and bright, the sun managing for once to defeat the morning mist rolling in from the bay. The Bards trooped into the Master's home armed with kitharas, pipes, and broad smiles for "their" apprentice. They settled themselves into their accustomed places in the ensemble room and testing on the kithara began.

Kaelin was fascinated by the instrument and found himself longing to play it. The kithara was closely related to the lyre, though it was larger and had more strings. The player, called a kitharode, played with his right elbow outstretched and his palm bent inwards, his right hand firmly plucking the strings with a leather plectrum. His left hand was used to dampen the strings. Kaelin, surreptitiously trying the position out on his lap, frowned slightly, hoping it wouldn't feel so awkward once his hands grew larger. He noticed some of the Bards were using kitharas of seven strings, while others were using kitharas of twelve strings, like his Master's.

The morning testing flew by quickly, and at lunch Master Bergid found himself watching his apprentice with satisfaction, noting the way he now participated in the conversation without having to be cajoled into doing so. Just as satisfying to the Master was the way his Bards treated Kaelin like their collective younger brother. *The more Bards on his side, the better. There are bound to be many at the Spring Council who will not be pleased to find an apprentice in their midst, much less one attached to a Master.* He glanced at Niall. "If you're done eating, you may pick up the composition test on my desk and take it to the practice room to complete. I'll send Kaelin to get you when the time is up."

The afternoon passed pleasantly, with five Bards performing two pieces each on the pipes. When everyone was finished playing, the Master began reviewing Kaelin's scoring and told him to fetch Niall. The Bard came out looking slightly dazed.

"Please score Niall's test for me, Kaelin, while I finish these," the Master said. "It will save us time."

"Yes, sir." Kaelin sat down and went carefully over the test, aware that the Bard was anxiously watching every movement he made with his quill. When he was finished, he handed it to his Master, who glanced up. "Niall, do you wish me to review the test Kaelin just scored?"

The Bard shook his head. "No, sir, I'm perfectly confident in Kaelin's abilities to score it well."

The Master nodded. "Then I will look it over only because I did so with everyone else's." When he was finished, he stood, picked up the kithara adjudication sheets and passed them out. "Congratulations to all of you," he said warmly, "for passing your level of testing. And to you as well, Kaelin, for the comments you made are quite in line with my own." He suppressed a smile as the Bards turned approving glances Kaelin's way, as proud as if they had molded the apprentice themselves. Then the Master went to collect the adjudication sheets for the testing on pipes.

"Once again, congratulations are in order," he said as he passed them out. "Although two of you could improve these scores, you all passed your levels. And Kaelin's scores came within two points of my own on two of these tests, one point on two others, and a match on one. Therefore, although his scoring does not count in any way, I am giving you his adjudication sheet as well, for I think you will find it enlightening to have comments other than my own from someone who, young though he is, is already a level five piper and a good adjudicator, and will one day be an excellent one."

The grins that were turned upon Kaelin were broad this time, and he flushed slightly at his Master's praise. Then Master Bergid handed Niall his test. "And the highest congratulations of all goes to you," the Master said, "for converting a dismally failing grade to an excellent score on your intermediate composition test, a score that precisely matched what I would have given it. Well done."

The Bard's face lit with pleasure as his colleagues enthusiastically applauded. Then Niall fixed a stern gaze upon Kaelin. "On your feet, apprentice, and come over here to take what you deserve," he ordered.

The surprised apprentice quickly stood and walked over to the Bard, who rose and enveloped him in a bear hug that left him gasping for breath. The Bards laughed and clapped even harder.

At last Niall released him and reseated himself with a groan of mock despair. "Now I'm doubly in debt to an apprentice," he moaned.

Kaelin grinned as he returned to his own seat. "An easy matter to fix, sir."

"How so?"

"You can play me *two* songs!" Everyone laughed.

"Two songs it is," Niall promised.

The Master cleared his throat. "Now, we'll proceed to my decision regarding releasing each of you for rotation this cycle." The room fell suddenly silent. "Flynn, you have served well on all five islands and are eligible to become a Master when an opening arises. Because of your excellent service on my island during this rotation, I would like to offer you my assistance in obtaining your new posting. Where would you like to serve next?"

At this unprecedented offer, wide eyes turned to Flynn, who

looked speechlessly at the Master for a moment. "That's a generous offer, sir," he said at last. "Unless you object to a back-to-back rotation, I would like to remain here and serve your island again."

"You are always welcome on my island," Master Bergid said warmly. "Your first assignment, then, will be to remain here on Kestrel when I leave for the Spring Council. During my absence, you will stay here in my home and function as Kestrel's interim Master. I'm sorry you'll miss seeing your colleagues on Elegy this time around, but I think you'll find the experience here invaluable. And it will count heavily in your favor when the time comes for a new Master to be selected."

Flynn's face split into a pleased grin. "I'll be more than happy to stay here for you, sir."

The Master nodded and turned his attention to the others. "The rest of you," he said with a smile, "will be happy to learn that you will all be released as well."

Smiles and pleased exclamations circulated as the Bards turned to congratulate each other. "An excellent first group this cycle, I must say," the Master continued. "I do not remember a single other group of six Bards who have all been released together. Congratulations." Bergid turned to the one Bard who wasn't smiling, who had offered his congratulations with considerably less enthusiasm than the others, and asked the same question he had asked one week before.

"Is there something wrong, Niall?"

The Bard smiled ruefully and gave the same answer, though in a far different tone of voice. "Well ... yes, sir, there is."

"Are you unhappy with my decision to release you?"

Niall shook his head. "After failing two of your tests and questioning your judgement, I had no reason to expect you to release me, and it would be the height of ingratitude to be upset that you have. But I would refuse it and serve here again if you would allow me to."

Complete silence fell, to the accompaniment of five pairs of astonished eyes. To refuse a Master's release for rotation was unheard of.

One of the Master's brows lifted. "On what grounds?"

The Bard studied the table for a long moment, then raised his head and looked directly at the Master. "I joined the Bardic Order because I was obsessed with music," he said. "I would think up a simple phrase, then spend hours changing it, counting up how many different ways those same notes could be played, and yet still sound like the phrase they came from. Then I'd think up another one and begin again. When I joined the Bardic Order I never mentioned this to anyone, because I thought no one would understand such a strange compulsion to *re*compose music, to rearrange the notes in a way that didn't destroy the original theme. I was happy to be assigned here for my second rotation because I thought that if anyone would understand, it would be the Master of Composition. But then I couldn't bring myself to tell you, because ... well, if *you* looked at me like I was crazy—" he broke off, unable to continue. No one spoke.

"Then maybe I was," Niall said at last. "I know now I should have come to you right away, but I let my own fear stop me. Even worse, I stopped trying, didn't ask for help, told myself I didn't care ... tried to make myself believe that becoming an arranger was just a foolish dream." He glanced at Kaelin. "Then your apprentice came along, and in our very first session, when he saw what I was doing, he told me what I should have realized all along."

"Which was?" the Master asked quietly.

"He told me that what I love doing isn't a useless obsession. He said it's a skill any good arranger needs to have, and that refusing to develop it would only drive me truly crazy. And, as young as he is, I knew that he spoke from his own experience, that he knew exactly what it was like to want something you were certain you couldn't have." The Bard paused for a moment and swallowed hard before continuing.

"So, this week I did the best I possibly could. Not just to pass the tests, but to find out if what he told me was true, that I could develop the skills to be good at doing what I've always wanted to do." He touched the test papers in front of him. "This score tells me he was. I know what everyone expects me to become—and I love my pipes—but what I really want is to become an arranger. I would like the chance to find out if I have the potential to become a good one before I'm rotated to the other three islands with little chance of returning here for at least nine cycles. For there is no better Master to learn such skills from than you." The Bard fell silent.

"And if I tell you that you must rotate, regardless?" the Master asked.

The Bard did not hesitate. "Then I'll obey you without question, knowing that you have good reason for it, and do my best to develop my compositional skills elsewhere until you allow me to return."

The Master abruptly turned his attention to his apprentice. "Kaelin, do you agree with Niall's opinion that he could be good at arranging?"

The apprentice stood. "No, sir." The Bard's eyes flew to Kaelin in hurt surprise, but the apprentice kept his eyes on his Master and continued. "Not just good. I'm convinced that Bard Niall could become the best arranger the Bardic Isles has ever seen."

Of all the surprised looks trained on the apprentice, none was more surprised than Niall's.

"Is that so?" the Master asked expressionlessly.

"With the exception of yourself, of course, Master," Kaelin amended, coloring slightly.

The Master chuckled. "And on what do you base this assessment of his potential?"

"One of the reasons Bard Niall didn't score well on his composition test is because he can't help but hear dozens of ways—

excellent ways—to write the same phrase, which slowed him down. Fixing his problems with theory first, then helping him realize that he must, in testing, maintain his focus on the first phrase he thinks of, gave him ample time to complete his theme, develop it, and add dynamics and articulation, none of which required any help from me. He could have passed both those tests after only one session."

"Why, then, didn't you tell him so and stop the sessions, saving you both a great deal of time?"

"To give him practice with his new theory skills, and because the higher his score, the more he would believe in his own ability. And someone with such talent," and the apprentice turned his gaze for the first time to Niall, "needs to believe in it, for how else can it be developed?"

For a moment, Bard and apprentice gazed at each other, then Niall looked at the Master with renewed hope.

"If you remain here," the Master warned, "I will work you as hard as I have my apprentice."

"Yes, sir!" the Bard replied, oblivious of the sympathetic look Kaelin gave him, or the smiles this elicited from his colleagues.

"You've convinced Kaelin of your ability; now you will need to convince me of your commitment. I will give you no more than a half cycle to pass the advanced theory *and* composition tests."

Niall's eyes were not the only ones to widen at this. "I'll pass them, sir," he said determinedly.

"If you do not, or you give me any reason to believe that you are not serious about your commitment and doing everything in your power to make your dream a reality, I will make arrangements for Master Talan to take you back for the remainder of the rotation. Nor will you return here until you have completed your rotations on the other three islands, which means it will be a minimum of twelve cycles from now before you have a chance to convince me again."

"Yes, sir," the Bard replied in a hushed tone.

"You will study the advanced forms of composition under Flynn until after the Spring Council, and then from my apprentice when I'm not available."

"Gladly, sir!"

"Then I rescind your release," the Master said in a gentler tone, "though you will still be credited with having completed your rotation here. Your rotation with me this time will be under very different terms, for you will not rotate amongst the other territories, but remain here in Kyet while you complete the advanced composition and theory forms. If you do well, you will stay here for the rest of your rotation, studying under me. I will expect to hear a good report of you from Flynn when I return from the Spring Council, for your half cycle to complete those forms begins now."

"Yes, sir. Thank you, Master Bergid!"

The Master nodded. "Very well, then, you and Flynn will stay here in Kyet, the other four of you will go to the Spring Council and rotate to your next island." This time all six Bards looked pleased. "Now then," the Master said, "whoever wishes to leave may do so. The rest of us are going to sit back and enjoy a sterling performance of two songs for pipes, from a Bard who completed all ten forms of that instrument before becoming a Piper."

Five Bards leaned comfortably back in their chairs.

Niall reached for his pipes. "Not just two songs," he said, his eyes resting on Kaelin. "I believe our apprentice has earned himself *three* songs ... and any more he may ever ask of me."

That evening, Kaelin rested comfortably against his Master's knee, almost drowsing as he looked into the hypnotic flames of the fire. "That was an amazing performance," he murmured.

"Yes," his Master agreed. "Niall has a true gift for the pipes. He could easily attain the status of Master Piper of the Bardic Isles if he chose to apply to the Council for it after gaining Master eligibility, which is what we all expected him to do. If the Council's vote in his favor was unanimous, he would gain the title, even without an island of his own, and would devote himself primarily to that instrument, the way Master Marek does to his flute and Master Grened to his Harp. He would also have the responsibility of testing all Bards on that instrument during rotation cycles."

Kaelin sat up in surprise. "You mean, Bard Niall is the best Piper in all the Bardic Isles, and he doesn't care?"

"Oh, he cares, but if his pipes were what he loved most, he would have leapt at the opportunity to rotate to his third island, on his way to becoming our Master Piper. Niall has decided that his dream of becoming an arranger is something he wants more." He glanced keenly at his apprentice. "Sometimes a person with a natural talent finds that it's almost too easy to pursue it and chooses instead to dream of something that seems out of reach, something that will take every ounce of his will and determination to attain. Niall's dream was never truly out of his reach, for all he needed to do was approach me. He let his own fear of rejection, and perhaps a fear of disappointing our expectations of him, place it out of reach. And I was so certain he would pursue his love of pipes that I didn't realize how torn he was and how that conflict was affecting his progress. It took my apprentice to see it clearly."

Kaelin was silent for a moment, thinking. "The morning you came to Vale," he said at last, "I was on my way to Craftmaster Arnor's workshop to accept his offer of an apprenticeship four cycles earlier than usual." He bit his lip, remembering. "I didn't want to, but Laena had to work so hard to provide for us." He shrugged. "And it's not like I didn't enjoy working with wood. It came easily to me, like I guess playing the pipes does to Bard Niall, but it just ... wasn't what I truly wanted. Then I heard you play my music in the village square, and I knew you were my one chance to go after what I wanted more than anything else, something I thought was impossible. So, I followed you." He paused, thinking of the Bard who could play the pipes better than anyone.

"I didn't know about Bard Niall being torn between two choices like that," the apprentice said at last. "But I saw how his face lit up when he thought of a theme, how he couldn't stop himself from changing it over and over. I could see how good he could be at arranging, and how he had convinced himself it couldn't happen. I remembered what it felt like to be convinced I could never become a Bardic apprentice, and I just ... gave him the chance to talk about it. I think he was able to because, well, an apprentice isn't nearly as intimidating as a Master is."

Bergid suppressed a smile. "Is that so?"

"Yes, sir," his apprentice assured him.

They sat in comfortable silence for a while, watching the fire. "You never told me I was in competition with the Woodcarving Craftmaster of Vale," the Master said dryly.

Kaelin smiled up at him. "It wasn't much of a competition, but I'm glad you were, because if I hadn't decided to accept his offer, I wouldn't have seen you in the square. I'd have missed my chance."

The Master shook his head. "I would not have left Vale until I found you."

"Truly, sir?"

"Truly."

Kaelin smiled and leaned his head back against his Master's knee, thinking that his variation of the kestrel's song must have been better than he'd thought, to have captured the Master's interest so strongly. He watched the flickering flames, trying not to think of the six new Bards who would appear at the door the following morning and view him with surprise and distrust. He felt his Master's hand suddenly rest on his shoulder.

"Don't worry about tomorrow," the Master told his apprentice gently. "I'm sure you'll have all six of them thinking of you as their very own personal apprentice before the week is half over, just as the first six did."

"You're getting awfully good at reading my mind," Kaelin grumbled, "if all you have to do is look at the top of my head." He frowned, firmly steering his thoughts away from what his Master must never know ... just in case.

Bergid chuckled. "Be that as it may, I'm quite aware that you've had a difficult week of it, not only dealing with six Bards you've never met, but a Master who hasn't cut you any slack."

Kaelin stared into the flames of the fire for a moment. "I don't want you to," he said at last.

"I know. That's why I haven't."

Kaelin smiled and leaned even closer. "I love you, sir," he said under his breath.

The Master gave no indication he had heard, but the hand on the apprentice's shoulder tightened for a moment before it was removed.

The following morning, Kaelin opened the front door, smiled at six astounded Bards, and bowed. "Bards Dugal, Marran, Connan, Ruairi, Donn, and Veryn," he said deferentially, looking each Bard in the eye as he named him. "My name is Kaelin. Welcome, sirs, and please come in."

For a moment, no one moved. Then Dugal softly chuckled. "By the Maker," he said. "Even if Master Bergid told you all our names, how could you possibly know which of us is which?"

"I asked my Master to describe you," Kaelin said simply.

"Your ... Master?" the Bard echoed faintly. "Well, then, thank you for your welcome, Kaelin." One by one, each Bard nodded at him as they entered, mixed expressions on their faces, amazement foremost on each.

Here we go again. Kaelin squared his shoulders and quietly closed the door.

Chapter 14

Three weeks later, Kaelin closed the door on the last group of Bards to finish their testing, wondering at his conflicting emotions. It was good to once again have his Master to himself, but he was going to miss the Bards, too, or at least most of them. There were two he would not miss, one from the third week, the other from the fourth. Both were older Bards, but unlike the easy-going Flynn, they proved staunchly resistant to the outrageous idea of a Master having an apprentice at his side. Nor had discovering how advanced the apprentice was in composition, theory, pipes, harp, and above all, flute, done anything to soften their attitude. They had kept their opinions to themselves, but made them known nevertheless, in subtle ways that the apprentice was in no way oblivious to. Kaelin took care to treat them with the utmost deference, not daring to take the liberty of speaking without being spoken to, much less bantering with them the way he had become accustomed to doing with the others. If all he got for his efforts was a thin veneer of tolerance, he'd take it and count himself fortunate. He wondered uneasily how many Bards attending the Spring Council on Elegy would feel similarly. The apprentice shook off his misgivings as his Master spoke from his favorite chair by the fire.

"I believe the two of us are in need of a vacation."

Kaelin's expression brightened as he went to sit on the floor in front of his Master. "I've never had one," he said eagerly, "though I've heard of them. What does one do on a vacation?"

"Whatever one wants to," the Master replied. "That's the whole point ... or so I've been told. I've never actually had one, either."

"Then you're *way* overdue, Master," Kaelin admonished him. "You should take a vacation every month for the next three or four cycles until you're all caught up."

"Impudent apprentice," his Master growled. "I'd have you fetch my switches—I'm sure they're around here somewhere—but unfortunately my hand is too sore to put them to use."

Kaelin laughed and went to get the salve. When the Master thanked him and reached for it, though, the apprentice shook his head. "Let me do it for you." He took the Master's hand and gently rubbed the salve into it. The Master sighed in relief and closed his eyes.

"What would you do on your vacation?" Kaelin asked curiously.

"Anything that doesn't involve the use of my right hand sounds good to me," the Master replied without opening his eyes. "Visit a friend, perhaps. I haven't seen Rassek for nearly a cycle, and heaven knows I'd better bring you to see him before he gets wind that his 'gift' arrived, and I didn't tell him. And since there's no school tomorrow, his son won't be equally upset with me for bringing you when he isn't there. The last time the two of them ganged up on me, I wound up with an apprentice, and," the Master said with comic dismay, "one of those is quite enough."

Kaelin chuckled. "How long a vacation should we take?"

"I'm thinking a full two days," the Master said expansively. "One day doing whatever *I* wish to do, and one day doing whatever *you* wish to do. How does that sound?"

"Completely unfair, sir," Kaelin said disapprovingly. He shook his head at the brows lifted in his direction. "An apprentice's vacation should not be the same length as a Master's," he said sagely.

The corners of the Master's mouth twitched. "Is that so? Well, then, as an expert in the Bardic hierarchy, how much longer do you think a Master's ought to be?"

Kaelin cocked his head, considering the matter. "A Master's rank is five levels higher than an apprentice's," he said decisively, "so your vacation should be five times longer than mine."

"Hmm ... sounds like an extravagantly long time." Bergid sighed heavily. "But you make a compelling case. Five days for me, then, and one for you. I'll send a note to Flynn first thing in the morning, instructing him to handle my affairs for the next six days."

Kaelin nodded in satisfaction and began to rub salve into his own sore hand. To his surprise, the Master took his hand in his own, waving away his apprentice's objection.

"It feels much better when someone else does it for you," the Master said, gently rubbing the salve in. "We'll start off tomorrow by visiting Rassek. The next day, we'll do some shopping. You start thinking about what you'd like to do the day after that, then the last three days will be mine. For all six days, no lessons, no assignments, no work that isn't strictly necessary. And," he added with a decisive nod at his flabbergasted apprentice, "since we're being recklessly extravagant, we'll take our meals at the inn!"

The next morning, the two of them enjoyed a leisurely breakfast at Gannet's Inn, then headed for Rassek's holding. Though it had rained heavily the previous night, the spring morning was clear, with only a few wisps of fog shrouding the harbor. Blossoming crab apple trees and gorse shrubs dotted the hillsides with pink and yellow. Scattered stands of aspens seemed to converse, the wind teasing rhythmic music from their rustling leaves. The Master lifted his walking staff and pointed out the spit of land jutting out some distance east of the harbor.

"That's Rassek's holding," Bergid told his apprentice. "A bit of a walk, but a scenic one, with the bay on one side and the hills on the other. I rarely get to see it, for I generally make my visits in the evenings." They took their time, talking and laughing as they walked. If it weren't for the difference in scenery and the absence of Poor Oran, Kaelin could easily believe he had been transported back in time to when he and his Master had traveled together across the length of Kestrel.

They soon approached the house and could see the Holder out in his fields, plowing furrows into the moist earth behind a sturdy plow horse. Before they could call out, a young boy working in the garden near the house leapt to his feet with a glad cry.

"Master Bergid!" The boy stared speechlessly at Kaelin for a moment, then appeared to lose his mind, racing toward the fields as though in pursuit of his own wits, and yelling at the top of his lungs.

"Father! Father, look! The Master's here, and he has our *gift* with him. Our wish came true!"

The Master shook his head and followed the crazed boy. "Come along, lad," he said to Kaelin in a resigned voice. "We might as well get this over with."

The Holder reined in his horse and went to meet his ecstatic son. "Well, now, didn't I tell you that, with both of us wishing for the same thing, it was bound to come true?" He clapped his son's shoulder, then strode to the Master with a broad smile. The two clasped arms.

"Good to see you again, my friend! It's been a long time."

"I've been ... away."

"So I've heard. And no one seemed to know where."

Bergid shrugged innocently. "It's hardly *my* fault you neglected to have your gift sent to my home. I had to trudge the length of Kestrel to pick him up myself."

The Holder chuckled. His son was gazing at Kaelin as if the apprentice had appeared by magic and might disappear at any moment.

"*Look*, Father!" the boy exclaimed. "Everything we wished for came true! He's about three cycles older than me, and he has a Bardic apprentice robe and everything. And his eyes are the most amazing color ... and we didn't even wish for that!" Rassek briefly looked Kaelin over, then exchanged a glance with his son, and they both burst out laughing.

The Master sighed. "I *told* you he'd be insufferable, didn't I?" he demanded of Kaelin.

"Yes, sir," the apprentice said with a grin. "That's by far the most insufferable laughter I've ever heard."

"Exactly," agreed the Master sourly, as the laughter continued. "And he's infected his son as well. Perhaps we ought to fetch a Healer, one who's good at treating *mental* ailments."

Kaelin stifled a laugh. His Master favored him with a glare, and the apprentice began laughing too, the Master silently glowering at them all. Then the corners of the Master's mouth began to twitch, a laugh escaped all his efforts to silence it, and suddenly all four of them were laughing helplessly at the edge of the partially plowed field. The horse turned his head in their direction and shook his mane in equine bafflement.

"Let's go inside," the Holder finally managed to gasp. "Unhitch Feathers, son, and take him to the barn for me. I couldn't lead him in a straight line right now to save my life, and this is a story I must hear immediately. The fields will still be here tomorrow."

"Don't tell it without *me*, Master Bergid!" The boy ran to do as he was told.

"Feathers?" Kaelin asked, looking skeptically at the stolid creature.

Rassek snorted as they began walking toward the house. "As

if I would name a plow horse!" he said, rolling his eyes. My son insisted on naming him after the horse helped me bring a Healer here in time to save his life. Claims the markings across his shoulders look like feathers and that's why he was able to gallop so fast for a plow horse. My frantic whacking of him apparently had nothing to do with it," he added dryly.

Once inside, the Holder brought his guests a tall pitcher of cool honeyed tea and a platter of little cakes, explaining somewhat defensively that he had baked them for "yet another one of the Schoolmaster's infernal meetings." The Master promptly choked on his tea. He recovered to find the Holder glaring at him.

"I very much doubt," the Master said mildly, "that Stevyn would have asked for your help with *that*. His one culinary pleasure is making little cakes for his meetings. Indeed, one might think the meetings were just an excuse to bake cakes." The Master suppressed a chuckle as the Holder continued to scowl at him. "However, I'm sure your *son* enjoys them."

At that moment, the Holder's son rushed in and began firing questions at the Master.

"Hold on!" the Master said, laughing as he raised both hands to stop him. "I think the two of you should be properly introduced to my apprentice first. This is Kaelin. Kaelin, this is Holder Rassek, an incorrigible friend of mine, and this is his son, Sean."

Kaelin stood and bowed to the Holder. "It's good to meet you, Holder Rassek, and you, Sean. I understand that I'm in your debt."

The Holder raised a brow at Bergid. "You told him?"

"Not the whole story. Just the fact that we ... traded wishes."

Rassek chuckled. "We certainly did." He gave the apprentice an appraising look. "I'm sure my son will enjoy telling you the whole story later on. It's a pleasure to meet you as well, Kaelin, but there's no need for such formality here."

"You're my elder, sir, and the friend of my Master."

"Well, then, since I'm guilty on both counts, I'll forgive you for it this once," the Holder said. "Just don't let it happen again."

Kaelin grinned and sat back down. "Yes, sir."

"Now can we hear the story, Master Bergid?" Sean asked eagerly. "I want to know how you found your gift!"

The Master chuckled and set down his tea. "I'll happily tell you the whole tale. But no interruptions! You can pepper me with questions afterwards if I don't do it justice." He glanced at Kaelin and began telling their rapt audience of two how he had heard the music of a small flute deep in the mountains of Kestrel. When at last he reached the clearing, there was no one there, so he went to the nearby village of Vale the next morning and played the song he had heard. And the village boy who recognized his own music had followed him afterwards with nothing more than his flute, not even some food or a cloak to keep himself warm that night.

Kaelin watched Sean, who was listening with his mouth partially open and a look of wonder on his face, as though the Master were telling a story of magic ... a faery tale, perhaps, or a myth from times long past. Maybe, the apprentice thought, all tales had a basis in facts that only gained their magic with the telling. In reality, he thought ruefully, there was nothing even remotely magical about spending the night hungry and cold.

Sean gave a sigh of pleasure at the end of the tale. "Just think," he said in a hushed voice. "In all the woods of Kestrel, you passed by that exact spot just in time to hear Kaelin's flute." He turned to his father. "Our wish did that," he said proudly. "It brought the Master right where he needed to be, at exactly the time he needed to be there to get his gift! Just like the Master's wish brought you to the inn at exactly the time you needed to be there to get yours!" He beamed at Kaelin. "I'm a gift, too," he told him. "The Master gifted me to Holder Rassek, and now I'm his son. Did Master Bergid—"

"Make me his apprentice?" Kaelin deftly inserted. "Yes, he did."

"Oh ... well, I guess that's okay, then, if that's what you wanted most," the boy said doubtfully.

"Before you met Holder Rassek, what did you want more than anything?" Kaelin asked him.

"I wanted a father who would give me a name," Sean said without hesitation.

"And you became the Master's gift and the Holder's son. Before I met my Master, I wanted to be a Bardic apprentice more than anything."

Sean nodded and grinned at him. "And you became *our* gift and the Master's apprentice! It worked!"

"We both got what we wanted most, because someone else wished it for us," Kaelin agreed, then smoothly switched the subject. "You know what? My Master has a mule named Poor Oran. If you'll introduce me to Feathers, we can trade stories about how they got their names."

Sean jumped up, grabbed Kaelin's hand and happily pulled him outside.

"That's a remarkably courteous and perceptive boy you have there," Rassek observed.

The Master pulled his gaze away from the doorway. "Yes ... yes, he is."

"And you took him as apprentice to a Master, something that is against all Bardic tradition. Not that it's any of my business, but I can't help but wonder what the *other* Masters think of that."

"'We'll find out soon enough at the Spring Council next month." Bergid shrugged at his friend's raised brows. "My apprentice, without playing a single note, has managed to convince twenty-two of my twenty-four Bards that he belongs at my side," he said. "Four Masters shouldn't be too much trouble."

The Holder snorted. "Masters," he said dryly, "are nothing *but* trouble, present company included." He looked keenly at his chuckling friend. "What are you going to do if they won't let you keep him?"

The chuckles abruptly stopped. "No one is taking Kaelin from me," Bergid said flatly.

"Not even the Council of Masters?" When Bergid made no reply, Rassek continued expressionlessly. "Of course, if you took the boy as your—" Flashing blue eyes warned him to go no further. "Well," he quietly concluded, "they could hardly take him away from you then." He nodded toward the open door. "And that apprentice of yours would certainly not object to the idea. He clearly worships the ground you walk on ... in case you haven't noticed. And you clearly think the world of him ... in case you think *I* haven't noticed."

The Master brooded silently for several moments. "Perhaps they couldn't take him from me then," he finally allowed, "but they could take away his robe and rank. And Kaelin belongs *in* the Bardic Order, not out of it." He glared at the Holder as though Rassek had just insisted otherwise. "He has a Gift, Rassek ... a Gift that hasn't been seen since the exodus. I will fight for this boy's right to his robe and his Master!"

Rassek leaned back in his chair and studied his friend for a long moment. "I'd say he has more of a gift than that," he observed. "I do not doubt you will fight for the boy you love." He lifted a hand at the frown Bergid gave him. "Come, my friend, I can hardly fail to see it. I, more than most, know the look of one who cannot say those words to someone who needs to hear them."

"As my friend, then, leave it be."

"Really, Bergid? *You're* the one who forced the issue with me—in the public streets of Kyet, no less—and thank the Maker you did! Can't I do the same for you, in the privacy of my own home?" When Bergid's expression remained set, Rassek sighed. "Very well, my friend. I'll leave it be. For now."

In the barn, the two boys were laughing together, sharing every funny story they could remember about their respective guardians. Kaelin was enjoying himself more than he would have thought possible, unaware until that moment how much he missed having a friend, even if this one was nearly three cycles younger. For the first time since leaving Vale, he didn't have to be careful of what he said or how he said it to those of higher rank. He could relax and just have fun, something this carefree youngster was reminding him how to do. He glanced at the boy, who was standing on the second slat of the paddock's gate and reaching out to pat Feathers. It was good, Kaelin decided, to remember what it was like to be a normal boy, not one trying to fit into the world of Bards and Masters cycles before his time. He reached out to pat Feathers himself. He liked Sean's cheerful grin and forthright manner. Spending the day with him was a pleasure worthy of a vacation day, even if it was technically his Master's day, not his own. He removed his cord and robe, placed them on top of the butter churn, and decided to enjoy it.

The two of them had a grand time together for the rest of the morning, romping through the Holding and the surrounding woods. They were high up in an oak tree, their legs swinging in unison as they sat next to each other, when Kaelin gave in to his mounting curiosity.

"So," the apprentice said, "how did your father end up finding *his* gift?"

Sean grinned and began to tell his story, a series of events that held Kaelin as spellbound as Sean had been at the Master's tale.

"So, you see," Sean said at the story's conclusion, "if it weren't for Master Bergid's wish, I wouldn't have a father or a name, because only a father can give you one, and I didn't have one."

"Wouldn't Master Bergid have found you a new family?" Kaelin asked.

Sean frowned. "He did find me one, but I begged him not to make me go. If I couldn't be the Holder's son, I didn't want to be anyone's."

"I think I can understand that." Kaelin was silent for a moment, thinking of the Master he wouldn't trade for any father in the world. "I can't even imagine what it would be like not to have a name, but I sure like the one your father gave you."

The youngster's face lit up. "I like it, too, though search me why he gave me a name that means 'wise one.'" He shrugged. "Maybe he's hoping it'll rub off. C'mon, let's climb back down. I've got a lot more to show you!"

By the time the sun had passed its zenith, they ended up where they'd begun, clinging to the paddock gate and petting the placid plow horse once again.

"You're afraid, aren't you?" the younger boy said, the question apparently popping into his head from nowhere.

"Of Feathers?" Kaelin asked in surprise.

Sean laughed. "Of course not!" He gave the horse a final pat, then turned and cocked his head at Kaelin. "You're afraid of losing your Master."

Kaelin stared at him, at a loss for words.

"It's okay," the youngster said with a shrug. "For a long time, I was afraid of losing the Holder, too. I guess that's why I can see it in your eyes. You look at him like you're memorizing his face in case you don't see it again. That's what I used to do, too." He jumped down from the paddock gate, and Kaelin stepped numbly down beside him. They regarded each other for a moment, like two friends recognizing each other after cycles of being separated.

"I don't know why you're worried the Master will send you away," Sean continued matter-of-factly, "and Father would tell me it's none of my business, either. But I've never seen the Master look at anyone the way he looks at you, so—" he shook his head. "I don't think you have anything to worry about. He's never going to send you away. He loves you."

Unexpected tears sprang to Kaelin's eyes, and he fought to keep them from spilling down his face.

Sean took no notice and hopped nimbly onto a bale of hay, perching there like a young sage. "Sometimes they can't say it—you know? Grown-ups are like that. My father couldn't say it for ever so long." He shrugged. "You just have to wait." He frowned disapprovingly toward the house as if he were cycles older than either of the men inside. "Eventually they figure it out."

Kaelin laughed, unable to help himself, and went to sit beside his friend. "I think your father gave you the perfect name," he said.

Sean rolled his eyes and changed the subject. "You told me about your sister. Do you have a brother, too?"

Kaelin shook his head.

"Me neither. I always wanted one, though."

"Me, too."

"Do you think the two of us might—" Sean twisted the hem of his tunic between his fingers. "I was just, well, wishing—" He fell silent.

"I was wishing the same thing."

"You were?" Sean looked up at him hopefully.

Kaelin nodded thoughtfully. "I'm not sure how we're supposed to do it, though, or even if anyone else ever has."

"We could be the first!" the youngster said eagerly, hopping down off the bale. "And we could do it the same way Master Bergid did for me and the Holder." He glanced at Kaelin's apprentice robe lying folded on the butter churn. "We could use your apprentice cord," he suggested helpfully.

At Kaelin's nod, Sean ran to fetch it. He stood next to Kaelin and held out his right hand. "Master Bergid tied my right hand to Father's left," he said, frowning, "but maybe we should use the same hands, left to left, since we're gonna need our right hands to wrap this cord around them."

"I suppose, since we're the first ones, we can do it any way we want to," Kaelin agreed.

"You should put your hand over mine, 'cuz you're older."

Kaelin obligingly laid his left hand over Sean's, then both of them maneuvered the black cord around their hands several times, binding them together. "Now what?"

"We speak vows with our own words," Sean said with certainty. "You want to go first?"

"Okay." Kaelin thought for a moment. "I take you for my brother," he said at last. "I'll never say or do anything to hurt you, and I'll always be there for you when you need me." He cocked his head. "Is that okay?"

Sean beamed at him. "It's perfect! Now it's my turn. I take you for my brother, too. I'll never say or do anything to hurt you, either, and I'll always be there for you when you need me." Then his face fell. "I forgot."

"Forgot what?"

"We're supposed to have a witness, and we need a Master to pronounce us brothers. I don't think Feathers counts as a witness, and we can't pronounce ourselves."

The two of them stared blankly at each other for a moment, and then a voice spoke unexpectedly from behind them. "You're in luck, then. You have an eligible witness *and* a Master." Both boys looked up, startled to see Master Bergid and Holder Rassek observing them from the door.

"But what you are doing," the Master continued sternly as he walked toward them, "requires permission first, which you have not yet asked for." He glanced at Sean, one brow raised. "Permission from your father," he said pointedly. He turned his attention to his apprentice and raised the other one. "And permission from your Master."

Kaelin bowed his head. "I'm sorry, sir ... I guess we didn't think it through. May I have your permission to take Sean as my brother?"

"Such an action cannot be undone," the Master gently warned. "Are you certain you wish to be bound as a brother to a boy you've only known for a few hours?"

"Yes, sir, I am." He glanced at Sean. "Even though we only met today, I feel as though I've *always* known him. I want to be his brother and have him as mine." He looked back at his Master. "If you'll permit it."

The Master held Kaelin's gaze for a long moment, then he nodded. "You have my permission." He suppressed a smile at the happiness that transformed Kaelin's face and turned gravely to Sean, who was listening to this exchange with wide eyes. "Well?" the Master said, glancing pointedly at the Holder.

Sean turned hopeful eyes to his father. "May I have your permission to take Kaelin as my brother, sir? Please?"

The Holder frowned slightly. "You've known Jared far longer, yet I don't recall you ever wishing *he* was your brother. Tell me why you want Kaelin to be."

"Jared's my friend ... a good friend, but it took time for that to happen. Kaelin is who I'd choose for my brother, and it didn't take much time because ... well, because he already *is*. Just like when Master Bergid wrapped the cord around our hands, he was just formal ... something." He frowned.

"Formalizing?"

"Yeah. He was formalizing something that was already true."

"I see. So, you're saying that you and Kaelin are brothers already, with or without the ceremony?"

"Yes, sir. Because we both wish it." Sean's eyes lit with joy when his father slowly nodded.

"Then you have my permission," the Holder said.

"Now," the Master said sternly, "before we proceed any further, you will both promise me that you will never again attempt to hold your own Bardic ceremony without first obtaining permission from your guardian and the consent of a Master. Bardic Law is quite particular about such things." He accepted their hasty nods.

"Well, then," the Master continued in a gentler voice, "you

both have permission, you've wrapped a Bardic apprentice cord around your hands, which I will accept in lieu of my own cord, and spoken vows in front of a witness. All that remains is for a Master to complete this ceremony." He placed his weathered hand over the youngster's bound ones.

"I hereby pronounce the two of you brothers," the Master said solemnly. "Though I unwrap this cord, the binding between you is permanent, for no one's hand can undo it, not even a Master's. You are brothers now, as truly as if you were born to the same parents. You must keep your vows to never say or do anything to hurt the other, and to always support each other as brothers do." So saying, the Master unwrapped the cord and handed it to Kaelin. The apprentice had barely taken it when he was knocked flat by his younger brother, who hugged him exuberantly.

Kaelin laughed. "Hey, little brother, didn't you hear Master Bergid? He said you must keep your vow not to hurt me!"

Sean sat up, glowing with pleasure. "Little brother ... I like that! C'mon, big brother, I'll take you to my secret hideout down on the beach. I've never even shown it to Jared! There's a cave there and the best flat rocks for skipping when the waves aren't too high. And I even found a huge ball made out of sea glass ... *you'll* see!" He raced off without waiting to see if Kaelin would follow.

The apprentice got to his feet and stood looking at his Master. "Thank you, sir," he murmured. Then he tossed his cord on top of his robe and ran after Sean, looking like any other young boy running after his little brother.

Master Bergid turned to find the Holder regarding him steadily. "That was kindly done," Rassek said.

"The two of them will be good for each other. However," Bergid added, "it looks like we'll be eating lunch alone."

"They'll be along soon enough when their stomachs start telling them what time it is." The Holder cleared his throat as they began walking back to the house. "Contrary to what you apparently believe, I am not ignorant of Bardic Law, my friend. I know perfectly well there *is* no Bardic ceremony for turning two youngsters into brothers. Kaelin, at least, will find that out sooner or later, and then what?"

Humor sparkled in the Master's eyes. "You, of all people, ought to know that what a Master binds together stays bound. As for Kaelin, my apprentice is no more ignorant of Bardic Law than you are."

Rassek halted in his steps. "He did that only for my son's benefit?"

"I think he did it as much for his own. And perhaps," Bergid added drolly, "I should see to it that the ceremony the two of them just invented *is* entered into Bardic Law. Why, just think! Even two consenting adults would be able to call themselves brothers, if they were so inclined."

The Holder looked suspiciously at the innocent look on his friend's face. "Not a chance," he growled, "and don't even *think* of using your sorcerous music to change my mind. I share my secret hideout with *no* one!"

Chapter 15

Their six days of vacation flew by quickly, far too quickly for Kaelin, who wished every day could be as wonderful. They had spent the entire first day at the Holder's, not returning until late that night. The second day had been spent in the marketplace of Kyet, where they had a pleasant time browsing and nibbling their way amongst the shops and stalls. The Master introduced his apprentice to several of the shopkeepers, including Craftmaster Lanek, the leather Craftmaster of Kyet. The Master bought Kaelin a new belt in the leather shop, the finest belt the boy had ever seen. It was sturdy yet supple, and carved into the leather were each of the seven Bardic instruments. The Master also bought his apprentice a new pair of boots, for Kaelin had worn his nearly to shreds, and the Craftmaster had been horrified beyond speech at first sight of them. Before the Master had a chance to order them, Lanek had swiftly set Craftsman Aidan to measuring Kaelin's feet for new boots and summarily instructed him to toss the old pair out. To Kaelin's astonishment, the Craftmaster then fixed the Master with a hard stare.

"If you think that I'll allow a member of the Bardic Order, however young he might be, to leave my shop in *those*, you are sorely mistaken!" he said, with a final scandalized glance at the boots in question, which his Craftsman was bearing out the back door like a pair of dead rats. "He'll leave in *new* boots, or he'll leave barefoot! Now, are you going to order them, or must I gift the boy a pair?"

Kaelin stared wide-eyed at the Craftmaster, half expecting a lightning bolt to incinerate him after such audacity to a Master, but Bergid only laughed. "Well, we can't have my apprentice ruining the reputation of the leather Craftmaster of Kyet, now, can we? Consider them ordered, Lanek. I'll be back in a little while."

"Your..." Lanek stared speechlessly at the Master as he left his shop, then turned to give Kaelin an appraising look. When Aidan reappeared, the Craftmaster waved him off impatiently, saying he would cobble the boots of the Master's apprentice himself. It wasn't long before Kaelin was walking out the door in the finest pair of boots he had ever seen, much less owned. His Master then took him to a clothing shop, where Kaelin was measured for new tunics and trousers, despite his objection that his Master was spending far too much coin on him.

"You're my apprentice, lad," his Master reminded him, "and it's my responsibility to see that you're properly clothed. I ought to have seen to it the moment we came to Kyet."

After arranging for their many packages to be delivered, they enjoyed a good supper down by the wharf, then headed home. "This wasn't a very good vacation day for *you*, sir," Kaelin said with a slight frown. "I wound up with a fine new wardrobe, new quills, a stack of my own manuscript paper, treats in the marketplace ... and you wound up with nothing!"

"On the contrary," the Master said with a smile, "I wound up with the memory of a wonderful day ... a day I spent doing exactly as I wished to, as per our agreement." A small hand inserted itself into his, and they walked on without speaking.

Kaelin decided to spend his vacation day taking the ferry across the Bronig and walking to Lynd to visit Laena and Donal.

The Master accompanied him and took his flute along, laughing off Kaelin's objection that playing for the villagers was work and should not be allowed while on vacation.

"This is your vacation day, lad, not mine," the Master reminded him, "and playing for the villagers will be a pleasure now that my hand has recovered." He glanced at his silently disapproving apprentice. "What do you have planned for *your* vacation evening, after we return?"

Kaelin's face lit up. "I'm going to use some of that manuscript paper you bought for me! I have three new compositions I can hardly wait to—"

"Now, now," the Master said, shaking his head in disapproval, "composing is clearly work, and strictly forbidden on vacation."

"But, *sir,* that's not work, that's—" he broke off at the amused expression on his Master's face. He sighed in defeat. "Play for the villagers of Lynd as long as you like, Master."

"Why, thank you."

They looked at each other and laughed.

On the morning of their fourth vacation day, the Master told Kaelin to pack up whatever he needed for the next couple of days. "I've been thinking of making a trip to visit Master Marek," he told his surprised apprentice, "and have arranged for you to stay with Holder Rassek. I'll meet you at the docks at noon the day after tomorrow."

"I'll be there, sir."

"I'm sure Sean is beside himself with excitement at the thought of having his big brother all to himself for two whole days," the Master said dryly. "His father is even letting him miss school for the occasion. Mind that he doesn't skimp on his chores and get himself in trouble."

Kaelin spent three wonderful days with Sean, and the Master evidently enjoyed his time as well, for he met Kaelin in good spirits. They ate lunch in a small eatery near the wharf, and when Kaelin asked his Master what he had planned for the remainder of his last vacation day, the Master waved his fork in the air. "I've spent quite some time planning a surprise for this day," he said expansively, "and," he warned, "I'll tolerate no questions about it."

"But—"

"Not a single one."

Kaelin stared at his Master, who returned to his meal and stabbed a chunk of lamb with a satisfied air. The Master began describing the beautiful coast of Zephyr, but Kaelin barely heard him, too preoccupied with wondering what the Master's surprise was. By the time they trekked up the hill and approached the door of their home, the apprentice was half mad with curiosity. *How could a surprise be here at the house when he hasn't even been here?* He opened the door for his Master and quickly scanned the living room but saw nothing that could be considered a surprise. He looked thoughtfully at the Master's pack. *Maybe he brought me something from Zephyr!* He sighed in frustration when the Master hung his pack up.

Bergid chuckled.

"You're enjoying driving me crazy!" the apprentice accused. "Sir," he belatedly added.

The Master laughed, then shook his head when Kaelin sighed and hung his pack on its customary peg by the door. "Such laziness," he said reprovingly. "Put your things away properly, lad, in your room where they belong."

Kaelin stared at him, and Bergid sighed. "What else is a Master for, if not to set a good example for lazy apprentices?" Suiting action to words, the Master hefted his own pack and walked down the hallway.

Kaelin picked up his pack and followed with a puzzled expression. Neither of them ever kept their packs in their rooms. The apprentice was even more confused when he opened the door to his room and his Master turned around and followed him in. Then

Kaelin caught sight of his room and gasped, so astounded that he dropped his pack.

Three days ago, his room, extravagantly spacious by his own standards, had only contained a bed, a small desk, and a chair, with a chest at the foot of the bed for his clothes. Now, by some miracle he could not comprehend, his room had changed into what could only be described as the room of his dreams. The wall between the two guest rooms was gone, creating one enormous room. At the western end stood a large, comfortable-looking bed with several pillows. Next to this was a nightstand with a pitcher and bowl on it. Two huge wardrobes of curly maple were set against the inner wall, one for hanging clothes in, and one bearing an assortment of drawers of various sizes. Both wardrobes had a large cabinet near the top, providing him with more storage space than he could ever imagine needing.

The eastern end of the room, which now abutted the living room, was set up for practicing. An oak music stand stood there invitingly, with Kaelin's Bardic flute resting on a pedestal next to it. Pegs on the inner wall silently promised a place for future instruments. A comfortable chair without arms stood nearby in case he tired of standing. The walls were paneled with pine, and a shelf in the center of the eastern wall displayed the carving of the village square of Vale, where Kaelin had first seen the Master.

All this was wondrous enough, but the crowning glory of the room stood against the southern wall, which now sported six large windows, three on the right and three on the left, overlooking Kyet and the bay beyond. Kaelin could see the mouth of the Bronig to the right of the bay, the docks with three Bardic ships moored there and one coming in from the open sea beyond. He could even see the promontory to the east of Kyet where his brother and Holder Rassek lived. And between the two trios of windows stood an exact replica of the Master's composition desk, complete with drawers and cubbyholes. Quills stood in a rosewood holder, an ink pot next to it ready for use. A shelf above this held his new pile of manuscript paper, begging to be filled with the music that even now flooded his mind. Dozens of cubicles were attached to the wall above the shelf, waiting to be filled with compositions. *His* compositions.

Kaelin regained the use of his muscles and turned to the wonderful sight of his Master's smile. The overwhelmed apprentice tried to speak, but not a single word would come out. Bergid opened his arms and Kaelin ran into them.

"Master," Kaelin managed to say, "this is—I can't believe—there's just no words I can find to thank you enough!

The Master chuckled. "This hug and the look on your face was thanks enough, lad."

Kaelin stood back and tried his best to look disapproving. "You must have spent a fortune! And what will you do now for a guest room?"

"I had one of the practice rooms converted into a guest room," the Master told him. "One practice room and the ensemble room are all I need most of the time, and the converted guest room can also be used as a practice room if needed. You are not my guest. This is your home, and I wanted you to have your own place in it, somewhere that's just yours, where you can practice whenever you want to and compose whenever you feel like it. The walls have been doubled, with padding in between, just like the practice rooms, so you can play without disturbing anyone."

"And ... all this," Kaelin's eyes swept the room in disbelief, "was done in less than three days?"

"With Flynn's help. I had the plans drawn up before we returned to Kyet, and everything was made off-site so it could be easily installed." He gave Kaelin a mock scowl. "The only way I could get rid of you for a couple of days without suffering an onslaught of questions was to imply that I was leaving for Zephyr and send you to Rassek. Then I returned here so I could answer any questions the workers had ... and put in a few finishing touches myself." He smiled at his apprentice's shocked expression. "If you recall," he said dryly, "I told you I was *thinking* of taking a trip to visit Marek ... perfectly true. I thought it over for an entire minute."

"You also told me to meet you at the docks," Kaelin reminded him.

"Did I say I would be arriving there by ship?" There was a mischievous glint in the Master's eyes. "I wanted this to be a surprise."

Kaelin grinned. "It was the best surprise ever! Thank you, sir."

The Master smiled at him. "Well, then, since it's my last vacation day, I'm going to spend the rest of it at my composition desk, and you may spend the rest of it at yours as well, if you like. We'll have our last vacation dinner at the inn later." He turned to leave, but Kaelin touched his arm, stopping him.

"It's not *my* vacation day. Let me make you a special dinner, to thank you," Kaelin said eagerly. "I've some coppers left from my allowance. I'll go to the marketplace and get some fresh ingredients and be right back."

"That would be wonderful," the Master admitted. "I'm actually getting a bit tired of eating out. What are you going to make?"

Kaelin grinned. "I've spent an entire minute planning a surprise for this meal ... and I'll tolerate no questions about it," he said in a deep imitation of his Master's voice.

The Master assembled a stern look. "Is that any way to speak to—"

"Not a single one!" With an impish grin, Kaelin snatched up his pack and raced from the room, leaving his Master chuckling behind him.

That night, after proudly serving the Master his favorite dinner of fresh trout with tubers and asparagus, followed by tarts from their favorite bakery, the apprentice lay sleepless for a long time in his comfortable bed. A slivered moon hung over the bay, a liberal dusting of stars gracing the canopy above. His eyes slid to his wonderful new composition desk, and he swallowed hard. No one would make such a room as this for their apprentice. Most apprentices of other crafts and trades had no room of their own at all, making do with a sleeping mat in the barn or woodshed, or, if they were lucky, the floor by the fireplace. Kaelin would have been perfectly content with any accommodation that placed him near his Master, but instead he had been given the unheard-of luxury of an entire guest room for his use. And now *this* room! The Master wasn't treating him like an apprentice at all. He was treating him like a—

Kaelin caught his breath and refused to allow the word admittance. He would not torture himself by imagining such a thing. His Master was just being incredibly kind. And this was just a room, he told himself firmly. An amazing room, but nothing more. And one he would have to leave behind when he was sent away. For a horrible moment, Kaelin envisioned his Master looking at the room he had created, empty of his apprentice, whom he had sent away forever. The devastation in the imaginary Master's eyes caused tears to spring to his own. Kaelin rolled over and pretended he was lying in an oversized guest room, not meant for permanent occupancy.

That's when he saw it. Hanging on the wall to the left of the two wardrobes was a picture. Hidden from view from anywhere else in the room, it was clearly visible from where he lay in his bed. Made of beautiful pieces of inlaid wood, it was a picture of a stream, a few graceful branches from a willow tree touching its surface. Near the bank was a large boulder with something etched on its surface. His eyes filled with tears, blurring the names carved there ... the names of his parents, with Laena's and his own carved below. It was the gift from his father that had hung in Kaelin's bedroom.

How did my Master get this? Laena told me it was gone, and she didn't know where it was! A choked laugh escaped him. *She never said she didn't know what happened to it. He must have gotten to her first and sworn her to secrecy.* He brushed the tears from his eyes and went to the picture, taking it carefully down from the wall and back to his bed with him.

Much later, when the Master went to his own bed, he looked in on Kaelin and found the boy fast asleep, the picture from his father nestled in his arms.

All in all, it had been the perfect vacation, and both were sorry to see it end. The next day, things got back to normal, as defined by the Master. Kaelin, having no idea what Masters normally did, spent the first week privately amazed and appalled by turns, for it seemed that Masters, whatever else they might be entitled to, had no free time whatsoever. Every moment was filled by something or someone—either a Bard coming to the door with a problem, or a Merchant or Craft dispute that required the Master's mediation, not to mention Bard reports arriving from all six territories of Kestrel that must be reviewed and answered. Indeed, the procession of things taking up the Master's time was endless. For the first time, Kaelin began to understand and truly appreciate the difficulties his Master had faced by spending so many months with him in the mountains. *No wonder the Phantom Bard was kept so busy!* Kaelin's respect for Bard Flynn grew even more as he realized how much of the Master's usual work had been handled by the capable Bard.

Even most of the evenings were taken, for on top of everything else, the Master also rotated groups of Bards to his home for ensemble work and lessons. Kaelin helped as much as he could with both, giving composition and theory lessons when the Master was working with ensembles, and occasionally helping with ensembles when the Master was called away. Although he never played with them, Kaelin critiqued the ensemble groups in much the same way his Master did, which often ended in lively and productive discussions. These he thoroughly enjoyed, and although his comments were always delivered with deference, he defended his opinions when challenged and rarely needed to retract his words. Even Ferrin, one of the two older Bards who frowned upon Kaelin's position as Master Bergid's apprentice, had grudgingly admitted to Flynn that the boy certainly knew what he was about with regard to music. Nevertheless, he insisted, that did not give him the right to take up a Master's time, which should be given to the many responsibilities that came along with that position, not the least of which was his Bards.

"Do you truly feel Kestrel has been mismanaged this cycle because of Kaelin?" Flynn asked incredulously. He had known Ferrin for many cycles, both of them attaining Master eligibility at the same time.

"No," Ferrin admitted, "which is the only reason I have not submitted a formal complaint to the Council."

Flynn stared at him, aghast. "You would have done such a thing to our Master?"

"I would not have wanted to," Ferrin said. "Don't misunderstand me! I have the greatest respect for Master Bergid, but if *any* Master disappeared for three seasons and left his island to flounder, I would have no choice. Nor would you. We are sworn to do what's best for the Bardic Isles, not for one Master, no matter how highly we regard him. Master Bergid took extensive steps to ensure that his affairs were taken care of, thankfully giving me no cause for complaint, except perhaps for the additional work it caused many of us older Bards, as you know better than anyone. But that doesn't mean I agree with his decision to take an apprentice, however talented he may be."

Flynn threw up a hand in exasperation. "So, you would pass Kaelin off to an Instrumentalist and leave him to be instructed by someone who knows far less than he does?"

Ferrin snorted. "The boy should never have been taught so much in the first place!"

Flynn refused to back down. "Would you hold him back from learning altogether simply because he's so quick? I, for one, am glad Master Bergid took him under his wing."

Ferrin glared at him. "Hopefully the Council will have better sense, then, and pluck him out from under it." He turned and strode away.

Flynn watched him go, thinking that this was one Spring Council he would be glad to miss. If Ferrin's opinion was echoed by any of the Masters—and he believed it would be—things were likely to get tempestuous on Elegy.

Meanwhile, Kaelin's instruction continued. The apprentice had his lessons with the Master first thing every morning, finished his assignments after breakfast, then practiced the rest of the morning in his wonderful new room. After lunch, he had an hour and a half of free time. His Master had reduced this from the usual two hours so Kaelin could spend a half-day with his new brother every week, much to the delight of both boys. The apprentice never took his flute with him and continued to avoid playing for anyone but his Master. Though the Spring Council loomed ever closer, Bergid still refrained from pressing the issue. He often wondered if perhaps Kaelin had confided in Sean the secret he was so unwilling to share with anyone else, but though he searched his apprentice's face carefully each time he returned from the Holding, there was no indication that he had.

In fact, Kaelin had come close to confiding in his younger brother, for his desire to tell someone was increasing as rapidly as his fear of his Master finding out. Sean was aptly named, being indeed a "little wise one," as his father affectionately called him. Kaelin found himself not only enjoying Sean's company, but sincerely admiring him. Certainly, the boy without a name had paid dearly for his wisdom during the cycles before he came to Kyet and met the Holder. Kaelin thought he himself would have been overwhelmed with anger and bitterness, but Sean was refreshingly free of either, despite what life had dished out to him. Kaelin had willingly told Sean about his life in Vale with his parents and sister … and of the old Flutist, who had related tales of Bardic Lore as if he himself were an eyewitness. Kaelin described traveling across the mountains of Kestrel with his Master and how hard the sense-deprivation test had been. He even told his little brother about the Bardic testing month at the Master's house and the Bards' reactions to unexpectedly finding an apprentice greeting them at the door. But he avoided talking about the reason he was afraid of losing his Master, and when Sean finally asked him outright, Kaelin frowned and shook his head.

"If I could tell anyone," he said at last, "it would be you, little brother. I know I could trust you not to tell a secret."

"Of *course* I wouldn't," Sean said indignantly. "Brothers keep each other's secrets safe."

Kaelin nodded. "I know." He bit his lip, thinking for a long moment. "I did something terrible," he said hollowly. "Something no one could forgive."

"Not even Master Bergid?"

"Especially not Master Bergid."

"That's why you think you'll lose him? You think he'll send you away if he finds out what you did?"

Kaelin nodded and sat down on the ground. Sean sat down next to him and said nothing for a few moments. "Are you sorry for what you did?" he finally asked.

"Of course I am," Kaelin said in a small voice. "I never meant for it to happen at all."

With no warning, a small fist connected painfully with his shoulder.

"Ow! What was *that* for?" the apprentice demanded.

"That's for thinking *I* couldn't forgive you," the youngster told him. "Especially for something you didn't mean to do! You better never tell me what I can and can't forgive you for. Nobody decides that but me. Okay?"

The apprentice smiled ruefully as he rubbed his shoulder. "Okay, I guess I deserved that."

"Yeah, you did." The youngster brooded silently for a moment, then spoke as though to himself, not looking at Kaelin. "I did something terrible once, too," he admitted. "When I first came to Kyet, I hadn't eaten for a long time ... and I stole a loaf of bread from the bakery. I hid under a building to eat it, and I heard Master Bergid holding a meeting right above my head. He was charging someone in his Order for stealing. He said thievery would not be tolerated in the Bardic Isles, and the man had to work for three whole cycles for the merchants he'd stolen from. If he didn't satisfy his debt to them, he'd be taken to the Council of Masters. And then he took his instruments from him and told him he was no longer a member of the Bardic Order. He said, since he admitted his guilt, he could ask for re ... re something ..." Sean frowned.

"Reinstatement?"

"Yeah. He could ask for that after he satisfied the merchants, but not before." Sean twisted the hem of his tunic. "Even though I was so hungry, I couldn't eat the rest of that bread ... it made me choke when I tried. I threw it to a stray dog that night and found a place under the inn to live where no one would find me and take me to the Master. I thought, since he hadn't forgiven that man, he wouldn't forgive me, either, and I'd be punished the same way." He looked into his brother's astonished face.

"But when Master Bergid found out," the youngster said wonderingly, "he didn't punish me at all. He said I'd already punished myself worse than he would ever dream of doing. He understood why I did it and let me decide for myself to go to the Baker and work off my debt." He glanced at Kaelin. "You don't have to tell me what you did, but I'll bet there was a reason for it. A reason your Master would understand."

Kaelin found himself unable to speak, but Sean didn't wait for him to recover his wits. He jumped to his feet with a grin.

"C'mon, I'll bet the tide's coming in. Let's go see if anything more floated into our hideout!"

Later, when Kaelin returned home, he found himself glancing sideways at his Master, thinking about his wise little brother's words. *Maybe he's right, and it isn't my decision to make for my Master. Maybe he would understand.* He bit his lip hard and tried to focus on his assignment. *But how can anyone understand and forgive it, when I can't?*

So, one by one the days slipped away like pearls from a string until the Spring Council was almost upon them, a subject neither Master nor apprentice wished to discuss. On the tenth day of the last month of spring, Kaelin turned twelve cycles of age. His Master declared the day a partial holiday, released Kaelin from all assignments, and kept the evening free of ensembles and teaching. He even insisted on making their evening meal himself, roasted lamb chops, fresh vegetables, and honeycakes. After they cleaned up together, the Master gave his apprentice permission to do whatever he wished for the rest of the evening.

"Anything I wish?"

"Did I not just say so?"

"Yes, sir, you did," Kaelin said triumphantly. "So, you have to grant me my wish!"

"I didn't say you could *have* whatever you wished, lad. I said you could *do* whatever you wished."

"Exactly," Kaelin cheerfully agreed, "And what I wish to do is listen to you play. For as long as you're willing to."

The Master gave him a surprised look. "Do you not hear me play often enough?"

Kaelin shook his head. "You play for my benefit, to demonstrate, to help me with phrasing and technique. Even when you play late at night, you do so to teach me songs of our history, in case I'm still awake and listening. I leave my door open at night so I can hear as much as possible before I fall asleep. But tonight, I wish to hear you play for yourself."

The Master held his apprentice's hopeful eyes for a long moment. *I give him a gift, and he turns around and gives me a greater one! I caught a wild kestrel ... and he has captured my heart like only two others ever have.*

The Master Bard abruptly turned, collected his instruments and settled himself near the fire. Kaelin happily sat at his Master's feet, listening to one composition after another, on one instrument after another, far into the night. He watched and listened intently as his Master composed two new pieces, one each for flute and harp, learning more about composition from this than he would have from any exercise. The Master jotted down the main themes to be fleshed out later, then took up his flute and asked Kaelin to choose five notes. The apprentice thought for a moment, then told him his selections, and the Master began to improvise, weaving the notes into an exquisite composition that took Kaelin's breath away. As the music coming from the Bardic flute filled the room, colors, rich and vibrant, filled the listening apprentice's mind. And it seemed to him in that moment that the music and notes were a path connecting the two of them, Master and apprentice, together. *Is this real, or just my imagination?*

Deciding he didn't care whether it was real or not, he closed his eyes and immersed himself in the blend of colors and sound. For this, he knew, wasn't just a beautiful song the Master was playing. This was an experience, shared with the person who meant more to him than any other. An experience that he instinctively knew would grow and change with every hearing of it. When it was finished and the Master put down his flute and took up his harp, Kaelin stopped him.

"Surely, Master, you will write down such a song as that!"

The Master smiled. "I already have," he said gently, "for I know that every note of it has engraved itself in your mind, never to be forgotten. It is my birthday gift to you." He returned to playing one of his harp compositions, leaving Kaelin stunned at the beauty of his Master's gift, worth far more to him than anything the Master's coin might have bought in the marketplace.

With a sigh of pleasure, the apprentice turned his attention back to his Master's playing. Kaelin was familiar with many of these pieces from the Master's extensive collection of scores and had played many of them himself. Hearing them now, played by the composer himself, was an experience Kaelin knew he would never forget. For whether the piece was light and whimsical, filled with the unbridled energy of a stormy day, or so wistful and tender that it brought tears to his eyes, every note of it was important. Every phrase, he realized, was a deep expression of the composer's inner being. Words the Master had spoken before blocking Kaelin's eyes and ears echoed in his mind.

You desire knowledge of musical instruments, which is well and good, but never forget one thing. You yourself are the most important instrument you will ever play. A life spent mastering that instrument, whether you ever play a Bardic one or not, is a life well spent.

The Master of music who played so expressively for him this night had most assuredly mastered more than his instruments. *It's not really his instruments he's playing,* Kaelin thought drowsily. *He's playing himself.* Thinking that this was the best birthday he could ever remember, he drifted off to sleep. He was scarcely aware of being guided to his bed and gently covered. He roused for a moment, though, when the Master briefly touched his cheek and murmured words he barely heard.

"Sleep well, my kestrel."

The Master quietly left, and the apprentice lay smiling into the darkness for a long moment before slipping back into sleep, the song he had been gifted still playing gently in his mind. Even better was the Master's touch on his cheek, yet another wondrous birthday gift, never to be forgotten.

Two days later, the Master sat at his desk watching his apprentice, who was trying to see how long he could hold a high note on his flute at the softest pianissimo level. He laughed as Kaelin broke off with a gasp and stood looking at him reproachfully.

"I don't suppose, Master, you would care to take me on?"

"Ha!" The Master's brows lifted at the challenge in Kaelin's voice. He strode to his instrument packs and removed his flute. "At the downbeat, lad!"

They began playing the same note, so softly that a listener passing by the Master's home would never have heard it. The single tone hung delicately in the air, perfectly pitched, matched in vibrato, never faltering in its sweet constancy. Finally, Kaelin broke off a mere moment before his Master. They stood panting and laughing at each other.

The Master Bard wiped his eyes and tried to look stern. "There, you young scamp. That ought to keep you in your place!"

"By a whole fraction of a second!" Kaelin grinned in delight at his Master's bristling eyebrows.

"Impudent apprentice! Your penalty for losing will be to make our dinner."

"But I always make our dinner," Kaelin said with a laugh. "What if I had won?"

"Then," growled the Master, "you would have had to clean up afterwards as well!"

"Sounds like a perfectly normal evening to me. Perhaps," Kaelin said solemnly, "you need a refresher course in how to punish impudence ... sir." With another laugh, he scuttled quickly into the kitchen before his Master could prove otherwise.

When Bergid came to the table, however, he seemed disinclined to begin eating. Kaelin waited, wondering at the Master's pensive mood, unwilling to take up his fork before his Master did. At last, Bergid looked up.

"Well, lad," the Master said gently, "I'm afraid it's time."

Kaelin met his Master's eyes and braced himself.

"We must leave tomorrow morning for the Spring Council," the Master told him. "My Bards that are rotating this cycle usually accompany me, but many of them have been delayed arriving here, so I've decided you and I will go on ahead, and they will follow us tomorrow." He picked up a roll and began buttering it.

Kaelin looked at his own plate in silence, his appetite abruptly gone. He knew many issues were discussed and decided upon at the Spring Council and that one of those issues was going to be his apprenticeship. What he didn't know was why he was being taken along. Surely such an event was reserved for Bards and Masters, not lowly apprentices, even one who had a Master for a teacher. He swallowed hard, wishing he could ask to stay with Sean until his Master returned, then castigated himself for such a cowardly thought. If his Master was willing to stand up for his apprentice against the Council, surely the least that apprentice could do was accompany him there. Instead of protesting, Kaelin tried to comfort himself with a memory.

Can they make you send me away?

Nothing could ever make that happen.

The next morning, they rose early, packed their bags, and headed for the docks and the ship that would take them to Elegy.

Movement Three

The Spring Council

Chapter 16

Kaelin leaned against the rail, looking southward expectantly. Every now and then the spray from a large swell scored a direct hit across his face, but he didn't mind. The lookout at the top of the mast above him had shouted "Land!" a few moments ago, and the apprentice was eager to see it for himself. Landing on Elegy after the exhilarating ride over the waves was a welcome prospect to his queasy stomach, even if the rest of him had no desire to arrive there.

"I see it!" As the faint outline of the island grew clearer, Kaelin whistled softly in admiration of the lofty peak that rose southwest of the coastal bluffs. "Is that Bardic Mountain, Master?"

"It is indeed," Bergid replied. "The Spring Council is held on its northeastern foothills."

Whereas Kestrel boasted a range of three peaks, Elegy had but one, the largest in the Bardic Isles. Wind and surf had transformed the northern coast of Elegy into a series of steep cliffs. The only place ships were willing to risk a short stop was at Bard's Landing, and then only in fair weather. Here, a narrow bay provided enough protection for the beaching of small craft. As its name implied, this was a destination for Bards and Masters only, who held their meetings here. Trade was handled in the larger, more convenient port of Tryl, on the populous east coast. Tryl did a brisk trading business with Lyssa, its sister port directly east of it on the southwest coast of Lyra.

The Master Bard had explained this to his apprentice on the day-long voyage, and Kaelin looked with interest at the sheer cliffs rising before him. *So, this is where Master Cyral chose to spend his last cycles. What a beautiful place. Beautiful ... and lonely.* He forgot his churning stomach for a moment as a melodic line, filled with the stark beauty of the cliffs and the voice of the wind, took shape in his mind.

"Come, lad, put aside your new composition for now," his Master said dryly. "It's time to get our packs."

Kaelin grinned and hurried after him. Not only could his Master tell when music arose in his mind, Kaelin was convinced he could probably read the full score just by looking at his face. They gathered their gear and were lowered into a boat, where two sailors sat ready to man the oars. The cries of the gulls mingled with those of the ship's crew, who leaned over the rail to thank Master Bergid for his songs and stories. More than a few of them sent curious glances Kaelin's way, some of them frankly sympathetic. The apprentice felt his face grow warm. *They probably think I've done something terrible and am being taken to answer to the Council for it.*

Master and apprentice took their place at the stern as the sailors plied the oars and the little boat skimmed over the waves toward the beach. White cliffs rose on either side of them. The Master's hair blew wildly in the wind. Then, with a last surging swell, the boat grated against the sand. The sailors helped them disembark, then made their farewells and rowed quickly back to the ship. Kaelin turned away from the water to see well over a dozen figures striding across the beach toward them, all in uniformly light blue robes and silver cords. *So many Bards!* He suddenly felt like a lowly intruder on the beach, the only one dressed in the dark grey and black cord of an apprentice.

The Bards bowed together to the Master and chorused a

greeting. Master Bergid smiled and returned it, then surveyed the large group.

"Quite the welcome for only two of us," he said expressionlessly. He glanced at his apprentice, standing motionless beside him. "This is Kaelin," he told the Bards, all of whom were staring at the apprentice, startled by the color of his eyes and even more so by the color of his robe. Clearly, the apprentice's existence had not become common knowledge outside of Kestrel. "Considering the circumstances, Kaelin, a single bow for all will suffice, and we will forgo names until a later time."

"Yes, sir," the relieved apprentice replied and quickly bowed to the Bards. "It's an honor to meet you, sirs."

Nods and a few smiles were returned to him. The apprentice kept his eyes lowered, all too aware of the few who were frowning his way with stiff disapproval. When no further explanation of Kaelin's presence was given, willing hands took the Master's packs and they made their way along a steep, well-traveled path that switchbacked its way up the cliffs.

Kaelin waited for the Bards to precede him, then, left to shoulder his own packs, followed along behind. At the top of the cliffs the trail led into the woods, continuing to climb east toward the mountain. The apprentice had begun to wonder how far they were going when his Master was suddenly at his side. Without a word, he slipped the heaviest of Kaelin's packs off the youngster's shoulder, slung it over his own, and continued up the hill, his staff punctuating the sound of his footsteps as he went. The Bards stared after him in surprise.

One of them, a tall, sandy-haired young man, suddenly chuckled. "I believe we have just been reprimanded for discourtesy, and rightly so." He turned to Kaelin and gave him a nod. "Welcome to Elegy, Kaelin. My name is Darryk, and I would consider it a privilege to carry the rest of your packs." He took them from Kaelin's unresisting arms, while another Bard hurried to unburden the

Master.

Kaelin bowed. "Bard Darryk," he said respectfully, looking directly into the grey eyes and relaxing slightly at the friendly acceptance he saw there. "Thank you for your help, sir."

"A Bard should need no reminder to offer it," Darryk said as they began walking together. "Your arrival with the Master Bard of Kestrel was ... a bit of a surprise. We had expected him to arrive with sixteen of his Bards. I was one of the two Bards sent to greet your Master. The others," he shrugged apologetically, "well, there *was* a rumor going around about a youngster traveling with the Master this past cycle, and I suppose that explains why there are so many of us. I'm afraid we're all a little confused."

Kaelin grinned ruefully. "So am I."

Darryk laughed, and Kaelin felt at ease for the first time since coming ashore. This Bard, he thought, could have easily followed the Master's demonstration of courtesy by simply offering to take the apprentice's pack and continuing on with his friends. Darryk needn't have stayed with him, much less taken the time to explain matters.

The tall Bard proved a pleasant companion as they continued climbing. They passed by an immense tree that Darryk said was likely the oldest one in the Isles. He pointed out a dark cavern in the side of a cliff and told Kaelin that it was the entrance to a tunnel.

"Bardic Mountain has many of them, some large and twisting their way deep into the mountain." Darryk gestured upward with pride, as though the mountain were his own custom-built home. "It's a fascinating place."

"Before you joined the Bardic Order, did you used to live on Bardic Mountain?" Kaelin asked.

The Bard looked startled. "Why, no ... no one does, Kaelin. But there are often Bards here in the foothills, and not just for Council sessions. Many of us are here now because this is a rotation cycle, which occurs every three cycles. Since the Bards freed for rotation from Kestrel did not arrive with Master Bergid, can I assume they will be coming on the next ship?"

"I think they're arriving from Kyet tomorrow." Kaelin looked at the Bard curiously. "Are you here to be rotated to another island, too?"

Darryk nodded. "I just completed my rotation on Eyrie with Master Talan, the Instrument Master. I'll find out where I'm headed next when the Masters post the rotation assignments at the end of the last Council meeting. We Bards use the Meeting Hall for our own meetings." He nodded toward the mountain in the west. "As for the mountain, it's not a place to live. Though it doesn't look like it now, when so many of us are here, it's a place to be alone in, to renew your strength ... to restore your music." He shrugged slightly. "It's not easy to explain, but it's the reason why the Masters allow us to come here alone at least once a cycle."

It didn't need to be explained to the apprentice walking alongside him. Even from this distance, Kaelin had only to glance at the mountain to hear its song ... strong, vibrant, and very disturbing. He quickly looked away from it. What was disturbing to him was undoubtedly soothing and healing to those whose Gift did not cause anyone else harm. "I think I understand," he said. "Being here all alone, with no distractions ... well, sometimes it takes silence to appreciate sound."

Darryk cocked a brow at his serious young companion. "I think there is more to you than meets the eye."

Kaelin grinned. "I'll take that as a compliment, sir."

"It was intended as one."

They traveled for nearly two hours, climbing steadily southwest until they reached a large clearing filled with many Bards, all of whom came forward to greet Master Bergid. More curious glances and frowns came Kaelin's way. The intimidated apprentice moved a bit closer to Darryk, grateful the Bard had not left him, and turned his attention to a great stone building on the northern

edge of the field. The structure was impressive, all the more striking for its isolated location. Massive stone plaques, each with one
of the seven Bardic instruments deeply carved into its surface,
stood prominently above two sets of open doors.

"We're now standing on the Meeting Grounds," Darryk informed him, "and that building you're inspecting is our Meeting
Hall, which is also used as a warmer living area during autumn and
winter when few of us are here. Inside there are grooves crisscross-
ing the floor, and panels that can be easily slid along them, giving
us a variety of ways to divide the area into smaller rooms. Since this
is a rotation cycle, it will be kept open for our large morning meetings. And," he added with a wry grin, "since the Council Grounds
of the Masters is open to the sky and weather, which can rarely be
trusted, they occasionally move their meetings here, leaving us to
the mercy of the elements."

"It's a wonderful building," Kaelin said, impressed with the
time and effort it must have taken to create such a structure here,
where materials would have to be carted up the cliff and mountain-
side. "Where do the Bards sleep at night now?"

"You'll see many campsites as you travel through the woods,
with small shelters and a fire pit for use during the spring and summer." He waved a hand at the dozens of Bards conversing in small
groups around the clearing. "Especially now, when there are too
many of us to stuff into the hall."

Kaelin nodded and quickly turned his attention away from the
groups of Bards, many of whom were staring in his direction.
"Where do the Masters stay? If I'm not asking too many questions,
sir," he quickly added.

"Not at all." The tall Bard indicated a broad path leading further uphill through the trees. "That leads to the Council Grounds,
not too far from here and closer to the Mountain. Each of the Masters has his own cabin near it, situated according to seniority. Since
Master Bergid is the Senior Master of the Council, his is the first

one you'll come to, just east of the Council Grounds and closest to its entrance. Masters Grened, Rial, Talan, and Marek have their cabins situated further away. The Bards of Elegy take turns seeing that the cabins are made ready for the Masters' use whenever a Council meeting is held." Darryk glanced at the apprentice. "I'm not sure if you'll be staying with Master Bergid or with us, but you're more than welcome to share my shelter and campfire." He pointed out a path that led past the Meeting Hall. "It's the first one you'll come to along that path."

Kaelin gave him a surprised look. "Thank you, sir. I appreciate the offer." He could see his Master laughing and talking with a few Bards nearby. He felt, rather than saw, a change come over the clearing as an older man with steel grey hair, dressed in the white robe of a Master, entered it from the path leading to the Council Grounds. His manner was decisive, his glance bristled with authority. When it was suddenly turned upon Kaelin, the boy drew a sharp breath and stepped back as though from a blow. He felt his face burn as if he were guilty of some grave, unforgivable misdeed, though he had no idea what it was. Unexpectedly, he felt his hand taken firmly in Darryk's as the Bard stepped back next to him and nodded respectfully to the Master. The Master paid him no heed and continued to glare at the apprentice, who lowered his head and fervently wished himself back on Kestrel. Darryk's hand squeezed his reassuringly.

The cheerful voice of his own Master released Kaelin from the fierce scrutiny. "And a warm welcome to you, too, Grened."

The Master Bard of Elegy's baleful expression scarcely altered as he turned toward his colleague. "What is the meaning of this, Bergid?" he demanded, gesturing toward Kaelin as though the boy were an offensive object on his island that required immediate removal.

Master Bergid sighed. "There seems to be a singular lack of courtesy on Elegy these days," he said to no one in particular. "I shall make it a point to compose a few songs on the subject for local distribution." He looked about him in mild reproof, then directed a meaningful gaze at the Master Harpist. "As for your question, I would hardly consider it a topic for open session. Now, if you'll excuse us, we're a little tired from our journey."

"Yes, I imagine so," Grened said acidly, "especially after such a *bitter* winter as Kestrel apparently had this cycle, though it was remarkably mild everywhere else." He brusquely called one of the Bards to his side and strode from the clearing, his manner stiffly disapproving.

Darryk released Kaelin's hand as Master Bergid joined them and spoke as though nothing unusual had happened. "Thank you for your courtesy to Kaelin, Darryk."

"My apologies for not having offered it earlier, sir. Please consider my camp open to him at any time."

The Master nodded. "Thank you. Kaelin will be staying with me, but I will take you up on your offer during the Council sessions, which can run quite late."

"It would be my pleasure to have him."

The Master nodded and turned to his apprentice. "Come along, lad."

"Yes, sir."

Kaelin walked silently at his Master's side along the well-maintained path heading toward the Council Grounds. Darryk and two other Bards came along behind with their packs and the provisions for their cabin. The apprentice's thoughts were gloomy. If this was the reaction of one of the Masters to his presence, what would the reactions of the others be? Was every Master going to be outraged at finding a lowly apprentice in their midst? Kaelin sighed. This was going to be far worse than the four weeks of Bard testing had been.

A reassuring hand was laid on Kaelin's shoulder. "Don't let Master Grened's crustiness bother you," his Master said. "He has little tolerance for the breaking of tradition—which I am guilty of, not you—but he is the Master Bard of Elegy and deserving of respect. Indeed, I hope you have the privilege of hearing him play while we're here. It would take only a few measures to demonstrate why he is the Master Harpist of the Bardic Isles."

Kaelin's eyes widened. He had forgotten that Master Grened was more than just the Master Bard of Elegy. As they continued their hike, the apprentice wrestled with the idea that the intimidating Master he had just met and the greatest Harpist in the Bardic Isles were one and the same person. *Maybe there's more to Master Grened than meets the eye, too.*

The Master's cabin on Elegy proved to be much larger than his cabin near the Bronig River on Kestrel. A beautiful fur rug adorned the center of the floor, and wood carvings of the mountain hung on the walls. A large oak table had six chairs around it, and four other chairs were arranged around the fireplace. The kitchen area was small compared to the Master's home in Kyet, but neat and serviceable. There was a small bedroom whose open door revealed a large, comfortable-looking bed, a desk, a chest, and a dresser. The Bards put down the traveler's packs and hung their instruments on pegs carved into musical symbols. Darryk insisted on preparing their dinner, waving aside Kaelin's objection, and soon had the apprentice mesmerized by his vivid description of the Council Grounds and the performances held there. The other two Bards unpacked for the Master and arranged Kaelin's bedroll on the floor near the fireplace. Then they took their leave, Darryk with a smile for Kaelin and a promise to see him again soon. After eating the delicious fish and potato soup Darryk had prepared, Kaelin, more tired from the day's excitement than he had realized, lay wearily on his mat and fell deeply asleep.

Sometime during the night, a voice called to him ... a strangely inhuman voice. The musical sound pulsed with loneliness, and Kaelin found himself on a grassy knoll, looking out over a wooded valley, the winding ribbon of a river below. In the distance, the dual peaks of a mountain gleamed in the sunlight. The voice cried out to him again, rising in song from the larger of the two peaks. With a shock, Kaelin realized that the voice belonged to a harp, echoing the music of a golden scroll in another dream. Once again its compelling beauty wrapped around him, drawing him toward the mountain as it had toward the Master's drawer.

I'm coming, he silently promised it. *Wait for me!*

Kaelin sat up with his heart pounding and his breath coming in ragged gasps, but all was quiet in the cabin. The fire was a bed of glowing embers, and he could hear his Master's soft snoring through the open door of his bedroom.

It's only a dream, and I'm staying right here. Why would I go any closer to that mountain? He shivered at the thought, then pulled the covers over himself with trembling fingers and eventually fell back to sleep.

Kaelin awoke before dawn the next morning, feeling refreshed and ready for music. He glanced through the open bedroom door at his sleeping Master, then got dressed and moved quietly toward his flute, thinking to find a place outside to play.

"There's a striking view from the hill behind the cabin," came his Master's voice from the bedroom. "Just the spot for serenading the sun into the sky."

"I'm sorry I disturbed you, Master. Should I get your breakfast first?"

The Master chuckled. "A bit early for that, lad. Wash up, then go on ahead. I'll join you soon."

Kaelin made quick use of the basin and pitcher of cold water the Bards had set out for them, then brought the fire back to life and heated a pot of water for his Master. Then he took his flute into the bracing, early morning mountain air and followed the narrow path behind the cabin. He soon found himself on a grassy hillock overlooking a valley. Below him wound a shining river. Far to the west, Bardic Mountain rose majestically into the morning sky, its twin peaks shining in the first rays of the sun. Kaelin stood motionless, staring at a scene that was unexpectedly, disturbingly familiar.

It can't be. It isn't possible.

A short while later the Master Bard stood looking down in concern at his apprentice's pale face. Kaelin's flute bag was still slung across his shoulder, and he seemed to have forgotten it entirely.

"Kaelin?"

"I—I don't understand," the boy stammered.

"Understand what?"

The apprentice gestured toward Bardic Mountain. "I know I've never been here before, but I saw it last night in a dream. I looked out from this exact spot. Every detail, every peak and ridge. And there was a voice ... a voice that spoke in harp music instead of words. It was the same music I heard from your desk drawer, Master, and the same mountain with two peaks." He shook his head wonderingly. "We could only see one peak from the ship, so I didn't know it was Bardic Mountain I've been seeing in my dreams. What does it mean?"

The Master Bard was silent. Over the last month, he had played every piece of music contained in Master Cyral's scroll for his apprentice, but Kaelin had not recognized any of them. "I don't know, lad," he said finally, "but a dream doesn't persist without reason. I'm sure it will be made clear to you—"

"In the fullness of its own measure?"

The Master chuckled, relieved at the mischievous light that had returned to Kaelin's eyes. "Precisely. So, then, how about that serenade of yours? The sun still appears to need a boost!"

Kaelin eagerly removed his flute, looked into the rosy glow of the sunrise, then closed his eyes and placed the flute to his lips.

Only a few notes later, he gasped and stopped playing.

"I'm sorry, sir, I … don't think I can play here."

"What's wrong?"

"I'm not sure how to explain it." Kaelin thought for a moment. "It felt like when you handed me your instruments during the sense-deprivation test. The music from each of them entered my mind and it took all my strength to push it back out." He stared at the distant peaks. "It's like the mountain itself is a huge instrument, one with a mind of its own. Its music started to force itself into my mind … to make me play it. I don't want to do that, sir."

The Master's frown deepened at the fear he saw on his apprentice's face. He glanced at the mountain and spoke gently. "Perhaps you'll be able to play out of its sight, then. But, if it happens again, you're to stop playing immediately. And I think it might be best if you do not play your own music while you're here. A week or two reviewing flute forms nine and ten will do you no harm, nor will further practice on harp and pipes."

"Gladly, sir."

"Come along, then. Let's get some breakfast."

Kaelin followed obediently, but his thoughts remained focused on the mountain behind him. He remembered Darryk's words. *It's a place to go to renew your strength … to restore your music.* He shook his head, confused by the feeling that the mountain wanted to take his strength instead, to drain him and leave him empty of his music. He shivered in the warmth of the rising sun.

The remainder of the morning was spent in the clearing outside the cabin, in a useless attempt to recapture the interest and intensity of Kaelin's usual lessons. Although he could play, his mind kept straying to the mountain like a tongue probing a gap left by a missing tooth. His Master's voice startled him.

"Kaelin, wherever you have gone, I suggest you return for lunch. We may as well eat early, since we seem to be wasting our time." The Master sounded more perplexed than reproving.

Kaelin lowered his flute and forced his mind away from the mountain. "I'm sorry, sir. I can't seem to concentrate."

The Master frowned. "Is it the mountain that's bothering you?"

Kaelin nodded. "Not like it was on the hill, but I can't stop thinking about it. It wants something from me." He flushed. "I know that sounds crazy, Master, and I've no idea—"

A cheerful voice came from behind them. "Good morning, Master Bergid ... Kaelin."

Startled, they looked up as Darryk crossed the clearing. The apprentice quickly got to his feet and bowed to the Bard.

Darryk gave Kaelin a smile and spoke to the Master. "I'm sorry to disturb you, sir, but I have a message from Master Grened, who instructed me to await your reply." He drew a thin scroll from his belt and handed it to the Master.

Bergid slit the seal with his belt knife and read the message, then glanced at Darryk. "Perhaps Kaelin can entertain you for a few moments while I write a reply." He rose and headed for the cabin.

The Bard turned to find the apprentice staring after his Master with a mixture of surprise and panic on his face. Darryk glanced at the Bardic flute in Kaelin's hands. "Is flute your primary instrument?" he asked.

The apprentice nodded reluctantly.

"I would be honored to hear you play it."

Kaelin felt his throat constrict. He had no way of knowing for sure if this Bard was Gifted like his Master, and if he wasn't— "Oh, you wouldn't want to hear me play that, sir," he blurted. "I'm not allowed to play anything but music from the flute forms right now."

Darryk smiled easily. "Well, then, perhaps you would like to borrow my harp." He began unslinging it from his shoulder.

Kaelin's eyes fastened on Darryk's entreatingly. "Sir, you are a Bard, and I am an apprentice. If you command me to play for you, I must obey. Please don't, sir."

Darryk looked at him in astonishment. "Certainly, Kaelin. I had no wish to distress you." His eyes lit with humor as he settled his harp back on his shoulder and surveyed the relieved apprentice. "I must say, a modest apprentice is a rare thing."

"It isn't modesty. I just—" Kaelin bit his lip and hesitated. "I just don't want anything to happen," he said in a low voice.

"Happen?" the Bard echoed blankly.

"Well, actually," Kaelin said hurriedly, "I've never played for anyone but my Master before, except once."

Darryk was doubly astonished. "You mean, no one at all? How then did Master Bergid come to take you as his apprentice?" He lifted his hand suddenly. "My apologies. I didn't mean to pry into things that are clearly none of my business."

"I don't mind, sir. He heard me when I was playing my flute in the woods."

They were interrupted by the Master's return. He handed a scroll to Darryk, who promised to deliver it immediately to Master Grened and turned to leave.

"One moment, if you please, Darryk. I would like a word with you." The Master glanced at his apprentice. "I believe you need to practice the duet in the third section of harp form five."

"Yes, sir." Kaelin bowed to them both, then went into the cabin, closing the door behind him.

"Harp form five? Most impressive for one so young," Darryk commented. "Especially since flute is his primary instrument."

"Did you ask him to play it for you?"

"I did, Master Bergid, and offered him the use of my harp as well, but he practically begged me not to make him play." Darryk shrugged helplessly. "I had no intention of forcing him. He said he has never played for anyone but you, except once."

"Except once," the Master echoed. "I wonder what happened that one time." He shook his head. "I would appreciate it if you tried to help him, Darryk. He may well be required to play for the

Council. I do not wish him forced to do so against his will ... by them, or by me."

Darryk's eyes widened. An apprentice of such tender cycles playing before the Council of Masters? Except for the adjudicated ones done by lottery, coveted performances on the Council Grounds had to be earned. He himself had played his harp on those grounds the previous cycle, having been recommended by Master Grened himself. He knew firsthand how intimidating the experience was for someone who was thrilled to be there. The thought of a young boy too afraid to play for anyone at all being forced to do so...

Darryk shook his head. "I hope it doesn't come to that, Master Bergid. I'll be glad to help him if I can." He smiled. "I find myself quite taken with him."

"Kaelin has taken to you also, far more quickly than with any of my Bards. I'm hoping that, where all the rest have failed to gain his confidence, you might succeed, for he has already told you something he has told no one else." He frowned. "The Council's first session is this evening. I'll send Kaelin to you then. Whatever the source of his fear, it is deeply rooted, and I've not been successful in freeing him of it. I will not force his confidence." He smiled grimly. "If someone like our good Master Grened gets hold of him, however—"

"The Maker forbid! I assure you I'll do my best."

The Master nodded in appreciation. "If you do manage to get him to play, make no comment about what you experience ... to him or anyone else except myself." He smiled at the Bard's look of bewilderment. "If you are fortunate enough to hear him, you will understand."

"I'll do as you say, sir."

"I need not mention, of course, that this conversation is strictly confidential."

"Certainly, Master Bergid." The tall Bard bowed respectfully and left.

The Master returned thoughtfully to the silent cabin, very much aware that not a single measure of harp music had come from it. He found Kaelin sitting motionless near the fire, the Master's harp in hand. "Are you having difficulty tuning my harp?"

Kaelin flushed. "No, sir." He turned his attention to the harp and began to tune it.

The Master stifled a sigh as he settled into his chair. He hadn't really expected Kaelin to play for Darryk, but apparently he would not so much as tune his harp in the Bard's vicinity, even with the sturdy walls of a log cabin between them. He could only hope that the growing rapport between the two would draw the youngster's reason out, and that Darryk could convince Kaelin to confide in his Master.

"You seem to enjoy Darryk's company," the Master commented, glancing at his apprentice.

This elicited a smile. "I like him," Kaelin affirmed. "He doesn't treat me like an apprentice, three ranks beneath him. Of course," he added hurriedly, "I won't forget that myself, sir. It's just that ... well, Bard Darryk treats me like I'm a person who matters to him, not just an apprentice he's curious about."

"And my Bards did not?"

Kaelin gave the Master a startled look. "They treated me fine ... it just took some time before they could accept me. I had to prove myself first ... except for the Phantom Bard," he added with a grin. "But then, he already knew about me."

It was the Master's turn to look startled. "The phantom ... ah, Bard Flynn, I presume?"

Kaelin nodded. "The one responsible for the pack that kept appearing and disappearing from our campsite."

The Master's mouth quirked. "You noticed that, did you?"

"Of course I did," the apprentice said, his words laced with indignation. "You couldn't have been reading the same letters over and over again. And woodworking tools, rosewood, and apprentice robes aren't things you would have packed for your journey."

Bergid chuckled. "Why didn't you just ask me about it?"

"Trying to catch a Phantom Bard in the act was more fun."

Chapter 17

Kaelin paused at the edge of a small clearing in the woods near the Meeting Hall, his flute slung over his shoulder. He was happy to spend the evening with Darryk, but not with his Master's comment that his composition of the morning needed work. It hadn't been a direct order to play, but Kaelin was accustomed to complying with his Master's slightest wish. Yet how could he possibly work on his composition with Darryk right there, listening? An old and terrible memory rose vividly in his mind, and he forced it back down.

Why can't I just forget? Hard on the heels of this thought came his own harsh answer. *I can't forget because I don't deserve to! It was my own fault.* He took a deep breath, entered the clearing, and bowed deeply.

"Bard Darryk. I hope I'm not disturbing you, sir. I came at my Master's request."

"Welcome, Kaelin," came the cheerful reply. "I was expecting you and will enjoy having your company this evening instead of spending it alone." Darryk thought wryly how difficult such privacy had been to achieve. He had needed to shoo away nearly a dozen curious Bards, who suspected he would be hosting Kaelin during the meetings and relished the idea of quizzing the young apprentice. Not only was the youngster several cycles away from coming of age at fifteen, the youngest age for anyone to apprentice to the Bardic Order, but was he actually Master Bergid's own apprentice? And Master's apprentice or not, what was he doing here, where only Bards and Masters were allowed? Had he been brought here to answer to the Council for misconduct? If so, what could so young an apprentice have possibly done, that he must answer to the Council for it? The novelty of such unanswered, intriguing questions was irresistible.

"Perhaps," one of the Bards of Elegy had whimsically suggested, "he stole an apprentice robe and refuses to take it off!" The laughter that followed was quickly quenched by glares from most of the Bards of Kestrel. They had arrived that morning to a crowd of Bards on the beach, who had interrogated them all the way to the Meeting Grounds. Not a single question had been answered. The Bards of Kestrel adamantly refused to discuss the matter with anyone ... which, of course, only inflamed the desire for answers. The relief on Kaelin's face, however, instantly rewarded Darryk's efforts to ensure their privacy.

They sat by the fire and talked, but Darryk's attempts to put his nervous young guest at ease met with little success. "The Bards of Kestrel arrived this morning," he said conversationally. "I suppose you got to know all twenty-four of them during the month of testing?"

"Yes, sir."

When Kaelin ventured nothing further, Darryk suppressed a sigh. *Wrong question.* "Did you enjoy their performances?" This, it seemed, was the right question. The apprentice's face lit up.

"Oh, *yes*, sir, especially the ensembles! So much wonderful music to listen to, even if I was busy learning how to adju—" The apprentice broke off, his face coloring.

Darryk was stunned. "Master Bergid taught you how to adjudicate?"

"Mine didn't count, of course," Kaelin said hurriedly, "except for the composition and theory tests." His flush deepened.

"Composition and theory—" Darryk's voice failed him. He wondered briefly what the Bards of Kestrel had thought of having their composition and theory tests scored by an apprentice.

"Master Bergid reviewed them," Kaelin said hastily, "and we went over my adjudication sheets every night. After two days of writing, I could barely play myself. But the ensembles were wonderful," he added wistfully. "Like listening to musical conversations."

Yes, and this conversation is getting stranger by the minute! "Well, then," the Bard said with a smile, "would you like to converse with me in a duet?"

The apprentice's face closed at what was apparently another wrong question. Darryk motioned toward Kaelin's flute bag and swiftly changed the subject. "I see you brought your flute. Would you mind if I looked at it?" He shook his head reassuringly at Kaelin's alarmed expression. "Don't worry. I can see that you still prefer not to play, and I would never command anyone to play against his will."

Kaelin relaxed slightly and slid his flute out of its bag. He handed it to Darryk and watched as the Bard handled it carefully, almost reverently. "What a beautifully crafted instrument! And made of rosewood, no less."

The Bard's words of praise put the apprentice at ease. "Thank you, sir! Master Bergid instructed me through every step."

Darryk found himself stunned yet again. *"You* made this?" He shook his head as though to clear it. "I'm sorry, Kaelin, I'd just assumed that you were using one of your Master's flutes and was surprised he had given you the use of such a valuable one. Only three men I know could have crafted one this fine, and all of them are Masters."

"I made it," Kaelin confirmed, "with my Master's tools, since I haven't any of my own. In Vale, I had the use of Craftmaster

Arnor's, but—"

"Craft ... *master?*"

"He's the woodcarving Craftmaster of Vale," Kaelin explained as he took back his flute, oblivious to the Bard's astounded expression. "He wanted me to apprentice with him, and I almost agreed, even though I didn't want to, but then Master Bergid came, and I heard him play my—" The apprentice frowned. "Well, I heard him play, and I followed him." When the Bard made no reply, the apprentice glanced anxiously up at him. "I apologize, sir, if I'm talking too much."

"No, Kaelin, not at all."

"I can hardly wait to begin a set of pipes," the apprentice continued eagerly, "or even better, a harp of my own!" He colored slightly. "Although my Master has done so much for me already, I would never dare ask him."

Darryk regarded him thoughtfully. "The flute is not an instrument I'm proficient on yet, as Master Bergid could easily tell you. I can, however, hold my own on anything with strings, particularly the harp, my primary instrument." He cleared his throat. "Both the playing and the making of it. The excellent construction of your flute tells me you have the woodworking skill to construct a harp. Perhaps, if I spoke to your Master, our evenings here during the many Council sessions could be put to good use." He looked at Kaelin inquiringly.

"I'm only an apprentice, sir," the apprentice said hesitantly, his words belying the hope on his face. "I shouldn't be taking up the time of a Bard."

"If the Master Bard of Kestrel believes you to be worthy of his time," Darryk said dryly, "you are certainly worthy of mine." He handed Kaelin his flute. "You won't be able to finish your harp in the week or two you'll be here, but you can make a good start on it, and I can give you detailed instructions on how to finish it yourself. Your Master can easily help you with any further questions you might have. I'll speak to him when he returns for you tonight."

"I don't see how I can ever repay you, sir," Kaelin said softly, his amber eyes shining in the firelight.

The tall Bard studied the boy for a moment. *It's not just Master Bergid who's been captivated by this youngster. I believe I already trust this boy more than I trust a few Bards I've known far longer.* Darryk came to a sudden decision. "I'm not doing it for payment," he said, "but there is something I'd like you to do for me." He ignored the uneasy glance the boy gave his flute and extended his arm toward him. "Not in return for helping you make your harp, but only if you desire it, as I do. I would like you to stop calling me 'sir' and consider me your friend."

The apprentice inhaled sharply and stared at the proffered arm, more moved by Darryk's gesture than the Bard could have known. In Vale, Kaelin's only friend had been Erik, but that had been a childhood friendship of shared mischief and escapades, and who knew if they would ever meet again? In Kyet he had Sean for his bonded brother, but the three cycles between them was a gap that only time would lessen as his little brother grew older. Though the age difference was even greater with Darryk, this friendship would be grounded in a shared love of music, a friendship he hadn't realized he had longed for until now. As much as he wanted to grasp the arm extended to him, however, he hesitated at the enormity of the gift being offered him. The status of a Bard was far above that of an apprentice. He didn't know what his own Master would think, but he could well imagine the expression on Master Grened's face and likely on those of the other three Masters he had yet to meet. Kaelin dropped his gaze and studied the ground intently.

"Surely, sir, a Bard would not wish to be seen on equal terms with an apprentice."

"This Bard would."

Kaelin looked up into the friendly grey eyes, then reached out and clasped the arm extended to him. "Darryk." The name was spoken with a respect bordering on reverence.

Darryk smiled and shook the arm of his new friend. "Perhaps someday, when you want to, you'd consider helping me with my flute playing, my friend. It isn't what a Bard's ought to be, something I must rectify before my rotation to Zephyr." He grimaced. "Which I devoutly hope doesn't happen this time around. I'm in sore need of help before going there, and I've an idea that, with as fine an instrument as this, you must be an excellent flutist."

Kaelin's eyes widened. An apprentice giving lessons on a Bardic instrument to a Bard? Master Grened's shock at their open friendship would be nothing compared to his outrage at such heresy as this. *But then,* he thought with sudden pleasure, *it's not an apprentice instructing a Bard. It's a friend helping a friend.* "I'll help you with your flute right now, if you like," he offered with a grin.

The rest of the evening passed quickly. Kaelin found his new friend in dire need of Master Bergid's breathing exercises. "No foundation? No stable building! No deep well? No lasting water!" the apprentice intoned deeply, in faultless mimicry of his Master's voice. Darryk stared at him for a moment, then almost fell over laughing. However, when it came to transferring this advice to the flute itself, Kaelin found it difficult to teach with words alone. Unthinkingly, he picked up his own flute.

"Like this, Darryk." A sweet, perfectly controlled sound emerged from Kaelin's flute, swelled into a beautiful vibrato, then died away without loss of pitch or quality. The apprentice dropped his flute to his lap, horrified at what he had just done. "I'm sorry!" He turned panic-stricken eyes toward his new friend. "I shouldn't have done that!"

"Why not?" Darryk said, utterly perplexed. "Your tone is absolutely beautiful! I don't believe I've heard a Bard who can match it."

His words only seemed to upset Kaelin more. "You don't understand! I might have hurt you!"

Darryk frowned. "I will admit to having felt distinct pain at the sound of a practicing apprentice before," he said dryly, "but you certainly do not qualify as such. Short of bashing me over the head with your flute, how could you possibly have hurt me?"

Kaelin was silent for a long moment. He had never told anyone, not even his sister ... *especially* not his sister. He had been unable to tell his Master, who would surely take away the robe and cord he had given him and regretfully send him away, telling him there was no place in the Bardic Order for someone whose music could hurt others. He hadn't even been able to tell Sean, unwilling to see his little brother's respect and admiration turn to fear. Erik would not have understood, and Kaelin could never have trusted him not to tell anyone. Maybe *this* friend—a Bard who would respect a confidence, a friend who wouldn't take him to his Master—might be someone he could tell. Everything within him rose in protest.

Don't be a fool! Friend or not, he's still a Bard! Even if he doesn't want to, he'll take you to your Master! You'll be sent away with nothing ... and no way to go home, for how will you return to Kestrel without a Bardic apprentice robe to give you free passage? You haven't enough coppers to pay for it, and you're not old enough to be hired on. No one in the Bardic Order will help you once your Master sends you away. Not even Darryk.

He blocked out the furious upbraiding his mind was giving him and closed his eyes against the overwhelming need to tell someone, to release the pressure of the terrible secret he had kept for so many cycles. Words Laena had spoken to him came suddenly to his mind.

It's okay if you can't tell me what happened, but I hope that someday you're able to tell someone. Whatever this burden is, it's too heavy for you to carry alone.

She's right. It is too heavy ... and no matter what happens, I can't carry it anymore. Kaelin felt something break inside him at the admission. Words came in a sudden, disjointed rush, as though reaching frantically for this unexpected chance to be released.

"How could I possibly hurt you? With my music!" The apprentice's cry erupted so suddenly that Darryk's mouth fell open in surprise. "It *hurts* people! I had to keep it inside, so it only hurt me until Master Bergid heard it. It doesn't hurt him because he's a Master." Kaelin was far too upset to notice the confusion on his new friend's face. "But it hurt ... two others. They ... died. I—" His voice broke off.

Darryk waited, watching his young friend struggle to continue. Kaelin abruptly turned away, staring into the fire as though searching it for words and the strength to say them. Neither of them noticed a silent figure approaching behind them.

"I killed my own parents," Kaelin whispered his confession to the flames, "with my music."

Darryk didn't move; only his grey eyes reflected his shock at this astounding statement. Kaelin drew his knees to his chin, as though to make himself as small as possible before continuing. His eyes did not leave the fire. He didn't want to see Darryk's face, didn't want to know if he had just lost the friend he had so recently made. He would finish what he'd begun and somehow find the courage to look into Darryk's face afterwards.

"I'd just turned seven," the apprentice told the flames, "when I saw a piece of wood at Old Torin's house that looked the right size for a flute. I asked him if I could have it, and he gave it to me. I used my father's woodworking tools and made my own flute with it ... just a small one. It wasn't much, but I did the best I could. When it was finished, I tried to play it, but it wouldn't even make a sound! I kept trying and trying until I got angry and almost threw the flute away. But I tried it one more time ... and it worked." The boy studied the flames for a moment, then continued in a low voice. "Then my parents got sick. They were sick for weeks and I was always being sent outside, so I took my flute into the woods and practiced until I could play a song of my own. The music had been going around and around in my head, and when I could finally play it without stopping, it felt … wonderful! I thought it might make my parents feel better, so I ran home to play it for them." He paused, his throat constricting as he saw it happen again in his mind.

"Laena wasn't there." Kaelin's voice rose, choked with panic. "My parents were awake. They were too weak to speak, but when I asked them if they wanted to hear my music, they nodded, and my mother even smiled." He broke off, shaking. "I … played my music … and I felt them *with* me, somehow. I was remembering where we'd been the month before—up on the slopes of Skellig Mountain to celebrate my mother's birthday—and it was like they were there with me, seeing it too. But when I stopped playing—" He looked down abruptly, as though unwilling for even the flames to hear his confession. "Their eyes were shut, like they'd fallen asleep. But they didn't wake up. They *never* woke up again!" His face twisted in pain. "I never thought my music would do something so awful! I just wanted to surprise them, to make them feel better. Truly!" he insisted, as though the fire had disputed this statement. "That's all I wanted!"

He stumbled to his feet and turned unexpectedly into the arms of his Master. Kaelin's face drained of color as he realized what had just been overheard. "I didn't mean it!" he cried into the white robe. "I didn't mean to kill them!"

"I know, Kaelin."

"Now you'll take my robe and send me away—" His voice broke with anguish.

"Didn't I tell you that *nothing* could ever make that happen?"

"But you didn't know what I'd done! And if there's no place in the Bardic Order for someone who lies, how could there be any place for someone who … who kills—" Kaelin broke off, his breath coming in ragged gasps.

The Master lifted his chin firmly. "What makes you think your music killed your parents?"

"It had to be my music … they both died right after listening to it!" Kaelin lowered his eyes, unable to bear his Master's gaze. "They were so weak from their sickness. They didn't have the strength to hear me play, the way you do."

"It takes no strength to hear you play," his Master said gently. "Why do you think it should?"

"Because my music takes all of *my* strength! And after what it did to my parents, it hurt, worse and worse every cycle. If every note hurt me, how much must a whole song have hurt my parents? They were too sick to defend themselves, too sick to beg me to stop!" Kaelin forced himself to look up into his Master's eyes, and the compassion he saw there nearly undid him. His Master would not want to send him away—was looking for any excuse not to—but in the end, he would have to do it anyway.

"So, this is why you forced your music into that cage inside you," the Master said softly, as though to himself. "This is why you've refused to play for anyone but me."

"What else could I do?" Kaelin cried, bitterness lacing his words. "I couldn't let it hurt anyone else, so I ran to my place in the woods and buried my flute there. I thought I could forget what happened if I could just forget the music that *made* it happen. But I couldn't get rid of it, no matter how hard I tried. The pain and the pressure got so bad that I had to release some of it before it drove me crazy! So, a cycle later I dug up my flute and only played it there, where no one could hear, so I wouldn't hurt anyone ever again. And then *you* came and played my music without hurting anyone with it, and I realized that there's nothing wrong with my music." Kaelin's face twisted with pain. "There's something wrong with *me*. And I knew then that I could never play anything for anyone else." He looked imploringly at the Master. "Please don't tell Laena what really happened to our parents. I couldn't bear to look at her if she knew what I did. Please," he whispered hoarsely. "It's awful enough that the two of you know, and she ... she's the only family I have."

"There is nothing wrong with you *or* your music," the Master stated, "and I would never lie to your sister and tell her that you were responsible for the deaths of your parents."

"But ... I am." Fresh tears streaked a crooked path down Kaelin's cheeks. "I know I should never have accepted an apprenticeship in the Bardic Order when I knew I couldn't stay in it and didn't deserve to ... but you wouldn't keep me if I refused. I didn't stay with you so I could put on this robe. I put on the robe so I could stay with you, at least until you found out. I know I should be sorry for it, for wasting your time ... but I'm not!" Defiance and grief danced a slow dirge across his face. "I'll *never* be sorry for a single minute I had with you!"

"Not one of those minutes has been a waste of my time," said the Master firmly. "What happened to your parents wasn't your fau—"

"It was, sir! You can't help me with this or make a variation of it I can accept. No lesson can fix it. I *know* what happened ... and it *was* my fault."

The Master's eyes never left the anguished eyes of his apprentice as he picked up Kaelin's flute and held it out to him. "Play the song you played that day."

Darryk looked up in surprise. The quietly spoken words were not a request.

Kaelin took a step back from his flute, glanced at Darryk with panic-stricken eyes, and frantically shook his head. "I can't! I made a vow—to *you*, sir—never to use my music to harm anyone. You're commanding me to break it!"

"Do you think I would ask you to play if there was the slightest chance that any harm would befall Darryk?" The Master's expression was uncompromising. "Play that song."

"No!" The first refusal he had ever given his Master was ripped from his throat in agony.

The Master said nothing more. He placed Kaelin's flute on top of its bag, then settled himself by the fire and stared into its flames. Darryk, taking his cue from the Master, did likewise. Time slowed to a trickle.

Kaelin fell to his knees by the silent Master. "Please don't make me," he whispered hoarsely. "I've done everything else you've asked of me. *Please* don't ask this. It's an awful thing to ... to live knowing I killed my own parents. If it happens again—I can't risk that, sir! I *can't.*"

When the Master made no reply, Kaelin tried again. "When I heard you play my music and nothing awful happened, I knew it must be because you're a Master ... and maybe, just maybe, you could help me. So, I followed you and you didn't send me away. You helped me free my music so I can play it without pain for myself and one other person ... you, the only person who isn't hurt by it. And now you want me to risk doing it again, risk killing someone I care about! I beg you, Master ... don't make me do it."

Darryk, struggling to keep his own face impassive, wondered at the Master's ability to remain deaf to such entreaties. Master Bergid sat calmly gazing into the flames as though he heard nothing. The Bard stared at his own set of flames and grappled with the astounding idea that music could kill someone. It was possible, he admitted to himself. Master Cyral's music had been just that powerful and had undoubtedly killed a great many warriors. But Master Cyral had been uniquely Gifted and highly trained, his acts committed with full intent. Darryk glanced at the desolate boy kneeling next to his Master. The idea that an untrained youngster could unwittingly kill his parents with the music of a crudely-made flute was almost laughable ... and yet Kaelin clearly believed it. *He thinks he's fighting to save my life. He honestly believes that if I hear him play, it might kill me!*

Kaelin sat back on his heels in total frustration with his Master's silence. *How can he order me to risk Darryk's life? I won't do it!* He closed his eyes, and the darkness shrouding his inner turmoil reminded him of his sense-deprivation test. He remembered the feel of rocks and feathers and the frustration of trying to sort them. He remembered the Master's withdrawal the few times Kaelin lost his temper with them, giving him time to work it out on his own.

Time. He's giving me time.

Kaelin looked at his flute, lying on its travel bag beside him, and gently touched it. If it weren't for his Master, he wouldn't have such a wonderful instrument. He wouldn't be able to play it, or the pipes or harp, or be able to write down his music. He thought of how horrible it would be if he were still in the village of Vale, apprenticed to Craftmaster Arnor ... his inhibited Gift an ever-increasing agony within him, playing his little flute only in the privacy of the woods. It had been nearly a cycle before he could bring himself to do even that. It had taken time.

Time can change things. And I made him a promise. I told him I would do anything he asked of me. Anything, no matter how hard. The boy felt the tight band of resistance inside him break apart and melt away. He did not trust his music, but he trusted his Master. If his Master was asking this of him and had assured him that nothing would happen to Darryk, then surely Kaelin could trust that nothing would. He glanced at Darryk and saw no judgement or fear on the Bard's face as he quietly studied the fire.

The apprentice stared at his flute and swallowed painfully. Slowly he picked up the treasured instrument, put it to his lips and closed his eyes. He would obey his Master's last command to him. He would play one final song as an apprentice before he removed his robe and left. He would not look at his Master's face while he did so, and if anything happened to Darryk, he would never play another note on this, or any other instrument, again. He took a deep, trembling breath and began to play.

The notes came without conscious effort, notes the flutist had not played since he was seven, but which were branded on the walls of his mind forever. He could see his parents' room clearly as he began to play. He could see the bed, his parents lying on it, their eyes fastening on him as he smiled at them and proudly showed them his flute. He saw his mother's smile, and he almost broke under the memory of it ... but he forced himself to keep playing. Unbidden, the place he had thought of when he composed the song came to his mind. The familiar banks of a stream up on Skellig Mountain ... the willow tree overhanging it ... all their names inscribed on the flat side of a boulder nearby. He saw it all clearly and felt his parents' presence with him in that special place. Then, with a surge of fresh anguish, he stared uncomprehendingly at his motionless parents, slight smiles erasing the pain on their faces. He felt the small flute drop from his hands, heard cries come from his own mouth that sounded nothing like his own voice, begging them to wake up. But they didn't rouse to his cries. They didn't stir at all. They were as motionless as if ... as if—

Kaelin barely managed to lay his flute down without dropping it. Shaking from the trauma of replaying those accursed notes from the past, his eyes fastened on Darryk. The Bard sat with his head bowed, silent but unharmed. With a gasp of relief, Kaelin got to his feet and fumbled with his cord, fully intending to remove his robe and leave. But before he could unfasten it, his Master was standing in front of him, gripping his shoulders and commanding his attention with fierce blue eyes.

"*Think*, Kaelin! Two healthy adults who became ill at the same time, yet you and Laena didn't, who weakened over the course of several weeks, then died at the same time? This doesn't sound like a normal illness, this sounds like poisoning! Your parents must have eaten something that you and Laena didn't. You had just been up on Skellig ... did you bring back any mushrooms with you? Mushrooms that only your parents ate?"

Kaelin thought for a moment, then slowly nodded. "But ... they didn't get sick when they ate them."

His Master's expression turned grim. "There are several varieties in the mountains here that are poisonous. Most of them cause problems quickly, but one variety takes many days for symptoms to develop. Nausea, vomiting, burning thirst, headaches, chills without fever—" He nodded as Kaelin's widened eyes confirmed his suspicion.

"There is truly nothing anyone could have done," the Master said gently. "No Healer could have prevented their deaths. Laena would have known the end was near, and gone to find you so you could say good-bye to them."

When Kaelin made no response, the Master gently shook his frozen apprentice's shoulders. "Do you hear me, Kaelin? Your music did *not* kill your parents! They died of poisoning, and you gave them a great gift at their passing, a gift that eased it better than any Healer could have done. Far from hurting them, your music was their elegy. A beautiful elegy played by their only son."

Incredulous joy swept over Kaelin, a surge of freedom surpassing even the regaining of his sight and hearing, a release more profound than the freeing of his music. He uttered a choked sob and found himself enveloped in his Master's arms. His tears flowed, washing away the guilt he had borne for nearly five cycles. His Master did not release him until his sobs abated and his trembling body relaxed. Bergid led the boy to Darryk's mat and sat beside him until he fell asleep.

The Bard raised his head like one waking from a dream as the Master returned to the fire and laid more wood on it.

"I hope you do not think me too cruel, Darryk."

"No, Master Bergid." The Bard shook his head slowly. "It was the only way to help him. But his *music,* sir! How is such a thing possible?"

"You were there, too?"

"Yes, I saw everything! The room, his parents, the boulder with their names engraved on it. I saw—no, I *experienced* his memory, exactly as he himself lived it, as if I were him! An unspeakably horrible memory ... but an incredible experience."

The Master nodded. "And impossible to believe if not experienced for oneself. The first song I heard him play was a variation of the song of a kestrel. I tell you, I was instantly airborne, soaring high above the mountains of my island! Not something I can tell anyone without them questioning my sanity or wondering what kind of mushrooms *I'd* been eating." He shook his head. "To think that I should have stumbled upon such a Gifted youngster while camping in the woods! Kaelin has an extraordinary Gift ... one, I might add, that he is totally unaware of."

Darryk gave the Master a surprised look.

"Oh, he knows he has a gift for composing," the Master continued, "and an equal one for playing what he writes. But I'm quite certain he has no idea that his music has the power to transport his listener to the very place he is thinking about, or experience a memory like this as if we were him." He frowned slightly. "I feel such a Gift is best left to develop slowly, allowing Kaelin to realize what he possesses gradually as he is able to bear it and use it wisely. A true Gift does not come without cost, and such a Gift as this could exact a terrible price." His eyes rested compassionately on the peacefully sleeping apprentice. "As it already has," he said softly, as though to himself. "Why must everything I do to help him be so painful?"

"Not everything," Darryk ventured to say. "You love him. Kaelin knows that and values it above any pain. It's the only reason he was able to play the music of such a memory as that."

The Master frowned. "I've never told him so."

"If I may be so bold as to contradict a Master, I think you have, sir," the Bard said quietly. "More often, perhaps, than you know."

The Master sat watching Kaelin for a moment before turning

back to the fire. He did not speak.

Darryk rose and stretched wearily. "Kaelin can remain sleeping where he is if you would like to stay the night here. I took the liberty of borrowing a couple of spare mats from the Bard's storeroom in case any of your sessions run late."

The Master nodded. "I appreciate not having to disturb him." He gave the Bard a keen glance. "You look in need of some sleep yourself."

Darryk grimaced. "I must admit those fiendish breathing exercises of yours have tired me beyond belief. Why anyone would want to play such a torturous instrument when they could play a nice, comfortable *stringed* instrument—" He shrugged, clearly at a loss.

The Master Bard chuckled. "You took a flute lesson from my apprentice?"

"I did," Darryk admitted, "and profited from it, too." He hesitated, then looked fully in the Master's face. "I also extended my arm to him, and it was accepted. Kaelin will do a great deal for a friend that he would not do for a Bard."

The Master gave him a keen glance. "Was that your reason for offering it?"

Darryk gave him a startled look. "I offered what I truly desired to give. I had no thought of gaining his confidence by doing so. I hope my action has not displeased you."

The Master's expression did not change. "And if it has, would you take it back?"

The Bard's face grew noticeably paler in the fire's light, but he shook his head. "No, sir. I would not hurt Kaelin to save myself your displeasure. The apprentice who went up against his Master to save my life deserves better."

Master Bergid smiled. "Your action enabled Kaelin to unburden himself and confide in you, something he could not do with his sister, his younger brother, or his Master. An older friend is exactly what he needed. He could not have asked for a better one, and your action, unorthodox as it may be, could not have pleased me more. However," he added dryly, "let's hope Master Grened does not hear of it before we're safely off his island."

Chapter 18

Kaelin bounced back from his emotional epiphany of the night before at a tempo that left Master Bergid and Darryk shaking their heads at the resilience of youth. Breakfast preparations were made with more exuberance than skill, prompting Darryk to shoo the youngster away and take over, much to the Master's relief. In short order, they all sat down to hot griddle cakes, sausages, and mash seasoned with fresh herbs.

"Perhaps," Master Bergid said after taking an appreciative bite, "you could both profit from an exchange of talents." He waved his spoon at each of them. "Flute and cooking lessons!"

Darryk laughed, but Kaelin looked chagrined. "Has my cooking been that bad?"

"Not on any other day," replied the Master as he scooped up another bite. "But have a taste of that griddle cake and tell me what *you* think."

Kaelin did as instructed, then eagerly repeated the task. "I think trading lessons is a great idea! Not even my sister can match this."

Darryk rolled his eyes. "I know when I'm being manipulated," he grumbled, "and you'll notice I did *not* ask if my flute playing has been that bad."

The Master cocked an eye at him. "That's because you know

the answer as well as I do. Your first rotation to Zephyr is likely to be your last if you don't do something about it," he said pointedly. "Marek lets no Bard leave his island until they've reached form seven. Where are you now … form two?"

"Almost," Darryk replied in a small voice. He flushed under the matching scandalized expressions of Master and apprentice. "I always intend to make better headway," the Bard said defensively, "but my harp just seems to wind up in my hands instead." He shrugged helplessly, as though his pushy harp were to blame.

"In that case," the Master said mildly, "perhaps you should hand your harp over to me for safekeeping until you've progressed to form two. If you spend even half the time on your flute that you spend on your harp, I'm sure you'll receive your harp back before the end of the Spring Council."

The alarm on Darryk's face made Kaelin stifle a laugh.

"You wouldn't really do that," the Bard asked tentatively, "would you, sir? That's my primary instrument!"

"A harpist who has passed all ten levels of his instrument isn't going to backslide in the space of a week or two," the Master said expressionlessly. "However, a level one flutist, given the right incentive, is likely to make a great deal of progress."

"What if I promise not to touch my harp until I've practiced my flute for two hours, every day that I'm here?" the Bard pleaded.

"Hmm … and you'll take lessons every morning with my apprentice?"

"I won't miss a day, sir!"

The Master pursed his lips, considering the matter. "Very well," he decided. "Make it *three* hours and you can keep your harp with you, but if you do not test with one of the Masters into form two before the end of the Spring Council—" He looked meaningfully at the Bard's harp.

"Consider it done, Master Bergid!"

"And you will reach form three before the end of the cycle," the Master continued. "If you do not, you will give your harp into the keeping of the Master of the island you rotate to, until such time as you do."

Darryk groaned.

"At that time, I will decide if an extension of our ... little agreement ... is needed to help you attain level four."

The Bard nodded morosely, and Kaelin gave him a sympathetic look.

"I suppose," the Master continued thoughtfully, "there's a reason each of us becomes enamored of a particular instrument. I, for instance, can clearly remember the Flutist who came to our house for dinner when I was only four, and played a song for us afterwards. I couldn't take my eyes off that flute, and begged him for another song ... and another, until my father sternly told me to stop pestering the poor man. The Flutist laughed and played me one more song before putting it away. From that moment on, I gave my parents no peace until they let me begin lessons ... with that same Flutist, who said that any youngster who kept begging for flute music was a student he would make time in his schedule for." He looked quizzically at Darryk. "I imagine you were mesmerized in similar fashion by a Harpist?"

The Bard chuckled. "I was, indeed, and I also clearly remember the occasion. My father took me with him to Kyet the summer I turned six, and—"

"Kyet?" Kaelin echoed in surprise. He flushed at his Master's raised brow. "Forgive me for interrupting you, Darryk, but I didn't realize you grew up on Kestrel."

"Yes, I'm a fellow Kestrelian like yourself," Darryk said whimsically, "if there is such a word. I grew up in one of the northeast coastal villages, so going to Kyet was a long and exciting trip for a child. When we got there, my father headed straight for the marketplace and began going from shop to shop, checking things off his own list and the lengthy one my mother had given him. He was in the leather shop so long that I asked if I could wait for him outside, where I could watch the people and carts passing by. He told me to stay right outside the shop, but the moment I slipped outside, I heard wondrous music coming from somewhere down the street, and promptly forgot everything except the desire to find it. A few streets away, I reached the square and discovered the music was coming from the most beautiful harp I'd ever seen, played by a man in a white robe. Dozens of people were sitting around him, listening. I stood there behind them and listened to song after song … until my father grabbed my arm and marched me into an alley, where he gave my backside several stinging reasons why I'd best never disobey him again, wondrous harp music notwithstanding." He looked at Master Bergid's astonished expression and grinned. "Yes, sir, you were the reason I did not sit down for the remainder of that day."

"So," Kaelin said, glancing mischievously at Darryk, "it seems we both had our lives changed forever by encountering the Master Bard of Kestrel, and without him speaking a single word! Perhaps we should warn the parents of Kestrel not to risk letting their children near him."

"Unless, of course, they have plenty of extra coin to spend on Bardic instruments."

"Or they're allowed to send the bill to him."

"Well, that sounds fair."

"Absolutely."

The Master rolled his eyes. "If the two of you are quite finished, I'd like to know what happened after you regained the ability to sit down, Darryk. Did you beg your father for a harp?"

"Just once, on the way home," Darryk replied. "My father did his best to convince me to choose another instrument, one we already owned, like a lyre or lute, for after all, he pointed out, did they not have strings as well? I stubbornly insisted it had to be a harp. He brooded for a while, then told me he would only buy me a lap harp if I could go a whole cycle without once disobeying him or getting into any kind of trouble."

Kaelin grinned. "In that case, you must have bought one yourself after you came of age and got a job."

The Master chuckled and Darryk gave the apprentice a withering look. "On the contrary," the Bard said, "I was the child of my father's dreams for an entire cycle, prompting him to wish he had made it two cycles instead of one. But, though he moaned about the expense, I got my lap harp, made for me by the Instrumentalist who lived in our village, and lessons with him as well. My father said that if he was going to be subjected to daily harp music played by a child of seven, it was going to be *good* harp music, and the sooner the better."

"And did you return to your incorrigible lifestyle after that?" the Master asked.

"I made a few valiant attempts to do so, but my father quickly discovered that all he had to do to keep his son in line was to threaten to take away his harp." Darryk grinned ruefully. "Still claims it was the best investment he ever made." The others laughed, and the Bard turned toward the apprentice.

"What about you, Kaelin? We know you made your own flute when you were seven, but what made you want to play such an uncomfortable, breath*taking* instrument in the first place?"

"Well, we didn't have any instruments in our family," Kaelin replied, "and there weren't any Bardic instruments in the whole village until Flutist Torin retired there. But when I was around five cycles old, I started hearing music from things ... a rock or feather or whatever I picked up and studied."

"You heard—" Darryk broke off at a glance from the Master. "Pardon my interruption, Kaelin. Please continue."

"Well, I liked the music," Kaelin said, "so I started humming it sometimes, and it felt good, like I was releasing some kind of pressure inside me. Things started happening after that—strange things—and I didn't realize that they only happened when I was humming until I asked Laena to teach me how to climb a tree. We started climbing, and when I studied one of the branches, trying to decide if I could reach it, I heard the tree's song. It was the first time I'd ever heard music from something alive, and it was more beautiful than anything I'd heard before, and—" he shrugged, "well, you know what that's like. I told Laena there was music coming from the tree, but she just looked at me like I was crazy and started climbing again. So, I started humming it to show her what it sounded like, and my sister fell and broke her ankle. Later, she told me she felt pulled by my humming somehow. She said it wasn't my fault, but we never climbed trees together again. She always had a reason why she couldn't do it. So, I started to worry that ... well, that something was wrong with me. Everyone else could hum or sing whatever they wanted, but if *I* did, weird things happened to the people around me."

The Master and Bard exchanged glances. "What happened when you started school?" the Master asked.

Kaelin frowned. "I was excited at first, thinking I would finally get to play an instrument, but all we got to play were these silly little drums and whistles! I wanted a *real* instrument ... something I could play real music on. So, when I heard that a Flutist had retired to Vale, I skipped school and went to see him. He was hard to talk to because he kept falling asleep, but he played a song on his flute for me, and I thought it was the most beautiful thing I'd ever heard. I begged him to teach me, but he said he was too old to take students and wouldn't change his mind, even when I offered to do all his chores every day. So, I just kept visiting and let him talk. And he'd tell me all kinds of interesting things and play for me, saying an audience of one was better than no audience at all. I learned a lot that way, but he never let me play his flute. He taught me how to write down the short pieces he composed, though, for his fingers were too sore to do it himself."

Bergid's eyes widened slightly. *So that's how Kaelin knew so much more than what's taught in school.*

"I could hear music all the time by then," Kaelin continued. "The pressure was getting worse, and humming didn't help much anymore. Then I made my own flute." A look of pain crossed his face.

Darryk smoothly filled the brief silence that fell after this. "Well, then," he said lightly, "since you've already made *two* flutes, it seems you're quite overdue for a serious stringed instrument like a harp. Speaking of which ..." He told the Master about his offer to help Kaelin make a Bardic harp of his own.

Kaelin's face lit up as he turned hopeful eyes to his Master.

"Hmm ... he'll need seasoned wood, of course, and strings," the Master said consideringly.

"Yes, sir, he will."

"And woodworking tools, which I do not have with me."

"He's welcome to use mine."

The Master cocked an eye at his apprentice. "With the exception of Master Talan, Master Grened, and myself, there is no one better qualified to teach you the intricacies of making a Bardic harp than Darryk. You will, of course, obey him in every detail, for in this matter he will be acting as your teacher, not your friend, and I will be expecting a good report."

"Yes, sir!"

"Is this a lap harp we're speaking of, or a full-sized harp?"

"I'll happily accept either one," Kaelin said, his eyes traveling longingly to his Master's harp. "But, if I have a choice..."

Bergid chuckled. "A full-sized harp it is. Very well, then, I'll see about having the wood sent here from Tryl as soon as possible." He smiled at the happiness on Kaelin's face and turned to Darryk. "Would rosewood, spruce, and beech suffice?"

Darryk's eyes widened. "Rosewood? Why ... certainly, sir!"

The Master rummaged in his pack and brought out a scroll

and quill. He wrote for a few minutes, looking amused about something, then sealed the missive and handed it to Darryk. "I would appreciate it if you saw to the quick dispatching of this order to Merchant Cathal in Tryl for me," he said, "and make no mention of it to anyone, particularly Master Talan."

"I'll see to it right away and mention it to no one." The Bard took the scroll and stowed it carefully in his pack.

"And the next time I visit the northeast coastal villages," the Master said casually, "I think I'll look up your father. I'm sure he'd be delighted to hear that the threat he used on you twenty cycles ago is still as effective as ever."

"He certainly would," the Bard wryly agreed, "and the two of you would enjoy each other's company. You have a great deal in common." His eyes looked briefly into the Master's. "And that's a compliment, sir." He slung his pack over his shoulder and left to obey the Master's instructions.

"Do you think you'll have to keep threatening to hold Darryk's harp hostage until he reaches flute form seven?" Kaelin asked in a hushed voice.

"Not if his young friend can inspire him with a desire to reach it himself," the Master said, suppressing a chuckle when Kaelin cast a determined look in the direction the Bard had gone. *Darryk may not know it yet,* the Master thought, *but he doesn't stand a chance.*

The two of them departed for the Master's cabin, Kaelin so lighthearted that Bergid whimsically told him he wasn't leaving any footprints.

Kaelin laughed. "Nothing can keep me on the ground today, sir!" With a whoop of pure joy, he ran on ahead, leaving his Master to follow at a more relaxed tempo, smiling as he went.

❧

Unlike his light-footed apprentice, the Master felt all the weight of his own footsteps as, later that day, he strode down the grassy path to the Council Grounds in deep thought. This was the second session of the Spring Council, and he doubted he could keep the talk steered away from Kaelin yet again. He chuckled grimly to himself. Being a month older than Grened, and thus Senior Master of the Council, was a distinct advantage at times. Bergid had the right to lead the Council meetings and had made full use of it the night before. Still, he couldn't avoid the issue forever and it wouldn't be wise to try. Grened, his friend for nearly four decades, was practically seething with unanswered questions and Bergid did not wish to alienate anyone else. Rial, the Master Bard of Lyra, was a conservative man, likely to side with Grened over anything controversial. Talan, Master Bard of Eyrie, was much more open-minded, and Bergid anticipated little trouble convincing Marek, the young Master Bard of Zephyr. Of course, they would all want to hear Kaelin for themselves before coming to a decision. *Perhaps, thanks to Darryk, that might yet be possible. Still, time will work to Kaelin's advantage.*

As Bergid approached, he heard loud voices drifting up from the Council Grounds. The path he was on soon brought him to a stone stairway that descended to a polished stone floor. This was a natural amphitheater, surrounded by cliffs in which tiers of seats had been laboriously carved. Its surprisingly excellent acoustics made it a coveted place to perform, and the Masters used it for their Council meetings when weather permitted. The sound of raised voices resounding from below was not unusual, but the Master hastened his steps. He had a feeling he knew the topic of debate.

Silence fell as Bergid walked across the Council Grounds, confirming his suspicions. Giving his colleagues no chance to wonder how much he had overheard, he strode past them to the head of the stone Council table and stood waiting for them to assemble themselves in order of seniority. Grened, Master Harpist and Master Bard of Elegy, took the seat to the right of him, his hazel eyes fixed upon Bergid with stiff disapproval. The others bowed to him before being seated, varying degrees of worry evident on their faces. Rial, the stolid, barrel-chested Voice Master and Master Bard of Lyra, seated himself to the left of Bergid. He tapped the table distractedly, his sea-green eyes half-shuttered, as though unwilling to meet the Senior Master's gaze. Talan, Instrument Master and Master Bard of Eyrie, sat next to Grened. The tallest of the Masters, he pursed his lips and studied the table as though it were a Bardic instrument in dire need of repair. Marek, Master Flutist and Master Bard of Zephyr, sat beside Rial. He ran his hands distractedly through his blond hair as he glanced at Bergid with concern.

Lining the outer perimeter of the grounds were eight torches in intricately carved stone holders, lit in readiness for the fast-approaching dusk. On the table stood two similarly carved lamps, ready to be lit when needed. Directly in front of the Senior Master stood a highly polished set of graduated chimes hanging from a frame of twisted silver. These were the same chimes that had been brought from their homeland, chimes that had graced the marble table of the Council of Masters in Aille-Mara for untold cycles. The Senior Master picked up the mallet that lay beside the chimes and struck the smallest three times. The silvery tones filled the Council Grounds, then died away.

"The second session of the Spring Council is now open." The Master's brow lifted. "Since so little was accomplished at our first session, I propose to begin this one by airing a subject that seems to be occupying your minds to the exclusion of all else."

The expressions around the table altered. Marek and Talan looked relieved, Rial glanced up in surprise, and Grened's frown deepened.

"I therefore open this session," Bergid continued, "to the questioning of myself concerning Kaelin, my apprentice." He sat back and waited for the explosion.

It came, predictably enough, from his right. "*Your* apprentice?" The Master Harpist was incensed. "I do *not* believe it! Why, you speak as though you've acquired nothing more than a new composition desk! When I heard a boy was traveling with you, I assumed you were taking him to a new home. I thought he must be a boy who had lost his parents, but instead, it seems he's the apprentice of a Master who has lost his mind! So, *this* is why none of the Bards of Kestrel will say one word—"

The Senior Master stopped the outburst with a sharp tap on the medium-sized chime. "I remind you that this is a questioning session, not a grievance session. If you have any questions, ask them. Otherwise, let someone else speak."

"Very well, then," Grened said acidly. "Exactly when did you stumble across this ... boy of yours?"

"Almost a cycle ago."

"And is he the reason you refused to attend all Council sessions for the past *cycle* and ignored all of my queries concerning your absence?"

"I would have willingly attended any session which dealt with a matter of more importance than what I was doing at the time. This cycle was refreshingly free of such matters." Bergid shrugged. "Your queries were sent to my home. By the time I arrived there, I had already received your summons ... which I did, in fact, respond to. I told you I would be happy to answer your questions at this Spring Council. And here I am," he favored Grened with an obliging smile, "doing just that."

Grened stared at him, at a momentary loss for words. "You value this boy so highly that you left your island unrepresented?"

"Kestrel was not left unrepresented, as you know perfectly well," Bergid said evenly. "I sent Bard Flynn, who is eligible to become a Master, to the sessions I missed for the express purpose of delivering my own hand-written votes on those matters, and to take detailed notes on the proceedings, which he brought back to me. None of my own votes were altered in the slightest by those notes, and all of them fell in line with this Council's voting, which in all cases was unanimous. Did you not receive my votes?"

"Well, yes, but that's hardly—"

"Then you lost nothing by my absence, and I was kept fully informed."

"Flynn may have kept *you* informed," Rial said testily, "but he was singularly uninformative on the whereabouts of the Master he was replacing at this table!" The Voice Master's finger stabbed the marble top for emphasis.

The Senior Master sighed. "Must I again remind you that this is a question—"

"Very well, Bergid," Rial interrupted tersely. "*Why* was Flynn so uninformative when asked to tell us where you were? He refused to answer any of our questions, and for a Bard to refuse to answer this Council is clear insubordination! I came very close to formally charging him with it."

"I gave Flynn explicit instructions to tell you that I was occupied with a personal, private matter, and that I would give you the details myself, in person." Bergid gave his colleague an inquiring look. "Did he not do so?"

"Well, yes, but—"

"And am I not giving you the details in person, precisely when I informed Grened I would?"

"But—"

"I also instructed Flynn to answer no questions about it, for a private matter is, by definition, *private*." Bergid's voice grew steely. "I'm sure we would all agree that a Bard who obeys the Master he is serving a rotation under can hardly be charged with insubordination."

Rial's eyes narrowed as he stared at Bergid, his expression mutinous. "You dared to order him not to answer to this Council?" he growled.

Bergid met the Voice Master's eyes unflinchingly. "Concerning a private matter of my own that no one has the right to discuss without my permission or presence? Yes, I did." He raised a brow. "I would be curious to know what charge you could possibly bring against me for it."

Rial sat back in surrender. A smile of admiration crossed Marek's face.

"How old is this youngster?" Talan smoothly interjected.

"Kaelin," Bergid said pointedly, "turned twelve cycles on the tenth of this month."

Grened snorted in contempt. "So, you took this *boy* on when he was barely eleven, when no one is accepted into the Bardic Order before coming of age at fifteen? Just how many cycles of expert instruction did he have before coming to you?"

"I took Kaelin as my apprentice last autumn, when he was still eleven. He had no instruction at all prior to mine." The Senior Master spoke calmly, but his words lifted the brow of every Master at the table.

"Do you seriously mean to say, Bergid," demanded Rial in a scandalized voice, "that you took on a completely untutored boy of eleven, disappeared into the hills with him, and left the island of Kestrel without a Master Bard for three *seasons?*"

"To answer each of your questions, I do seriously mean to say that I took on a completely untutored boy of eleven cycles. I did not, however, disappear, nor did I leave the island of Kestrel without its Master. You will find all of Kestrel's affairs to be quite in order." A slight smile tugged at the corner of his mouth. "We did live for some time in the hills."

Marek chuckled. "Perhaps, Bergid, it would be best if you explained the matter from the beginning. I, for one, am consumed with curiosity, and I do not believe for a minute," glancing defiantly at Rial, "that the island of Kestrel has suffered a moment's mismanagement during this cycle or any other."

Talan nodded in agreement. "I also would prefer hearing the sequence of events in order, instead of picked out question by question."

"As would I," Rial said with a terse nod.

"Agreed!" Grened growled. "Provided we have the opportunity to question what we hear."

Once again the Council Grounds filled with the sound of chimes.

"The format of our session is now changed. Questions and comments on the recitation are allowed, providing they are not disruptive." Bergid relaxed in his chair, closed his eyes for a moment, and began.

"As you all know, my knee injury kept me away from the mountain villages three cycles ago, when I would normally have visited them. But after leaving the Spring Council last cycle, I decided my knee was finally up to the challenge of a trek through the mountains, so I made arrangements for the Captain to let me disembark on the western shore. I left a missive with him for my Bards, telling them of my plans and placing my island in Flynn's capable hands for what I thought would be no more than six weeks. I procured a mule and headed east through the Skirling mountains, spending a day or two in each village I came to. One evening, while camped near the village of Vale, I heard flute music. It was a beautiful, original composition coming from a small village flute, but that was not what held my attention." The Master paused, carefully considering his next words.

"This," he said suddenly, with an authoritative glint in his eye, "is where I must ask your indulgence. I will not, at this time, tell you what compelled me to discover the identity of that flutist. Suffice it to say, I slept that night in my camp, and early the next morning, I entered the village." He held up a hand to forestall the interruption he saw coming from his right. "Hear me out first, Grened. I have good reason for what I am saying ... and for what I am *not* saying."

Grened subsided with a frown. The Senior Master took a deep

breath and continued. "As you can well imagine, I had no lack of candidates to screen when I reached the village square. However, no composer or flutist approached me, so after repairing a few instruments, talking to the villagers, and waiting for a crowd to gather, I began to play my flute. Near the end, I modulated my music to the melody I had heard the night before, watching the crowd carefully." He paused, reliving the moment.

"I was as astonished as any of you would be to see a young boy look up startled into my face. When I ended, he lingered, as if wanting to speak to me, but not daring to do so." He paused for a moment. "I rose and left the village, knowing that, if he was indeed the flutist I had heard, he would follow me. I did not, however, expect him to fetch his flute and leave home for good, without so much as a change of clothes or a bedroll to sleep in, but that is precisely what he did." There was a snort of amusement from Rial's direction.

"I made him return and obtain permission from his only relative, an older sister," continued the Master Bard, "then we headed east together. I told him I would take him for a month on a trial basis, then perhaps get him an apprenticeship with a Flutist in Kyet. He would never have had the opportunity had he been left in Vale, for as I soon discovered, the lad was too frightened to approach a Bard for help."

"Frightened?" questioned Marek. "Of Bards?"

"Of his own music," Bergid replied. "Kaelin was under an immense strain. There was no denying the Gift he possessed, but it was locked ... buried deeply within him for reasons I did not, at the time, understand. Though he was not yet a member of our Order, I decided to give him a Bardic test, the only one that stood a chance of enabling him to free his music." He paused, knowing the eruption his next words would cause. "I gave him the sense-deprivation test."

The stunned silence that followed his words was shattered by several voices at once.

"No Master would do such a thing!" exclaimed Marek. "Certainly not *you*, Bergid!"

"Sense-deprivation? On a boy of *eleven?*" Rial's horror-stricken voice projected to every corner of the Council Grounds.

"You have indeed lost your mind!" Grened's open hand slapped the table. "That's a test for *Bards,* not untutored village boys!"

"How long did you torture the lad?" Talan demanded to know. "Surely not for the entire week!"

The sound of chimes filled the Council Grounds, effectively ending the clash of questions. The Master Bard of Kestrel closed his eyes until the silvery music died away. His eyes opened to rest on the youngest Master.

"I'm afraid, Marek, that under the right circumstances, which these were, I would indeed do such a thing. I took no pleasure in the necessity. Yes, Rial, I gave the sense-deprivation test to a boy of eleven. I assure you I have not misplaced my mind, Grened, and am fully aware that this test is normally given to Bards after careful preparation. I am also quite aware, Talan, that what I did could well be considered torture, but I did not do it against his will. Understand that this was a boy filled with music, every note of which was causing him intense pain. Kaelin took this test by his own choice and was free to stop it at any time, but he did not do so. I ended it myself when he finally came to terms with the music inside him and stopped resisting its expression." He paused, looking at Talan. "His sight was restored at six weeks, his hearing at eight weeks, and his speech at nine."

The Masters of the Bardic Isles sat stupefied. They all clearly remembered their own week of sense-deprivation. The difficult test had given them a new sensitivity and greater depth to their music. The thought of a young boy choosing to endure such an experience for several times longer than they themselves had was unbelievable.

The Master Flutist was the first to recover. "I have never, and am not now," Marek said slowly, "doubting your word, Bergid, but it is nevertheless an incredible thing to hear. I have never known anyone to undergo that test for longer than the required week, let alone a mere boy like Kaelin."

The Senior Master nodded in understanding. "I have, though I grant you it's unusual. My own testing went on for three weeks," he said, enjoying their fresh look of surprise. "The music of a composer sometimes lies deeply buried and can require a longer time to be freed. I knew what Kaelin needed, but was not sure he could endure such a test, which is why I left the choice to him and gave him leave to end it at any time. He surpassed all my expectations."

"And you have surpassed all *mine* for the most unusual actions ever taken by a Master Bard," growled Grened.

"Unusual actions for an unusual boy," Bergid swiftly countered. "I have kept Kaelin as my apprentice since then. We moved to my cabin north of Kyet, where I could discreetly ensure that the management of my affairs continued to run smoothly throughout the winter months. We then returned to my home, where I resumed handling them myself, including holding the Bard testing for this rotation. If anyone here has any accusations of negligence to bring against me," he said with bristling brows, "he had best be prepared to prove them!"

"None of us have any such ridiculous accusations, Bergid," replied Talan, with a glance at Rial. "However, I believe I speak for us all when I say that, although you have told us a great deal, you have explained nothing." He paused, and the other Masters nodded in agreement. "Obviously, this youngster must have a remarkable ability for you to have gone to such lengths for him, but even so, isn't the training of apprentices better left to our many Pipers, Flutists, Harpists, and Instrumentalists? Bards don't have the time for it, and *Masters* most assuredly do not."

"I haven't explained, because it can't be explained in words,"

Bergid stated firmly. "Kaelin's Gift has to be experienced, like the sense-deprivation test or the strength to be drawn from this mountain. But I tell you now," the Master said with quiet authority, "a Flutist or Instrumentalist may have the time, but not one in all the Bardic Isles has the skill to train him. Not only has Kaelin's level of playing already surpassed theirs on three instruments, he has also mastered every advanced form of composition I've given him and passed all three levels of Bard tests on composition and theory with perfect scores." His eyes swept the astounded group. "If any in the Bardic Order surpassed me in musical composition, I might consider giving Kaelin to him, but I will *not*," he said emphatically, "hand him over to anyone less. I have barely the skill necessary myself."

The Masters of the Bardic Isles were stunned for the third time that evening. Grened stood, his voice challenging. "If the Master of Composition, the best one we have had in untold cycles, has barely the skill to train an *apprentice*, then I, for one, wish to hear this apprentice for myself!" He looked around at the other Masters, who nodded in emphatic agreement. "Let us have this 'experience' of yours, Bergid, and if it's judged to be as you say, you may keep your apprentice as long as you like. I warn you now that I will not be easily convinced. Our traditions serve a purpose and should not be set aside lightly."

"And if it is not judged to be as I say?" queried the Senior Master, holding Grened's eye.

"Then the boy must be sent to a Flutist, as Talan suggested. Or an Instrumentalist ... one of your own choice, if you like." Grened snorted in exasperation as he reseated himself. "What else?"

"There is always another way to modulate a phrase."

The Master Harpist frowned at the enigmatic words and made no reply.

Bergid glanced at the others. "I realize, of course, that you must hear Kaelin for yourselves, which is why I brought him with me. Unfortunately, Kaelin is not yet ready to be heard. He had an experience at a young age that left him too afraid to play his instrument for anyone. It was only last night that this fear was dealt with, and he played in the presence of someone other than myself." His fingers tapped a rhythmic staccato against the table, punctuating the intensity of his voice. "Kaelin must be given time to come to grips with the idea of coming before such an intimidating audience as we are. Forcing him here against his will, half scared to death, would be a mistake. I will not have him pushed back into fear when he has so recently been released from it, so I must insist on waiting until our last Council session to bring him here."

Marek nodded approvingly. "Terrorizing apprentices is not in my repertoire, and I'm happy to be reassured that it's not in yours, either. I'm quite willing to grant Kaelin's need for time."

"And what guarantee have we that this 'time' will not expand beyond that?" demanded Grened. "I wish to be sure this matter is settled before the end of *this* Spring Council." He stopped at the disconcerting frowns of three Masters.

The Master Bard of Kestrel was on his feet. "If you wish a guarantee beyond my word on the matter, then I pledge my robe on it!"

The fourth shocked silence of the evening was by far the longest. To pledge one's robe was a drastic step, and in the two hundred cycle history of the Bardic Isles, there was no record of a single Master ever doing so.

"Surely, Bergid," Marek's voice gently broke the silence, "you would not risk your position as Master Bard for this young prodigy, however fond you may be of him." He glanced at Grened. "I'm sure none of us will hold you to those words if you wish to retract them."

"I retract nothing, Marek. My pledge stands." The Senior Master loosened the golden cord from around his waist and placed it deliberately in the center of the table. Four Masters stared at it, aghast. Bergid, his white robe billowing loosely about him, picked up the mallet and struck the largest chime with it.

"A decision has been reached by the Council." Bergid's voice was clear and strong. "Kaelin will appear before you at our final meeting. If he does not, or if any of you are dissatisfied with his performance and feel he is not entitled to study under the Master of Composition, you may have my robe and my position as Master Bard of Kestrel. As dictated by Bardic Law, my cord will remain here as a token of my pledge." Every eye except Bergid's turned to the cord lying on the table. Flickering torchlight danced along the smooth coils. "Until then," the Senior Master said firmly, "this matter will not be discussed further at these sessions, and I ask that you keep it between yourselves elsewhere. Are there any objections to this?" He looked at each Master in turn until he received a quiet, negative reply from each. Then he tapped the large chime three times.

"The decision stands as stated." It was with a noticeably weary hand that the Master struck the smallest chime thrice. "This session of the Spring Council is ended."

Chapter 19

Kaelin's amber eyes flashed with challenge as his new friend peered doubtfully into one of the Bard's storage sheds. "If you don't think I'm telling the truth, Darryk, get a blindfold and test me yourself!"

Darryk gave him an exasperated glance. "I don't doubt your honesty, but someone must have forgotten to replace the lantern, and it's pitch black in there. It's impossible to tell which of those pieces are beech, or find the few pieces of spruce that are left. Patience, my young friend. It won't take me long to go borrow a lantern."

"I don't need a lantern *or* my eyes," Kaelin insisted. He removed his cord and wrapped it twice around his eyes.

"You can't be serious!"

"Just tie this for me, and I'll have your wood out here in no time."

The Bard sighed and tied the cord securely. He had made the mistake of telling Kaelin he could begin practicing the construction of his new harp on spare pieces of wood, which had prompted cries for immediate action.

Darryk shook his head as Kaelin disappeared into the dark shed. The sound of rummaging was heard for a few minutes, and then the apprentice reappeared, triumphantly carrying an armful of spruce and beech.

"I don't believe it," the Bard said flatly. "No one could do that without seeing what they were looking for!"

"As I tried to tell you, feeling is as good as seeing."

"Maybe for *you* it is. Is this some inborn ability of yours, or did you have to learn it the hard way?"

Kaelin grinned. "Definitely the hard way. One of my Master's lessons. Now, are you going to help me carry this back, or are you going to just stand there and let a poor apprentice do all the work?"

"Better watch it, youngster," the Bard threatened as he took several pieces of wood out of Kaelin's arms. "Your *teacher* might just command you to find your way back without removing that blindfold."

The apprentice laughed and walked off with the remaining wood, heading unerringly in the direction of Darryk's camp.

The Bard's jaw dropped. He latched the door of the shed and hurried to follow. "How in blazes are you staying on this narrow trail when you can't see it?" he demanded.

"Pay attention to your feet instead of your eyes for a moment," Kaelin advised. "Is the trail level from side to side?"

"Well, of course it's level!"

"No, it isn't," the apprentice said patiently. "The sides of the trail are higher and the center of the trail, where everyone has been walking, is lower."

The surprised Bard scanned the trail. "Hardly enough to notice."

"Enough to feel it under your feet. Enough to keep a blind apprentice on the trail and not wandering off into the woods."

"But not enough to keep him from tripping over a root or a rock," Darryk suggested hopefully.

"Have I tripped over a single one of the four roots behind us?"

Darryk glanced incredulously behind him. "Well, no ... and how have you managed that?"

"That's a lesson for another day," Kaelin said loftily, and the

Bard rolled his eyes.

When they reached the camp, Kaelin slipped off his cord and Darryk brought out his tools. "You must have excellent basic woodworking skills to have produced that flute of yours," the Bard allowed, "but making a harp is different. Your flute was made from a single piece of wood, but the harp is made of three types of wood, which have to be fitted perfectly together. You can learn by fitting together spruce and beech first," he told the watching apprentice. "Then, when you gain the necessary skill, you can begin your harp with the seasoned wood Master Bergid has ordered from Tryl for you. It should arrive tomorrow afternoon."

Kaelin smiled agreeably. He had not spent three cycles under Craftmaster Arnor's critical eye for nothing. Darryk, observing the proficient ease with which the apprentice handled the tools, expertly shaping and fitting various pieces of wood together, sighed.

"You might have *told* me that, in addition to being a superb flutist, you're also an expert woodworker," he said reproachfully.

Mischief lit Kaelin's eyes. "I did mention being offered an apprenticeship to the woodcarving Craftmaster of Vale four cycles before coming of age," he remarked innocently, and laughed at his friend's withering glance.

"Well, then," Darryk said, "let's stop wasting time and wood, and start drafting your plans." He picked up his own harp. "The main frame of a harp is comprised of three sections, the column, neck, and body," he lectured, indicating each part as he spoke. "I hope you haven't spent so much time in the woods with your flute that you're lacking the mathematical and drawing skills these plans are going to require."

"Not to worry," Kaelin said with a grimace. "Bardic Instruments aren't the only things made of wood that require detailed planning, and the Craftmaster's instructions were delivered only once."

"What happened if you forgot something?" the Bard asked

curiously.

"He swiftly ordered the offender to bend over their work desk so he could 'explain it to them more clearly.'"

Darryk whistled softly. "No wonder you have such a good memory. How many ... sessions ... did it take to develop it?"

Kaelin shrugged. "A few of them a month, I guess, but not for forgetting anything. It was usually for using too much wood when trying out designs of my own, or for cursing when a tool slipped."

"Cursing? You?" The Bard was incredulous.

"Well," Kaelin said uncomfortably, "I helped make our coppers go further by talking vendors into giving me samples for breakfast and lunch. You hear a lot of cursing in a marketplace, and..." he shrugged again. "I can't help it if I have a good memory. You needn't worry, though," he assured his friend. "What no one in Vale could manage to do in four cycles, my Master did in a single lesson. Your sensitive Bardic ears will be quite safe."

The rest of the evening passed quickly and productively. The Bard was soon satisfied with Kaelin's abilities, his math skills being sufficient for the task and his drawing abilities exceptional. Finally, Darryk called a halt and began putting his drafting tools away. "Master Bergid should be returning any time now. How about spending a few minutes refreshing a tired and overworked Bard?" He gestured invitingly toward Kaelin's flute.

Unable to refuse such a request from his friend, Kaelin took his flute and began to play, keeping his thoughts firmly away from the mountain. Mindful of his Master's instructions not to play his own music on his flute, he played a village song that had been Laena's favorite. *I wish I had been able to play it for her. The next time I see her, I will.* He ended the song on a note of sadness, then looked up to find Darryk gazing into the fire with tears in his eyes.

"Are you all right?" Kaelin asked in concern.

"Yes, of course," came the husky reply. "It's just that she's ... I mean, your song was beautiful."

Kaelin glanced at his friend curiously. *Darryk must have been thinking of a girl, too.* Before he could ask, Master Bergid spoke from the edge of the clearing.

"Beautiful indeed, and just what I needed to hear after a long and trying Council session." The Master walked wearily to the fire and warmed his hands, his robe billowing slightly around him.

"Master!" exclaimed Kaelin in surprise. "What happened to your cord?"

Darryk stared at the Master's unrestrained robe in shock, and Bergid gave him a quick warning glance.

"I left it at the Council Grounds," replied the Master calmly. "How did your harp-making go tonight?"

"Oh, very well, sir! The plans are almost finished. Darryk is a good teacher."

Darryk smiled wryly. "I must say I learned a few things myself." At the Master's inquiring gaze, he continued. "Such as not to underestimate an apprentice."

The Master Bard chuckled. "Not this one, at any rate." He sat down by the fire. "Darryk, if you wouldn't mind us imposing on your hospitality tonight, I would as soon not bother returning to my cabin until morning."

"Certainly, Master Bergid." Darryk rose to make his guests comfortable for the night, insisting that the Master use his own bedroll. He himself would be quite comfortable on one of the thinner spares. "After all," he said, glaring at Kaelin, "I have to set a good example for that piece of impudence over there."

Kaelin looked up innocently. "Me, impudent? To a Bard?" He shook his head. "Not a chance. To a *friend,* though … that's a possibility."

The Master looked from one to the other and chuckled. "I'll be sure to look into this tomorrow. Now, if you two youngsters will let a tired old man sleep..."

ⅅespite the Master's professed desire for sleep, Darryk awoke late that night to find his guest sitting motionless before the fire. The Bard slipped silently from his bedroll so as not to awaken Kaelin. "Is there anything I can get for you, Master Bergid?" he asked quietly. "Some tea, perhaps?"

"No, thank you, Darryk."

"You pledged your robe tonight."

It was a statement, not a question, to which the Master made no reply.

"On Kaelin."

Though this was also not a question, the Master nodded. "On his appearance at our final Council session, and on his performance satisfying the others of my right to retain him." He smiled faintly at the consternation on Darryk's face. "The pledge of my robe was necessary to convince them of my seriousness in this matter. If he plays satisfactorily, I will receive it back again."

"And if he doesn't?" Darryk asked with difficulty.

"In that case, I would relinquish my position regardless."

"Sir!" the Bard exclaimed, shocked. "You can't take such a drastic—"

"Can't I?" The Master challenged the Bard, who fell silent. "I will not allow Kaelin to be taken from me, whatever the cost to myself," Bergid said firmly. "That boy is more important to the Bardic Isles than any position of mine. And handing him over to an Instrumentalist who knows far less than he does is not an option."

The Bard remained silent for a long moment, considering this astounding endorsement.

"I must ask you not to discuss any of this with anyone," the Master said, "including Kaelin. His knowledge of Bardic Law does not extend to such details as the inner workings of the Council. He doesn't understand the significance of my missing cord, and I prefer it to stay that way."

"As you wish, sir."

Darryk did not look happy with the Master's command, and Bergid abruptly changed the subject. "By the way, what was all that about impudence?"

Darryk related the events of the evening. "I couldn't believe my own eyes when he came out of the shed with that wood, and then went marching off down the trail with his cord still wrapped around his eyes," he ended ruefully. "I thought perhaps he had been born with the ability to see through objects—and his own eyelids—but he laid the credit at your door."

Bergid chuckled and relayed the details of Kaelin's sense-deprivation test. "His sense of touch and hearing are acute, and if I were you, I wouldn't make any bets with him concerning either one of them."

"I'll keep that firmly in mind," Darryk said in awe. "I haven't yet undergone that test myself." He glanced sideways at the Master. "Perhaps, when the time comes, I'll apply to you, sir," he said expressionlessly.

"Whenever you like, Darryk," replied the Master with a glint of challenge in his blue eyes. "And, as I've often told my apprentice, there's no time like the present. Shall I fetch my wax?"

Darryk rose hastily. "I wouldn't dream of imposing on you during the Spring Council."

The rumor of a golden cord lying on the Council table circulated quickly among the Bards, brought to life by the one in charge of maintaining the Council Grounds. And the Master Bard of Kestrel's unrestrained robe made it clear who had pledged his position to the Council. Though none of the Masters had mentioned the matter, it was naturally assumed that the pledge had something to do with Kaelin. Darryk, keeping fully his promise to Master Bergid, blocked all probing questions, stating flatly that the matter was none of his affair. He didn't hesitate to give broad hints that it was none of anyone else's, either.

As for Kaelin, his curiosity about his Master's missing cord soon grew into a deep-seated worry. *Why has he chosen to leave it at the Council Grounds? And why did he take it off in the first place?* He turned back to his harp, grateful to have something to distract him from the increasing pressure coming from the mountain, and a place to go that wasn't as close to it as his Master's cabin was. He could no longer play anywhere near the cabin, and what little practice he could get in had to be done at Darryk's camp.

One afternoon, Bards Brent and Fenadal visited Darryk's camp and inspected the small heap of pegs lying next to Kaelin. The apprentice was working on one of them, carefully carving a detailed picture on the flat of the peg, often turning it to work the same lines onto the other side.

Brent shook his head. "You're doing beautiful work, Kaelin, but why such painstaking detail on pegs? After all, the instrument will sound the same with or without the carvings, won't it?"

"Yes, sir," came the reply, "but the feel and look of a thing is also important."

"Hmm ... so much effort on these tuning pegs, yet the column is unadorned," noticed Fenadal. "Isn't its feel and look important, too?"

Kaelin nodded. "I'm leaving its carving for later, after the harp is finished. I can do that on my own, but I must get Darryk's help with the main construction while I can." He glanced at the pile of pegs yet to be carved. "I would leave these, too, only they'd be too difficult to carve once they're attached to the neck."

Kaelin returned to his work. He was happy with his harp and was now at ease with the Bards that frequented Darryk's camp. Though many brows had lifted at the open friendship between Bard and apprentice, nothing was said, and Kaelin found himself treated with friendly respect from most of the Bards. Darryk knew that this was largely thanks to the Bards of Kestrel, Brent included. Though they refused to discuss the apprentice with anyone, all but two of them made it quite clear that anyone making a derogatory comment about his presence would find himself ostracized from their ranks. In the face of so many silent champions, the detractors took another look at the apprentice ... and except for a handful of traditionalists, who would have made Master Grened proud, soon revised their hasty opinions.

Darryk looked up from the pile of harp strings he was sorting. "Come, you two, let him get on with his work, or he'll never get those pegs put where they can be of some use." He glanced at the idle Bards. "Speaking of useful objects, why don't the two of you give us some music to work by, since sorting harp strings is apparently beneath you?"

Brent snorted. "We know perfectly well you wouldn't let us touch a single one of your sacred strings! And if it's a singing song you want, Fenadal's been working my voice over every night for the past week, on the chance that I'll be assigned to Lyra. I'm as hoarse as a raven."

"Well, that leaves you, Fenadal," said Darryk with a grin. "I know it goes against your grain not to deliver an entire concert, but I've strings to sort and an apprentice to teach and haven't got all day. How about entertaining us with 'Cyral's Harp?' That seems appropriate ... and it's the shortest song I know. Might leave enough time for Brent to give us a song or two on his harp and spur Kaelin on to finishing those pegs."

The others laughed as Fenadal, with an air of offended dignity, rose to get his lap harp. Pointedly turning his back on Darryk, the Bard began to sing.

Out of the east, long cycles past,
So say the tales of lore,

Came five ships across the sea,
Fleeing their native shore.

Driven by winds and currents strong,
Escaping from evil hands,
Westward they sailed, far over the sea,
Searching for other lands.

O Cyral's Harp! O Cyral's Harp,
How far away you roam.
What land awaits your music fair,
What place can be your home?

The Master took his Harp in hand
And played both day and night.
The winds blew true; the Bardic Isles
Were glimpsed ... a glorious sight!

O Bardic Isles, sweet Bardic Isles,
May you forever hear
The music of my people sung,
In voices free and clear!

The sound of the music faded softly into silence. *A compliment of the highest order,* mused Kaelin, remembering his Master's words. "Someday," he spoke softly, "if my Master allows, I would like to learn to sing with such a voice, if you will give me lessons, sir."

Fenadal cocked his head in Kaelin's direction. "Perhaps, if I'm assigned to Kestrel after your voice changes, that could be arranged. It's never too early," he said with a meaningful glance at Brent, "to prepare for Master Rial."

Soon after Brent and Fenadal left, Darryk brought a pile of

carefully chosen strings to Kaelin. "These will make fine strings for that fancy harp of yours." He waved aside Kaelin's thanks and looked through the pile of carved tuning pegs. "These are truly beautiful," he murmured. "You might well be starting a new tradition. I wouldn't be surprised to see Bards and Masters industriously carving their tuning pegs before the month is out."

The apprentice chuckled at the thought and began putting his pegs away.

Darryk cleared his throat. "I realize you're busy with your harp, but perhaps you should take advantage of the Bards that come by, to practice playing for an audience." His young friend stiffened slightly. "I'm just trying to help, if I can," the Bard gently added.

"I know." Kaelin hesitated, trying to sort out his thoughts. "It isn't fear that's stopping me ... at least, not fear of playing. It's the mountain." He gazed toward the west as though the darkness were no obstacle to his vision. "It gives me strange dreams at night. And during the day, if I'm within plain sight of it, I can't concentrate on anything else." He turned to Darryk with a rueful expression. "It's worse when I play. I can't even play village songs without it interfering. And it's even started to bother me here, so I just ... don't play. I'm afraid I'll lose control and play the mountain's song, the music I hear it whispering over and over." He shuddered slightly and turned away, his voice barely audible. "Its song is trapped somehow ... just like my music was trapped. It scares me."

Darryk frowned. His young friend's words were disturbing and left him at a loss. "Have you told Master Bergid about this?" he asked at last.

"We haven't talked about it much, but he knows. That's why he stopped my lessons and is having me stay here most of the time. I don't want to bother him with it, because he ... well, he seems worried lately. I guess with the Council meetings and all—" The apprentice fell silent for a moment. "Darryk, why hasn't Master

Bergid retrieved his cord from the Council Grounds?"

The Bard frowned slightly, wondering how to answer this without telling Kaelin he was forbidden to explain it. "Masters sometimes do things that make no sense to us," he told his young friend. "When that happens it's best to realize that if they don't explain their actions, it's their own business and not for any Bard—or apprentice—to question. After all, they are in a position to know things they're not always willing or able to share. I've found that, in time, their actions always do make sense." He smiled into the eyes fastened so seriously on his. "Don't worry about it, my friend. When he wants you to know, he'll tell you."

Kaelin nodded and began putting his tools away. "Do any of the other Masters have eyes like mine?"

"Eyes?" Darryk repeated, surprised by the unexpected question. "Of your color, you mean?" When Kaelin nodded, he shook his head. "Yours are the only amber eyes I've ever seen. What makes you ask?"

Kaelin shrugged. "Just a dream I keep having. I hope the Spring Council ends soon, so we can go back to Kestrel. Maybe from there, I won't dream as much or hear the mountain's music anymore. Yet in a strange way, I'll miss it." He shook his head at the seeming contradiction. "I'll miss you too," he added sadly.

"Well, Bard assignments will be posted at the end of the Spring Council," Darryk reminded him. "My first rotation was to Elegy, and my second was to Eyrie, so there's a one-in-three chance I'll be assigned to Kestrel." He smiled at Kaelin's delight. "I hope that I am, and not just so I can continue to be pestered by a certain apprentice I know. I think highly of your Master and look forward to the chance to serve under him. Come, I'll show you how to make a Bard's coddle. It's getting late, and I'm sure Master Bergid will be hungry when he gets back."

"He most definitely is," the Master said as he entered the clearing and seated himself by the fire with a sigh. "Thank you,

Darryk. I hope you don't mind if we stay the night here again. I do apologize for imposing on you so often."

"You're always welcome, sir! And so is that scamp over there."

Kaelin rose to help his friend prepare the coddle, which turned out to be nothing more complicated than a stew of sausages, potatoes, and onions. The three of them ate together in unusual silence. Kaelin was mulling over what Darryk had told him about the actions of Masters not always making sense to others. Darryk was worried about Master Bergid, who was clearly exhausted. He wondered if the Master was thinking of his cord, still lying on the Council table. The Bard himself could not get it out of his mind.

In fact, the Master was thinking of his apprentice. He was aware that Kaelin wasn't playing at all anymore, and the fearful glances he gave the mountain made it clear why. *How can I ask it of him? Yet, how can I not?* He frowned at the dark shape of the mountain in the distance and came to a sudden, final decision.

"The last Council meeting will be held tomorrow night."

Kaelin looked up in surprise at the announcement. Darryk held his breath.

"We finished earlier than usual this cycle," the Master added with a wry smile. The Masters had found it difficult to enter into their usual prolonged, spirited debates with the Senior Master's gold cord shining before them. "I thought you ought to know, Kaelin, so that Darryk can show you how to finish the parts for your harp tomorrow. We'll leave early the following morning." The Master turned back to his meal, his manner clearly forbidding questions.

Kaelin frowned. *Something is wrong. Why won't he tell me?*

Darryk started to speak, but a swift glance from the Master stopped him. The Bard abruptly set aside his meal, then rose and turned to Kaelin. "I'll be happy to help you tomorrow, my friend," he said quietly. Then he bowed to the Master. "If you don't need me for anything, sir, I believe I'll go for a walk." At the Master's nod, the tall Bard left the clearing.

Kaelin's eyes narrowed, wondering at the look of grief he had seen in the Bard's eyes as he left. Whatever was bothering his Master, Darryk evidently knew about it. Surely his friend would have explained it to him, unless the Master had forbidden him to. *Whatever is wrong, then, has something to do with me.* He studied the loose robe his Master wore. *And it has something to do with his missing cord no one will talk about around me. And why hasn't my Master told me whether or not the Council has approved my apprenticeship? Maybe that's what's bothering him ... maybe he's going to ask them tomorrow. Or maybe they've already given him their answer, and he doesn't want to tell me yet.* He looked at the silent Master, who had put aside his own meal and was staring into the flames of the fire. Kaelin hesitated a moment, remembering Darryk's advice not to worry about what a Master chose not to divulge.

"Master?"

Bergid did not reply.

"I would do anything for you. You know that ... don't you?"

His Master's reply, when it finally came, was barely audible. "Yes, Kaelin. I know."

Darryk did not return to the campsite until long after Kaelin had gone to his bedroll. He said nothing, but his closed expression did not go unobserved.

"You might as well say it," the Master advised.

"What I have to say, sir, is not something a Bard has any right to say to a Master," Darryk said stiffly.

"Say it, nevertheless."

"You're *wrong*, sir!" The words burst from Darryk with unexpected vehemence, startling them both. "You're wrong not to tell Kaelin. You're not giving him a chance! And you're not giving yourself one, either."

The Master made no reply, and the agitated Bard turned toward him, his words impassioned. "All Bards respect the Masters, and each of them is deserving of that respect, but *you,* sir, are the one we respect the most ... the one we can least afford to lose! I would understand it if you had no choice, but you only have to ask him to play. You know he will do it for you, no matter how frightened he might be of the Council." He glanced toward the shelter where Kaelin lay sleeping. "If he had any idea of what's at stake—what you're giving up for him—he would *run* there, whether you asked him or not. I beg you, sir ... please ask him!"

Still the Master said nothing, and Darryk pressed his head against knees held tightly to his chest. The words he spoke were barely audible. "Not telling my friend what his Master is about to sacrifice for him is the hardest command I have ever been given, and I doubt Kaelin will be able to forgive me for obeying it." He looked up at the silent Master.

"I deserve to be punished like an apprentice for speaking so to you," Darryk said quietly, "but I just can't stand by and watch the Bardic Order lose the best Master Bard I have ever had the privilege to know."

"I'm not offended," replied the Master calmly, "and you may be quite right in thinking that I should ask Kaelin to play. The Maker knows I've gone back and forth over the matter dozens of times myself." He leaned back with his hands on his knees and closed his eyes. "Has he told you about the mountain?"

"Yes, just before you returned tonight. I know it would be difficult for him to play, but surely—"

The Master shook his head. "Were it merely difficult, I would have asked him. I certainly intended to when I pledged my robe to the Council." He sighed. "You and I might not be able to understand the incredible pressure that mountain is exerting on him, but it's very real. I was hoping it would lessen with time, but instead, every day it worsens, and the strain he is under increases. I've come to believe that allowing Kaelin to play on the Council Grounds would not only be difficult, but dangerous."

Darryk was taken aback. "I know Kaelin is afraid of the mountain, but how could it be dangerous?"

"You and I are the only two people in all the Bardic Isles who have heard Kaelin play. You know what it's like to be pulled into his music and experience it exactly as he does himself. Now imagine if the first time you felt that pull was when you were up in a tree, reaching for the next branch."

Darryk's eyes widened. "No wonder his sister fell."

The Master nodded. "And that was caused by mere humming. Who knows how many other small things happened as his Gift grew stronger, each of them increasing his uneasiness about his music, until at last he played for his parents and was utterly convinced it was his music that killed them. His Gift is by no means full-grown yet, any more than he himself is. It is still growing and developing, and the Maker only knows how powerful it will eventually become." The Master saw the frown on Darryk's face and shook his head at the protest he saw coming.

"Before you say anything more, take a moment to think about his Gift. Try to understand it, if any of us truly can." The Master swept a hand around them. "Everything in this world was created by the Maker with its own music. Even something as small as a blade of grass holds a song we haven't the ears to hear or the wit to appreciate." He gestured toward the unseen peak of Bardic Mountain. "Bards and Masters come to this mountain to renew ourselves, yes, but with precious little idea of what we're renewing ourselves *in*. We tell ourselves it's the beauty or peace of this place that renews us, but it's the *music*, the inherent song of the mountain itself, placed there when it was first created, that truly refreshes us." He paused, looking for a moment as young as his companion. "Bardic Mountain, for whatever reason, has such a strong current of music running through it that even we can sense it, however faintly. But I tell you," he stated emphatically, "if we had the ears to truly hear, we wouldn't need to come to this mountain at all. We could as easily refresh ourselves listening to the song coming from a sunset, or a leaf lying on the ground." He glanced at the motionless form of his apprentice.

"And now a boy like *this* comes along, who can hear the music in everything around him and translate it directly through his instrument. More, he can take his listeners with him to experience whatever he does himself, as if we were him." He wagged a finger at Darryk. "You have marveled at mere exercises and village songs. You've heard his first piece, composed when he was only seven. But his compositions now are far more powerful. He may be barely twelve cycles of age, but he is already a highly trained composer and flutist, with a Gift which hasn't been seen since the days of Master Cyral. A Gift that commands incredible power and died out, for reasons none of us know, after our arrival in the Bardic Isles. And now, without fanfare or warning, it reappears over two hundred cycles later in a village boy from Vale!" The Master paused and exhaled deeply, suddenly looking every one of his sixty-three cycles.

"Objects, trees, past experiences ... these things drain him when he plays their music, even while they fulfill his need to express it. Yet they are small matters and safe enough. But Bardic Mountain," he said grimly, "is no small matter. The music pulling relentlessly at him is, I fear, stronger than the vessel it seeks to release itself through. Perhaps one day Kaelin will play its music, but he is not ready now." He frowned. "Performing on the Council Grounds, so near the strength of that mountain, would take an immense amount of control and pose too great a risk. I will not put him in harm's way to save myself." He glanced at the silent Bard. "So, I will not ask him to play. Right or wrong, I will not ask that of him." With a sigh, the Master Bard settled himself on his bedroll.

Darryk sat with his head bowed over his knees for several moments, then banked the fire and went to his own bedroll.

A short distance away, Kaelin lay wide awake. He stared into the darkness, trying to come to grips with what he had just overheard. He should have let them know he had woken up during their conversation, but what his Master was saying was so unbelievable that he had been too stunned to interrupt. Could it possibly be true that the Masters of the Bardic Isles were not Gifted, as he had thought? Not even, it seemed, his own Master? That instead it was only himself, a village boy from Vale, who was? *That's absolutely crazy! How could I possibly be the only one in the Bardic Isles who is Gifted?* But if this crazy, unbelievable thing was actually true, then no wonder he was the only one disturbed by the powerful music emanating from Bardic Mountain. He was the only one who could hear it! Kaelin frowned into the darkness. Apparently, this ability was part and parcel of the Gift. This Gift that no one else had.

Even more astounding was the notion that others could experience what he was experiencing when he played his music, which must also be part of this inexplicable Gift, something he had never asked for and was no longer at all sure he wanted. Kaelin felt himself go cold. *That's how my Master knew about the tree with our family's names carved into it! I was sure I had never mentioned it, and yet he knew. He saw it ... they both saw it when I was playing. And when I played Laena's favorite song, Darryk wasn't just thinking of some girl he knew. He saw Laena as I saw her in my mind! How is that possible? And why does my Master need me to play for the Council? Needs me to ... but won't command or even ask me because he thinks the mountain might hurt me somehow.*

The apprentice lay motionless, wrestling with the unanswerable questions spinning through his mind. His inexplicable, growing fear of the mountain was becoming hard enough to deal with, but the idea of playing before all the Masters of the Bardic Isles filled

Kaelin with a far deeper dread. He thought of the grim expression on Master Grened's face and shuddered, imagining it reflected on the faces of three other Masters he had never met. He would rather face all the Druids of Eire than ... *them!* It was long before his troubled thoughts settled sufficiently for sleep to overcome him.

Chapter 20

The sun had risen well above the eastern hills before Master Bergid awoke, astounded to see Kaelin still asleep. "Good heavens, lad! When a young boy like you outsleeps an old man like me, something is far wrong, indeed." He indicated the motionless form of Darryk. "Of course, I expect no better from a shiftless loafer like that Bard over there, but I thought I had trained my own apprentice better." He scowled in mock outrage as his two companions rose sheepishly to their feet.

"Shiftless loafer," muttered Darryk. "Fine thing, indeed! It's obvious that this apprentice of yours purposely overslept so he could skip making breakfast and begin with lunch. After all, he knows perfectly well that we count on all his racket in the morning to awaken us."

The Master chuckled and decided an early lunch was a good idea. At a discreet nod from Darryk, Kaelin went to work preparing a cottage pie over the fire. As the apprentice mixed dough and measured herbs, Darryk made a point of staying far away and making not a single comment or correction. When Kaelin proudly served slices of the steaming pie, oozing fragrant gravy, they all tucked in with good appetite.

"This trading of skills between you and Darryk has turned you into an excellent cook, Kaelin," the Master said with an approving nod.

Kaelin flushed at the praise. "Thank you, sir. Darryk is a good teacher."

"Yes, I can taste the evidence myself," the Master agreed, forking up another mouthful of tender lamb. Master Grened had a fine appreciation for the culinary arts, and his Bards kept everyone at the Spring Council well provisioned with fresh ingredients, brought in twice a week from Tryl. Master Bergid arched an eyebrow at Darryk. "And what of Kaelin's teaching abilities?"

Darryk grinned. "According to Master Marek, there may be hope for me yet. He summoned me just yesterday to verify the rumor that a Bard who is woefully deficient in flute skills was receiving instruction from an underaged flutist, who is apparently running loose near the Council Grounds. After demonstrating my progress, I was promoted to form two and advised to keep the young vagrant if I manage to catch him."

The Master chuckled and rose. "My congratulations. You'll be keeping your harp with you until the end of the cycle, then ... unless you manage to pass form two."

"I'll pass it, sir," the Bard promised.

"I'll leave you two to your industrious pursuits, then. There are a few people I would like to see before leaving tomorrow." He slung his pack and instruments over his shoulder and left the clearing.

Kaelin spent the afternoon learning the technique of attaching tuning pegs and strings to the frame of his harp. "I'll do it as soon as I'm done carving the rest of these pegs," he told Darryk. "Thank you for all your help."

"It's been my pleasure." The Bard looked at the frame of Kaelin's harp, laid carefully on its grey travel bag, which the Master had ordered sent with the harp's materials. "Have you thought about what you're going to carve into the column?"

"I'm going to carve symbols of the Bardic Isles. Bardic Mountain at the base, for the island of Elegy. At the top, a kestrel in flight, for the island of Kestrel." For a moment Kaelin stared at the un-carved frame and spoke as though to himself. "My Master once told me I was like a wild kestrel with a broken wing." He glanced up at Darryk. "I'll put symbols for the other three islands between those someday, after I've seen them for myself."

"Your harp is going to be stunning, Kaelin. I hope I can see it when it's all finished."

"You will." He put his harp away and glanced at the sky. The sun was beginning to set behind Bardic Mountain.

$\mathcal{B}$ergid spent the afternoon with his colleagues at Grened's cabin, having requested that they meet him there with their instruments. He brought with him several of his most recent compositions for quintets, and they spent a pleasant time playing and critiquing them. No mention of the imminent final Council Meeting was made, and if Bergid seemed more reticent than usual, no one mentioned it. Nor did the Master of Composition seem inclined to leave, bringing out one piece after the other until at last, the afternoon slipping away, he brought out one final piece.

"Now, for an encore," he said with a smile, "let's see what you think of *this* one. I wrote it just this week and am looking forward to hearing it played." He raised a brow as he passed out the parts. "Best have a look first," he advised. "There's a bit of preparation needed."

Marek looked over his part and chuckled. "So it seems." He put down his flute and began placing three of his other instruments close to hand. The other Masters glanced at their own parts and began arranging various instruments around themselves as well.

Grened scowled at Bergid. "You're giving me three whole beats to switch from kithara to harp, are you? How very generous!"

"You're welcome," Bergid said. "Two beats would have been ideal, but considering your advanced cycles—"

Grened snorted and picked up his pipes. "Not quite as advanced as your own, my friend. How many beats did you give yourself?"

Bergid chuckled.

"I see our reflexes are going to be well tested," Rial said.

"Yet you only have three instruments, while the rest of us have four," Talan observed with a teasing glint in his eye.

"Have you forgotten my primary *Bardic* instrument?" came the Voice Master's tart reply. "Just because I don't need to pick it up and put it together, and it's always in perfect tune—"

"Now, then," Bergid quickly intervened before the two Masters could renew their cycles-long debate over the voice being a qualified Bardic instrument. "Is everyone ready?" He picked up his flute and glanced at Rial, who was holding his lute on his lap in readiness. Leaving it resting there, the Voice Master of the Bardic Isles began to sing. Even Talan glanced at him in awe as the clear voice emerged, blossoming from the softest pianissimo. One by one, flute, harp, pipes, and kithara joined him.

The instrumental melody began to sweep upward, swirling around the room as though a faery from Eire had appeared and dusted the cabin with magic. At the peak of the crescendo, the solo voice disappeared as Rial switched deftly to his lute and the individual voices broke apart in a lively dance, two partners dancing around Bergid's flute, which took to the skies above them in a burst of joy. Then the dance segued into another one, as Masters quickly switched instruments and, without missing a beat, partnered anew around the bass line of Talan's pipes. Again it changed, as new partners danced light staccatos under Grened's masterful harp arpeggios. One more set of partners danced playfully around Marek's flute, which spiraled them upward once again. At its peak, Rial set aside his lute, and the clear, poignant voice returned. Four instruments followed it down, as they had followed it up at the beginning. One by one, the instrumental voices disappeared in the opposite order of their arrival, until only Rial's voice remained, sadly leaving the dance until it, too, vanished in the distance. Four Masters of the Bardic Isles sat stunned into silence. Bergid set down his harp, a look of profound sadness on his face.

Marek shook his head in wonder. "Truly, Bergid, you have outdone yourself! This is a piece that will last long after we are gone, as a testament to your skill."

"A stunning piece," Talan murmured, "with such a clear, beautiful story. I would not change a note of it."

"It was a privilege and a pleasure to be the first ones to play it," Rial said emphatically, "and I would ask that we also be the first to perform it on the Council Grounds. What a wonderful way to end the Spring Council!"

Grened, observing the gleam of moisture in Bergid's eyes, snorted indignantly. "Not until he edits my part and gives me another beat to switch to harp. He gave himself four!"

Laughter filled the room, and everyone began putting their instruments away. Bergid opened his pack and removed four wrapped packages, which he passed out to the others. "This is the score and parts to the piece you just played."

His colleagues looked at him in surprise. "Surely, Bergid," Grened said, "such music as this should be sent first to Caer Wynd to be archived before being distributed."

"It is a gift," came the quiet reply. "Use it as you will." Before anyone could respond, Bergid took up his pack and instruments and left.

Darryk was putting away his tools when Master Bergid returned, looking weary. The Bard went to fetch the dried bramble leaves for the Master's tea, but Bergid raised his hand.

"No need, Darryk," he said. "I must admit to a loss of appetite, even for tea." He looked around in surprise. "Where is Kaelin?"

"Why, I don't know … he was here a moment ago."

"Perhaps it's just as well that he isn't here." The Master spoke calmly, but lines of tension crossed his forehead. "Bardic Law states that when a member of the Bardic Order pledges his robe and forfeits it, he is demoted one rank, which in my case would mean becoming a Free Bard. There's a small chance that the Council might allow a Free Bard, who is not assigned to any particular island, to keep an apprentice at his side, and such a position would also allow me to help the new Master Bard of Kestrel more easily." He shook his head slightly at the hope that lit Darryk's eyes. "I know my colleagues. Two will be for it, and two against, which will not give me the majority vote I need to keep Kaelin. Therefore, I will refuse the rank."

"And … what will happen then, sir?"

"I will be demoted another rank, to that of a Bard. This I will also refuse, for none of them will agree to a Bard keeping an apprentice. That will demote me to an Instrumentalist, which I will accept, having every right then to keep him."

Darryk was outraged. "If that happens, you'll be the most overqualified Instrumentalist in the entire history of the Bardic Isles! I should think the Council would be embarrassed to demote their Senior Master so far."

Bergid's mouth quirked. "Then hopefully one of the two traditionalists on the Council will agree with you and give me the third vote I need to become the first Free Bard ever allowed to retain an apprentice. And if not, then at least my overqualification ought to win me enough students to support myself and Kaelin. And, come to think of it," he added with some amusement, "I'll earn a stipend for teaching him, as well." He chuckled softly at the idea of the Bardic Order having to pay him for the apprentice he was demoting himself to keep.

Darryk, however, saw no humor whatsoever in the prospect. "Every Bard who has ever served a rotation under you will rise up in protest to the Council if they do such a thing," he stated flatly. "And, although I have not yet served on Kestrel myself, I will gladly lead them!"

The Master gravely surveyed the rebellious Bard. "I appreciate the loyalty that prompts those words, Darryk," he said mildly, "but the Council will simply tell you what I'm telling you now. The Masters are bound by Bardic Law and will not break it for me, any more than they would for anyone else. My word has been given, my robe pledged. With Kaelin not appearing before them, there is no possibility whatsoever that I will be returning here as a Master. The loss in rank I sustain this night is by my own choice, not by any desire on their part to inflict it. Every one of them would far rather hear Kaelin successfully play than be forced to take my robe." He held the stormy grey eyes firmly until Darryk reluctantly lowered them.

"We will be assigning Bards this evening," the Master continued, "and being Senior Master gives me first choice. I assume Master Talan has released you for rotation, or you would not be here."

"Yes, sir, he has."

"I believe I heard you tell Kaelin that you look forward to serving my island. Have you any objection to a rotation on Kestrel, then, outside of running the risk of becoming a competent flutist before you land in Master Marek's clutches? Regardless of what happens tonight, Kaelin and I will be staying in Kyet, not only to give whatever aid the new Master Bard of Kestrel might need from me, but also to be within walking distance of Kaelin's sister and brother. During the times you are assigned to Kyet's territory, I can help you prepare for the Master Flutist's scrutiny."

Darryk's face broke into a smile tinged with sadness. "I would be delighted to be assigned to Kestrel."

"Excellent. Kestrel will be without a Master until the Council can select a new one. I left Flynn as interim Master primarily in case such a thing happened. Selecting a new Master will take some time, so I'm being especially careful about my choice of Bards. You have quite impressed me with both your knowledge and discretion. You didn't hesitate to offer Kaelin your friendship, regardless of what anyone may have thought. You also had the courage to challenge my decision not to ask Kaelin to play. Few Bards would have done that." The blue eyes glinted with approval. "Your priorities are decidedly in the right place, and I would welcome you as a Bard to my island whether I am its Master or not."

Darryk was stunned by the Master's praise. "It would be an honor to serve your island. Thank you, Master Bergid!"

"I'll be back shortly," the Master said quietly.

Darryk's heart wrenched at the sadness in the Master's eyes as he turned to leave, then the Bard frowned at the empty campsite. *Where is Kaelin?* he wondered. *And where,* he thought in sudden alarm, *is Kaelin's flute?*

$\mathcal{M}$aster Bergid walked the familiar path to the Council Grounds in deep thought. He paused at the top of the bowl, but not a single voice broke the stillness below. He began to walk down the many steps, reflecting sadly that this was the last time he would ever do so as a Master. He knew he would never regret his decision, but he would deeply miss being the Master Bard of Kestrel. He loved his island and the many responsibilities of caring for it, and he would miss his colleagues on the Council. At the base of the steps, he looked up and saw that the other Masters were already seated, so still and silent that they might have been carved from the same stone as the table.

All rose as the Master Bard of Kestrel made his way to the head of the table, an act of respect that surprised and gratified him. He picked up the mallet and struck the smallest chime three times.

"The final session of the Spring Council is now open," Bergid said. "We have two items that remain to be settled tonight. The first is the posting of Bard assignments, this being the third cycle since the last posting. As you make your selections to replace the number of Bards you have released, please give first choice to those who have not yet been assigned to your island, so that each may eventually complete his five-island rotation and the Bard tests required for Master eligibility." He glanced at the Instrument Master, seated next to Grened. "I believe you have the list, Talan?"

Master Talan nodded and handed it over to him. The Senior Master set his mark for the island of Kestrel beside Darryk's name. Then he passed the list to Grened, who made his choice and passed it to Rial. The list continued to circle the table in order of seniority until every Bard who had satisfied the requirements of his previous rotation had been reassigned to a new island. Only nine Bards were eligible for the position of Master at the moment, all of them over forty cycles of age.

The Senior Master leaned forward and handed the completed list to Grened. "I would appreciate it if you would post this for me in the Meeting Hall. I'm sure every Bard will be anxious to see it first thing in the morning."

Grened frowned as he accepted the list from Bergid's hand. It was customary for the Senior Master to do the posting. As Bergid calmly sat back in his chair, the thought that perhaps the Master Bard of Kestrel did not expect to *be* Senior Master in the morning had occurred to them all. Four pairs of eyes were drawn to the golden cord gleaming in the center of the table.

Bergid did not glance at it. "The appointment of Bards is complete. We will now deal with the second item on our agenda." Unaccountably, the Master fell silent.

Grened broke the silence in his usual gruff manner. "Well, Bergid, when is your boy going to be here?"

"Kaelin will not be coming."

"What?" exclaimed Grened. "Your own apprentice refused you?"

"No, Kaelin would not refuse me." Bergid looked directly into

Grened's eyes. "I did not ask him to come."

The Masters glanced at one another uneasily. Finally, Marek spoke. "Bergid, I think we should hear why you did not."

The Master shook his head. "Without having heard him yourself, my explanation would sound like the ravings of an old man bereft of his senses. I'm going to leave here without my robe tonight, but—" he smiled tightly, "I will keep at least the appearance of sanity firmly wrapped about me." He rose to his feet. His voice was clear and strong as he spoke the words no Master at the table wanted to hear. "My pledge is forfeit. My position as Senior Master of this Council, Master Bard of Kestrel, Composition Master of the Bardic Isles, is hereby rescinded."

"*No, sir!*"

All five Masters turned in shock as Kaelin stepped onto the Council Grounds. He saw the golden cord lying in the center of the table, and its significance burst fully upon him. For a moment the pull of the mountain's song, which had grown distressingly stronger with every step taken toward its source, had no power over him. His jaw tightened with determination as he loosened the black cord binding his apprentice robe and walked purposefully toward the open end of the table.

"Kaelin—" Bergid said urgently, but the boy's steady gaze stopped his words.

"I followed you once before, Master, and you didn't send me away when I needed you. Please don't do so now, when there's something I can do for you." He glanced at the golden cord lying on the table between them. "This is where your cord has been all this time," he said softly. "You were willing to give up everything—your robe, your rank, your home—to keep me from being hurt." He shook his head decisively. "I can't let you do that, sir."

The apprentice laid his own cord over his Master's, and the two cords seemed to join together, a gleaming river of gold and black. Kaelin glanced at the other Masters, who were staring at him in astonishment.

"I will play for this Council and satisfy my Master's pledge," he told them. Then he turned to his Master. Though the apprentice's voice was deferential, there was steel in his gaze. "Give me your permission, sir, to play my own music."

Bergid did not answer. Blue eyes and amber held each other motionless across the length of the table. At last, the Master spoke.

"Why not a variation ... of the kestrel, perhaps?"

Kaelin shook his head. "It needs to be my own music, not a variation."

Bergid frowned and did not reply.

The apprentice spoke softly. "You caught a wild kestrel with a broken wing and cared for it. Let's see if it can fly."

The Master fell heavily into his chair and closed his eyes. "And if it dashes itself against the mountain?"

"Then it will be grateful for its moment of freedom ... and for the Master who made that possible." The apprentice unslung the instrument bag from his shoulder and placed it on the table. He slid the case from it, assembled his flute, and laid it gently down. Then he stood waiting. Bergid did not open his eyes.

"Master?"

Bergid slowly nodded, his face pale in the flickering torchlight.

Kaelin picked up his flute, rested the headjoint against his shoulder, and turned his gaze to the mountain. The song of Bardic Mountain instantly responded to the boy who could hear the music of anything he focused on. It whispered across the Council Grounds and echoed from the empty tiers of stone. The flames of the fire danced to its silent strains. The chimes trembled, filling the air with sudden disharmony.

Four of the Masters stared at the young flutist before them, watching as Kaelin's fingers moved over the keys, silently playing music he alone could hear. Though he stood before all the Masters of the Bardic Isles, his battle with Bardic Mountain was fought alone, where no eye could intrude. He moaned in pain as he strained to force his fingers and mind free of the mountain's song that flooded his senses, demanding expression. The apprentice, however, was no stranger to denying the expression of an overwhelming musical force. Effortlessly he recreated the cage that had held his own music captive for nearly five cycles, then opened the door invitingly.

The force that swept through the Council Grounds increased, as though incensed at such brazen opposition. The flames flared high in their sconces; the chimes clashed in dissonance. Four Masters tried unsuccessfully to rise from their chairs, their hair blowing wildly as the sudden wind kept them seated, their cries of alarm lost in the maelstrom. Bergid's hands clenched to fists in his lap, but he did not open his eyes and made no attempt to rise.

The apprentice was aware of nothing but the battleground in his own mind. The shimmering notes of the mountain's song battered him, whirling through his mind like thousands of fireflies. Desperately he caught them and forced them into the cage. Hundreds he caught, until the translucent walls of the cage glowed with the brightly shining notes, and yet there seemed no lessening of the ones that swarmed his mind. Alarmed at the realization that he was tiring, Kaelin shouted his defiance to the mountain.

Part of your song is trapped now and will stay that way! Is that what you want? I may not be able to defeat you, but I can cripple you! My mind has room for many cages. If you'd like to lose more of your song, I can make another—and another—and yet another. Leave me now, and I will free the notes that belong to you.

For a moment, the notes beleaguering Kaelin seemed to hesitate, as though considering the offer. Then the battle resumed with increased fury, the notes inside the cage surging against the walls like a stolen phrase frantic to be reunited with its composition. Kaelin fell to his knees in pain, his fingers still dancing across the keys, silently playing the mountain's song that he refused to give voice to, yet at the same time, badly wanted to. The desire to give in to that powerful song, to play it, to *experience* such passionate music, only grew as he struggled to deny it. Slowly, almost imperceptibly, the headjoint began to move toward his lips. He fought to keep it down.

You are not my Master! I will play only for him! Battered nearly senseless by the powerful music that flooded his mind and senses, aware that he was losing the battle to keep the flute from his lips, Kaelin cried out in his mind to the one who meant more to him than anything or anyone else.

Master!

Though the cry was inaudible, Bergid's eyes flew open. He saw his apprentice on his knees, saw the pain contorting the young face as the flute approached his lips. Closing his eyes, the Master answered the boy in the same silent way, using all his strength of will to say three simple words that he had not uttered for over forty cycles.

Under the onslaught of the mountain's song, Kaelin heard the words his Master had never spoken, words that were written in his eyes, that showed on his face, that spoke to him from every twist and turn of the golden cord lying in the center of the table. He perceived the words as musical notes in his mind, three notes of such incredible power, such overwhelming brightness, that the storm of music besieging his mind faded before them, lost its hold, and left him. Marveling, he released the cage, and the walls in his mind dissolved. A paean of sparkling notes burst forth and fled before the brilliant, incomparable music of those unspoken words.

For a single horrifying moment, the force sweeping the Council Grounds increased as though in a fit of pique at the Master who had supplanted it. The chimes in front of him fell before its fury, landing with a clash against the Council table. The flames of the torches billowed and seethed. Then gradually, reluctantly, the force howling through the Council Grounds abated. The dissonance of the chimes faded away. The flames subsided. Kaelin slowly rose from his knees as four disheveled Masters stared at him, their wide eyes fastened on this young musician who had yet to play a single note. Bergid, his face pale and haggard, sat motionless, his eyes still closed.

Though his own eyes were also closed, Kaelin's mind was alive with images. He saw the cords lying on the Council table, mingled rivulets of light and shadow. He saw his Master's eyes, looking into his in the village square of Vale. He thought back to the days he had spent making his first flute, the frustration of trying to play it, the joyful release of producing that first, uncertain tone.

Listen, he silently told his audience. *Listen, and understand.*

Keeping his eyes closed and his memories vividly open, Kaelin lifted his flute, took a deep breath, and began to play.

If the listeners expected to hear a brilliant rush of notes, they were disappointed. For the flutist began with a single low note, held within the confines of its own vibrato until the listeners despaired of it ever changing. At first a bare whisper of sound, it gradually increased in volume, and with it came a feeling of intense longing to be free of this, the lowest note ... to break away from the intolerable bonds the deep tone imposed.

The music of the flutist suddenly swept upward in a complex arpeggio, leaping gracefully across undulating inversions to rest abruptly on a high tone of perfect clarity. The listeners gasped, their minds drawn upward without warning in the wake of a powerful crescendo. The open air around them thrummed with dissonance as the flutist began playing a disturbing melodic line. Far below, breakers pounded against the cliffs of Elegy in forceful counterpoint to the music filling the air. The harmonics of the wind blended with the unresolved notes of the flute as the minds of the listeners were drawn swiftly northward, over the waves. North, to the island of Kestrel.

The rushing sound of the wind faded as the dissonant music of the flute took the listeners high into the mountains, to a small clearing in the woods. They found themselves seated at the base of an oak tree, carving a small wooden flute. They concentrated with all their might on carefully boring the last of seven holes. Bringing the flute to their lips, they took a deep breath and blew, devastated when no sound came from it. Again and again, they tried to produce a note on the instrument, but without success. The listeners rose in anger, trying to decide whether to throw the flute down or break it in two with their own hands. Stubborn resolve brought the flute back to their lips, and once again they blew across the hole, lips pursed with anger. A sound, breathy and uncertain, whispered across the clearing. Elation filled their minds as the music which had brought them here lingered on a major triad, then took them swiftly away.

The major triad modulated subtly to its relative minor. The listeners found themselves in a dimly lit room. The shadowy outline of two people lying on a bed filled one corner. The troubled music of the flutist continued, but the listeners barely heard it, riveted by the lifeless figures before them, staggered by the horrific thing they were certain their music had just done. The music became a dirge. A profound sense of loss and guilt overwhelmed them, raking their minds with serrated edges of despair. The flutist caught his breath; the phrase was nearly broken. Then, the dynamic crescendo straining with effort, the music lifted them up and bore them away.

The flutist increased his tempo with deft fingers. The listeners found themselves in the woods, running in step with the music, choking and sobbing through branches that slapped their faces, through unseen roots that tripped them and sent them sprawling into the dirt. The music forced them to their feet, raw grief and guilt lashed them forward again, and they stumbled on as though trying to outrun the suffocating weight of their own emotions. At last, they fell sobbing at the base of an oak tree and began digging feverishly between the roots. Grief flung the wrapped flute into the hole; guilt covered it completely. Their fists pounded the packed earth until their hands ached with the force of each blow. Traitorous music surged within them, and they forced it ruthlessly behind the walls of an invisible cage. With a cry of intense pain, the listeners turned and ran from the instrument and music that had betrayed them.

The flutist lingered over the notes of a diminished triad, allowing their poignant suspense to increase. A disquieting mood was deftly woven from the chord, swelling within the listeners to the point of physical pain. Anger, frustration, and confusion filled their minds. They heard nothing but the agonizing sounds within them, felt nothing but raw, tearing emotions. They begged to be released, but no one heard. Tears made silent paths down their cheeks, but no one saw. They stood once again in the woods, the small flute pressed against their lips, desperately trying to play the music surging against the walls of its prison, intense pain increasing with every note. They broke off with a gasp, longing to free the music causing them such pain, and terrified of what might happen if they did. They turned their attention to a leaf lying on the ground, focusing intently on it until they heard its song, the notes of it almost drowned out by the turbulent music inside them. Hesitantly, they played a simple variation of the leaf's song, gaining a measure of peace, and the restless music behind the walls subsided. Then the vision of a kestrel eyeing them from the branch of an oak filled the listeners' minds. A wild fragment of the kestrel's music flowed through the small flute in a spontaneous variation that took their senses into the skies for a single, glorious moment of freedom.

The music of the flutist modulated to a despairing minor, and a figure appeared in the listeners' minds. An old man seated in a village square, dressed in the white robe and golden cord of a

Master Bard. In shock, they heard their variation of the kestrel's song echoed by the Master's flute. They looked for a moment into vividly blue eyes. When the Master rose and left, they felt an aching sense of loss ... then a thrill of joy as the music of the flute climbed a major arpeggio and propelled them forward, following the Master.

The flutist began to play a series of alternating arpeggios in the lower register. The sensation of music trapped, denied all expression, grew until the listeners felt suffocated by its pressure. Then, in deft counterpoint, fragments of memories chased each other through their minds. The Master played his harp by the fire, singing a song of Bardic lore. He held his hand out with the palm up, his expression stern. He laughed merrily as he danced a jig in a village square. He held out an empty manuscript with challenge on his lifted brows. He read through a filled one and closed his eyes, nodding in approval. The whirlwind of memories climbed upward, and the listeners soared with it. They caught their breath in wonder as the flutist lingered for a moment on the highest note ... then slowly they began to descend.

An unreasoning dread filled them as each descending note became softer than the one before it in a relentless diminuendo. The vivid imagery in the minds of the listeners abruptly faded. Darkness overwhelmed sight, silence abolished sound. They waited in growing panic, blind and deaf, until the terrible pressure of the music trapped within them became an agony. Silent, unplayed notes whirled in their minds, surging against the walls of their cage in a bid to be heard. The listeners refused, screaming in defiance of the music they refused to give expression to. Music they couldn't trust. Music that filled them with intolerable pain. Music that could kill.

The flutist lingered on the lowest notes of his instrument, stretching each beyond its measured length. Time melted, no longer bound in rhythmic consistency. The listeners tried to cry out but could not. They groped in the darkness, searching. The unexpected feel of strong arms lifting them up, followed by a gentle hand covering their own, dissolved their panic and banished the horror of their nightmares. They felt a procession of various objects under their fingers: the end of a rope pulling them forward, a pile of rough stones, the soft fluff of a feather. The listeners sat stunned, caught between powerfully conflicting emotions as the music of the flutist faded, drifting into silence like the tide slipping backward over the sand.

The listeners strained to hear the music of the flutist, but it was no longer audible. Their eyes ached from trying to see, but the blackness was impenetrable. They felt a set of pipes—a harp— a flute. A confused tangle of songs came from each, and the music within the listeners strained to escape the walls of its cage and reach the instruments that could give it voice. Racked by terror and longing, the listeners came within a heartbeat of freeing their eyes and ears and giving up. Only the thought of the Master kept them from doing so.

The listener's own small flute replaced the Bardic one in their hands. Joy filled their minds at its touch, a welcome silence gave them peace. Yet even the fierce desire to unite the music within them with the small instrument was not enough to overcome the fear they had lived with for so long. Forced to choose between their fear or the Master, they chose ... and discovered that what they could not do for themselves, they could do for the Master they had followed. For the first time, they focused on the music behind the walls, recognizing it as an intrinsic part of themselves, and marveled at what they heard.

With breathtaking suddenness, the translucent walls dissolved, and music surged forth, free at last, becoming one with the fingers that danced over the holes of the simple instrument. The sensation of music trapped within them, the dissonance of constant frustration that had filled their minds, was dispelled so suddenly, the release so profound, that tears of exultation sprang to their eyes. Music flowed unhindered through the small instrument in pure, uninhibited song, a song all the sweeter for having been so long confined.

Without warning, the music of the flutist exploded into the upper register in a burst of ecstatic sound. The listeners, their hands unknowingly stretched out in the darkness, were bathed in its bright light. Color, rich and pulsing with life, filled their minds with a transparent beauty that left their senses reeling. They reveled in it, bathing in its rainbow glow with the abandoned joy of childhood. Intricate trills, rippling masterfully across a three-octave stretch, flooded their minds. Every phrase bespoke the music of unnoticed things: the fall of a leaf, the rustle of a branch, the lone chirp of a bird. Then the sound of a voice, a thrillingly human voice lifted in laughter. The voice of the Master Bard of Kestrel. The feel of the Master's hand. The challenge in the Master's brow. The love in the Master's eyes.

The music paused for a moment on a deeply satisfying, resolved tone, then slowly receded, disappearing like the last trickling droplet of rain at the end of a stormy day. The flutist put down his instrument.

The listeners were released.

None of the Masters could afterwards recall how long they remained lost in the wonder of what they candidly admitted was the most incredible performance they had ever experienced. The sun was still low on the horizon, but it felt like hours or even days might have passed. They found themselves blinking back tears and staring at one another in wonder. The Master Bard of Kestrel sat motionless, his eyes still closed. Kaelin stood breathing in labored gasps, his face streaming with sweat. He was utterly spent, but his spirit sang victoriously; the mountain had not defeated him. He placed his flute on the table with shaking hands, then walked unsteadily to the head of the table and knelt by his Master's side, half falling in his exhaustion.

Master Bergid opened his eyes and smiled. "My kestrel can fly," he said gently. "He can mount up on wings and fly like none other. And I could not be more proud of him than I am at this moment."

A smile transfigured the youngster's face, then he leaned against his Master's knee and closed his eyes.

Bergid glanced at Grened. "As you can see, my friend, though I am admittedly guilty of setting aside tradition, I did not do so lightly." His gaze swept the table. "Do any of you have any further doubts?"

No one seemed capable of speech, let alone the voicing of doubts. Finally, Marek roused himself and managed a wry smile. "If anyone does, it's their hearing and not your head, Bergid, that needs examination."

Rial's eyes were full of wonder. "Never in all my cycles have I heard ... have I *experienced* ..." The Voice Master's primary instrument failed him utterly.

"None of us have any doubts, Bergid," said Talan, rousing himself with difficulty. "But I'm sure we all have even more questions than before." A chorus of agreement broke over the table as three revived Masters began exclaiming at once.

"Yes! How could such imagery ... was it just me, or did all of you—"

"Did you hear the incredible—"

"Hear! Did you *see*—"

"And what was the force that swept over us before he played a single—"

"Yes! Where did *that* come from?"

"From the mountain itself, do you think?"

"What else could possess the power to nearly blow us—"

"He can *hear* it? The song of the mountain itself? A Gift of such magnitude as that—"

"And the pain of his repressed Gift ... the horror of what he thought it had done—"

"The release of it was absolutely beyond description!"

"The colors ... the sounds ... I thought being sense-deprived a mere *week*—"

"I almost want to blind and deafen myself again for a *month*, just to experience such—"

"How is it possible? Every detail seen so clearly, every emotion felt as if it were my own!"

"I feel as though I apprenticed with Bergid myself!"

"Indeed, why should *Kaelin* be the only one given such an honor? Why, I think we should *all* apprentice with Bergid!"

Kaelin, leaning wearily against his Master's knee, chuckled softly.

"Hmph!" Bergid snorted. "Your analysis and questions, if they can be answered at all, must wait. My apprentice," he said pointedly, looking directly at Grened, who alone had remained silent and whose eyes still rested appraisingly on Kaelin, "is far too spent to answer any of them." He closed his eyes briefly. "And so, I must admit, is his Master."

Grened, second in seniority, rose, and all eyes turned to him. His own were fastened on Bergid's as he quietly spoke.

"You and I became Bards together. This cord of mine was wrapped around my waist only two cycles after yours was, and I was proud to take my seat at this table as your colleague and friend. But I have never been more honored than I am now, to be the one to return *this* cord to where it rightfully belongs." He picked up the golden cord lying on the Council table and bowed formally to the Senior Master.

Bergid, his eyes glistening with moisture, rose and returned the bow. The Master Bard of Elegy bound the golden cord around the waist of the Master Bard of Kestrel with his own hands.

"Your pledge stands fulfilled."

The other Masters rose as one and bowed to the Senior Master, whose smile seemed to lighten the growing dusk. The Master Harpist then took the plain black cord from the table and stood before Kaelin. "I am also honored to return *this* one," he said. Seeing that the boy hadn't the strength to rise, he stooped down and bound it around the apprentice's waist.

"You went up against the mountain with a flute, boy, and you won," Grened said. "Only the Maker knows how, for the Master of this island most assuredly does not. Regardless, your pledge also stands fulfilled. You are acknowledged by this Council as the apprentice of the Master Bard of Kestrel, unless you wish to accept the robe of a Flutist ... the youngest one in Bardic history."

Kaelin looked up in wonder at the other Masters, who were nodding their agreement with this offer. "Thank you, sir," he said quietly, "but I consider my robe of apprenticeship to the Master Bard of Kestrel to be of higher honor."

Grened nodded. "So be it."

Chapter 21

The following morning, Master Grened posted the list of Bard assignments in the Hall, and the Meeting Grounds were soon filled with dozens of Bards ready to leave for their new islands. Kaelin was fast asleep at Darryk's camp, having been carried there from the Council Grounds by Master Marek, for Bergid would not allow his apprentice to stay any closer to the mountain. Unwilling to leave Kaelin's side, Bergid sent Darryk to tell the new Bards of Kestrel to leave for the island without them and report to Flynn. To their surprise, Master Grened insisted on staying as well. He sequestered himself and two of his Bards in the Meeting Hall, equipped with a full kitchen and close to Darryk's camp.

"This is my island," the Master Harpist said gruffly to Bergid when the Master of Composition had protested that it wasn't necessary, "and you are my guests, even if you insist on sleeping out of doors. A host does not leave before his guests. My Bards will keep you well-provisioned, and if you need anything, send Darryk to me and I will see to it. I've some bone broth simmering over the fire that will be good for the boy when he awakens." With a glance at the sleeping apprentice, he turned and left.

Kaelin slept through the day and roused at last in the late afternoon. He was able to sit up and devour Grened's soup, laden with chunks of meat and vegetables and seasoned with fresh herbs.

"I don't think I've ever tasted anything so good in my whole life," Kaelin said as he regretfully put the empty bowl down.

Darryk chuckled, then, catching a meaningful glance from the Master, cleared his throat. "I'll convey your regards to the culinary genius of the Bardic Isles, then, and see if I can wheedle another serving or two out of him. Your Master, I think, could use a bowl of it himself." He smiled at his young friend, nodded to the Master, then snagged his harp and left the clearing, humming as he went.

Kaelin scrutinized his Master's face. "Are you okay, sir?"

His Master waved his concern away. "I'll be fine after a good night's sleep," he said firmly.

"Couldn't you sleep last night?"

"I wanted to be awake in case you needed me during the night," Bergid told him. "Now that you've demolished a meal with your usual voracious appetite, I'll be fine. Now, then, if you're up to a short conversation, I would like to hear your reason for following me to the Council session last night. Darryk assures me he did not tell you what I intended to do."

"He didn't, not even when I asked him about your missing cord. He just said that Masters sometimes do things that make no sense to the rest of us, and when that happens, it's best to trust that they know what they're doing."

The Master's mouth quirked with amusement. "Why, then, did you follow me? Do you not trust your Master to do what is best?"

"For me? Absolutely, sir. For yourself ... not so much." Kaelin frowned. "As you've proven yet again by not getting any sleep last night on my account." He hesitated as the Master chuckled, then continued in a subdued voice. "Are you upset with me for following you?"

"No, lad, I've no intention of chiding you, I'm simply satisfying my curiosity. I've never been more happy in my life that you did something you knew perfectly well I would have forbidden, had you asked me first." He cocked an eye at his apprentice. "I wouldn't, however, advise you to make it a habit."

"No, sir, I won't," Kaelin quickly assured him. He studied his empty bowl for a moment. "I couldn't be the cause of you losing your robe," he said in a low voice. "I did ask you for permission, but I would have played my own music regardless," he admitted.

"I know. Which is why I gave it," the Master said with a smile. "I would hate to be in the position right now of having to chastise my apprentice for disobedience to his Master. For it is because of what you were willing to do … and how very well you did it … that I am still in possession of this robe."

"What would they have done to you if you had forfeited it?" Kaelin asked.

"You would very likely be the apprentice of an Instrumentalist, and I would now be garbed in a sapphire robe and silver cord."

"You meant what you said," Kaelin said softly, "when I asked you if the Council could make you send me away."

"Did you ever doubt it?"

"No."

Master and apprentice sat in comfortable silence for a moment, then Bergid gathered up Kaelin's few dishes, shaking his head when his apprentice tried to object. "I'll take care of these," the Master said firmly. "You lay down and get some more sleep."

"I'll lie down," Kaelin promised, then sighed deeply. "But I won't be able to get any sleep."

"And why is that?"

"An apprentice can't sleep when his Master is suffering from lack of it," Kaelin informed him.

"Is that so?"

"He'll spend all night worrying about his Master's health."

"Will he, now?"

"And then he'll probably get sick and need a Healer … and who knows how long it will take for one of them to get here?"

"Well, we can't have that, now, can we?"

"No, sir."

Bergid sighed and placed the dishes back on the ground. He settled himself comfortably on his bedroll, then quirked a brow at Kaelin. "It's still not clear to me," the Master said, "if no one explained the significance of my cord being left on the Council table, why you thought I might be about to do something at the last session that was not in my own best interests."

It was a moment before the apprentice answered. "I didn't intend to eavesdrop, but I woke up and heard you talking to Darryk the night before. You said you wouldn't put me in harm's way to save yourself."

Bergid was silent for a moment, considering this. "So that's why you said it needed to be your own music, not a variation. You chose the memories you played for the Council deliberately, knowing they would experience them as if they were you."

"I wanted them to know what it was like to be me ... and to experience having a Master like you, who didn't send me away and did so much to help me. It was the only way to make them understand and let us stay together."

"You could not have chosen a better way to convince them."

"Does Darryk know what happens when I play the music of something I focus on?"

"I've never told anyone about your abilities. Darryk and the Masters know about one of them because they experienced being transported into your memories for themselves. They do not know about your ability to travel inside an object, and I think it would be best to keep it that way, at least for now."

Kaelin nodded in agreement.

"There is something, however, *you* need to know," the Master continued, "and I think now is a good time to tell you. Your listeners experience *whatever* you are experiencing when you play. Which means they don't just travel with you on the wings of your thoughts or memories ... they also follow you into objects."

Kaelin gave his Master a startled look. "You mean, when I entered that feather with my Gift, you were there, too, seeing everything the same way I was?"

The Master nodded. "A truly incredible experience."

Kaelin shook his head as though to clear it. "At the time, I thought you knew all about it because you were Gifted and had seen everything before. Then, when I overheard you talking to Darryk and realized you weren't Gifted, I thought you must have known about it from reading our historical records, or something only Masters are allowed to read. But ... you didn't know any more about it than I did? Why didn't you tell me?"

"Because the timing was terrible," the Master said. "The music inside you had just recently been freed. The last thing I wanted to do was give you reason to fear your Gift again. Telling you that you were the only one in the Bardic Isles who was Gifted, and that your Master was as ignorant about the Gift as you were, might well have made you too afraid to explore your Gift at all."

Kaelin nodded thoughtfully.

"I'm aware that you could, with some justification, accuse me of lying to you—" Bergid began, but his apprentice shook his head.

"You never told me you were Gifted. I assumed you were. You didn't have to tell me otherwise."

"I may not have lied outright," the Master said, "but I am guilty of lying by omission to someone I demand total honesty from. For that I sincerely apologize. It is something I have often castigated myself for doing."

"You did so for my benefit, Master ... and you were right. I *would* have been too afraid."

"You won't be, once the time comes to continue that exploration. But," the Master added sternly, "you *will* be far more careful."

Kaelin nodded solemnly, then remained sitting, wondering how to ask what he most wanted to know. "So, you knew from the beginning that I was Gifted? Just from hearing me play a variation of the kestrel's song?"

The Master's brow lifted. "What else could have taken my senses up into the skies, if not the Gift of old?"

"And that's why you helped me free it?"

"After I was certain it had been given to a boy who would use it well, yes."

"And ... was it also why you took me for your apprentice?" Kaelin held his breath, waiting for the answer, which was a few moments in coming.

"It was one reason, yes," the Master said quietly, "but it was not the only reason."

The apprentice smiled and lay down. Silence fell over the clearing as shadows began to dance with the flickering flames of the campfire.

When Darryk returned later that evening, he found them both sound asleep, Kaelin with a slight smile on his face. Darryk regarded his young friend for a moment, marveling at the strength of the youngster's Gift, one that had swept the Council of Masters into unanimous agreement. Not everyone was pleased with the endorsement of Kaelin as the Master Bard of Kestrel's apprentice, but word that the Master's pledge had been fulfilled and his cord recovered had sent every Bard into a state of fist-pumping jubilation. None of them, however, were as delighted as the Bard looking down on the two peaceful sleepers, chuckling at the duet produced by the soft snoring of Master and apprentice in unison octaves.

The next morning, Kaelin perked up at his Master's broad hint to Darryk that so much free time could be put to good use on flute form two. "If you'd like any help torturing Darryk, Master," the apprentice offered, his eyes dancing with mischief, "I'd be happy to take over for you. After all," he said solicitously, "you're going to be too busy pretty soon, with four more apprentices to give lessons to—" Kaelin struggled to maintain a serious expression. "And four sets of wax plugs and eye patches to make—" The apprentice's voice began to shake. "Not to mention four ropes … to attach to … to Poor Oran—" The youngster abruptly disappeared into his bedroll, which shook violently as paroxysms of helpless laughter came from within it.

"Don't ask," the Master growled at the confused Bard, then picked up his instruments. "Grened's expecting me … and *I'll* be expecting that you've practiced your flute before I return." He strode from the clearing, chuckling as he went.

Darryk stood for a moment, listening to the helpless laughter still coming from within Kaelin's bedroll. There was a simple way to sober his young friend and find out what was going on. The Bard had only to obey the Master's directive. He grinned and picked up his flute.

That afternoon, Kaelin woke to find his sister hovering over him. He blinked. "Laena! Am I dreaming? What are you doing here?"

"I'm wondering when my lazy brother is going to wake up and say hello," she said with a smile.

"But why … how—"

"Master Bergid sent for me. He said you've been through quite an ordeal since coming here, and although there's nothing physically wrong with you except exhaustion, he thinks a conversation between us is long overdue and will aid in your recovery. Donal took me straight to the ship, where I discovered that your Master had not only paid for my passage, he'd given me his own berth!"

Kaelin sat up and looked around the empty campsite, still somewhat dazed.

"Your Master and Bard Darryk left after lunch to play ensembles with Master Grened and his Bards," Laena told him, "and won't be back until later this afternoon. Regardless of what Master Bergid said, you don't have to tell me anything you don't want to."

Kaelin shook his head. "It will be a relief to tell you. You were right when you told me I was underestimating my Master."

Laena smiled. "I figured you must have finally told him."

Kaelin shook his head. "No, I don't think I ever could have. He overheard me telling Darryk."

His sister's eyes flew open in surprise. "You're friends with a *Bard?*"

"He's the best friend I've ever had," Kaelin told her.

Laena nodded slowly, digesting this. "So, then, the Master overheard you and didn't send you away, as you feared he would. Did he ... fix whatever it was that broke you?"

It was some time before Kaelin answered. "The day our parents died," he finally said, "you knew they were close to death and left them to go find me, didn't you?"

Laena's eyes widened. "How did you know that? I went to find you so you could say goodbye to them. But I couldn't find you anywhere, and when I came back, they—" Tears stood in her eyes. "I still feel so bad that no one was there with them at the end. When you finally came home that night, I knew someone must have told you they died, because you were too upset to speak to me, or even go into their room."

"No one told me," Kaelin said softly. "But someone was with them, Laena. I was."

His sister gasped. "You—"

"I was in the woods, practicing my first flute song all that morning, and went home to play it for them, thinking music would make them feel better, like it did me. They were awake, barely able to nod when I asked if they'd like to hear it. Mother ... smiled at me." He stopped for a moment, swallowing his emotion. "I played my song, and when I was done ... they wouldn't wake up."

"By the Maker himself," Laena exclaimed in horror, "you thought your music ... killed them? Oh, *Kaelin,* I'm so sorry! What you must have gone through—" She caught her breath in a sob and began to cry.

Her brother shook his head. "Nothing that happened was your fault or mine. You couldn't have known what would happen when you left, and I couldn't bring myself to tell you what I thought I'd done." He had barely finished his sentence before he was enveloped in Laena's embrace. Her tears dropped unchecked onto his shoulder.

"It should never have happened at all," Laena said brokenly.

Kaelin pulled her tighter against him. "I think things happened the way they needed to, somehow."

Laena sat back and stared at him through her tears.

"Everything I went through with my music," Kaelin said slowly, "happened for a reason. It led me to my Master ... made me who I am now." He shrugged. "Maybe this doesn't sound sensible, and I'm not saying it wasn't an awful thing to go through, but to be here right now, in this moment ... I wouldn't change a thing."

Laena smiled. "You've grown up, brother of mine. But how did Master Bergid convince you that your music didn't kill our parents?"

Kaelin grimaced. "He told me to play the song I played that day, and when I finally obeyed him, he saw them in their sickness and realized they were close to death. He told me it was probably the mushrooms up on Skellig Mountain that poisoned them."

"Healer Telon said the same. You were so young, and I was so upset ... I just didn't think to explain things to you like I should have." She frowned. "Wait. What do you mean, the Master *saw* them?"

"He and Darryk saw everything when I played. Remember how you told me my humming seemed to pull you just before you fell out of that tree? I've found out that my music pulls my listeners into whatever I'm thinking or experiencing when I play, so they see exactly what I see, and feel what I feel." He gave her a rueful glance. "So, it really *was* my fault you broke your ankle that day. I can't explain it any better because I don't understand it myself." He looked regretfully at his flute, lying with his pack against the corner of the shelter. "It would be far easier to show you by playing something, but I'm forbidden to touch my flute until my Master thinks I've recovered enough."

Laena shook herself out of her amazement and smiled. "Well, then, it seems you've underestimated your Master yet again. He told me you would want to play, and that you had his permission to do so as long as I felt you weren't overtiring yourself."

"As long as *you* felt!" Kaelin said indignantly.

"That's what he said, brother of mine," Laena said in a teasing voice. "Obey him, or I'll tell."

"You would, too," the apprentice grumbled. "Sisters never change."

Laena laughed and brought him his flute. She whistled softly as he removed it from its leather case. "Unless it's grown as fast as you have, that certainly isn't the flute you showed me before."

"No, this is the one I made under my Master's instruction," Kaelin told her.

"It's beautiful! No wonder Craftmaster Arnor was so upset when I told him you weren't coming back." Laena settled herself to listen. "What are you going to play?"

"Well, first I want to show you what I showed our parents just before they died ... unless you'd rather not see it."

"Of course I want to see it!"

Kaelin nodded, swallowed hard, and began to play. Laena gave a little gasp of wonder as she felt herself pulled into her brother's music.

The music lifted them up, then out over the open sea to Skellig Mountain, on the island of Kestrel. They hovered for a long moment over the village of Vale, the small house they had grown up in directly below them. Then they sped over the woods, flying above the trail they had so often followed on foot. Both of them could have sworn they heard the sound of their own laughter mingling with that of their parents' on the trail below. They wound their way through the trees, skirting meadows splashed with golden buttercups and powdery pink centaury. Butterflies lifted gracefully from the petals at their passing. They crossed splashing brooks and rivulets as they climbed ever higher up the slopes. At last, they came to the banks of a stream with a strong current, and a willow whose graceful limbs swayed over its banks. Next to it stood a large boulder, the side facing them flat and smooth. Four names were carved deeply into it, their parents' above, their own below. The music lingered here for a long moment, then gently took them away.

When Kaelin stopped playing, he found his sister sitting close to him, her eyes closed.

"What you just did," Laena said, her voice filled with wonder, "defies belief." She reached out and touched the flute as though it were magical and might vanish at her touch. "Thank you for showing me. I'm glad ... so glad that you gave them one last glimpse of the place they loved so much ... and that they left us from there."

This time it was Kaelin who reached for his sister, and they cried together, thinking of the parents they loved who had been lost to them much too soon. Afterwards, they both smiled at each other, the shedding of those healing tears having brought them closer than they had ever been.

When Bergid and Darryk returned to the campsite, Laena smiled at the Master and nodded, as though answering an unspoken question. "Thank you so much for bringing me here, Master Bergid," she said simply.

"I'm sorry it can't be for a longer time," the Master said regretfully.

"I'm sure my presence here has caused you enough trouble already," she said with a laugh.

"If you'd like to stay with Kaelin, Master Bergid," Darryk said,

"I'd be happy to accompany Laena back to Bard's Landing."

"I'd appreciate that."

Laena gave Kaelin a final hug, then left the clearing with Darryk. The apprentice's eyes rested on his Master. "How could you have known how badly I needed to talk to her, when I didn't know myself?"

The Master smiled. "You have more than just the mountain to recover from. I knew you wouldn't completely heal from the trauma of your parents' death until you spoke to your sister, and since I'll have a whole crew of new Bards to train on our return, there'll be little time for it after we leave here."

"You went to a lot of trouble for me," the apprentice said softly.

The Master's eyes sparkled with humor. "It was worth it just to see the scandalized expression on Grened's face when he came out of the Hall and saw me walking through the Meeting Grounds with Laena. Before he had a chance to erupt, your sister walked straight up to him and thanked him profusely for allowing her to come, as though she owed her entire trip to his generosity and understanding." The Master laughed. "I've never seen Grened so flummoxed in my life! He could scarcely upbraid someone who was looking at him with such adoring gratitude, so he did the only thing he *could* do ... accepted her thanks and escaped as quickly as possible." The Master shook his head in admiration. "The next time I'm too busy dealing with an apprentice to attend a Council session, I believe I'll send your sister in my place."

Kaelin laughed, and his Master cocked a brow at the apprentice's flute, lying on top of its travel bag. "Your permission to play is hereby rescinded," he said sternly, "so pack it up, lad, and get some sleep!"

Chapter 22

On the afternoon of the fourth day, Bergid allowed his apprentice to finish carving the rest of his tuning pegs. Much to Kaelin's delight, his Master admired them openly and was caught frowning at the unadorned pegs on his own harp.

Darryk grinned. "What did I tell you, Kaelin? We'll be sharpening his tools for him this evening!"

The Master Bard shook his head. "I could never carve such intricate pictures on a tuning peg, much less achieve such uncanny likenesses." He ran his finger gently over the detailed face of Laena carved into the peg's surface. "I may be reduced to commissioning my own apprentice to do it for me." They laughed at his look of comic dismay. Stooping, the Master picked up another peg and confronted his apprentice with an air of injured amusement.

"Has your apprenticeship been under so hard a Master that you feel *this* to be its appropriate symbol?"

Darryk moved closer to examine the peg and chuckled. On its

surface was the simple, clear carving of a switch.

There was no amusement on the apprentice's face as he glanced at the peg. "I carved that as a reminder to value the power of my own words," he said quietly. He held out the peg he had just finished. "This is the symbol of my apprenticeship."

The Master Bard took the peg. Two cords, one smooth and tinged with gold, the other coarse and black, twined together on the wooden surface.

Darryk whistled in admiration. "That is both beautiful and appropriate, Kaelin. Where did you get such vivid dyes?"

"From Master Grened." He grinned at the look of surprise on their faces. "He came by yesterday while you were taking a walk and saw me working on this peg. He told me I could make dyes for it, black from a logwood tree, and gold from the bark of a black oak. He knows a lot about dyes and told me all kinds of interesting things about them. When I woke up this morning, I found this lying next to me." Kaelin picked up a small box with a tight-fitting lid and opened it. Inside were six compartments, each containing a dye of a different color, all of them deep and brilliant. "I've never seen such colors!" he exclaimed. "Craftmaster Arnor himself didn't have ones this fine. I'm going to use them to highlight the carvings on my pegs and harp frame." He closed the box carefully. When no one spoke, he glanced up and found them both staring at him. "What's wrong?"

Darryk found his voice before the Master. "Nothing, Kaelin. It's just that Master Grened is well known for his meticulously prepared dyes, but not for his generosity with them." He scowled and spoke in deft mimicry of the Master Bard of Elegy. "Good dyes take far too many hours of preparation to be carelessly handed out to fools too lazy to learn for themselves, so don't bother running to *me* for them!" He snorted contemptuously, so like Master Grened that his two listeners burst out laughing. Darryk glanced at the box of dyes. "So, you see, that's a rare and valuable gift you have there."

Kaelin touched the box gently. "How can I ever thank him?"

"By keeping his gift a deep, dark secret," the Master advised. "The two of us solemnly swear to never divulge it."

The two men looked at each other and chuckled. Darryk, seeing Kaelin's confusion, explained. "Master Grened has built up a reputation for being crusty and difficult to please. He would not like it known he'd gone soft, especially on an apprentice."

Kaelin nodded and looked thoughtfully at the few leftover pieces of wood from his harp sections.

Apprentice, Bard, and Master rose early on the morning of their departure. At the Meeting Grounds, they found Master Grened and his two Bards waiting for them, their packs ready for travel back to Tryl. The two Masters greeted each other, and when Bergid and Darryk began talking to the two Bards, Kaelin turned to the Master Harpist and bowed deeply.

"Master Grened. May I have a word with you privately, sir?"

The Master glanced at him, gave a curt nod and strode off across the clearing. Kaelin followed, then removed a slim package from the pocket of his robe and handed it to him. Master Grened frowned slightly, then unwrapped it to find a smooth, polished piece of rosewood with six intricately carved pictures gleaming on its surface. Three trees: oak, logwood, and acacia. Three plants: crocus, henna, and woad. Each were delicately tinged with the colors the Master had produced from them.

Kaelin spoke quietly. "I wanted to make you a sectioned box to thank you for your gift, sir, but I only had time to finish the lid. When the box is complete, I'll send it to you. The Woodcarving Craftmaster of Vale had good dyes, but these are by far the finest I've ever seen. Not just in the depth of the colors you produced, but the consistency as well. They apply smoothly and easily, even when using tiny amounts for tinting, so nothing is wasted. If Craftmaster

Arnor saw them, he'd pay top coin for them ... but I wouldn't sell, no matter what he offered."

The barest hint of a smile crossed the Master's face.

"Someday, I hope to learn how to make such colors as these," Kaelin said earnestly.

"The process is not an easy one, boy," Grened warned. "It takes a great deal of time and effort."

Kaelin nodded. "Yes, sir ... my Master has taught me that things worth the having are seldom easy."

The Master's eyes softened. "If you return to Elegy for a lengthy stay, then, I shall see to it." He nodded abruptly and strode back across the clearing with his customary frown.

It was a much easier walk down to Bard's Landing than the arduous climb up had been, and the group of travelers made good time. Once on the beach, the Bards built two signal fires. The Master told Kaelin that each fire's location informed a passing ship of the desired destination, so that in this case, only a ship bound for either Kyet or Tryl would stop. A few hours later, one set its anchor in the small bay and a boat was lowered to fetch the three travelers going to Kyet. The small boat soon reached the ship, and the crew helped them board. Courteous greetings were exchanged, with a few curious glances directed toward the apprentice. The passengers got settled and Kaelin was soon leaning against the rail, his eyes on Bardic Mountain as the sails above him caught the wind. His Master came up alongside him.

"On the Council Grounds," the Master said quietly, "I don't know how, but I heard you."

A smile crossed the apprentice's face as he stared at the mountain. "I heard you, too."

The Master nodded. He waited as the youngster began to chew his bottom lip, knowing there was something more on Kaelin's mind.

"Am I really the only one?" His apprentice looked at him as if begging to be told that there were numerous others scattered all across the Bardic Isles that his Master had forgotten to mention.

"The only one born with the Gift that most Bards and all the Masters of Eire once had? As far as I know ... yes, you are."

"Why me?" Kaelin's voice shook slightly. "I never asked for it! I thought I had a Gift that at least some of the Bards and Masters have, too ... that *you* have! What if I don't want it?"

"None of us have any control over what talents we are born with," Bergid said, "whether for craftwork, growing things, or hearing the music of everything around us. A talent, however, is useless if not developed, and that is something we *can* control. If you don't want the Gift you were born with," the Master said gravely, "then don't develop it."

The apprentice frowned slightly, his eyes fixed intently on his Master.

"Master Cyral was also born with the Gift you possess," Bergid continued, "and faced the same choice you're facing now. He chose to develop his Gift, and that choice ultimately led to him standing on that ship, facing another choice that only he could make because he was the only one whose Gift was strong enough to do what needed to be done to save us. Had his first choice been different, he would never have faced such a difficult one on that ship ... and we would not be here right now, discussing yours." He looked compassionately at his shaken apprentice.

"Your choices with regard to how you use your own Gift are dependent on that Gift being developed," the Master said gently. "If you choose not to, then there will be no choices regarding it in the future to face. You will simply face other ones, as we all do, and each of them will give rise to others. We make choices every day, many of them seemingly unimportant." The Master smiled. "Like deciding to camp in a small clearing before visiting the village of Vale. That decision led me to a Gifted young boy, where I faced another choice ... to take him with me or not ... to help him or not ...

to take him as my apprentice or not ... to let him explore his Gift or not. Each choice leads us down different paths. The path you're on now began the moment you chose to free the music inside you. Have you changed your mind now that you have a fuller understanding of what that means? Do you wish to leave this path and choose another?"

Emotion filled the amber eyes fixed on the Master. "If this is the only path that keeps me by your side, I will never choose to leave it."

Bergid shook his head. "It is the path of your Gift we are considering, not the path of music, though the two may often head in parallel directions. And I will never send you away unless you wish to go. So, no matter what choice you make, know that your place by my side will not be threatened by it."

Kaelin was silent for a moment, considering. "What would happen," he asked, "if I chose to leave the path of my Gift, yet remain your apprentice?" For this indeed seemed the brightest, easiest path to take.

"You would continue to study with me until you were ready to become a Flutist or Instrumentalist and take students of your own," the Master told him. "You would continue to compose and play your music, and it would continue to take your listeners with you, to experience it as you do. That much of your Gift will always be yours to use, for it is an inherent ability. But you would make no effort to explore your Gift and discover what else it has to show you, or what else it is capable of. You would not enter objects, or any other thing, by playing their music. That part of your Gift would still exist within you, causing you no pain, but it would remain as it is now, undeveloped, its boundaries fixed by your own decision not to pursue it."

Kaelin was silent for a long moment, staring at the frothing path that stretched from the stern of the boat to the receding beach of Bard's Landing, then to the switchback trail leading up the cliffs and on to the Council Grounds, and from there— His eyes lifted unwillingly to the mountain. "And later on, if I decided—" He fell silent.

"There is always the option to adjust your course," Bergid said, "but keep in mind that, as you are discovering right now, it is not always easy to do so, for we become accustomed to the path we're on." He indicated the taut sails above. "And sometimes the winds of life blow us too far from the path we left for us to easily return to it." Sadness crossed the Master's face like a passing shadow, causing Kaelin to wonder what path his Master had left that he had not been able to return to.

"You need not make such a choice now," his Master said gently. "You will not come of age for another three cycles, the earliest I will allow you to begin developing your Gift. Nor need it begin then. You may have as much time as you like to decide."

Kaelin nodded and returned his gaze to the distant island of Elegy. They stood there for a time, looking out over the waves together. The apprentice thought about the decision he would need to make. The idea of staying by his Master's side without the pressure of developing a dangerous Gift that no one knew anything about was a pleasant one, an easy choice to make. And yet—

Above them the wild, staccato cry of a kestrel split the air, and they looked up, startled to see a large male arrowing down toward them from the south, coming within a few handspans of the Master's head. The magnificent bird cried out again, circled above them twice, then headed swiftly north, toward Kestrel.

Kaelin, watching the bird fly off, heard faint strains of music— music he had heard before—and was assailed with vivid memories. He knelt at the base of a twisted oak, looking up into the eyes of this same kestrel, envious of its freedom to fly the skies above. He heard the beginnings of the wild, glorious music that had later pulled him into the world of a feather. He felt the thrill of flight when he played a variation of that song, unaware that not far off a

Master stood, listening and experiencing it with him. He heard the words his Master had spoken after his performance at the Council session.

My kestrel can fly. He can mount up on wings and fly like none other. And I could not be more proud of him than I am at this moment.

Kaelin smiled, remembering. Then he turned and, looking up into the eyes of his Master, made his decision. "When my music was freed, I told myself that I would never cage it again," he said. "So I won't bind my Gift with a decision not to use it. Your kestrel will fly free, sir, or he will not fly at all."

His Master nodded. "When the time comes, you will work hard, then, to explore and develop your Gift?"

"I will."

"You'll accept an ungifted Master's guidance, for what it is worth?"

"As long as that Master is you."

Bergid smiled and laid his hand over his apprentice's. "I wish you had a Gifted Master who could teach you all the things you'll have to discover on your own," he murmured regretfully.

Together, they watched the mountain disappear in the distance.

"Do you think I'll ever play its song, Master?"

"One day, Kaelin," came the reply as the Master gently squeezed the small hand beneath his. "One day."

End of Book One of the Bardic Isles Series

Over Sea and Over Stone

Over sea and over stone,
Over cycles yet to be,
Lies a Bardic treasure caught
In time, for need alone to free.

Come, you Pipers, blow with might!
Come, you Harpists, play!
Masters, keep the land of song
From silence in that day.

Where, oh where, the young sprig growing
On an old tree, so alone?
Awake the Harp, the Master's Harp,
That lies forsaken, trapped in stone!

I hope you enjoyed your trip to the Bardic Isles!
If you would like to hear the music described in this book, all of
which was composed by the author, you can experience it in a
one-of-a-kind audiobook, available on all major audiobook
platforms, including Audible (Amazon), Spotify, Apple Books,
Google Play, Barnes & Noble, Audiobooks.com, Chirp, and Kobo.
Samples of the music can also be found on the author's website,
mhimedabooks.com, or scan the QR code below.
See the books ... hear the music ... experience the wonder!

Glossary of Basic Music Terms

Accent: (>) to play the note(s) with emphasis or stress
Adagio: a slow tempo, between largo and andante
Andante: a moderate, walking tempo
Allegretto: a moderately fast tempo
Allegro: a fast tempo
Arpeggio: the notes of a chord, played consecutively
Articulation: markings on notes that define their smoothness and duration, such as a staccato or accent
Augmented: a major chord with the top note raised; evokes uneasiness
Cadence: a series of chords that brings closure
Chord: usually three or four notes played together
Coda: a passage that brings the piece or movement to an end
Counterpoint: the combination of different melodic lines
Crescendo: a gradual increase in volume
Da Capo al Coda: a direction to go back to the beginning, then take the "coda" ending
Descant: the highest melodic line
Diminished: a minor chord with the top note lowered; evokes suspense
Diminuendo: a gradual decrease in volume
Dominant 7th, or V7: a chord comprised of a major triad and a minor 7th, such as C-E-G-Bb; has an unresolved sound
Dynamics: the range in volume of a piece
Embellishment: the ornamentation on a note, such as a trill
Fermata: a dot with a curved line over it that prolongs the length of a note or rest, at the discretion of the player
Forte: (f) loud or full in volume
Fortissimo: (ff) very loud or full in volume
Half Step: the closest possible distance between two notes

Interval: the distance between two notes

Inversion: a chord whose main (root) note is not the lowest; thus C-E-G (root) is inverted first as E-G-C, then G-C-E

Key Signature: a series of notes (most often a major or minor scale) that defines the tonality, the sharps and flats of which are usually notated at the beginning of the staff

Legato: to play smoothly connected, usually marked with a slur

Major Chord: the 1st, 3rd, and 5th notes of a major scale, played together; evokes well-being

Marcato: (^) to play the note(s) with strong accentuation

Measure: fixed number of beats between two vertical staff lines

Minor Chord: the 1st, 3rd, and 5th notes of a minor scale, played together; evokes sadness or melancholy

Piano: (p) soft

Pianissimo: (pp) very soft

Presto: an extremely fast tempo

Scale: a series of notes from which melodies and harmonies can be built, the most common being major and minor

Slur: a curved line connecting two or more notes to be played smoothly connected, or legato

Staccato: a dot above or below a note, played short and light

Tempo: the speed of a piece

Time Signature: convention defining how many beats are in one measure, and what kind of note receives one beat

Tonic: first note of a major or minor scale, or a chord built on it

Tremolo: two notes played rapidly back and forth

Trill: a note played in rapid alternation with one a whole or half step higher

Vivace: a very fast and lively tempo

Whole Step: an interval comprised of two half steps; notes a whole step apart have only one possible note between them

Acknowledgements

All stories are an evolution of ideas and dreams, penned to inspire others to think and dream as well. This story was birthed over thirty years ago, from a love of making up stories for my children. Thank you, Charis, Shawna, Kristy, and Kevin, for all the practice you gave me! I would also like to thank Anne McCaffrey for the inspiration provided by Master Robinton.

The initial writing was helped enormously by Merle McKaig, whose eagle eyes spotted errors and lapses in logic that authors so often can't see themselves. It reached another level from the advice and encouragement given by Michael Larsen and Elizabeth Pomada. My deepest thanks to you all!

Now, so many years later, that initial story has developed into a series of musical fantasy books, thanks primarily to Charis Himeda's superb editing of the manuscripts. She also provided the original cover art concept (brought to life by Maxx Marshall), help with interior art designs, and invaluable advice on navigating the maze of the publication process. Without her unfailing encouragement and support, this series would not exist. My sincere thanks also goes to Jenny Hasenjaeger for her help with my first website, and to Matthew Howard for the time he took to teach me the painstaking steps to producing a good Kindle version. A huge thank you to Jeff Brown, who created the current cover right before my eyes, expertly capturing the magic of the Bardic Isles and the music that all things are created with! And finally, a heartfelt thank you to Will Hahn for his wonderful narration of the audiobook and his enthusiastic support for my compositions for them.

About the Author

Marla Himeda is a lifelong musician who taught piano and clarinet for eighteen years at Punahou Schools and for over half a century in her own studio. She composes all the music for the audiobooks of her Bardic Isles Series, teaches theory and composition courses, coaches ensemble groups, and is a prolific arranger of chamber music for winds. She has performed in the Seattle Opera House, the Seattle Art Museum, and many concert venues in Hawaii, where she lives near Mount Olomana, whose twin peaks sparked the birth of Bardic Mountain. She is a member of the National Music Teachers Association, Opus 5 Winds, and the Honolulu Wind Ensemble.

Titles in the Bardic Isles Series have won many international awards, including the IAN Awards Fantasy Book of the Year and Young Adult Finalist, the IP Awards overall Oustanding Audiobook and Gold medalist, the Readers' Favorite Audiobook Gold & Silver Medalist, the B.R.A.G. Medallion Honoree, the BookFest Awards Audiobook Silver Medalist, The Wishing Shelf Awards Fiction and Audiobook Finalist, and The BookLife Prize Semi-Finalist. The Bardic Isles Series is a merging of two passions—music and writing—and portrays a unique world that the author unabashedly admits loving to escape to. She believes everyone should have a Master Bergid in their lives, and her own life was blessed with three of them: Michiko Miyamoto and Professor Randolph Hokanson, both amazing piano teachers, and Frances Walton, an inspiring Youth Symphony director.

Visit her at mhimedabooks.com

9 781959 900009